MAFIA CROWN

L. STEELE

1

Some say the world will end in fire,
Some say in ice.
From what I've tasted of desire
I hold with those who favor fire...
-From Fire and Ice by Robert Frost

Theresa

"Who are you?" His blue-almost-indigo-colored eyes bore into me. Considering he's been unconscious for two weeks, he shouldn't seem this alert. But nothing about this man has been predictable from the moment I laid eyes on him.

"Don't you remember? You stepped in front of me; you took a bullet for me." Shit, hadn't meant to blurt it out like that, honestly, but it's the only thing I have been able to think of in the time I have sat here staring at him.

"Bullet?" He tilts his head, then winces.

"Your temple," I gesture to the bandage around his head, "the bullet hit your temple. You lost a lot of blood, and they had to put you in an induced coma so that you could heal faster."

The expression on his face doesn't change. If he's surprised, he doesn't show it. He raises his gaze back to mine, then glances around the room, before staring at the glass of water on the side table.

"Oh, are you thirsty?"

He doesn't reply. Simply looks at me again.

Of course, he's thirsty. What an insane thing to ask. His gaze tracks me as I reach his bedside. I raise the glass of water and hold it out. He stares from my face, to the glass of water, then back at me.

"Oh, right." I lower the glass until the edge of the straw stuck inside it brushes his mouth. He parts his lips and sips from the straw. The tendons of his throat move as he swallows.

Awareness prickles up my spine. I've stared at him so closely over the past couple of weeks that I know every ridge of his face, every crease at the edges of his eyes, the jut of his nose, the strong squareness of his jaw, the way his lower lip is pouty and fat and almost too feminine for the rest of his face; the way his dark hair curls over his forehead, how his long lashes brush across his cheekbones, the width of his shoulders which strain against the hospital gown they draped on him, the tan of his skin, still dark, even after all this time in the hospital, hinting at his bloodline. A bloodline that I know well, considering I had been in love with his triplet before he died. A man I'd crushed on since I had been a child. A man who is now gone, never to return, and instead... This man, with the face of my past love appeared out of the blue to take his place. It has to be a sign, surely, that his path and mine have crossed. Xander is dead, but this guy is alive. And he saved me from the bullet. Surely, there is no logical reason he'd do that... Not unless he felt pulled toward me, even though neither of us knew each other. Of course, I know who he is now, but the intensity with which he's watching me indicates he has no clue about how we are connected.

When he slumps against the pillow, I place the glass back on the bedside.

"Uh, I think I need to call the doctor." I shift forward in my chair before rising.

"The doctor?"

I nod. "You've been in a coma for two weeks."

He frowns.

"Basically, since you got shot, you've been out. We, uh, had to rush you to the hospital—"

"We?" His scowl deepens.

"We, as in me—even though I was on the verge of a nervous breakdown, seeing as I was covered in your blood—and your brothers were—"

"Brothers?" His gaze intensifies. "Did you say my brothers?" he asks with slow deliberation.

"Yes." I nod. Surely, it's okay to tell him about his brothers, right? I mean, he does know about them, doesn't he? Why else would he have sought them out and intruded on the gathering at Christian and Aurora's place?

Unless he doesn't really know about their existence, or that he is one of triplets, or the fact that one of them is dead. Oh, crap. I swallow. Maybe I shouldn't have spoken to him, and called the doctor instead. Surely, it isn't good for him to get all worked up, and that's exactly what I'm causing right now.

His eyebrows knit, a wary gaze in his eyes. He clenches and unclenches his fingers, and my gaze is drawn to his arm. Scars run up the length of his forearm. They should be ugly, except there are tattoos inked into either side of the blemishes. I've had two weeks to study them while he was unconscious, and I still find them fascinating. The designs are flames that have been drawn into his skin. The patterns enhance the scars, showcase them, and turn them into a work of art. It must have been painful, though. It looks like he had been badly burned, and a while ago, by the state of the blemishes.

"What happened?" I burst out.

His features tighten. "None of your business," he snaps.

I firm my lips. "Jeez, keep your shirt on. I was only trying to be sociable."

"Well, don't be," he rasps. His voice is rough, probably because he hasn't used it over the last two weeks, but hell if it doesn't sound sexy. Damn it, the man is recovering from a coma. He has no business being this attractive. *And you have no business wanting to jump into bed with him when he's this weak.*

"Okay then." I pull out my hair tie, and my hair flows around my shoulders. "I think it's best I get the doctor."

I turn to leave, then gasp when he grabs my wrist. Electricity travels out from the point of contact. I glance down at where the darkness of his fingers contrasts with the paleness of my skin. It's as if I'm the one who's been unwell, considering my pallor.

"For someone who's been unconscious for two weeks, you seem to have retained most of your strength," I mutter.

"No doctor," he rasps. I glance up to find his face is definitely a few shades paler than earlier.

"You're in a hospital, and you've just emerged from a coma. I really do need to call the doctor."

"No..." Sweat beads his forehead.

"No doctor." He glances between my eyes. "Please," he seems to force the word out, "no doctor."

"Look, I'm not sure why you are having such a panicked reaction to the idea of a doctor checking you out, but they saved your life. If it weren't for them, you might be dead."

There's still no response from him. His hold on my arm seems to tighten. Jesus, this man must have been in peak physical condition if he's this strong emerging from a coma. To be fair, he had moved so quickly when he stepped in front of me that I hadn't even realized what was happening. Not until I'd heard that sickening thwack of the bullet piercing through his flesh and then... I swallow. Then, a part of me knew how close to death I had been. As he stumbled back, I knew he'd stepped in front of me to protect me. I jumped forward to try to catch his fall and had half collapsed under the weight of his body before sinking to my knees with him sprawled across my lap. And even then, I didn't know who he really was, until Christian had taken off the stranger's mask and I had seen Xander's face, as if resurrected from the dead. My heart begins to race in my chest as I take in the features of the man on the bed. Even now, I can't believe just how similar the two of them look.

Christian and Xander were twins, but they hadn't been identical. But this man, he resembles Xander so much, it makes my chest hurt just looking at him.

"Okay," I nod, "no doctor ... for now, but someone is going to come and check in on you, eventually."

He doesn't reply, doesn't let go of my arm either. "Who are you?" he asks again. "Do I know you? Have we met?"

"Not until you stepped in front of me and took the bullet."

He winces.

"Does it hurt?" I glance at the bandage around his head. "Damn, I knew I shouldn't have agreed not to call the doctor. Look, I don't want anything to happen to you, okay? They need to come and check you out and make sure that you are okay and—"

"I'm okay," he rasps.

"You don't look okay." I take in his features, which have definitely gone paler in the past few seconds. "You look like you're about to lose consciousness again, and that's not good, that's really not good, I—"

"Will you calm the fuck down, woman?" he growls.

"Excuse me?" I stare. "What did you say?"

He blows out a breath. "I'm fine. I don't need you making a fuss over me."

My chest rises and falls. I've been waiting for him to wake up all this time. I had practically chained myself to the bed and kept vigil and prayed that he'd open his eyes, and now that he has... He tells me to fuck off?

"Let go of me," I say through gritted teeth.

"Not until you tell me how the hell I came to be in this hospital room."

"That's what I've been trying to explain, if you'd put your paranoia aside for one moment and listen to me."

"Paranoia?" He scowls. "What the fuck gave you that idea, anyway?"

I glance down at where his fingers are still curled around my wrist, and his grasp tightens.

"You're my insurance," he says in a hard voice. "I'm not letting you go until I understand what kind of a situation I'm in."

"You're in a hospital, and I should've called a doctor, who's going to be pissed that I didn't at the first sign of your waking up; that's the kind of situation you are in," I scold. "Now, will you let go of me, please?"

"Why are they keeping me here? Who are these brothers you spoke about?"

"You don't remember?" I study his face. "And for the record, as I have already explained, no-one is keeping you here. You were shot, so they brought you to the hospital—"

"Who's they?"

"The paramedics who your brother Michael called."

"Michael?" He frowns. "And he is..."

"Your oldest brother."

"How many brothers do I have, anyway?"

"Um ... five? No, there's four, actually."

"Which is it, four or five?"

"Four." I bite the inside of my cheek. "Xander, your triplet—"

"Hold on, did you say triplet?"

Oops, I didn't mean to reveal that yet, but he would've eventually learned about it, one way or the other, right? So, it's okay for me to tell him that he has a triplet. I mean, he must have known, considering he turned up at Christian and Aurora's wedding, right?

"Umm, yeah ... and then you have two half-brothers, so including you, that makes it seven brothers again."

"Again..." He scowls. "What do you mean by that?"

"Xander is ... you know—"

"No, I don't know." Sweat beads his forehead, and his grasp on my arm loosens. "What happened to Xander?"

"He's ... uh..." Damn, it's not easy to break the news to him, especially when he's only just woken up from a coma. Speaking of, how the hell can he be so lucid so soon? "It's best you hear about it once you recover completely."

"Tell me ... now..." He begins to slur. "Tell me..." His eyelids flutter, "I ... in-insist." He releases me, then slumps back against the pillows. His features go slack. I hesitate and watch as his breathing deepens. Best to call the doctor now, before he wakes up again and insists that he doesn't want anyone to examine him.

I turn to leave, and that's when the window of the hospital room shatters. The glass pieces scatter across the floor as a man jumps into the room.

2

Axel

A scream pierces through the blankness in my head. What the hell? Who's that? I try to open my eyelids, but they seem to be weighed down. Darkness crowds in on my subconscious, and I push it away. I crack open my eyes as she screams again. I turn my face in the direction of the scream and watch as the tiny dark-haired woman grapples with a man wearing a pair of black pants and shirt. The lower half of his face is covered with a mask. He has a gun.

He has a gun.

My pulse rate ratchets up. The beeping of the machine linked to me increases in intensity. The man raises his free hand and strikes the woman. The force of the blow carries her across the floor. She hits the wall and crumples there.

The beeping speeds up even further, until it's one long discordant note. Anger slices through me, and it's not because I know her... Or do I? I'm not sure, but it's wrong to hit a woman... Especially that woman. *My woman.* Jesus, she's not my woman. Where the hell did that thought come from?

I push up from the bed, only my arms give way, and I collapse back. The man pulls out his gun and raises it in my direction. My heart slams into my ribcage.

Asshole points his gun at me and takes a step in my direction. Adrenaline floods my veins. I push over onto my side and roll away just as the pillow next to me explodes.

Fucking hell. Bastard's going to kill me, and I'm lying here unprotected. Every part of my body screams in protest as I force my muscles to obey my commands. I roll over further and drop to the floor. The needle stuck into my arm is wrenched out, and the tape rips out the hair on my arm. Fuck! Blood spurts from the wound, but that's the least of my concerns. Pain squeezes up my spine. Another bullet slams into the floor next to me.

Motherfucker! He's gonna take me out, and as if that's not bad enough, when I'm in a hospital gown. Nothing against hospital gowns; it's just that I'd prefer to go without my ass on display to the world at large.

I glance up to find him standing over me. Fuck, fuck, fuck. I will not die. Will not. The skin around his eyes tighten, and I know the asshole is laughing. Anger squeezes my chest. Blood pumps in my ears. Sweat pours down my face as I grab the edge of the bed. Every muscle in my body protests, and my arms and legs tremble as I push up to my feet. Or try to, anyway. My biceps spasm, and my body refuses to obey me.

I collapse against the floor, and the impact knocks the breath out of me. *F-u-c-k.* Sparks flash behind my eyes. My stomach twists, and bile sears my throat. Darkness flickers at the corners of my vision. I shove it aside and glance up and into the barrel of his gun. He depresses the trigger; I squeeze my eyes shut. Then, I hear the thump of the bullet as it embeds into the floor next to me.

I snap open my eyelids to find the man is no longer standing over me. Turning my head, I lock my gaze with my would-be-assassin's sightless eyes. Blood trickles out of a wound between his eyebrows.

The breath rushes out of me, the tension drains out, and my arms and legs tremble.

"Here, take my hand."

I turn my face in the direction of the voice and come face-to-face with features which are so damn familiar.

"Fuck," I growl. That's when darkness overwhelms me.

**

When I open my eyes next, I'm on the bed again and he's standing in front of me. The intruder's body is gone, along with the blood, and all of the pieces of glass have been swept away. I glance at the window to find the pane has been replaced. Huh?

"My men cleaned the room." The man scowls at me. "Also, replaced your bedclothes. You're welcome."

"How is she?" I rasp.

"If you mean Theresa, she's shaken, but she'll survive."

Theresa, so that's her name. "Asshole threw her against the wall." I try to ball my fists and find I'm clutching something between my fingers. I glance down to find I'm holding something purple in color … something that resembles a hair tie. *Her* hair tie? Green eyes, thick auburn hair, curves that could drive a man to madness. Anger sweeps through me as I close my fingers around the colorful restraint. "He pointed a gun at her." I cough.

"Now you know," the man retorts in a hard voice.

"What the fuck do you mean by—" I burst out coughing. When the bout subsides, I sink back against the pillows.

The man, who is not me, but looks a helluva lot like me, snatches up the glass of water with the goddamn straw and holds it to my mouth. Fuck, if I don't hate being an invalid, but the burning in my throat demands that I lock my lips around the straw and suck. The water trickles down my throat, soothing it somewhat. He places the glass back on the table. "I would introduce myself, but you know me already."

"Do I?" I rasp. My throat hurts, my head throbs, and underneath it all is a lingering heaviness, probably from whatever drugs they are pumping into me.

"You shot at me?" The man curls his fingers into fists.

"Join the queue," I drawl. "You're not the first man that I pointed a gun at, and you won't be the last. But as to who you are?" I reach into my memories, but a white haze engulfs my brain. "Nope, sorry; don't remember. Clearly, you weren't anyone of consequence, else it might have stuck in my mind?"

His jaw tightens. "To answer your earlier question, you held a gun to my wife's forehead, you *testa di cazzo*."

"Did I, now?" I pretend to think, not that it matters. I can't remember shit of what happened to land me here in this bed.

"Yes, you did, you *stronzo*. You pulled a gun on her. You blackmailed her into helping you spy on me and my family, or don't you remember that either?"

That seems about right, though I can't say I remember all of the details. Apparently, the one time I'm telling the truth, no one wants to believe me. What a fucking joke. I roll my shoulders. Hold on, do I know my name at least? "I'm Axel." The words are out before I can stop myself.

The man scowls at me. "Evidently, you can remember your name."

"It must be instinctive," I say slowly. The breath whooshes out of me, and my muscles relax a little. Thank fuck, I was able to remember my name, at least, but why the hell did I shoot at this man, who is, clearly, related to me? Or pointed a gun at his wife.

"What else do you remember?" The man's jaw hardens.

"What's it to you?" I yawn, and his features grow angry.

"I should have let that motherfucker's bullet take you," he snaps.

"Why didn't you?"

His features contort. He closes the distance between us, then grabs the front of my hospital gown. "Now listen here, you *pezzo di merda*, if you think I'm going to let you get away with this pretense of losing your memory, then you don't know me, you—"

"Christian, let go of him," a man admonishes as he enters the room.

I take in his build, his features, the dark hair. He resembles the other guy, so I guess his features resemble mine. Authority rolls off of his shoulders as he pauses on the other side of my bed.

"Let go of your triplet, Christian."

"Triplet?" I stare between them as Christian releases me and steps back. "Did you say triplet?" I ask again.

She, too, mentioned triplets, didn't she?

"Didn't you notice the resemblance?" the newcomer asks.

"He's nowhere as good-looking as me," I retort.

Christian's features grow stonier.

The new guy chuckles, then turns it into a cough. He jerks his chin in my direction and says, "Good to have you back, *fratello*."

"Can't say I share the sentiments, *fratello*." Christian glares at me.

"Another swear word, I take it?"

The other guy's eyebrows shoot up. "You don't speak Italian?"

"Not a word," I assure him.

"We'll have to rectify that." His lips quirk.

"And you are—?"

"Michael." He holds out his hand.

"Axel," I murmur. "You'll forgive me if I don't shake your hand; trying to conserve energy here."

"As you should." He peers into my features. "That's quite a brave thing you did back there, taking a bullet for Theresa."

"Can't say I remember any of it." *And good thing too, because taking a bullet for someone else? Nope, not something I'd do.*

"The doc says it's because of the bullet you took," Michael informs me. "While it didn't hit anything vital, it was a shock to your system, which has resulted in some parts of your brain shutting down to protect you. It's normal to be groggy and unsettled for some time as you recover from your coma."

"Are you siding with him on this?" Christian glares at Michael. "After everything he did to me and Aurora, you're giving him the benefit of the doubt."

"It's the doctor's diagnosis," Michael says mildly. "There's no reason for him to lie, is there?"

"No reason to believe this *stronzo* when he says he doesn't remember the events of what transpired, is there?" Christian shoots back.

"Chillax." I tip my chin in his direction, and even that motion sends vibrations of pain thudding through my head. "I wish I were lying, but this time, sadly, I speak the truth—a first for me, I assure you."

"At least, you're truthful about lying." Michael's lips curl.

"Got nothing to lose. In fact, it's in my interest to tell the truth, considering I'm not going anywhere for a while."

"Hmm…" Michael strokes his chin. "What's the last thing you remember anyway?"

I narrow my gaze on him. "A phone call. I had a phone call for a new assignment, and then…" I shake my head. "Nothing after that."

"How convenient," Christian scoffs, at the same time that Michael narrows his gaze on me.

"An assignment?" he asks. "What kind of assignment was it?"

"I don't remember all the details." I shake my head. "I'm sure it will come back to me, but from what I recall, it was related to..." I squeeze the bridge of my nose, "...related to tracking down you guys."

"You mean killing one of us? Namely, me?" Christian snorts.

"I was just obeying orders; it was nothing personal."

"Nothing personal?" Christian's features harden. "I almost died, you *carogna!*"

"From what I can see, you're still alive." I smirk.

His jaw tics, his nostril's flare, color smears his cheeks, and he reaches over and grabs the collar of my gown.

"Hey." Michael grips his shoulder. "Let him go, Christian."

His grip tightens on me. I cough.

"Now," Michael snaps.

Christian grits his teeth, but he releases me. I collapse onto the pillows, draw in a lungful of air, and my chest hurts. Fucking hell, I really am weak at the moment. No sense antagonizing these chaps when I'm unable to hold my own against them. "Trust me, I have no reason to be lying about my predicament."

Michael lowers his arm to his side. "I do believe he's telling the truth."

Christian turns on Michael. "So, you're willing to forget the fact that he threatened you, as well?"

Michael surveys my features. "Only because the doctor backs him up."

"Maybe the doctor is wrong," Christian growls. "Maybe this asshole got to him and has been able to get him to lie on his behalf."

Michael tilts his head and looks at me. "Have you gotten the doctor to lie on your behalf?"

"Me?" I widen my gaze. "Of course, not."

"See?" Michael raises his shoulder.

"Fucker's lying." Christian tightens his fists at his sides.

"Stay back, *fratello*," Michael says in a soft voice. "You're still grieving for your triplet, and seeing him is bound to trigger memories."

"Fuck that." Christian shakes his head as if to clear it. "This asshole can't be my brother."

"The resemblance is uncanny, you have to admit." I shrug. "Not that it isn't creepy to be talking to someone who looks very much like me."

"The resemblance is all we have in common." Christian widens his stance. "After what you did to my wife, I'll never accept you as my brother."

"Speaking of…" I glance between them. "Does our triplet have a name?"

Christian's shoulders go solid.

Simultaneously, Michael says, "Xander. His name is Xander."

"So, when do I get to meet this Xander?"

Christian draws himself up to his full height. "You don't." Spinning on his heels, he heads out the door.

"What was that about?" I frown after him.

"Xander's dead."

I turn to Michael "He's … dead?" *Wait, I think Theresa mentioned that…*

"He was the unfortunate victim of a car bomb that our father planted in my wife's car."

Damn, can't trust family these days, can you?

"So, let me get this straight. You tell me that I'm one of a trio of triplets, then inform me in the next breath that one of them is dead?"

"You can see why it feels to us like you are Xander returned to us?" Michael murmurs.

"I'm not Xander, though."

"And no one knows it better than I. I was the one who had to identify his body at the morgue."

"It was us who buried him, though … all of us." Another man strides into the room, then pauses when he sees us. His features pale, before he wipes all expression from his face. He walks over to stand next to Michael. "I'm Luca," He jerks his chin.

"Axel," I mutter. "Let me guess; you're another brother?"

"The second." His features close.

O-k-a-y, what happened there? Seems like it's a touchy topic for Luca to be born the second. "Guess you're the spare, huh?"

Luca scowls. "What the hell do you mean?"

"You know, the heir and the spare." I raise my shoulder. "You're the spare."

His features grow thunderous. "Fuck you," he says in a low voice.

I chuckle, then wince when the pain in my head intensifies.

"Anyone else in this infernal shit-show I still need to meet?" I drawl.

"You're not in control of your emotions; being shot at and then attacked can do that to a man," Michael drums his chest, "so I'll forgive you this indiscretion."

"Indiscretion?" I laugh. All the muscles in my body seem to seize up, pain clouds my vision, and I gasp in a breath. "What indiscretion?"

"Since you don't seem to remember, let me enlighten you. I am the Don of the Cosa Nostra."

I furrow my eyebrows. "And that's supposed to mean something?" Something brushes up against my mind, only to fade away.

"He's only the most powerful man alive, this side of the Atlantic," Luca cautions me. "If I were you, I'd be careful in what I say to him, you—"

Michael raises his hand. "You do get a wide berth in what you can get away with. After all, you are one of my brothers."

"How many of your brothers are there?"

"Seven." Michael's voice softens. "We are seven again, now that you are one of us, *fratello*."

Not sure what to make of that. I wait for something in my memory to confirm that I knew I had brothers, but there's no spark of recognition, nothing that tells me I was aware of their existence.

"Gentlemen, I'm aware of your importance, but the health of my patient is my number one priority." A doctor walks into the room. "If you don't mind, I need to ask you to leave"—he nods toward the doorway—"now."

Michael seems like he's going to refuse, then nods. "I expect a full report on my brother, Doc." He turns and stalks out.

Luca folds his arms across his chest, as if settling in to wait.

"That goes for you too." The doctor scowls at him.

"I'm staying for his safety," he nods in my direction, "so why don't you get busy and start checking him out, because I'm not going anywhere."

"But I need to examine the patient," the doctor protests.

"I'm not stopping you."

The doctor hesitates, then looks in my direction. I shrug, and he blows out a breath. "Fine, can you stay out of the way until I'm done, please?"

I'm not sure how much time has passed, but when I open my eyes again, I spot Theresa curled up in the only chair in the room. It's a typical, straight-backed hospital chair. The kind that's meant to cause as much discomfort to the occupant as possible, because that's what hospitals specialize in, apparently. Her head is pillowed on the back of her palm. Her lips are slightly parted, and the skin of her face is flushed. She's wearing another dress, I think, also black, with black tights and black shoes. Her hair is loose and flows over the back of her chair. She seems like a princess in mourning. *Is she mourning Xander? Did she love him?* I raise a shoulder, then wince; doesn't really matter.

Either way, she's not my type. For one, she's not as busty as the kind of women I prefer. Likely, she's also intelligent. She looks like a woman who has an above-average IQ and who doesn't hesitate to verbalize her thoughts. I blow out a breath. Everything that makes me run the other way. I prefer my women on their knees, or on their front, or back… Doesn't matter, as long as they have their thighs open and mouths shut—or stuffed with my cock. As long as they take what I give them, do as they're told, and leave when I'm done with them.

Yep, so that's rather predictable, and perhaps, misogynistic in a man, but hey, I don't claim to be a saint. Also, I don't hide behind the polite veneer that society demands of you. Scratch the surface, and most men will admit that they are basic creatures at heart. That what they want is a woman who satisfies their desires, who does as she is told, and who, ideally, also cooks for them. See, the last, I don't ask them for that; it's one of the things I'm good at. I like to eat good food, and it turns out, most women aren't that competent in the kitchen either. Why do you think there are so many male chefs, eh? And considering I have been on my own since I turned eighteen, I had to learn to cook in order to feed myself, and I'm proud to say, I've eaten well.

Now, Theresa, on the other hand? She seems like the kind of woman who'd probably be able to cook as well… A theory I'm not going to test because I don't want anything to do with her. Of course, if she offers herself up to me… Well, I wouldn't say no. I mean, I could fuck her. I drag my gaze down the slope of her breasts, the tiny waist that flares into hips which are curved enough that I can hold onto them when I fuck her from behind. My balls tighten. Huh? Didn't expect to get turned on that quickly. Especially not when the rest of my body feels like I've crashed into a brick wall. It's a relief to know that part of my anatomy is working, and that I, at least, recall the kind of woman I prefer. So why the hell am I attracted to her? And why can't I recollect what went down the day I was shot?

I sit up and wince when my muscles protest, but I ignore it. If I'm going to get out of here, I need to get my body moving.

Theresa stirs. She shifts around in her seat, then her eyelids flutter open. Her green eyes fix on me. She blinks, then sits up. "You're awake?"

I take in the bandage on her temple, and anger rips through my veins. "What the hell are you doing here?"

3

———————

Theresa

"Uh, I wanted to make sure that you were okay."

I blink rapidly. Why is he angry? Is it because I fell asleep while waiting for him to wake up? No, that doesn't make sense. After the intruder shoved me aside, I hit my head and blacked out. I woke up in another room in the hospital to find a nurse dressing my wounds. They offered me painkillers, which I didn't want to take, but I finally relented in the hope that it would reduce my headache. The pills helped, but they made me drowsy, which is why I

fell asleep in the chair, and woke up to find him glaring at me.

"You shouldn't be here," he says in a hard voice.

Goosebumps pop on my skin. Hell, why is it that my body responds this way to him? I swallow and push myself to my feet. "Considering you're flat on your back and not even able to walk without help, I don't think you have much say in the matter, do you?"

His lips firm. "Where's Luca?"

"He took a break." I gather my hair over one shoulder—damn it, why do I keep losing my hair ties?—then walk over to stand next to him. "You're feeling better, I take it?"

"I'll feel better when I'm out of this goddamn hospital."

"Can't say I blame you." I sniff. "The color of this hospital gown is playing havoc with your complexion."

"Eh?" He stares at me as if I've grown a second head. "What do you mean?"

"Just that you, ah, look pale. I mean, you're still tanned, of course. In fact, your skin color definitely shows that you spend a lot of time outside, but the hospital gown is a dirty cream color. Of course, flowers in that color look so much better."

"Flowers?" He blinks.

"I own a flower shop. I'm a florist, you know? I specialize in tulips. Did you know there are more than 3000 registered varieties of tulips in the world? Of course, I don't showcase all of them, but it's my dream to do so one day. I'll have to wait until my flower shop makes a lot more money, considering some of these tulips are so rare, they go at $2500 a bulb."

He stares at me as if I've grown another head or sprouted a flower—a tulip flower, to be exact. Argh. *What the hell am I doing, blathering like an idiot?* Why does he make me so nervous that I seem to blurt out whatever comes into my head?

"Umm, okay, now that I've thoroughly embarrassed myself..." My voice trails off. "Forget it." I turn to leave.

"What's the name of your flower boutique?"

I pause. Did he refer to it as a flower boutique? That's really creative. No one has ever referred to it like that before. I glance at him over my shoulder. "Do you really want to know?"

He merely tilts his head. The silence stretches. My skin begins to feel too tight for the rest of my body. A bead of sweat slides down the valley between my breasts, and I know I have to speak before I lose the ability to form words. *"The Tilting Tulip,"* I murmur.

"A fan of Don Quixote, I take it?"

My gaze widens. Oh, my god! Nobody, and I mean nobody, has guessed the origin of that name, to date. Not even Xander. Not even Elsa, my friend and sole employee who has helped me with the flower shop almost since the day it opened. So how did this guy figure it out? It scares me more than the fact that he has such an uncanny resemblance to Xander.

"Umm, okay. Bye. I have to leave now." I spin around and dart toward the doorway.

"Theresa," he growls, "get back here." His voice chafes over my nerve endings and does funny things to my insides. My belly trembles. My core clenches. Moisture beads my pussy. Hell, the man is on his back, trying to recover from a coma, but he's far from helpless. He only has to call me by my name, and I want to throw myself down at his feet and beg him to lick me all over… Especially in that throbbing place between my thighs. Definitely across my breasts. Maybe I could beg him to pluck at my nipples and tweak them hard until I come. Maybe I could—

"Theresa."

I squeak. "Y… yes," I stutter as I bite down on my lower lip.

"Turn around and face me."

My steps slow until I come to a halt. I draw in a breath, then turn and meet his gaze. Those blue eyes, so like Xander's … yet not. The look in them is so much more intense, like I have his entire attention. Did Xander ever look at me that way? Like I was the only one in the world, and he couldn't take his attention off of me?

"Why are you here?" He scowls. "What do you want from me?"

I want you to be Xander. I want you to be the man I loved and lost, the one I hoped would one day love me back. The one my heart still belongs to because I've had a crush on him for so long that I no longer know how to go on without him.

"I…" I twist my fingers together. "I want you to get better soon."

"Is that all?"

No.

No.

"Yes." I nod. "You saved my life, and I don't like seeing you in pain because of it."

"You have a soft heart," his lips twist, "but I'm not sure it warranted my taking a bullet for you."

I gape.

"You see, I'm not the kind of man who'd do something so selfless. And I definitely wouldn't put my life at stake for someone else, especially not someone who—"

I narrow my gaze on him. "Someone who?"

"Someone like you, who's clearly not the kind of woman I'm normally attracted to."

I open and shut my mouth. "Jesus, do you hear yourself? For someone who can't even pee by himself at the moment, you sure have a big ego."

"Not the only thing that's big." He smirks.

I throw up my hands. "You're a horrible man, and your jokes are sexist."

"So I've been told." His grin widens.

Goddamn it, he's even more attractive when he smiles. His features light up in a way Xander's never did. Xander was more introspective, more troubled about the state of the world, more brooding about his own internal conflict, while Axel… There's a recklessness to him that comes through in the gleam in his eyes. In how he sprawls back in the bed, making the entire space feel too small for him. How he sucks up all the oxygen in the air, how he draws my attention to his face, to his chest, the length of his body partially hidden under the sheet. Even though his muscles will need rehab to regain his strength, thanks to the coma he's been in… Still, there's an aura of power that to clings to him, a cloak of dominance that seems to cover him from head to toe, a lazy authority that oozes from his very pores. It's as if he has the best of all the Sovrano brothers, and more. All that charisma locked away and ready to be unleashed on some poor, unsuspecting mortal like me. Hell, without even trying, he's positively overpowering me… How the hell will he be when he's on his feet and dressed to kill? I'll probably combust if I'm in his presence then. Not that I'm not all hot and bothered now. A bead of sweat runs down between my breasts, and I shiver.

"Hey." He snaps his fingers, and I blink. "You okay?" he asks.

"Don't I look okay?" I demand.

"No need to get defensive; I was just being polite."

"I see you're awake?" Both Axel and I turn toward the door.

Luca swaggers in, then throws himself down on the chair I recently vacated. "This one," he jerks his chin in my direction, "deserves a medal. Not only has she been by your bedside since you were brought out of surgery, but the first thing she did after regaining consciousness earlier was ask about you."

My cheeks flush. "I was simply doing what was right," I mutter.

"But you might be wasting your attentions on the wrong guy," Luca warns.

I glance from Luca to Axel, whose face is wiped of all expression. If that offended him, he isn't showing it. Damn, but it's so difficult to get a read on this man. He seems to keep everything bottled up inside... Except for his ego, of course, which pushes him to make stupid remarks like he did earlier.

"I'm not sure that's a nice thing to say." I scowl at Luca.

"It's a fact." He raises a shoulder. "Best to say what's on my mind, right?"

"Don't let us stop you," Axel says dryly.

"You couldn't, even if you wanted to." Luca looks him up and down pointedly. "How long is it going to be before you get on your feet again?"

"The doctor thinks it's going to be at least a month of intensive rehab. I bet him I'll be walking again in two weeks."

"Two weeks?" I turn on him. "You were unconscious for two weeks. No way, can you regain your muscle strength and get back on your feet that quickly."

"You challenging me, Sunshine?" he drawls.

And whoa, what's with that nickname? I shoot Luca a glance and find him absorbed in something on his phone.

"I'm not challenging you." I turn to Axel. "It's just..." I lower my voice. "I don't want you to push yourself so hard that you end up hurting yourself."

"You took care of that already, didn't you? Doubt I can hurt myself further."

My heart slams into my chest. I stare at him and feel the tell-tale pressure of tears behind my eyes.

"You really are a selfish prick; you know that? I was just worried about you—"

"Don't be." He reclines further back into the pillows, looking for all the world like he's the master of all he surveys. "I can take care of myself."

"I have no doubt. It's just, you're hurt and—"

"I'll mend. I have strong healing powers."

"I'm sure, but—"

"I understand Xander is dead," he drawls. "Did you know him well?"

I nod. "He was...

He was..." Truth is, I'm not sure what he was to me. Not my boyfriend, not my lover... I'm not even sure he reciprocated my affections, but since I first set eyes on him, I was sure that our destinies were interlinked. I had dreamt of the day that I would marry him.

"Did you love him?" Axel drums his fingers on the bed. "Is that why you want to take care of me, because I look so similar to him?"

"I ... I did love him," I admit, "but that's not why I'm here."

"Oh?" He tilts his head. "Why else would you spend so much time by the bedside of a perfect stranger, taking care of him?"

"Maybe it's because you saved my life, and this is my way of thanking you?" I tip up my chin.

He arches an eyebrow. "By spending every moment of the past two weeks at my side? I think not."

I open my mouth to speak, but he shakes his head.

"I'm not him, Theresa. I never will be him, so if you think by hanging around me you can transfer the fixation you had on him to me, then you're mistaken."

A hot sensation stabs at my chest. My heart feels like it's going to break into a million pieces. My stomach hurts, and I fold my arms around myself. "You're right. You're not Xander. Xander never would have been this unkind to me." I swallow down the tears that threaten to overflow. "I must have been crazy to think that you could have ever held a candle to him. You ... you're a terrible man. You may look like him, but you'll never be h-him." My voice hitches. *Don't cry. Don't you dare cry before this horrible man.* I turn and rush out of the door.

4

Axel

"Couldn't have toned it down, eh?"

I hear Luca speak, but can't turn my gaze off her retreating figure. Goddamn it, why did I have to say that? So what if I was feeling aggravated, angry, and wanting to lash out at someone? It just so happened that she was there and she, apparently, cares for me, even if she doesn't know me at all. She thinks she knows me, and that's even worse. I'm nothing like this Xander chap. So what, he was my triplet. We have nothing in common.

He didn't know poverty, or what it felt like to see your mother whore herself out. She wasn't accepted into her own family because of me, and she wasn't very good at fending for herself. When you were a Mafia princess brought up in the lap of luxury, you had no idea how to take care of yourself, let alone your child. Despite her shortcomings, she managed to put a roof over my head and food in my belly. By the time I was sixteen, she was dead. That's when I began to carve out my own empire. Guess the apple didn't fall far from the tree, in that sense.

My mother had never told me about my father's side of the family or the insignificant fact that I was one of triplets. Something she obviously knew, but for whatever reason, she kept hidden from me. All she told me was that she had a falling out with my father, had left him, and her own family hadn't accepted her back. Not after having bedded their enemy and falling pregnant with his child. She refused to go back to them for help, no matter how difficult it was for her. Another reason I was so clear that I was going to make it on my own. Without help from anybody. Definitely not my mother's family. So, if they think I'm going to go all sentimental on them, they're going to be sadly mistaken. All I intend to do is play along until I'm back on my feet and then... Well, I'm going to get out of here.

"Axel, hey, you okay?" Luca calls out.

"Why wouldn't I be?" I growl. "I'm laid up in this bed with you for company. What more could I want?"

"You sent away the only person here who is sympathetic toward you."

And fuck, if I don't hate myself for it. Why is it so difficult for me to accept her concern? Why do I feel threatened by the utter selflessness with which she wants to care for me? Why the hell can't I remember stepping in front of her and taking the bullet as she claims I did? Why would I do that anyway? I've always put my survival ahead of anyone else's... So really, it makes no sense that I would do that.

I rub the back of my head, and my arm trembles.

I hate being so damn weak. The doctor who examined me had told me that it's a miracle I managed to get on my feet and avoid the intruder who had broken in. By all accounts, I shouldn't have been able to move my limbs without assistance, not after being unconscious for more than two weeks. But the adrenaline pouring through my veins propelled me to fight back, and thank fuck I did, else I'd be in a coffin by now. At least, I'd have family at my funeral... My breath catches. The fuck am I thinking? These guys... While they may be blood relations, they're definitely not my family. They are... I'm not sure, exactly, what to call them... Acquaintances, at best. Enemies, at worst. More probably, the latter.

I push myself up to sitting position, then swing my legs over the side of the bed.

"The fuck you up to, brother?" Luca rises to his feet. "What do you think you're doing?"

I place my feet on the ground and push up to standing position. My thighs burn, my calves hurt, and sweat breaks out on my forehead. "Fuck." My knees tremble. Luca closes the distance between us and grabs my shoulder, but I shake it off. "Keep the fuck away from me, asshole."

"Hey"—he holds up his hands—"just trying to help."

"Well, don't." I grab the edge of the bed to steady myself, then holding onto it for support, I take a step forward, then another. My muscles protest, my arm hurts, and my head throbs with such intensity that the edges of my vision begin to darken. I take another step, and my entire body sways.

"You're a stubborn motherfucker," Luca says mildly.

"Didn't get to where I am by being lazy," I say through gritted teeth. I take another step, and my knees give way. I topple forward and hit the floor. "Fuck," I growl. Pain shoots through my chest and arms. My legs feel like they have turned to jelly. I manage to turn over on my back and lay there panting. "The fuck, asshole?" I glare at him. "You could have, at least, stopped me from falling."

"Thought you didn't want my help." He smirks, then holds out his hand.

"Fuck off." I grab the side of the bed, pull, but my muscles refuse to cooperate. "Fuck, fuck, fuck." I grit my teeth, hold onto the side of the bed, and push up, only to fall back panting.

"Come on; don't be an idiot." Luca lowers his arm until his palm is in my line of sight. "Take my hand, asshole," he drawls. "It's not a sign of weakness to take help when you need it most."

I glower at his palm, then raise my hand and manage to grasp his. He pulls me to my feet, and I lean my hip against the bed. He releases me, and I fall back onto the bed and lay there panting. "Fuck, I need to get back on my feet."

"Keep pushing yourself like that, and you'll do more harm than good."

"We'll see about that."

"Do you really think you're going to be back on your feet in two weeks?" He arches an eyebrow.

"That's the plan." I haul myself up the mattress, then collapse with my head on the pillow. Sweat drenches my shoulders, and the hospital gown sticks to my chest.

"Want some more water?" Luca holds out the glass of water with the fucking straw—I hate that straw. When I'm better, I'm going to ensure I'm never near another straw for my entire bloody life. For now, though, I lean forward and take a sip of water, then another, until I have chugged down all of it. He places the empty glass on the bedside table.

"You know, you're as pig-headed as the rest of us."

"Spare me the comparisons," I growl. "I'm not one of you. I'll never be one of you—"

"Is that why you wanted to kill one of us? Because you hold a grudge against our family?"

5

Axel

Michael prowls into the room, followed by Christian and three men who I don't recognize, but with their dark hair and features that resemble Michael's, they must be some of the seven brothers Theresa alluded to.

Michael walks over to stand at the foot of the bed. Christian comes to a halt next to Luca. The biggest of the new arrivals stalks over to stand on the side of the bed opposite Luca.

"I'm Massimo." He tilts his head.

"And I'm Seb." One of the other guys jerks his chin as he comes to a stop next to Massimo.

"Adrian," the third guy offers. He walks over to stand between Michael and Seb. The brothers surround me. If they plan to show me how outnumbered I am, then they're not succeeding. What they don't realize is that I do best when I'm challenged. When the odds are stacked against me, I rise to the occasion—no pun intended.

A fourth guy closes the door behind them, no doubt, standing guard outside.

"Why did you threaten Aurora?" Christian folds his arms over his chest.

"Aurora?" I frown. "Who's Aurora?"

"Don't pretend you don't know her," Christian snaps. "You tracked her down in London and threatened her family. It's because of you that she returned to Sicily. It's you who followed us to the lodge in Cortina and shot at me."

"Did I get you?"

"No," he growls.

"Damn," I smirk, "so sorry; I'll try better next time."

Christian takes a step forward, and Michael slaps his arm in front of his chest.

"You're hurt and disoriented." Michael frowns at me. "It's normal, since you've just come out of a coma, but you're not doing yourself any favors by antagonizing us."

"Is that right?" I tilt my head, "I'm not afraid of you guys."

"And you shouldn't be," Michael agrees. "Like it or not, you're one of us. You're a Sovrano by blood. Not to mention you resemble a brother we lost who we dearly loved, so my preference is to not hurt you."

"You can try," I scoff. "I may resemble your brother, but I don't consider myself one of you."

"Why else were you trying to hurt one of us?" Seb growls. "You must have known who we were. You sure knew about our movements. You knew we were at a family getaway when you came after Christian. Who put you up to that?" He narrows his gaze on me. "It's time you came up with some answers."

"Even if I knew the answers"—I hold up my hand, which doesn't tremble this time, thank fuck—"I wouldn't tell you."

"Wrong answer." Luca scowls at me. "You're either a fool, or you know something we don't."

"And you don't strike me as a fool," Massimo drawls. "So why don't you tell us what you were after?"

"Because I don't remember it?" I glare at their faces. And fuck, if I can ignore the resemblance to my features again. It's disconcerting—this sense that they're my family overwhelms me. My head begins to hurt, and I close my eyes. "Look, the more I push it, the less I'm going to remember. It's best I rest and get my strength back. That way, hopefully, my memories will resurface. Not that I'm planning to share any of that with you." Christian makes noise at the back of his throat. I grin without opening my eyes. "Unless you ask nicely, and maybe not even then."

The frustration that pours off of the guys makes me smile wider. *I hold the cards here, assholes, and don't forget it.*

"Besides, once I'm on my feet again, I could try to track back on my movements, and perhaps, that might jiggle something in my head?"

"Already on it," Luca states.

I open one eye. "What do you mean?"

"Got a couple of guys making enquiries about your whereabouts."

"N-i-c-e." I smirk. "Good to know, at least, one of you is thinking on your feet."

Luca's features harden. His brow pinches. I can't stop the chuckle that rips out of me. Ouch! Now my throat hurts, but fuck that. It's worth it just to see another of my brothers grow hot under the collar. *And f-u-c-k, stop thinking of them as your family, asshole. You don't do family, remember?*

"Too bad you're not on your feet"—Massimo holds up his fist—"or I might have to knock some sense into you."

"You have to stop taking this older brother thing so seriously." I yawn.

Massimo's brow furrows. "Is this guy for real, or what? Maybe I should forget about the fact that he's recovering from a bullet, which he did take for one of our own, and—"

"Hold on; back up." I scowl. "What do you mean 'one of our own'? Are you talking about—"

"Theresa?" Adrian nods. "She is one of us."

"Is she related to you guys?" I scowl.

"No, she's not related to *us.*" Seb gives me a pointed look. "She was Xander's..." he hesitates, "...friend. So, by default, she comes under our protection."

The breath I wasn't aware I was holding rushes out. What the fuck? Why did the thought of her being with one of these jokers cause me such dread?

"Although, considering how you rebuffed her, I'm sure you wouldn't mind if one of us decides to pursue her, eh?" Luca adds.

A growl rips up my throat, and I blink. What the fuck? What do I care if she decides to hook up with one of them? Not my problem. They're welcome to her. A hot sensation stabs at my chest. I ignore it. "Go for it." I close my eyes again. "Now, if you'll excuse me, I need to get my beauty sleep."

"Not so quickly." I open my eyes, and Michael narrows his gaze on me. "As soon as the doctor agrees, we're moving you out of here."

"What do you mean? I'm not going anywhere with you. I plan to get on my feet, then..." *get out of here.* I don't say the words aloud.

"Exactly." Michael smirks. "Afraid we're putting you under an old-fashioned house arrest."

"Are you?" I tilt my head.

"Can't have you getting your memory back, and then you go rushing off to whoever it is you owe your allegiance to," Seb confirms.

"We're not letting you leave." Christian bares his teeth. "Not until we figure out who the hell is behind your actions."

"What makes you think I was following anyone's orders?" I manage to fold my arms behind my neck. My muscles grumble, my biceps hurt, but fuck that. I grit my teeth and force a bored expression on my face. "And I'm not going anywhere with you."

"Oh, you are," Massimo drawls.

"Keep dreaming," I say mildly.

"He has no idea." Adrian shakes his head.

"None whatsoever." Luca smirks.

"The fuck you talking about?"

"The fact that in about two minutes you're going to agree to everything we ask of you," Seb retorts.

"And I thought I was the one on painkillers." I chuckle. "What have you guys been imbibing, eh?"

"Wait for it..." Christian cups his palm behind his ears. "Wait for it."

"What the hell?" I stare at them.

"Any moment now," Adrian adds.

The door to the room opens, and the clack of heels hitting the floor reaches me.

"Axel, my boy," a woman's voice reaches me.

The guys move aside so I have an unrestricted view of the woman who has entered the room. Her hair is grey and cut in a bob which sweeps her chin. Her features are almost regal as she sweeps her gaze over me. She wears a pantsuit, and on her feet, she wears stilettos I'd expect to see on a woman half her age. She wears a string of pearls around her neck, which only adds to her aristocratic bearing.

"There you are." She brushes past Michael and bends to take my hand. "I'm so happy that you're awake. I was so worried about you, *nipotino mio*."

"Uh…" I turn to Luca. "What does that mean?"

"It means my grandson," the woman interjects. "I'm your grandmother, Axel."

"Grandmother?" I blink. "So, you're my father's—"

"Mother, yes." She nods. "Unfortunately, your father is no longer with us."

"I guessed." I frown back at her. "How did he die?" I raise a hand. "No, don't tell me. I'm guessing he was killed by one of you?" I glance around at the gathered men.

"Not so sadly; I take the credit for that," Michael retorts. "He wanted me out of the way, so I had to kill him first."

"Sounds like a fun family," I respond.

"I understand how it might come across to an outsider," my grandmother murmurs, "but make no mistake, we have each other's backs." She holds my gaze. "And you are one of us now, *ciccino bello*."

"That means my wonderful grandson," Luca explains.

"I gathered," I say wryly. "So," I turn to the older woman, "you are my grandmother?"

"You can call me Nonna." She pats my hand.

"Nonna," I murmur, "you're clearly a woman to be reckoned with."

"Oh, phst." She waves her free hand in the air. "The way you turn on that charm effortlessly, you remind me of my husband; God rest his soul." She releases my arm to cross herself. "Before he decided to stray from our marriage."

"Ah"—I close my mouth which I only now realize has fallen open—"is that good or bad? Not your husband straying from his marriage, but the fact that I remind you of him?" I hasten to clarify.

"It's good." She laughs. "He was a rake, but damn, if he wasn't charismatic. I fell for him the moment I met him, and stayed married to him until he died."

"You didn't kill him, did you?" I ask only half-jokingly.

She fixes me with that gimlet eye of hers. "I knew you were smart." She laughs.

"Eh?" I scowl, "So, you did … off him?"

"Not me, personally, but his enemies did finally get to him."

"Are you telling me you had a hand in it?"

"Now, now, I'm not the kind to kiss and tell, if you get my drift." She cackles.

That headache pounding behind my eyes turns up a notch. And I thought *I* had a bloodthirsty background? Hanging out with the Sovranos gives a whole new perspective on the meaning of *'nearer the blood the bloodier,'* as someone—whose name is inconsequential— once remarked.

"You've gone pale." Nonna's sharp gaze instantly spots my discomfort. "Do you need your painkillers?"

"No." I shake my head, then wince when the hammers behind my head turn up the intensity of their drumming. "No more painkillers."

"The man's as obstinate as the rest of you," Nonna says in an affectionate voice.

I feel my eyelids flutter down and force them open. "I want to make it very clear that I am not one of you."

"I think the man protests too much," Seb murmurs. "Why don't you get some shut-eye, eh?"

As they turn to leave, I call out, "Seb?"

He turns.

"I need your help."

He walks over to me, "What is it?"

"Can you get me a pack of cigarettes and a lighter?"

"Smoker, eh?"

I raise a shoulder.

"You're aware this is a hospital and smoking is not allowed, right?"

I gape at him, and he bursts out laughing, "Relax. The rules don't apply to the Cosa Nostra. I'll get it for you."

He pivots on his heels, then hesitates, and leaves.

I lay back and don't fight the sleep that overwhelms me.

When I wake up next, it's dark outside the windows. Illumination from the safety lights highlights the face of the person sleeping in the chair. The pale skin and the sweep of auburn hair flowing over the chair indicates it's *her*.

Her chest rises and falls, and she has her cheek cushioned in her palm. The dark curve of her eyelashes rests against her cheekbones. She stirs in her sleep, then settles again. When her breathing evens out, I glance away and spot the pack of cigarettes and lighter on the side table. Guess Seb came through for me.

I reach for the lighter, flick on the flame, then hold my palm around it. The warmth seeps into my blood, and I sigh. I click off the lighter, place it on the bedside, then swing my legs over the side of the bed. My feet hit the ground, then I take a deep breath and push myself to a standing position. My thighs burn, my calves hurt, and my knees threaten to give out from under me. I dig my heels into the floor, and thankfully, my legs seem to hold me up. I lower myself to the ground. Every muscle in my body protests, but I ignore the pain. I manage to lower my body weight onto my palms and feet, and fuck! My entire body trembles. My biceps spasm, and my calf muscles scream in protest as I bend my elbows and push down, then thrust upward. My shoulders convulse, and the still unhealed wound at my temple throbs. Fuck, fuck, fuck. I grit my teeth, push through the pain, and force my muscles to comply as I flow into another push-up. My vision flickers. Sweat trickles down my temple and trails down my chin to plop on the floor. My entire body turns into one pulsating vector of pain as I push down, then up. Again and again.

"What are you doing?"

I lose my balance and face-plant on the floor. "Fuck." I pant, try to roll over, but find my arms no longer obey my command. "Bloody fuck!" I growl, then stiffen when she grips my shoulder.

"Let me help you."

She sits cross-legged next to me and grips the underside of my shoulder. She leans in closer, and the scent of apple blossoms fills my nostrils. I draw in her scent, fill my lungs with it, and use it to center myself. Her pushing, combined with my own efforts, means I finally manage to turn over on my back. I collapse on the ground, my breath coming in pants. My heart thunders in my chest like I have run for miles. At this rate, it's going to be weeks, maybe months, before I return to my former strength. I cannot let that happen. I need to get back to full health as soon as possible.

I close my eyes, focus on regulating my breath, on getting my pulse rate under control. When I open my eyes, I find her scrutinizing my features.

"What?" I growl. "Happy to see a man falling apart in front of you?"

A stricken look crosses her features. Fuck, why did I have to say that? Why do I have to hurt her every time I see her? I close my eyes again. "I told you stay away from me, didn't I? I'm not good for you, Theresa."

"Let me be the judge of that."

I crack open my eyes and meet her gaze. She holds it, then color stains her cheeks. Jesus, how innocent is she that she can't even hold my gaze without blushing. How sheltered has she been? What little I know tells me the Mafia are protective about their women. And the Sovranos consider her one of theirs. So, chances are good she hasn't seen much of the world outside of Palermo, or been with any man except for Xander. Or has she?

"Are you a virgin?"

6

Theresa

OMG, that inevitable question. Why is it such a big deal for these men anyway? And why is he asking me that question now? Is he interested in me? Is that what this is about? But all of his actions so far indicate the exact opposite.

"What do you think?" I shoot back.

He blows out a breath.

"I'll take that as a yes."

"That's not what I said."

"You didn't need to." He tries to sit up, only to collapse back onto the ground. He growls in frustration, then pushes up off his elbows. This time, he makes it halfway up before gravity pulls him back onto the floor. "Fuck," he yells. "Fuck, fuck, fuck." The tendons of his beautiful neck strain, the skin glistening with sweat. The hospital gown he's wearing gapes in the front. I take in the groove between his pecs, the design of a tattoo that creeps up over his shoulder. It's something I noticed before, but now I can make out the intricate whirls, the pattern, the colors. Does it flow down his back as well? Does it cover his biceps?

A bead of sweat trails down his temple, and I lean down and lick it up.

His entire body goes solid. His shoulder planes tense. He glares at me as if he can't quite believe what I did. Truthfully, I can't believe I did it either. Maybe it's because he guessed that I'm a virgin. Maybe because I'm pissed at myself for having stayed a virgin for a man who may or may not have loved me; something I'll never know now because I didn't have the lady balls to confront him about it. For some reason, I have been given a second chance with Axel. Who is *not* Xander. I may have wanted him to be Xander when he was unconscious, but now that he is awake, now that his blue gaze bores into mine, now that the awareness behind those eyes is focused on me, it's clear to me that this man is nothing like Xander.

Xander had a laid-back charm about him, a goodness that seemed to permeate everything around him. He had a charisma which made me feel that the world could be a better place than what people believed. It's why I wanted to be with him. He gave me hope. He was everything Axel is not.

Where Xander was all light and brightness, Axel is darkness—he is deeper, more complex, more intense, more secretive in a way that makes me want to dig in and unearth what it is that he holds so close to his heart, what it is that he is concealing under the mask he shows to the rest of the world. And it's not only because his memories haven't returned completely… It's something else. Something I can't put my finger on, something that pulls me closer, makes me want to throw myself at him and sink my teeth into his skin until I unearth whatever it is that lurks just under the surface.

I bite down on my lower lip, and his gaze drops to my mouth. His nostrils flare. He stares at my mouth like he wants to taste me, consume me, absorb me into himself and never let go, and somehow, I have a feeling I wouldn't protest if he did so. I gulp, the sound audible in the silence.

"Don't start something you won't be able to see through," he drawls.

I scowl. "Good to know you already have a preset impression of me that has nothing to do with what I actually am."

"Oh?" He raises his gaze to mine. "And what are you?"

"I'm not as innocent as people make me out to be."

"Is that right?"

I tip up my chin. "Don't make the mistake of underestimating me." I lean in close enough for our breaths to mingle. "Don't mistake me for a wilting flower, because I am not."

He rakes his gaze across my features before meeting my eyes again. There's a flash of interest in the depths of his eyes, something I hadn't noticed before. It's as if he's seeing me properly for the first time. *Asshole.*

"When I make up my mind that I want something, I go after it. I can be very persistent." I stare at his mouth, and something hot unfurls in my chest. My core clenches, and my pulse rate ratchets up. I draw in his breath, and that musky, sweaty scent of his pours through my veins. I touch my lips to his, and the next moment, I'm pulled into his chest. I lose my balance, fall on him, and he groans.

"Oh hell, sorry, sorry, sorry." I try to push away, but even in his weakened state, his arm around me holds me in place.

The color drains from his face, but he doesn't release me.

"I thought you weren't able to use your arms and legs properly?"

"Turns out, I only need the right motivation." He smirks. "You were saying?"

"What?" I frown, unable to turn my gaze away from that gorgeous mouth of his. The hard planes of his body dig into my chest. Damn, he may need rehab to get back on his feet, but lying horizontal like this, with every inch of my body plastered to his, I feel smaller, softer, and overwhelmed by his masculinity. Every dip and ridge of his muscles, every indentation of his tendons, every hard plane of his body hints at the power coiled under his skin. Something only temporarily leashed by the position he's in now. It won't be long before he's back on his feet and then…

He'll leave. I know he will. He'll walk away and I… I won't have anything left to show. Again. And that … that I can't bear. Not again. I'm not going to lose this man… No, he is not Xander, I know, but something about him pulls me in a way that Xander never did. My head spins. I don't know this man at all, but no way am I letting him leave me. This time, I'm going to stake my claim. This time, I'm going to make sure that I don't commit the mistakes of my past.

"You said something about being persistent?" His smile widens. "Let's see how—"

I lower my head and smash my mouth to his. I must take him by surprise because he parts his lips, and I thrust my tongue inside his mouth. A groan rips up his chest. The next moment, he grips my hair and tugs, so I have no choice but to jerk my chin up.

"That's not how this works, Sunshine," he murmurs. "Just because I'm not one-hundred percent functional doesn't mean that you can take control."

"And here I was, thinking you didn't want anything to do with me," I say lightly.

"Oh, I still don't," he retorts.

"Um … excuse me, but are you living in a parallel reality? From where I am"—I push my pelvis into the hard column between his legs that tents the hospital gown—"it seems you want me a lot."

"I'm never one to turn down free pussy."

I gape at him "You're an asshole."

"So you keep saying, and yet you keep throwing yourself at me."

"I am not—" I close my mouth.

"You aren't?" He smirks. The bastard smirks as he takes in my flushed features.

"Okay, I admit, I'm the one who made the first move. From the moment you stepped in front of me and that bullet hit you, I haven't been the same." I swallow. "You remind me of Xander, and I know you are not him, but tell that to my heart, which can't seem to tell the difference. I lost Xander, and I don't want to lose you as well."

"You never had me to lose me," he points out.

"You think I don't know that? All the time you were in a coma, I kept watch over you, and I kept telling myself that you were not Xander, but a part of me refused to believe... I still can't get my head around how similar the two of you are."

"Put it down to being a coincidence," he offers. "I understand that it must be difficult for you to see him every time you look at me, but I promise you, I am not him."

"I know..." I close my eyes. "Please, can you release me now?"

"No."

I glance down at him. "What do you mean, no?"

"You set out to kiss me; you may as well do it properly."

"I don't want to kiss you anymore." I scowl.

"Too-fucking-bad, Sunshine. You started the job; you have to finish it now." He pushes down on my head until my nose bumps his, until my lips are poised over his, and I can't escape that searing gaze of his which holds mine. He presses his lips to mine. He brushes his mouth over mine with such gentleness that my breath catches. He nibbles on my lower lip. I open my mouth, and he sweeps his tongue across the inner seam of my lip. His tongue tangles with mine, and a flash of fire ignites low in my belly. I wriggle against him, and the thickness between his legs seems to lengthen further. Vibrations of awareness shoot up my spine. Still holding my gaze, he deepens the kiss. He sucks on my tongue, draws from me, seems to consume my breath, my taste, my very soul, which he's about to lay claim to.

No, no, no, he doesn't want me. He's made that clear. He only sees me as a willing body. Someone to play with while he regains his strength. Probably even fuck while he figures out what to do next. I know I'm the one who made the first move, but I didn't expect the attraction to be this potent. I wanted to lay claim to him, but I'm not ready to feel so much for him. What if he leaves me, after all? What if he has his fun with me and decides to go his merry way? I would be shattered.

I try to turn my head, but his grip on my hair holds me in place.

"Let me go," I murmur against his lips. "Please, let me go."

He loosens his grip, and I pull away. I rise to my feet and straighten my clothes. "I … I'm sorry; that shouldn't have happened. I don't know what came over me." I shake my head. "I … I'll get someone to help you to your feet."

I turn and rush to the door when, "Theresa," he calls out, "it's okay that you lost your head around me. It's normal."

"Excuse me?" I scowl at him over my shoulder. "What are you talking about?"

"It's just my charm. I'm irresistible; I understand."

"You …you…" I sputter. "Jesus, and I thought you had so much in common with Xander." I shake my head. "You know what? You're right."

"Oh?"

"You're not him. You can't be him. Xander would never treat me like … like…"

"Like a submissive?"

"What?" I blink.

"You're a natural submissive, Sunshine," he drawls. "No wonder the Sovranos decided to adopt you as one of their own. They must have realized that you wouldn't survive for one second out in the big, bad world. You, with your trusting nature and natural instinct to obey an order."

"Jesus Christ, do you hear yourself?" I ask. "I'm my own woman. I run a successful business. I have my independence and—"

"How much sexual experience have you had?"

I open and shut my mouth.

"Exactly." His lips kick up. "Doesn't matter how much you deny it; it's in your nature to obey. It's in your DNA to feel most secure when you're following directions. You're the happiest when you're serving your master."

"I… I…" I shake my head. "That's a load of bull."

"Your denying it doesn't change who you are." He sprawls on the floor, a predator in repose, a lion stalking his prey and biding his time. Shit, and I thought he was helpless? Ha, the joke's on me. And now he gives me that load of nonsense about being submissive.

"Whatever." I toss my head. "You deserve an early death thanks to your horrible habit."

"My horrible habit?" He frowns.

I nod toward the lighter and cigarettes on the side table. "I can't believe Seb would actually get that for you. I was going to remove it from your room, but you know what? I don't think I will now."

"Like I said," his smile widens, "you're a nurturer. A submissive with a soft heart who cares for others."

"Stop reducing all of my actions to sexual signposts." I throw up my hands. "Just for that, you deserve to be alone." I spin around and turn to leave, when he calls out.

"Stop."

As if I'm going to obey him? I reach for the door handle when he calls out, "Theresa." He lowers his voice to a hush. "Turn around and get your arse back here."

A shudder runs down my spine. My tummy flip-flops. Something shifts in my chest, and I can't stop myself from turning to face him. Goddamn it. I don't want to obey him. *I don't.* I take a step forward, then another. I reach him, then scowl down at him.

"See, that wasn't so difficult, was it?"

"What do you want?"

"Ride my face."

7

Theresa

"Wh-a-a-t?" Of everything he could have said, honestly, this is the last thing that I could have anticipated.

"You heard me"—he jerks his chin toward his chest—"sit on my mouth."

"Jesus," I gasp, "what the hell is wrong with you?"

"What's wrong is that you're still standing." He scowls. "Take your panties off now, and sit on my face, woman."

"And if I say no?"

"Don't make me force you."

"Ha," I flip my hair over my shoulder, "you couldn't even get back into bed after you fell to the floor."

"I can still use my tongue," he smirks, "and I can make you do anything I want."

"Don't bet on it."

"Want another demonstration?" He arches an eyebrow.

Yes.

Yes.

"Of course, not," I say primly.

"Then take off your panties and sit on my goddamn mouth, right now."

Only when my fingers brush against the underside of my panties do I realize that I have obeyed him. I can't stop myself from pulling my panties down my legs. I kick them off, and he nods. "Good, now fit your pussy on my mouth."

A shiver runs down my spine. I squeeze my thighs together, and one side of his lips kicks up. "Come on Sunshine," he coaxes, "get that sweet cunt of yours in between my lips."

I step over his chest then lower myself down to a squat over his face. My cheeks heat as my dress bunches up around my thighs. He stares up at the most intimate part of me. His nostrils flare, and his blue eyes seem to grow deeper in color. He licks his lips, and my knees almost give way from under me.

"Come 'ere," he growls, "slide that glistening flesh across my mouth. Now."

I lower myself, and when his hot breath sears my pussy, I almost cry out. When he swipes his tongue up my core, I *do* cry out. "Xan—"

He freezes, and only then do I realize my mistake. "Oh, hell, I'm sorry. I didn't mean it. I—"

He tips up his chin and fastens his mouth over my throbbing center.

"Jesus," I yell, "omigod, omigod, Axel, no, what are you doin—" He thrusts his tongue inside my channel, and my head lolls against my neck. My thighs do give way, and my knees hit the floor on either side of his head. I part my legs wide enough to avoid coming into contact with the wound on his temple.

My thigh muscles protest, and I huff when he thrusts his tongue in and out of me; in and out. He tongue fucks me; and my entire body shudders. I grab hold of his hair on the unhurt side of his head; a growl rumbles up his chest. The vibrations envelop my pussy and travel up my spine. He pulls out of my channel only to curl his tongue around my clit. He bites down on the swollen bud, and a trembling swoops up from my feet. It grips my thighs, my belly, and shoots up my spine. "Oh, god, oh, god."

He thrusts his tongue inside my channel again, and I explode. The climax grips me, and I slap my hand over my mouth to stop myself from screaming aloud.

He continues to eat me out, licks my core, sucks my already sopping flesh, and that's when I fall over. Literally, I smother his face with my pussy as I slump over him. He makes a humming noise in his throat, and my pussy instantly clenches again. Oh hell, I need to put some distance between us, only until I can work out what just happened. I pull away from him and collapse on my back next to him.

"Kiss me," he demands.

"What?"

"Taste yourself on my mouth."

I turn my head and see his glistening lips. Moisture clings to his chin, and I know that's my cum. Heat flushes my cheeks, and he smirks.

"Lick yourself off my face, Sunshine."

My nipples tighten. When he puts it like that... I lean over and kiss him, taste myself on his lips, and it's weirdly erotic. I lick his mouth, then his chin, then press kisses to his jaw, to the side of his throat. That dark, edgy scent of him, combined with the taste of my arousal is so hot. I kiss my way back to his mouth, then press my lips to his. Instantly, he closes his mouth around mine. He sucks on my lips, thrusts his tongue inside my mouth and deepens the kiss. My head spins as he once more fucks my mouth with his tongue. Jeez, that's one talented tongue he has there. Moisture beads my core, and I know if I stay, I'll simply fit my aching center over his dick and thrust down and take his entire length in one go and—

"What the hell is happening here?"

A voice cuts through the haze in my head, and I pull away, or try to, for he's once more gripped my hair and held me in place.

"Let me go," I hiss.

"Not a chance," he says in a normal voice.

"Clearly, you're recovering faster than expected." The doctor walks in followed by Luca, then Michael.

I struggle to try to pull away, but he doesn't let go. "My panties, you asshole, I need to grab them." He loosens his grip enough that I clamber over him, grab my panties, and shove them behind my back.

The three men don't seem to notice, or if they do, they don't let on.

Luca walks over to where Axel is still sprawled out on the floor. He continues to act like he owns the space.

Luca bends, grips Axel's shoulders, and helps him to his feet. Axel sways, then leans his considerable weight on Luca, who grunts. "Couldn't you have been a little lighter?" He helps Axel to the bed.

Axel collapses on the bed with a sigh, then jerks his chin toward the assembled men. "Isn't it a little early for visiting hours?"

The doctor presses his fingers to Axel's wrist and checks his pulse. Then, he straightens, pulls out his stethoscope, and proceeds to examine Axel.

"Well," Axel scowls at Michael and Luca, "what are the two of you doing here?"

Michael ignores him. "What do you think, Doc?"

The doctor lowers his stethoscope, then takes his time coiling it up and shoving it into his pocket before turning to Michael. "He's still going to need rehab."

"But he's out of danger?"

"That much can be concluded, yes," the doctor replies in a wry tone. "If he keeps up this rate of recovery, there's no reason why he can't leave a little earlier than expected."

"I'll be out of here in two weeks," Axel insists, "mark my words."

"Do you agree?" Michael turns to the doctor.

"Too early to tell, but if he responds well to the rehab, it's a possibility," the doctor murmurs.

"Told you." Axel smirks.

"Thank you, doctor." Michael shakes his hand. "I appreciate your assistance."

Luca gestures to the door. After a final look at Axel, the doctor leaves. Luca shuts the door, then turns and stands with his shoulders against it.

Michael turns to glance between us. "I've had my men working around the clock to fit out Xander's home with everything needed for your physical therapy."

"And you are telling me this, why?"

"Because that's where you're moving," he states.

8

Axel

"Into Xander's home?" Luca bursts out. "You're letting him move into our brother's home?"

"He's our brother too," Michael replies without taking his gaze off of me.

Luca seems like he's going to protest some more, then firms his lips.

"You want me to move into Xander's place?" I rub the back of my neck. "Are you sure about that?"

"If Xander were alive, he would have wanted you to move in under his roof, so he could get to know you better. Besides, his place is lying vacant, and he would have hated for it to be treated like some kind of a shrine." He raises a shoulder. "I've moved his things out of his bedroom and refurbished it to suit your needs. There are enough rooms to accommodate a physical therapist, as well, and household staff on call around the clock to help provide for your needs. As for his studio," Michael glances away, then back at me, "I have left it as it is. You and Christian can decide what you want to do with his paintings."

What he's saying makes sense, but I'm not sure how I feel about moving into Xander's home. Especially when I can't get over the suspicion that they are treating me as some kind of a replacement for him. I purse my lips. "And if I refuse?" I ask Michael.

"You won't," he states.

"And why is that?"

"Because you have nowhere else to go, and this is the only way you are going to stay alive."

"Brotherly love, huh? Gotta say, it hits me right here." I manage to raise my hand and thump my chest, then wince when even that small action causes my muscles to protest.

"The house will be guarded, of course," Michael adds.

"Of course." I tilt my head.

"For your own protection."

And so you can track my movements, no doubt.

"We haven't yet been able to trace the identity of the man who broke into your hospital room. Whoever he was, he's not on the police database, nor is he affiliated to any of our rival gangs." He watches me closely as he speaks "I take it that doesn't surprise you?"

"It doesn't," I admit. "The people we are dealing with are not amateurs."

"And you know that, how?"

"Just a feeling." I rub the back of my neck. "Doesn't matter. I don't have a clear recollection of my past. Instinct tells me the people I worked with are the ones who sent the man to kill me. And considering they were my associates, I can promise you they are professionals. They don't muck about."

"You were lucky Christian shot him when he did," Michael points out.

"Are you telling me this because you want me to apologize to him for what I did to him and his wife?"

"It would help." Michael's gaze narrows. "In this business, family is what has your back. Family is what makes you strong enough that you can take on your rivals."

"You mean, safety in numbers?"

"We have a lot of enemies. If we fight with each other, it only makes us weak."

I stay silent.

He watches me for a few seconds, then tilts his head. "I have arranged for the doctors to check you out regularly, and the physical therapists will help you get back on your feet."

"You seem as much in a hurry for me to get better as I am."

"You're my brother"—Michael raises a shoulder—"of course, I want you to get better."

"Don't bullshit me, Michael," I drawl. "What's the real deal here?"

"We need you to regain your memory so we can find out who put you up to killing Christian."

"Don't get me wrong. I'm aware that your arranging for me to stay here buys me time to get me back on my feet, but don't mistake it for weakness. I don't take kindly to orders."

We glare at each other, then Michael bares his teeth. "If it was your idea to kill Christian, then nothing in the world can save you, Axel."

"Wait…" Theresa walks over to stand between me and Michael. "You can't be implying what I think you are."

"You know I don't have a choice, Theresa. If he's turned against us, then I can't let him live."

"No"—Theresa shakes her head—"there must be some other way."

"Let's hope the reason for his actions doesn't turn out to be the kind that necessitates such action then."

"He's your brother, Michael," Theresa pleads with him. And for some reason, I hate it. She shouldn't be asking him to spare my life. Hell, she shouldn't be asking anyone for anything… Except. Me. She should be pleading with me for her orgasm. Pleading with me to spank her. Pleading with me to make her come. Pleading with me for my forgiveness. She should be allowed to only use that tone of voice with me, not anyone else.

"Please, Michael, don't do this."

"Theresa, stop. You don't need to beseech him for anything."

"I do!" She scowls at me over her shoulder. "He's the Don, in case you haven't noticed. He can take anyone's life at any time, and no one can say no to him."

"So can I." The words burst out of me, and I'm not sure where they come from. Perhaps instinct, or perhaps, I'm regaining some of my memory.

I glance up to find Michael and Luca watching me intently.

"What was that all about?" Theresa asks in a low voice. "Why did you say that? Is it because you're like Michael? Are you also a Don? But that doesn't make sense. If you were the head of a clan, you wouldn't be going around dirtying your hands. You would be putting others up to the job."

"Unless this was so personal—" Michael interjects.

"If I couldn't trust anyone else." I exchange glances with him. So we're on opposite teams, for all purposes, but damn, if the two of us don't think alike. If my brief interaction with my other brothers is any indication, Michael and I are the closest when it comes to how we approach a problem.

"So you understand why I need to keep you under guard for the moment?" Michael murmurs. "You may be my brother, but until you give me a reason to trust you, I'll have to treat you as I would a potential enemy."

"I'd have done the same thing in your position," I admit. "Doesn't mean I'm not going to be angry with you for doing this."

"I'd have the same reaction," Michael agrees.

"Jesus, for guys who don't like each other, you sure do think alike," Luca grumbles.

"For the moment, at least, we are on the same side." I shoot Michael a glance. "At least, until I'm back on my feet, you can be assured that I won't have the strength to come for you."

"I'm not holding my breath," Michael informs him. "And you, Theresa." He turns to me. "What are you going to do, now that Axel is moving out of the hospital?"

"She goes with me," I snap.

"No way am I going anywhere with you," Theresa retorts at the same time, then shoots me an angry glance. So fucking cute. Like she has any say in this matter.

I glare at Michael, who's watching our exchange with interest.

"Surely, Theresa has a say in this matter," Luca suggests.

"No," I retort.

"Yes, I do." Theresa wraps her arms about her waist. "I can go where I want, when I want, and no one can stop me."

She spins around and stomps to the door, but Luca blocks her way.

"Let me go," she says in a low voice.

"I'm sorry, but I can't do that," Luca replies, his tone gentle. "It's not safe for you to be without someone guarding you."

"What?" She tips up her chin. "Why? I have never had guards on me before."

"You were almost killed—"

"By mistake. I happened to be in the wrong place at the wrong time; the bullet wasn't meant for me."

"Probably not, but until we figure out who the person who shot Axel was aiming at, no-one in the family is allowed to go anywhere unprotected."

"So I'm supposed to walk around with guards in tow?" She scoffs.

"And you'll need someone in your home, as well," Michael interjects.

"What?" She turns around."That's terrible. I don't want anyone coming into my house."

"I agree." I widen my stance. "I'm not comfortable with any man in her personal space, either."

"Unless it's you, I presume?" Luca chuckles.

She glares at him, and he turns the sound into a cough. "Sorry, it was merely an observation."

"Not funny." She scowls at him.

"You may have a point," I say slowly. "She definitely needs a guard on her. She needs to be protected from everyone, except me."

"Oh?" Michael's eyebrows shoot up, "And why is that?"

"Because I took a bullet for her. Ergo, I'm the only one proven not to want to harm her."

She shuffles her feet then glowers at me. The look on her face indicates she doesn't believe me. She's right.

I may not cause her physical harm, but the havoc I could wreck on her body and to her emotions is something she won't be able to recover from quickly; and neither would I if I am to be honest.

"What are you saying?" Luca frowns.

"That she moves in with me."

9

Theresa

I glance out of the window of my room in Xander's home. I often imagined myself living here with him. I never thought I'd end up here as a houseguest of his triplet.

When Axel had demanded that I move in here, I wanted to refuse. But then he turned to me and used that tone of voice, the one I can't refuse, the one where he lowered his pitch and ordered me to move in with him, and I found myself agreeing. Damn it, why is it that I'm unable to stand up to him? Why is it that he only has to glare at me and something inside of me seems to melt instantly? My chest feels funny, my stomach wobbles, and I find myself saying yes.

What the hell is wrong with me?

I grab my phone, and review the messages from Elsa, my employee and friend. Dammit, I really do need to text and let her know that I'll be at the flower shop very soon. She's covered for me the last two weeks when I was by Axel's side. I know that it was a stretch for her, but she did it without complaints. She's already gone that extra mile for me, and I don't want to inconvenience her any further. I start typing a message, then erase it. If I message her now, she'll only message me back and ask me where I was, and honestly, that's a conversation I'd prefer to have face-to-face.

Instead, I dial Cass' number.

"Hey," her face fills the screen, "how are you?"

"I'm not sure."

"Eh?" She frowns. "Everything okay with Axel? I heard from Karma that he's awake?"

"Yeah…" I blow out a breath. "He is, and now I wish he weren't." I squeeze my eyes shut. "No, I don't mean that—aargh." I force myself to relax. "God-damn it, he ties me up in knots, that man."

"What happened?" Cass asks in a careful voice. "The man just woke up from a coma; surely, he can't be that much of a threat."

"That's what you'd think"—I shake my head—"considering he managed to get on his feet a few seconds after opening his eyes—"

"You mean, because of the break-in?" She must notice the confusion on my face because she adds, "I heard about it from Adrian. Must have been the adrenaline of finding himself under threat that made him do that, don't you think?"

"Yeah…" I hunch my shoulders. "When the intruder flung me away, I lost consciousness."

"I heard," she says gently. "I assume that's why you have a bandage on your forehead?"

"The doctor's think that burst of activity has set back his recovery time, though, as he put a lot of strain on his already weak muscles."

"I see," she murmurs. "How is he now?"

"He's in a room in the other wing."

"Eh?" She blinks rapidly. "So you are in the same house as him?"

"I am," I say glumly, "or rather, I'm in Xander's house that Michael decided to loan to Axel."

"So what does that have to do with you?"

"The men seem to think I need to be protected until they track down the guy who shot Axel at Christian and Aurora's wedding."

"Which makes sense, right?"

"I suppose." I scowl. "But why do I have to move in with him?"

"Hold on, so you moved into Xander's place, which is now Axel's place?" Her gaze widens.

"Not my idea, trust me."

"But you are in a different room?"

"Yep, and the house is guarded, and apparently, I need to be chauffeured around by one of the Sovrano brothers, at all times."

"That doesn't seem so bad, does it?"

"On the face of it, no," I say with reluctance. "It's just that—?"

"Your family is upset about it?"

"Not after Michael spoke to them and told them he'd be taking care of me." I huff. "He's the Don; obviously, they won't go against his word."

"So you're upset about it?"

"I understand. they think I need to be protected, but moving into the house that Xander lived in..." I pause to collect my thoughts. "When I'm in this house, I'm surrounded by memories of Xander. Can you imagine? I am stuck here, thinking of him, and then Axel is also here with me." I wring my fingers together. "It's driving me crazy."

"Hmm…" She bites the inside of her cheek. "Something you're not telling me, Theresa?"

"What? No." My cheeks heat.

"You're a terrible liar," she teases. "Are you attracted to Axel?"

I open my mouth to answer, and she raises her hand. "No, don't tell me. Clearly, you feel something for him. The question is whether you're able to resist him."

I hang my head.

"That's what I thought."

"It's not what it seems," I protest

"Oh?" She tilts her head. "Then how is it?"

"I, ah, didn't have a choice."

"What do you mean, you didn't have a choice? Did he force you?" She scowls, "Come to think of it, he's still recuperating; he couldn't have physically forced you."

"He didn't have to."

"Sorry, but I'm not understanding this." Her brow furrows.

"He asked me to move in with him, and I couldn't refuse."

"You couldn't refuse?" She repeats the words slowly as if I'm speaking a language that she doesn't quite understand.

"Yeah, when he orders me to do something, I seem unable to say no."

"Ah…" Her brow smoothens. "I see."

"What do you mean, *I see?*" I huff. "I don't like it when you use that tone of voice."

"What tone of voice?"

"That one." I point my finger at her—or rather, at the screen. "That smug tone of voice which seems to indicate that you know something I don't know."

"I do know something that you don't know."

"Oh?" I scowl. "Well, out with it then. What is it that you know and I don't?"

"I can't tell you." Her eyes gleam.

"Nooo," I groan, "don't do this. Please, don't do this, Cass. Don't be so mean. I really need to understand what's happening here, and if you know something and you're not telling me, then it's going to eat at me. I won't be able to sleep now, please, Cass—"

"You're in his power."

"Excuse me?"

"Okay, that came out wrong." She glances away, then back at the screen. "I mean, clearly, his will is stronger than yours, and you are attracted to him, so—"

"So?"

"So he's not above using his dominance to make you do his bidding."

"Ugh!" I glower at her. "I kind of guessed that, but this has never happened to me before. I've never found myself rushing to do someone's bidding like this."

"It's not like you're a particularly strong-willed person, Theresa, and I mean that in the most complimentary fashion."

"Umm," *I don't think that was a compliment,* "you make me sound like a … a weak, indecisive person."

"No, no…" Cass shakes her head. "All I'm saying is that you have a soft heart. You tend to feel things deeply and see everything from an emotional view point."

"And you think that's a bad thing?"

"It's something others can take advantage of."

"Like Axel?"

"Among others, yes."

"I can't help it." I begin to pace. "I've always been the kind of person who can see the other's point of view, you know? I understand where they are coming from. And if I can get by without hurting the other person, then well, I'd prefer that."

She stares knowingly at me.

"What?" I glower at her. "Just because I prefer for everyone to be happy, doesn't make me weak."

"No, it doesn't," she agrees. "It makes you very human, very soft, very..."

"Say it." I scowl.

"Submissive," she says reluctantly.

"I am not submissive," I snap.

"It's not a bad thing," she says in a soft voice. "It's also what makes the Sovranos want to adopt you into their family and take care of you, I think. It's also why—"

"Axel, can order me around, and I can't turn him down."

"I'm sure that it makes him happy when you obey him."

"Probably," I say dully. *And here I was, thinking that I had my own business, that I have proven myself to be someone who can take care of herself, stand on her own two feet without having to depend on anyone else, someone who has actually turned her passion into a successful career.*

"Being submissive doesn't take away from your other achievements," she murmurs as if she's reading my mind. "You actually hold the power, you know?"

"Right," I scoff. "When he glares at me and tells me what to do and I obey, despite not wanting to, trust me, it doesn't seem to me, then, that I hold the power."

"Oh, but you do. If you don't obey him, it'll upset him."

"But I do," I snap back. "That's the entire problem. I can't tell him no; know what I mean?"

"And by doing so, you are putting yourself in his hands and that's a big responsibility. You're allowing him to take care of you, to do what he thinks is right for you. If you're not happy with what he does, then he has to change tactics and figure out what does make you happy. You get me?"

"No." I glower. "You're confusing me. And for all that you said, it doesn't change the fact that even though I don't want to do as he says, when he commands me, I find my body seems to want to obey. My logical mind resists, but it's like a switch inside of me seems to flip, and then I scurry to do what he wants."

"So why don't you use that to your advantage?"

"What do you mean?"

"Do as he says, give him your assent, then use it to make him do what you want."

"And how do I do that?"

"That's for you to figure out." She smiles.

"You're really not helping me, you know that?"

Her smile widens. "I know it can seem confusing, but just trust your instinct."

"Easy for you to say; you haven't been in this situation."

"Haven't I?" Her smile is secretive.

I stare at her. "Shut up." I peer into her features. "Are you telling me this entire submission-dominance thingie is something you've experienced before?"

She makes a motion of zipping her lips. "Not saying anything."

"Aw, come on," I protest, "you're no fun; you know that?"

"This isn't about me anyway," she murmurs. "You're a smart person, Theresa. I'm sure that you'll figure out a way to have Axel wrapped around your little finger."

"Don't want him wrapped about anything." I scowl. "I just wish there were a way I could resist him."

She glances off screen. "Sorry, Theresa, but I've gotta go. I need to get dinner ready."

The screen goes dark. I place my phone down and turn back to survey my room. It's spacious, a suite actually, with a living room, a kitchen, a bedroom with an adjoining balcony from which I have an unrestricted view of the sea. The bedroom itself—which is where I am now—is comfortably furnished with a wooden floor, a large bed with plenty of cushions, a dresser and two doors, one of which leads into a closet and the other into a bathroom.

I walk into the closet and survey my clothes, which Michael had arranged to be brought to me. Overall, the Sovranos are supporting Axel in this move.

Even though, from the earlier conversation, it was clear to me that there are tensions simmering between Axel and the other brothers. Well, maybe not Seb; he and Axel seem to get along just fine. It was Luca and Michael who didn't seemed particularly happy with Axel. And of course, Christian. Axel's triplet was nowhere to be seen, though I assume, he met Axel at some point. So clearly, he is still coming to terms with Axel's appearance.

All in all, I feel completely unsettled, like someone pulled the rug out from under me. It was, somehow, easier when Axel was unconscious. I could stare at him and almost convince myself that he was Xander. But once he had woken, the awareness in his eyes, the way he commanded me to ride his face and made me orgasm, all of it was very unlike Xander. It leaves me with no doubt that I am dealing with an apex predator. Someone who will chew me up and spit me out; someone who could reduce me to a puddle of raw need by just looking at me; someone who makes me hate him and lust after him in the same moment. Gah!

There's a knock on the door to the bedroom.

I turn. "Who're you?"

10

Theresa

"Hello, I'm Sheena." The woman hovers just inside the doorway.

She wears pale pink scrubs, which should really be unglamorous, but with her petite figure and straight black hair that flows to her chin and her shining eyes, she looks smart. "The door to the suite was open," she explains, "so I walked in. I hope I'm not intruding?"

"Who are you, again?"

"The physical therapist; I'm in charge of Mr. Sutton's rehabilitation."

"Mr. Sutton?"

"Axel?" she clarifies. "That's his surname."

Of course, it is. He didn't grow up with the Sovranos, so why did I assume that he'd share their surname? I didn't even think to ask him what his surname is. And this perky little thing has found out about it before me. A hot sensation stabs at my chest. She's also going to help Axel with his exercises and get him back on his feet. And dammit, I'm even more jealous when she calls him by his given name. Wonder what kind of rehabilitation she has in mind for him? No doubt, she'll use the excuse to have her hands on him. And likely, he'll return the favor. Wonder if he commanded her to ride his face within minutes of their first meeting, as well. Okay, so it was the second meeting when he proceeded to eat out my pussy, but perhaps, he won't show the same restraint with this woman.

"Are you okay?" she murmurs, still standing by the doorway. "You went a little pale."

"I'm fine." I clear my throat. "I just haven't had anything to eat all day. I was too busy moving in here, so…" I raise a shoulder.

"I understand. Would you like to get something to eat?"

"Um…" I hesitate. "I'm not really sure."

"Don't be silly. There's a lot of food that has been catered in for the team that's helping Axel get back on his feet. There's more than enough for everyone."

"There's a team helping him?"

"Don Sovrano has roped in the best in the profession for his brother," Sheena informs me.

Why didn't I know that? To be fair, since the entire topic of my moving into Axel's place came up, I was so pissed off that I stomped out of his hospital room, and I haven't checked in on him since. In reality, I'm upset with myself for having given in to him so easily. Why does he have this influence on me? Why is it that I already find it so difficult to deny him?

I've decided it's best to stay out of his way, for the time being, at least. Best to stay in my room and get on with my life. It's time I return to my floral business anyway. It's a good thing I have a reliable employee, but it's time I resume my responsibilities. I've already been away from my shop for too long.

"That's good," I murmur. "He'll be back on his feet in no time, I'm sure."

"He's a fighter, no doubt about it," she agrees. "He's been pushing himself during the physiotherapy sessions. I had to caution him to go slowly, not that he listened to me."

"Of course, not," I snort. "That man has a mind of his own. Does he have to go to the hospital for the physio sessions?"

"No, Don Sovrano had a room converted into a studio with all the necessary equipment," she replies. "In addition to that, there is a team of nurses who will be taking care of him around the clock. Michael really has pulled out all the stops."

"Has he?"

She nods. "Axel is getting the best care possible, and his condition is improving by the minute."

"Thanks for the update." I scowl at her. "Although, I'm not sure why you're telling me?"

"Aren't you his girlfriend?"

"No," I snap. "Who told you that?"

"No one." She furrows her eyebrows. "It's just that you are the only other person living in this house so, I assumed."

"Well, don't," I snap, then blow out a breath. "I'm sorry; I didn't mean to be a bitch."

"It's okay," she says in a soft voice. "You must be under a lot of stress because of his injury."

"Yes. No." I shake my head. "Doesn't matter. I'm glad he's on his way to getting better." I grab my handbag from the bedstead, then head for the doorway and brush past her. I walk into the living room, and she follows me.

"I'm sorry if I upset you. I just thought you'd want to know about his condition."

"Thanks," I mutter. Good thing I've already showered and dressed. I have already messaged Adrian, my designated driver for this morning, and he told me he'd pick me up at 9 am.

I walk down the steps and toward the front door.

"Aren't you going to see him before you leave?" she calls out after me.

I hesitate, then shake my head. "No, I'm already running late."

"It won't take but a moment. I'm sure he'd be happy to see you."

But how will I feel when I see him? I can't risk allowing him to use his magnetism on me again. Can't risk agreeing to something else that he asks me to do. No, I'm going to hold off seeing him until I feel like I'm able to resist him … somewhat.

"I really have to go." I secure my bag over my shoulder, reach the front door of the house, and wrench it open. The man at the doorway nods at me as I race past him, down the steps, and toward the car waiting for me. Adrian pushes away from the back door and holds it open. I slip into the back seat. He slides into the driver's seat, then eases the car down the driveway.

We drive in relative silence. He halts at a signal, then eyes me in the rearview mirror. "You okay?" he asks.

I turn to face him, "Yeah…" I blow out a breath. "Still getting used to the idea of being chauffeured around," I admit. "Not to mention, it's unsettling to realize I'm under the protection of the Sovranos."

"It's safe for you," he reminds me in a gentle voice. "And it's only until they figure out who shot at you."

"I wasn't the target, though, was I?" I murmur. "I just happened to be in the path of the bullet."

"Probably," he agrees. "Still, you could have been shot."

"But I wasn't," I point out.

"But he did take the bullet for you," he retorts.

"What a mess." I turn to face out the window. "I wish I could get my life back, before all this happened."

"Were you happy then?"

"Yes," I say without hesitation. "Maybe I would have been happier if Xander had reciprocated my affections, but I was confident that I could get to him, eventually. I had … still have my business. I love what I do. I had a social life, friends—"

"Who you can still keep in touch with."

"Try to explain to them what you're doing under house arrest and living under the same roof as a man you barely know."

"A man who saved your life."

"That too." I scowl at the shops we pass by. "Imagine telling a normal person that you were almost shot, then see how they try to comprehend your life and fail."

"Your life was never normal," he remarks.

"Maybe not right now," I bite the inside of my cheek, "but it used to be."

"You sure of that?"

"What do you mean?"

He glances at my reflection in the mirror, then once more at the road ahead. "You were interested in Xander, who was the Don's son. Some part of you must have realized the road you were going down?"

"You mean realizing that, at some point, I was going to be shot at?" I say in a wry tone. "Not to mention, probably held under house arrest while having most of my freedom taken from me?"

"It's as good or as bad as you make it."

"Oh, I'm not complaining about it. I understand why I need to be guarded at the moment. Doesn't mean I can't, on occasion, think of a life outside it as well?"

We continue driving in silence.

"It's not that I'm not grateful for being protected," I finally explain. "I mean, it's nice of you to have taken the time to drive me to work today."

"Not like I had a choice." He smirks.

I must look stricken because he laughs.

"Not that I mind it. I'd rather be playing chauffeur than working on anything else."

"But surely, you must have a normal life—a family, things you'd rather be doing than be here."

Something flickers across his features. "You're right," he finally admits. "But since I'm not going to be making headway there at the moment"—he raises a shoulder—"I might as well be your chauffeur today."

"Hmm…" I lean forward in my seat. "Is it an affair of the heart we're talking about? Are you interested in Cassandra?"

He doesn't reply.

"Aww, come on. You've fallen for someone, haven't you?"

"That might be too strong of a word." His grin widens. "You know we Sovranos don't believe in love."

"And yet, Michael married Karma. Are you telling me he's not in love with her?"

"He did kidnap her first," he reminds me. "As did Christian with Aurora. He held her captive until she fell in love and agreed to be his wife."

A shiver runs down my spine. "Is that the Sovrano MO?" I ask lightly. "Take them, then hold them prisoner until they agree to do your bidding?"

"With the kind of background we have, I'd be surprised if the rest of us don't follow a similar path." He laughs.

"Axel wasn't brought up with you lot," I retort. "Not that I know much of his background. What are the chances that, in comparison, he had a more normal childhood?"

He raises his gaze to mine in the mirror.

"Yeah…" I blow out a breath. "Guess he's as screwed up as the rest of you, huh?"

"Maybe more?"

"Thanks." I slump in my seat. "Not that it matters or anything. I mean, it's not like I'm interested in him."

He chuckles. The smirk is back in full effect on his face. Ugh! Why do all of the brothers have this raw, feral appeal about them. It simply invites a woman to try to tame them.

I narrow my eyes. "Are you laughing at me?"

11

———

Theresa

He wipes the grin off of his face. "Of course, not."

"Good. And for the record, I do know that you and Cass have a thing going on."

His features firm. He narrows his gaze on me in the mirror, then returns his attention to the road.

I chuckle. "You do like her, don't you?"

No response. Not that I was expecting one. Still, I wouldn't have expected Adrian to turn out to be this chatty. I figure I might be able to get some information from him while he's still in a mood to talk to me... A mood which seems to have evaporated since I mentioned Cass.

"I spoke to her before I got in the car," I continue. "She seemed fine, in case you were wondering. Not that you asked me or anything. I mean, I'm sure you speak to her whenever you go to see Michael. I mean"—I hit the back of my head against the headrest—"now I'm putting my foot in my mouth, right? Are you taking the long way to the shop or what?" I laugh nervously.

Almost immediately, the car slows to a stop. I glance up and find we are at our destination. Finally. "Oh, here we are. Thanks for the ride." I push open the door and jump out before Adrian can come around to get it for me. I tap on the window on the passenger side, and he lowers it.

"I can find my way back."

He stares at me.

I blow out a breath. "No, seriously, I have lived in this town my entire life. I should be able to find my way back without any problem."

He merely holds my gaze.

"Fine!" I throw up my hands. "I'll be done by five."

"I'll be here."

I turn around and enter the *The Tilted Tulip*. When I glance back, the car is only just pulling away. So he waited until he was sure I was safely inside. Was it Axel who told him to do so? Doesn't matter.

I draw in a breath and the scent of roses, lilies, and hibiscus envelops me. I drag the scent of the flowers into my lungs, and my muscles immediately relax. It's always been this way. I walk into my shop and feel instantly calmer. This is my space, my little heaven that I've carved out in the middle of the craziness that is life. I may come from the Mafia, and when I'm with the Sovranos, I often end up falling into the stereotype of a meek woman, but I managed to give shape to my dream. I found a way to open this flower shop, didn't I? This is my baby, this business, and it means so much to me. Yet, one look at a wounded Axel, and I dropped everything to be by his side. That man has the ability to make me forget my priorities. Not to mention, when he asks me to do something, I seem unable to refuse him. It's like his dominance completely overpowers me and pushes everything else out of my mind.

I approach the counter, and Elsa glances up.

"Theresa!" she exclaims. "Finally—I've been so worried about you."

She comes around the counter and throws her arms around me. "The last time you messaged me was from the hospital when you said an emergency had come up and that you might not be able to come into the shop for a few weeks. Then you seemed to vanish off the face of the earth. I texted you so many times. Did you get my messages?"

"I did." I bite the inside of my cheek. "I'm so sorry I didn't reply to them." I hug her back. "It's just, I knew the business was in safe hands, so I could focus on what needed to be done and not worry about the shop. I owe you a big thank you, Elsa. If you hadn't been here to take over all the day-to-day operations of the shop, I would have never managed to take so much time off."

Elsa blushes. "I was only doing my job."

"No," I shake my head, "on the contrary, you went above and beyond what anyone else would have done. You treat this business as if it is your own, and I want you to know how much I appreciate you. In fact, I want you to take over the day-to-day running of the shop from now on."

"What?" Her gaze widens. "What are you saying?"

"Effective immediately, I'm promoting you to General Manager of the shop."

"OMG!" Her gaze widens.

"I'm also putting you on salary and raising your salary by twenty-five percent."

"Oh, vow!" She blinks rapidly. "Really? Are you sure? Not that I can't do with the extra money, but I have to ask."

"I'm sure!" I smile. "You deserve it, Elsa. It's because you are so capable and so dedicated that I could step away and not worry about the business going into decline." I step back and take her hands in mine. "How can I ever repay you for what you did?"

"By telling me what's going on."

"Umm…" I release her hands. "I was uh, busy. That's all."

"It's a man, isn't it?"

It's my turn to blush.

She chuckles. "Knew it!" Then she pauses and peers into my face. "Were you with a Sovrano?"

I hesitate.

"Well?" She tilts her head. "So you were with a Sovrano?"

"Not quite." I brush past her and into the back of the shop. I toss my bag onto the table by the window, then head over to the small kitchen alcove. I top up the espresso maker and set it on the stove.

"Now you have me really curious." Elsa comes to stand next to me. "Is everything okay, Theresa?"

"I'm fine." I turn to face her. "Everything is fine."

"I called your family, and they told me that you have moved in with the Sovranos."

"Not with the Sovranos; with *a* Sovrano."

Her gaze widens. "So you're living with one of the mob?"

"You know my family is connected to the Sovranos, right? My father is their gardener, and my mother used to clean their home, before my brother was born."

She nods.

"So when I needed the money to buy this place, Xander loaned it to me."

"Hmm.." She taps her toe on the ground. "You were in love with Xander, so I'm not surprised that you accepted the loan from him. But Xander was one of the Sovranos, so technically, that made his money mob money."

"He made the money from selling his paintings, so technically, it wasn't mob money, but yeah; I know what you mean. It wasn't a big deal for me, to be honest. I figured I'd end up married to him eventually, and anyway, the *Cosa Nostra* is part of life here."

"R-i-g-h-t…" She purses her lips.

"You cool with that? It's not something I thought to mention earlier. But it isn't exactly something I could bring up in everyday conversation."

"I am new to Sicily, so yeah, the *Cosa Nostra* is more of a concept for me. It's just, you know... Common sense dictates that one should steer clear of any mob involvement, that's all."

"So, you are okay with it?"

"I need this job. I enjoy working with you, so yeah, I'm fine. Besides, you are the only friend I have in Palermo, so you ain't getting rid of me that easily." She grins.

"Oh, thank God." I throw my arms around her and hug her. "I really value our friendship too."

She pats my shoulder.

I pull back. "I know you're not all that enamored with the Sovranos, but I did go to the same school as them, and I've known them all my life. They are very much like family to me."

"And now you've hooked up with one of them." She lowers her arms to her sides.

"I haven't." I step back. "I'm simply staying under the same roof as Axel, until the uh, danger passes."

"Danger?" She pales. "Are you in danger? Is that why you're hurt?" She gestures to the bandage at my temple.

Shit, I'd forgotten about that.

The espresso pot begins to boil, and I raise it off the stove and pour the fragrant brew into two cups.

"Here." I hand one to her, then grab a biscotti from the jar and walk over to take my seat behind the table. Elsa drops down into the seat in front of me.

"So," she takes a sip of espresso from her cup, "how did you get hurt?"

"I uh, there was an intruder—"

"An intruder?" Her eyes bug out. "Are you okay? Were you robbed?"

"He broke into Axel's hospital room."

"Axel?" She frowns. "He was the emergency, the reason you were incommunicado for the last few weeks?"

I nod.

"He's also one of the Sovranos, I take it?"

"He is." I shift in my seat. Why can't I get comfortable?

"Why were you in his hospital room?"

"I was uh, watching over him while he was in a coma."

"He was in a coma," she says the words slowly, "and you were watching over him?"

"Yeah." I blow out a breath. "The thing is, Axel looks like Xander."

"Hold on; back up." She places her cup back in its saucer. "So, this Axel guy looks like your ex-crush?"

"He's also Xander's triplet."

"Holy shit!" She opens and shuts her mouth. "Is it too early to drink something stronger?"

"It's barely 9:30 am," I say dryly. "Oh, and by the way, he took a bullet for me."

"Wait, what?" She gapes at me. "Someone shot at you?"

"Not me, per se. It was intended for one of the Sovranos, but I got in the way."

"And he stepped in front of you? Is he in love with you?"

"He didn't know who I was. I think it was instinct that had him placing himself between me and the bullet."

"Instinct, eh?" Her forehead creases.

"The bullet grazed his temple. He suffered significant blood loss, so the doctors had to induce a coma to help him heal."

"Wow…" She straightens. "So, he was in a coma for the last two weeks, and you were with him?"

I nod.

"But he's better now?"

"Yes." I drain my espresso and place the cup back in its saucer. "And now you know everything."

"Not everything."

I crunch down the biscotti. "Sure, you do."

"You mean, you and this Axel didn't…" She places the fingertips of both hands against each other.

My cheeks heat. "No, we, didn't," I mutter. "For heaven's sake, the man was unconscious until two days ago."

"But he's recovering quickly?"

"Very quickly," I murmur.

"Enough for the two of you to have done some hanky-panky, while he was prone on the bed."

I spring up from my seat. "I think I heard the bell of the shop door. Did someone just walk in? You know, we need to have someone at the front counter at all times, right? We can't afford to be seen as unprofessional."

"Hmph…" She rises to her feet. "I can take a hint. If you don't want to talk about it, you just have to tell me; no need to invent excuses.

She turns to leave, and I call out, "Really, Elsa, there's nothing more to it."

She raises a finger over her shoulder. "You know you can't lie to save your life, right? I'm going to get it out of you, one way or the other, Mother Theresa."

"Ugh, don't call me that, please."

"You can't blame me. You're too good-natured, too much of a do-gooder, and you can't lie for shit. If the shoe fits…" She chuckles as she walks out of the office. I slump back in my chair. She's right. You'd think running my own business would have made me savvy enough to pull off a lie? But that's not the case. I've managed to stay honest about most things, so I've never needed to lie. Plus, I know I'd never be able to pull a fast one on anyone. So I try my best to stay honest. But I can't talk about what happened with Axel to anyone. It's too soon.

. . .

Later in the evening, I walk inside the house. I locked up at 5 pm and rode home with Adrian. Walking up the staircase, I pass the floor on which his room is located and hesitate. Do I dare go in and check on him? What happens if he uses some of his stupid mind-magic on me again? But I want to see how he's doing. I can just peek in and not actually enter. That would be okay, right? Yeah, I can totally just pop my head around the door, check him out, make sure he's okay, and then run off, and he won't know it.

Mind made up, I head down the corridor, peeking into the first doorway to find the room is set up with the physiotherapy equipment that Sheena had mentioned to me. The next door is shut. I push it open and find it's a bedroom. The shower is running in the bathroom, so whoever is staying here, Sheena probably, is in the shower.

The door to the third is half open. I peek inside, then step through and walk across the floor of what seems to be a living room, and to the half-open door on its other side. I glance around the door and see him. He leans against the pillows on his bed, wearing a shirt and a pair of sweats.

The dressing around his head has been replaced by a smaller plaster.

His eyes are shut, the dark lashes an inky curve against his cheekbones.

His face seems to have regained some of its color, for he's not as pale as he was in the hospital. His chest rises and falls, his hands folded over his stomach. He's definitely asleep. I step inside the room, and reaching the bed, I stand over him.

At this proximity, I can smell that dark scent of his. Heat from his big body reaches out to me. A shiver runs down my spine. His t-shirt clings to his shoulders and outlines every ridge of his pecs, before it stretches across his concave stomach. The sweatpants ride low enough on his hips that I can make out the trail of hair that disappears inside the waistband. The fabric at the crotch is tented though… Hmm… Is he aroused in his sleep? Or is that just his general state?

I glance at his face again. His eyelids are closed, his breathing steady.

He's still on painkillers, right? Surely, he must be. He's definitely out of it. I reach down and palm the tented fabric. The warmth singes the skin of my palm. I press down and I swear, his dick seems to thicken. Goose bumps pop on my skin. My nipples tighten. I trace the outline of his length through the cloth, and my core clenches. Jesus Christ, the man is packing all right. My mouth waters. I want to taste him. I really, really want to drag my tongue across his shaft and find out if he tastes as dangerous as he smells. I lean over and rub my cheek against the thickness.

A shudder grips him. I glance up and find his blue gaze is fixed on mine.

12

Axel

I sensed her as soon as she'd peeked through the door. I felt a ripple of awareness curl in my belly as she walked over to me. It's good to know that, despite not being fully functional, physically, my senses haven't been impaired. As she stood next to my bed, I sensed her drag her gaze down my body, knew when she moved, and then she placed her palm on my crotch. Motherfucker! It took everything in me not to swoop down and grab her hair and push her face into my aching length. Instead, I watched as she surveyed the column of my cock outlined through my sweats. Her breathing sped up, and her lips parted. She fondled my dick, and just as I was sure that I couldn't pretend anymore, she leaned down and pressed her cheek to it. Like it was an object of worship and she was adoring it. Then, she turned her face up and spotted me.

Her mouth opens in an 'o' of surprise. Her cheeks flush. Her chest rises and falls, and I'm sure that she's going to turn and bolt. Instead, she wraps her hand around my length and squeezes.

"Fuck." A growl rumbles from my throat.

It seems to rouse her from of her reverie, for her blush deepens. She begins to straighten, and I shake my head. "Don't," I say in a low voice. "Don't go."

She bites down on her lower lip, and more blood rushes to my groin.

"Take me in your mouth," I order.

She swallows. "What if I don't want to?"

"Don't you?" I fold my palms behind my neck.

Her gaze widens. "How are you—"

"—Able to move my arms without trembling?"

She nods.

"Turns out, I'm improving at a rapid pace, thanks to working my butt off." I smirk. "Now, pull me out and take me into your mouth, will you?"

She hesitates, and I lower my voice to a hush. "Do it, Sunshine. I've been lying here thinking of your intoxicating scent, your sweet mouth, the way you moan when you come, your soft skin that I want to mark."

Her breathing heightens.

"Your gorgeous pussy that I want to bury myself in."

Her face flushes further.

"Your hot, tight, wet cunt that weeps for me even as we speak."

A moan bleeds from her lips.

"Your mouth that yearns to taste me."

"I … I don't," she says on an exhale, "don't want to"—she closes her eyes —"taste you."

"Taste me, Sunshine."

She squeezes her eyes closed and seems to get ahold of herself, then snaps her eyelids open, and fixes her gaze on mine. She grips my waistband and lowers it down my thighs. My cock springs free.

She gasps. "You didn't wear briefs?" she asks in an accusing voice.

"What can I say? I like to be prepared."

"What do you mean?" She scowls up at me. "You knew I would come to you?"

"I had hoped?" I lower my arm and cup her cheek. "To be honest, I missed you."

"You did?"

I nod. "I missed the taste of your pussy. And I was lying here, imagining your mouth around my cock as you pulled on it, as you took me down your throat and hummed around the crown and sucked me off."

She scowls. "Good to know that I'm good for only one thing."

"Oh, more than one thing," I assure her. "You have more than one hole, remember?"

"You're a jerk, you know that?" She breathes as she straightens. "I'm not going to stand here and listen to you insult me."

She turns to leave.

"Get back here, Theresa," I say in a hard voice, "and take my cock down your throat."

She hesitates, and I growl, "Do it, Sunshine."

She turns around slowly, her face pale. "I hate it when you make me do things I don't want to do."

"Or maybe you do want to, but you want me to take the choice out of your hands. How about if I absolve you of all responsibility? How about if you can blame me for your momentary lapse of reason?"

"Oh, I'm going to blame you, all right." She shuffles her feet. "Please let me go, Axel. Please."

"Fine." I lean back. "Leave, then." I cross my arms over my chest and close my eyes. I wait for a beat, then another, and hear her shuffle her feet. I sense her standing there, unable to make up her mind, then the mattress dips. *There you are.* I crack open my eyelids as she straddles my legs.

She shoots me a hateful look from under her eyelashes. "I really do hate you."

"No, you don't," I murmur. "But if it helps you justify this action in your mind, then by all means, feel free to tell yourself that story."

She shoots me another glance, then wraps her fingers around the base of my cock and squeezes.

"Fuck." I curl my fingers into fists. "Just like that, Sunshine."

She makes an angry sound at the back of her throat, then drags her fingers from base to crown.

"Harder," I order. "Grip my cock like you think it's my throat you want to crush."

She tightens her grasp at once, and my balls tighten, my cock lengthens, and a bead of sweat slides down between my pecs. "Just like that," I growl. "Now take me into your mouth."

Her chest rises and falls. Her skirt is bunched up around her, and the warmth of her pussy seeps through her panties to sear my legs. Bloody fuck.

She narrows her gaze on me, and without breaking the connection, she lowers her mouth to my shaft. She licks the crown, and heat sizzles up my spine. She draws her tongue from the head down the length of my dick to the base, then up again. She licks the head delicately and a groan rips from me. Her being this tentative is going to kill me.

"It's not an ice-cream cone, Sunshine," I groan. "Eat it like it's your favorite fast-food instead."

"Hmph." She firms her lips. "I hate fast-food."

"You Italians." I smirk. "What's your favorite food?"

"Pasta, of course." She rolls her eyes.

"Fine, suck it like it's a strand of past—"

She clamps her lips around my dick and hoovers it up, and Jesus-fucking-Christ, my cock elongates. My balls tighten, all the blood drains to my groin, and fuck, if I don't see stars. This woman is going to suck my soul through my dick if she keeps going like this, and frankly, I'd be just fine with that.

"Just like that," I coax her. "You're doing so well, Sunshine. Keep going; don't stop."

She takes me down her throat and promptly gags. The sucking sensation sends shivers up my spine. I draw in a breath, and my shoulders tighten. The wound at my temple throbs, and the pain only amplifies the pleasure from how she swirls her tongue around my length. I dig my fingers into her hair and tug. Her breath catches as I pull her back so my dick slips out. The swollen head stays poised between her lips. I hold her gaze, then apply enough pressure for her head to move forward. My cock disappears inside her mouth, and the sight is so erotic that I almost come right then. I pull her back, then forward, then again, as I fuck her mouth. The next time I draw her forward, my dick slides down her throat. She hums, and the vibrations crawl up my cock, and coil in my groin.

"Fuck, Sunshine, fuck." My balls draw up. "Touch yourself," I order. Even before the words are out of my mouth, she shoves her hand between her legs and strums her pussy lips. The scent of her arousal bleeds into the air; the wet sound of her flesh as she thrusts her fingers in and out of herself envelops me. I tighten my fingers in her hair, and she moans. I pull her back then haul her forward again and again. All the time, the sound of her fingers burying themselves inside her soaking wet channel is an erotic soundtrack.

"Grind the heel of your palm into your clit," I command and glance down to find she does just that. Her chest rises and falls, and her entire body jolts. A trembling grips her, and with her free hand, she holds onto my arm.

I pull her forward, then coil my fingers around her throat. The sensation of my cock gliding down her throat pushes me over the edge. My thighs harden, and my balls draw up. "Come with me," I growl, and her back arches. Her gaze widens as the orgasm crashes over her.

13

Theresa

The climax grips me, my orgasm pounds through me, and I come all over my fingers. That's when he comes down my throat. I slump against him; my eyelids can't seem to stay open. The next moment I'm being hauled forward and onto his chest. I snuggle into the muscled expanse of his chest and drag my fingers through his hair. My hand brushes his temple, and he winces.

"Oh, shoot. I brushed against your bandage," I try to sit up, but he doesn't let me.

"Fuck that." He pulls me in, and I curl up against him.

The heat from his body pours over me, surrounds me, cocoons me. I can't stop the sigh of contentment that spills from my lips. He wraps those massive arms around me and tugs me even closer as I pillow my cheek against the hard ridge of his pec. "*Tortiglioni,*" I murmur, "it's more like *tortiglioni.*"

"What?"

"Fat and thick with ridges across it."

"Hmm," he drawls. "Are you talking about what I think you are?"

"Am I talking about your magnificent dick, you mean?" Barely are the words out, when I slap my hand over my mouth. "Forget I said that." I squeeze my eyes shut.

"You think my dick is magnificent?" He chuckles, and the vibrations crawl over my skin.

"Like you need any more praise to bloat your already swollen head."

"You talking about the one on my shoulders?"

I sneak a glance up at him. "What else would I be talking about?"

His eyes gleam, and I huff. "That was a terrible joke."

"No more than you comparing my dick to a *tortiglioni*."

"Hey, you're the one who started it with your food porn talk."

"Had to come up with a comparison to get you on the right track," he explains.

"And how did I do?"

"You passed with flying colors." He smirks. "In fact, I think you should move into this room with me so whenever the mood strikes, we can trade more food porn talk."

"Hmm, no." I glance around the room. "I don't want to be the third wheel when you are 'working out,'" I make air quotes with my fingers, "with Sheena."

"So you met her, eh?"

"Not like I had a choice. She came to my room and introduced herself. Speaking of, I'd better get out of here before she comes back."

"She's not coming back tonight." He tightens his arms around me. "I'm done with the physiotherapy sessions for the day; though, I do need to have a bath."

"So go have a bath," I murmur.

"I'm going to need help; I'm not strong enough to bathe myself."

"A likely story." I huff.

"Would I lie to you?" His voice rumbles under my cheek.

"You know you'd lie to get your way with me every single time." I sit up, and this time, he doesn't stop me. I take in his features, the slight flush in his cheeks which wasn't there earlier, the way his hair is mussed up as if he's been running his hands through it. Overall, he looks healthier and more relaxed. If I hadn't seen him shot with my own eyes and then tried to stop him from crumpling to the ground, I wouldn't have believed it myself. He looks so much healthier, so much more like Xander. I bite the inside of my cheek.

"What's wrong?" He scowls. "What did you think just then?"

I shoot him an annoyed glance. "Jeez, can't I have some privacy with my own thoughts, or what?"

"No," he snaps. "Tell me what went through your mind just then."

"Xander." I hunch my shoulders. "I couldn't help thinking how much you look like him when you're relaxed."

"But I'm not him."

"Of course, I know that, and I have accepted it. In some ways, that makes it worse, though."

"What do you mean?"

"Nothing." I glance away. "I need to go."

"Not until you tell me what you're thinking about."

I push off his chest, but he grabs my arm and hauls me close. "Look at me, Sunshine."

I turn to glance at him. He peers into my features then nods. "Now, tell me what's troubling you."

"You," I burst out. "You're troubling me. I should be mourning Xander. Instead, I can't stop myself from tumbling into bed with his triplet. One who looks so very like him. It feels like I'm being unfaithful to his memory."

He holds my gaze. "That's understandable," he finally says. "It hasn't been that long since he died, so his memory is still fresh in your mind. But why did he not claim you as his when he was alive?"

I open and close my mouth. "You know what? I'm not having this conversation with you." I try to pull away, but his grip tightens.

"You'll leave when I allow it." The low hush of his voice causes that same strange feeling to coil in my chest.

"You're not my keeper." I scowl at him.

"But I am responsible for your safety."

"You can barely take care of yourself, let alone—" I squeak as he flips me over and braces himself over me.

"Oh, wow." I blink rapidly. "You've certainly made a lot of progress in the past few days."

He leans his weight on his arms. His biceps tremble, and he scowls. "Maybe not as much as I thought I had, apparently."

Sweat breaks out on his forehead, and he finally lowers himself onto the bed next to me. "Damnit," he growls. "I really need to speed up my recovery."

I laugh. "Seriously, you have made tons of progress. You're not a super-hero, you know."

"Aren't I?" he grumbles.

"Oh my god." I turn and take in his features which have lost some of that healthy flush I'd noticed earlier. "Do you seriously think that you can be back on your feet so quickly after getting hit by a bullet?"

"I do." He juts out his chin.

I burst out laughing. "You sound so confident, I almost believe you."

"Everything is in your mind." He taps his temple, the unhurt side. "If you believe in it, then it will happen."

"Is that your motto?" I ask. "Is that what makes you tick? This belief that you can do anything you want?"

"You don't believe me?"

I raise my shoulder, "I've had to fight hard for everything I want, so I'm not sure what to believe."

"What if I tell you that I can walk to the sofa"—he gestures to where a settee is pushed against one wall of the bedroom— "and back."

"Then I'm sure you can."

"Want me to prove it to you?" He repositions his sweats around his waist, rolls over to the side, then pushes up to sitting position.

"No, really, I don't. Besides, I don't think it's safe for you to exert—"

He swings his legs over the side of the bed, then draws in a deep breath. "Here goes." He pushes up to his feet and sways. I reach for him, but he rights himself. He takes a step forward, and his legs tremble, but he remains stand-ing. He takes another step, and another. His confidence seems to grow with each step he takes. He keeps his pace steady until he reaches the sofa, then sinks down onto it. He rolls his shoulders, his breathing heavy. He straightens his spine, raises his chin, and looks at me. "Well, what do you think?"

"I think…" I shake my head. "I think you're pushing yourself too hard."

"Fuck that." He rises to his feet. "I'm going to walk back to you."

"No, Axel, seriously, don't—" But he's already taking a step forward, then another. A third step and his body sways.

"Fuck," he swears. His body trembles, and he stumbles a little.

"Oh, hell." I jump off the bed and walk over to him.

I reach for him, but he holds up his hand. "I can do this."

"Let me help—"

"On my own," he says through gritted teeth as he glares at the bed. "I'm fine. I can walk without anyone's help."

He chants it like it's a mantra. It's as if he believes if he says the words enough, they'll become true. He takes another step and sways again from side to side. Sweat beads on his forehead and trickles down his temple. He takes another step and almost stumbles. I move toward him when he growls, "Fuck this."

He pushes forward, placing one foot in front of the other quickly, until he reaches the bed, then collapses onto it facedown. "Fuck," he growls, the sound muffled against the mattress. "Fuck, fuck, fuck."

"Hey." I walk over and sit on the bed next to him. "You okay?"

He doesn't answer.

I touch his shoulder, and my fingers come away wet with his sweat. His musky, earthy, male scent surrounds me, and my nipples tighten. My core clenches. Goddamn, this man is sex on a stick. I run my fingers through the hair at the nape of his neck. So soft, unlike the rest of him. I draw my fingers across his neck and over the ridge of his shoulder. His muscles bunch. I trail my finger down to the swell of his biceps. I poke at the muscle, which doesn't give a millimeter. "Holy shit," I whisper, "you really are a man of steel."

He turns his head to glare at me. "I am no fucking Superman. In fact, I always hated the bastard."

"I guess with your growliness and general grouchiness, you're more of a shoo-in for Batman."

"No thanks; not a fan of the bat ears."

I walk my fingers down to his forearm and tug at the fine hair there.

"What are you doing?" he asks in a soft voice.

"Just exploring." Jeez, I really should take my hand off of him. I should turn around and leave while he's still somewhat incapacitated, but if he's truly exhausted from over-exerting himself, he's not really a threat, is he?

I drag my fingers down to the back of his palm and trace the veins there. "Guess you work out a lot, huh? Your veins are so prominent."

When he doesn't reply, I glance up to find him watching me with a predatory look in his eyes.

"Oh, shit." I pull back my hand, but he flips on his back and grabs my wrist. He tugs, and I fall over onto the bed. "I… I … didn't mean anything by that," I swallow. "I was just curious."

"Want to see what your touch can do to me, huh?" He moves up toward the headboard, then pulls me closer. He presses my palm to his chest, and I feel the *thud-thud-thud* of his heart against my skin.

"Is your heart beating faster because of your earlier exertion?"

"You mean, when you sucked me off?"

"No," I scoff as my face reddens. "I mean, because of your crazed walk to the sofa and back, trying to prove some god-knows-what point."

"The point I was trying to prove is that I may be weaker than usual, but I'm not defenseless."

"Trust me, I'd never mistake you for that. Ever."

"And my heart is beating faster than usual, due to your proximity." His forehead furrows. "I can't believe I said that." He shakes his head. "I'm not supposed to feel anything for you."

"Gee, thanks." I strive to keep my voice light even as my heart rate ratchets up. He feels something for me? OMG, he feels something for me! Is that good or bad? Considering, he shot at Christian, threatened to hurt Aurora's family until she agreed to help him out, oh, and he also lied to the Sovranos about Aurora wanting to kill Christian. All in all, he's proven himself to be a psychopath, a sociopath, a misogynist, and someone who would not hesitate to lie simply because it causes more trouble for everyone else involved. Exactly the kind of man I should avoid. The kind I find attractive. I bite the inside of my cheek. What does that say about me?

I should be going out of my way to avoid this guy. I should stay as far away from him as possible. I should turn around and leave right now, while I can, before I do something that I'm going to regret for the rest of my life. I try to tug my wrist from his grasp, but he tightens his grip.

"Where do you think you're going, Sunshine?"

"Just t-to-to my room." Goddammit, and now I'm stuttering. Why the hell am I stuttering? It's not because of his nearness. Definitely not because of the way he's watching me with that intense gaze of his. Certainly not because the heat of his body surrounds me, overwhelms me, sinks into my blood and seems to coil in my lower belly. Absolutely not because he draws me closer to him … closer still. The tips of my feet bump against his. A shiver runs down my spine.

"Nervous?" he asks in a silken tone.

"N-no. Of-c-course, not."

"So why are you stuttering?"

"I-it happens. I t-tend to s-stumble over my w-words sometimes."

"Hmm," he looks me up and down, "we can't have that now, can we?" He tugs on my wrist, and I squeak as I fall into him. He wraps his arm around my waist and holds me immobile.

"L-let me g-go."

"Give me one reason why?"

"B-because I don't like you?"

"Are you asking me or telling me?" He smirks.

"N-neither. I'm stating a fact."

"Liar." He leans in and drags his nose up the side of my cheek. A shiver runs down my spine. He closes his lips around my earlobe, then bites down.

My entire body jolts. "Oh … hell." I whisper, "What are you doing?"

"Trying to stop your stuttering."

He drags his nose down my cheek then licks my lips.

My nipples tighten, and my belly clenches. "Don't do that," I whisper. "Please don't."

14

Axel

"It worked, though, didn't it?"

"What?" She blinks.

"You stopped stuttering," I point out.

"Oh"—her gaze widens—"that's true. But I still don't want you to kiss me," she says in a small voice.

I lean back and peer into her face. There's genuine distress and conflict in her eyes.

"What's the problem?" I murmur. "You want me, and I have made it very clear just how much you turn me on, so why can't we make each other happy?"

"It's not that simple," she replies.

"Is it because you're a virgin?"

She reddens. "I never said I was."

"You never denied it either."

"That's because, unlike you, I don't lie."

"What's that supposed to mean?"

"I was there when you lied to Christian about Aurora's 'bargain,'" she makes air quotes around the word, "with you."

"Did I?" I ask in a casual voice.

"Really, you're going to make me rehash what happened?"

I release her, then fold my hands behind my neck. "Go ahead, please enlighten me about my misdeeds."

She pushes away from me, then climbs off the bed as if wanting to put distance between us. I scowl. I don't want her to be wary of me. No ... hold on, that doesn't sound right. I don't care what she thinks of me, just as long as she submits to me.

"Well," I drawl, "what do you have to say?"

"Didn't you lie to Christian and tell him that Aurora had asked you to kill him?"

"She told me to distract Christian."

She stares at me. "So you remember things now? Your memory is coming back?"

I drag my fingers through my hair and wince when I brush the bandage at my temple; at least, the pain is bearable now. "When I don't make an effort, things seem to filter back into my consciousness."

"What else do you remember? Can you recollect why you made the deal with Aurora in the first place?"

"It doesn't work that way." I rub the back of my neck. "With every day that passes, my mind gets clearer. Then someone says something which triggers a thought, a layer shifts, and I recall another chain of events."

"So, she told you to distract Christian?" she prompts.

"Which is why I shot at him."

She stiffens. "You do realize that's not the same thing, right?"

"Isn't it?"

She gapes at me. "How can you say that? She told me that she specifically asked you not to hurt Christian, but at the most pivotal moment, you told him the exact opposite."

"So?"

She blinks rapidly. "So, that makes you a liar. Not to mention, what you did was so wrong. You clearly came between them. It's because of you that she returned to London."

"I'm sure that only made him realize how much he missed her. Bet he went after her."

She scowls at me.

"He did, didn't he? Poor bastard must have groveled in front of her and now they're together."

She flushes. "But they almost split up."

"Only, they didn't," I point out.

"Are you taking credit for the fact that they're together today?" She stares at me.

"You have to admit that it's only after my little push that he went after her?"

"Christian loves Aurora. He simply needed a little time to come to terms with it, and once he accepted it, he pursued her and brought her back."

"And all I did was hurry things along. If it weren't for me, they might still not be together."

"You are delusional," she mutters. "Fact is, you lied to their faces."

"I was simply testing them. They should be grateful to me that I gave them a chance to assess their relationship beforehand. They emerged stronger for it."

"Still doesn't change the fact that you lied. Also, you did threaten to harm her family unless she cooperated with you in spying on the Sovranos," she says in an accusing tone.

"So?"

"Jesus!" She throws up her hands. "Can't you see how wrong your actions were?"

"Nope." I make a popping sound with my lips. "I did what was needed to survive."

"Why, though?" She peers up into my face. "Why did you do all this? Why did you need to get information on the Sovranos? Although, considering you're right here with them now, you don't need anyone else spying on them. You can do it yourself."

"You have a point," I concede, "but since I'm unable to go anywhere, it's not the way I'd have chosen to get close to them."

"Why did you do it? Did someone compel you to get information on them? Is that why you threatened Aurora? Is that why you shot at Christian?"

I take in her earnest features, the flush on her cheeks, the way she folds her fingers together as if she's urging me to say that whatever I did was not by choice. "I'm not a good man, Sunshine. You do realize that, right?"

"So, neither are any of the Sovranos. I grew up as part of the Mafia clan; *you do realize that, right?'*

"I'm worse than the Mafia."

She scoffs, "What can be worse than the Mafia?"

"Someone who had a choice to leave the life behind, and didn't take it. Someone who's pursued revenge over anything else. Someone who won't hesitate to lie and kill, if needed, to get what he wants." I stiffen as I hear my words. Goddammit, it rings true. All of it. It's why I arrived at the deal with Aurora. It's why I shot at Christian. It's why I have been tracking the Sovranos obsessively most of my adult life.

"So, you do remember more than you let on?" An expression of hurt crosses her features.

My chest tightens. Why do I care that she's upset? She's just a means to an end, remember? So what, if I'm attracted to her? It doesn't mean anything. I roll my shoulders. "Like I said, I don't even realize what I have remembered sometimes until I have spoken it aloud."

"But you remember enough to realize that you want revenge?"

"What do you think?"

"I think you have spent most of your life searching for something. It's what brought you here, but you're finally home, Axel."

I stiffen. "The fuck you mean?"

She tips up her chin. "You are with your brothers. This is where you belong. You should have grown up with them in the first place. That didn't happen, but you're here now."

"For a reason. As soon as I'm better, I'll proceed with my plan."

"You may have come here to hurt them, but you're not going to do so now."

I stare at her for a second, then laugh. "You have a rather innocent view of the world, don't you, Sunshine?"

"You mean, I believe in the basic goodness of people?"

"I mean you're rather naive."

"I am not naïve; your problem is that you're too cynical. You think you're capable of hurting your brothers, but I don't believe you will."

"You don't know what I'm capable of."

"I know that you stepped in front of me and took a bullet for me."

"That was a mistake."

"I don't believe you."

"Better believe it." I look her up and down. "As soon as I'm better, I'm going to make sure that the Sovranos regret what they did to me."

"You are a Sovrano," she points out.

"I wasn't brought up as one. I sure as hell don't feel like one of them. And I'm definitely not going to join forces with them."

"Hmm…" She purses her lips. "I'm guessing you haven't been at the receiving end of one of Nonna's speeches. She's a very difficult woman to say no to."

"I've faced killers and survived. I'm sure I can handle an old woman."

She bursts out laughing and seems to laugh even harder when I scowl at her.

"Nonna's not your stereotypical old woman," she cautions me after a few moments. "Michael may be the Don, but make no mistake, Nonna wields a lot of power over all of the Sovrano brothers."

"You forget, I'm not one of the Sovrano brothers."

She blows out a breath. "You are; you just haven't accepted it yet."

"And I never will." I yawn. "Now, are you going to help me shower or—"

"No, I'm not. I told you already."

"If that's the case"—I nod toward the door—"get gone."

She opens and shuts her mouth. "You're so damn rude."

"Tell me something I don't know."

She shuffles her weight from foot to foot.

"Changed your mind?"

She shakes her head.

"So, what are you still doing here?"

She turns to leave. That's when Sheena pops her head inside the room.

"Can I get you anything, Axel?" She glances between us. "Oh, sorry, didn't realize I was intruding."

"You're not." I beckon her inside. "Theresa was just leaving."

"I can come back," she murmurs, and I shake my head.

"I do need your help with something."

"Sure. What can I do for you?" She takes a step forward.

"If you can help me to the bath and help me with my shower?"

"Of course." Sheena walks over to stand on the opposite side of the bed from Theresa, who freezes. She scowls at Sheena, then at me. She opens her mouth, and when I raise an eyebrow at her, she glowers at me.

"You staying or leaving, Sunshine?"

15

Theresa

I flipped him off then left without another word. I'm not someone who is normally rude, but this man... I stomped out of there, and he had the gall to tell me to shut the door behind me. I told him to get up and close it himself, since he's so strong. Only, I spoiled the effect by slamming it so hard behind me that it crashed against the doorframe. Small victories. I marched all the way to my room, then slammed that door shut as well.

I grab my phone and throw myself on the bed.

I start to dial Cass' number, then change my mind and FaceTime Aurora instead.

She picks up on the second ring.

"Hey," she says, her voice slightly breathless. "Long time since we spoke."

"I'm not the one who's newly married and who no longer has time for friends."

"Aww," she makes a face, "you know that's not true, Theresa."

"No." I slump down against the pillows. "Why Christian hasn't kidnapped you again and whisked you off to a honeymoon, I don't know."

"He wants to wait until all of this business with his triplet is resolved."

"Well, he won't have to wait too long, considering Axel is improving by leaps and bounds."

"I still can't get used to calling him by name," she confesses. "I still think of him as the stranger." She shudders. "He's scary, and not only because he's threatened me in the past. When I ran into him near the lodge while we were on the Christmas getaway, I swear, I thought that he was going to kill Christian. The look in his eyes"—she shakes her head—"it was like there was no emotion in the man. It felt like I was looking at someone who had all his feelings stripped away, leaving someone indifferent behind. He seemed like someone who was more dead than alive."

"Oh, he's very alive alright," I retort. "Trust me, I would know."

She stares at me. "Please tell me you're not considering a relationship with him."

"Oh, I don't think he's capable of a relationship. Sex, yes. Anything else, nope."

"Why would you want to sleep with him?" She grimaces. "The man is a sociopath."

"Believe me, I've been asking myself the same question." I blow out a breath. "I'm aware of what he did to you and Christian. I know what he's capable of. But it doesn't change the fact that he took a bullet for me."

"Maybe he did it by mistake."

"That's what he claims as well," I mutter.

"So, you've been spending time with him?" Aurora frowns. "Christian did mention to me that he'd asked for you to move into the same house as him, but you don't have to stay there, Theresa." She peers into my eyes. "Really, say the word, and I'll insist that Christian come over and get you out of there."

I hesitate.

"Please don't think twice. You shouldn't be near that man. He'll hurt you, Theresa."

"I know." I chew on my lower lip. "I know he's done things that I can't bear to think about. I know, at some point, I'm going to be done resisting him and give into him, but I can't stop myself. I can't, Aurora." I survey her features. "You'd think, knowing everything I do, I'd run far away from him. But I can't. I see glimpses of the man he really is beneath all that swagger. He's hurting,

Aurora. He's been through a lot—" she opens her mouth, and I raise my hand. "No, he hasn't told me anything specific, but I can guess. Whatever happened to him has made him into what he is, but when he's not being mean, I actually enjoy talking to him. He's so intelligent and so determined. You should see how he pushes himself every day to go through his physiotherapy exercises. It has to hurt, but he never complains. He simply throws himself into it because he's determined to be back on his feet as soon as possible. I've never seen anyone so focused, so strong willed. It's like he's literally bending destiny to suit his needs, you know?"

She purses her lips. "It seems to me, you're quite taken in by this guy."

"No, no," I protest, "I'm simply saying that he hasn't let being wounded or the fact that parts of his memory are still patchy stop him. He's really committed to recovering from his injury."

She merely stares at me.

"Aurora, honestly. I don't intend to have anything to do with this man."

"Then why don't you leave?"

"I…" I glance away then back at her. "I can't."

"Why not?"

"I can't leave him alone, not when he's still helpless."

"He has bodyguards posted around the house, plus an entire team of doctors, nurses, and physiotherapists."

"One physiotherapist, and don't get me started about her."

"What?" She frowns.

"Nothing, don't mind me." I bite the inside of my cheek. "You were saying?"

"That you need to get out of there before you are completely under his influence and can't tell right from wrong."

"I know what he did to you was wrong." I hasten to add, "But he took a bullet for me. I'd be dead if it weren't for him."

"Is that why you're staying, because you feel beholden to him?"

"Also, because he's Xander's triplet." I swallow. "Xan would have wanted me to help his triplet. He needs me."

"He doesn't need you." Aurora draws in a breath. "The man is a manipulator. He knows how to use people to suit his needs. And right now, it suits him to have you at his beck and call. Once he's back on his feet, he'll move forward with his life and he won't take another look at you. Not that the Sovranos will let him go anywhere. Especially, considering the fact that he did wound Christian, after all. But ultimately, he's one of them. They'll work things out, no doubt. Bet he'll come to some kind of an agreement with them that will compel them to set him free. And then he'll leave. He'll use you and discard you, Theresa."

"Gee, thanks," I murmur. "That's so reassuring."

"I'm not trying to reassure you." Her gaze intensifies. "I'm trying to keep you from being hurt. Well, more hurt than whatever it is that he's already done to you."

"He hasn't done anything to me."

"Are you saying that he hasn't made a move on you?"

"Umm." My cheeks heat.

"That's what I thought." Her frown deepens. "And I'll bet you weren't able to resist him either."

I rub my forehead. "I don't know... It's just... I..."

"You're falling for someone who is even more of a villain than the Sovranos are."

"Funny, that's what Axel said too."

"See…" she stabs a finger at me. "You can't go even a few minutes without bringing up his name."

"I was only trying to make the point that, at least, he is honest about his shortcomings."

"He's only saying that to try to lure you into a false sense of complacency. He's manipulating you. He wants you to try to prove it's not true."

"Geez," I scowl, "you really don't like him."

"Of course, I don't. You're not the one who was threatened by him. You weren't there when he shot at Christian when we were on the Christmas getaway. You—"

"Okay, okay," I cut her off. "I know he's done some things he shouldn't have done, but he's really not that bad. He saved my life, remember?"

"Something he's all but confessed was an accident," she scoffs.

My cheeks heat. Maybe it was a mistake calling Aurora. Clearly, she is so biased against Axel—and with good reason—that she'll never be able to give me an objective opinion about him.

"Look," I begin, but she cuts me off.

"You know what, Theresa? Nothing I say will dissuade you. I see that now. Just remember that I care about you. And I'll be here for you anytime you want."

"You mean, when I have my heart broken, you'll be more than happy to say 'I told you so' and help pick up the pieces?"

"That's not what I mean, I—"

"Oh, I have another call coming; gotta go." I disconnect. I immediately feel terrible. Ugh, why did I have to do that? She means well, and I really do like Aurora. And I understand what she's trying to say. It's just... I don't completely agree with everything she says. And she hasn't seen Axel pushing himself to recover, or seen him get frustrated and angry when his body doesn't obey him. She doesn't know what it's like to be kissed by him. I shake my head. No, no thinking about that. Separate the sex from the man. Ha, as if that's possible. Maybe I should call her back and apologize. I reach for the phone when it rings again.

Elsa's name pops up on the screen, and I answer the phone immediately.

"Hey." I smile as her face appears on screen. "I'm so happy to hear from you."

Elsa laughs. "Hey, you, what are you up to?"

"Nothing much." I roll over onto my front. "Just getting ready to head down for dinner, and then, I guess, I'll just read and go to sleep."

"That's boring, even for you."

"You know I much prefer to be curled up with a book boyfriend than a real one."

"That's only because you don't have a real boyfriend."

"How do you know that I don't?"

"Well, do you?"

I hesitate.

Her gaze widens, "You hooked up with Axel, didn't you?"

"Kind of," I murmur.

"OMG, tell me everything."

Let's see, he took a bullet for me, then I watched over him as he fell into a coma. When he came out of it, he had no idea who I was, and his memory was patchy because of his head wound. Oh, most likely, he's out to get the Sovranos, who will probably never let him get away with how he threatened someone close to them. Oh, wait, he's also a long-lost brother of the Sovranos, so it, in fact, makes him one of the Mafia, or worse.

"Well?" She scowls into the screen. "Have you slept with him? I mean, you are staying with him, aren't you?"

"I told you, I'm not staying with him," I rush to explain. "Just in the same house, but different rooms."

"Yeah, right." She snorts. "Bet you've already paid a few visits to his room." My face heats.

"Knew it," she crows. "So, how was it? Did he make you come? Have you guys slept together yet? And how many orgasms has he given you, anyway, you—"

"Stop." I hold up my hand. "It's not like that. It really isn't. Given the circumstances, it was best that I move in with him. You know that."

"Circumstances?" She frowns. "It can't be. You're not pregnant, are you? I mean, you only met him two weeks ago, so I suppose that's not impossible, but still."

I groan. "I'm not pregnant. Didn't you hear what I'm trying to say? I haven't slept with him."

"Aww, why not? You are attracted to him, and considering he asked you to move in with him, he must like you too. Why don't you make the most of the situation by, at least, getting a few orgasms out of it? Sleep with him; get him out of your system; just don't marry him." She stabs her finger in my direction.

"I'm not going to marry him." I laugh.

"I'm warning you, that's all." She tosses her hair over her shoulder. "These hot Italian men can be tricky. They use their cocks to manipulate you, then before you know it, you end up married to him, and you don't want that."

"Actually…" I bite the inside of my cheek. "I do hope to get married one day soon. I know it hasn't been an easy experience for you, but I hope I'll meet the right man soon."

"So, this Axel chap isn't the right man?"

"Of course, not."

"All the more reason to fuck him, and then you can share all of the juicy details with me," she says in a bright tone.

"I'll do no such thing." I scowl.

"So, you do have details, but you won't share them with me?"

"No, no, there are no details. There's nothing to share." My cheeks flush.

"You're lying. I can tell." She blows out a breath. "But fine, have it your way. I won't push."

"Thanks," I murmur.

"And there goes my chance to live vicariously." Her lips turn down. "I was banking on you to take my mind off of my own problems."

"Is your ex still causing you trouble?"

"He's an asshole," she says in a matter-of-fact tone. "If he has his way, I'll never get to see my baby girl again."

"I'm so sorry you have to deal with this, Elsa."

"Anyway, let's not talk about my problems. Why don't we go out tonight? You can bring Axel. That way, I can, at least get to meet him."

"Oh, no. He's not up to leaving the house. Besides, I know for a fact that he's otherwise occupied." I bite the inside of my cheek. Asshole wanted that … that … Sheena woman to help him with his bath. Right now, she's probably rubbing soap all over him, paying special attention to his dick, no doubt. She's probably on her knees sucking him off, even as we speak.

"Well, if he's busy, then why don't you come out to dinner with me?

He's probably digging his fingers into her hair and yanking her forward so he can thrust his dick down her throat. Then he'll groan as he empties himself, and she'll suck down every last drop of his cum, before she sits back on her heels and glances up at him adoringly. Then he'll lean in and kiss her on the lips. I squeeze my thighs together, even as my chest feels too tight. No doubt, he won't give me a second thought as he spends the rest of the evening with her. And me? Am I going to spend the evening locked away in my room, bemoaning the fact that I didn't take him up on his offer? I mean, I could have been the one in his bed, under him as he took my virginity. My nipples tighten.

"Theresa," Elsa calls, "you there?"

"Yes." I push away the images in my head. "And I have a better idea."

"What's that?"

"Let's go to a nightclub, you and me."

She stares at me, then bursts out laughing. "You want to go to a nightclub? You, who really does prefer staying home on a Friday night reading a romance novel, wants to go out and party?"

"And if I do?"

She peers into my features. "Now, I really do want to meet this Axel. He's managed to push you out of your comfort zone, hasn't he?"

I scowl, "Are you coming with me to the nightclub, or not?"

Forty-five minutes later, I walk into Venom, the most happening nightclub in Palermo. It's also owned by the Sovranos, which, I assume, is the only reason Seb—who's filling in for Adrian—agreed to drive me here. He'd turned up within fifteen minutes of my calling, which was just enough time for me to get dressed. He drove me in almost complete silence, and except for raised eyebrows when I mentioned my destination, he didn't react. He parked at the entrance to the nightclub, and a valet materialized out of nowhere. Of course, he's a Sovrano—they run this town. It stands to reason that a valet would notice his car and come over to park it right away.

He walks around, opens my door, and I step out. I pull down the hem of the dress I'm wearing, which comes to mid-thigh. It's still not as short as the dresses some of the other girls here are wearing, but it's the shortest dress I own. Thankfully, I had the foresight to pack this little black dress, which makes up for its plainness by the way it clings to my curves.

I walk toward the entrance with Seb right behind me.

"Theresa." Elsa materializes next to me. "So glad you could make it."

"Me too." I grin up into her flushed features. A heavy, wing-shape eyeliner outlines her eyes, and her thick blonde hair is pulled up in a messy bun. She's wearing a purple sequined dress which should look like too much, but really, it suits Elsa's partly flamboyant, partly messy style. With her thigh-high boots and bracelets that decorate her forearms up to her elbows, she looks like she's thrown on an eclectic mish-mash of items from her wardrobe, but somehow, it works.

"Come on!" She yanks me forward, only to come to an abrupt stop when Seb walks around to stand in front of us. He folds his arms across his chest and stares down at her.

"Who's this?" She tips her chin all the way back to meet his gaze.

"Ah, this is Seb, my uh, my bodyguard for the evening."

"Bodyguard." She shoots me a sideways glance. "You have a bodyguard?"

she asks in a whisper-scream, which is loud enough for Seb to hear above the noise that filters out of the nightclub.

"Yeh, uh, told you the Sovranos insist that I am ferried about for my own safety."

"OMG, I had no idea it meant you have your own personal bodyguard."

"Only because I wanted to go out," I murmur.

"Hmm…" She looks him up and down. "Well, we don't need you this evening. Why don't you go off and do whatever it is bodyguards do on their time off?"

Seb glares at her; she scowls back at him.

"Jeez, you are grumpy, aren't you? Maybe you should come along with us and have a few drinks to loosen up."

He turns to me. "I assume you know her?"

"Oh, yeah; sorry. I forgot to introduce you guys. Seb, meet my friend Elsa."

"Pleased to meet you." Elsa holds out her hand.

He ignores it, then spins around and prowls toward the entrance of the nightclub. The crowd parts in front of him, and we follow in his wake.

"He's rude." Elsa glowers at his broad back.

"He's a Sovrano."

"There seem to be more of them than the Baldwins," she retorts.

"What?" I glance at her. "What does that mean?"

"Nothing, just a joke. It's a film reference joke. One of my classmates from when I went to school—Summer West, was her name—she was so into movies that all her conversations were peppered with references to films. Some of it rubbed off on me."

"Do you miss England?"

"Not the weather. I miss London, though." Her gaze grows pensive. "It's a big city. It afforded me more anonymity than Palermo."

"You moved here to be close to your daughter, didn't you?"

"It was the only way I could get to see her." Her lips firm.

"Sorry, didn't mean to upset you."

"No, it's fine." She shoots me a smile that's so bright that I wince. "Let's have some fun, shall we?"

She hooks her arm through mine, and we follow Seb into the nightclub.

A wave of noise hits me as we walk down the short flight of steps and into the large room. The scent of sweat, perfumes, and alcohol all mesh into a strange bitter-sweet scent that overpowers me. The room has high ceilings and is cavernous enough for the music to echo back and be magnified. On both sides of the room, a bar stretches from end to end, and in between is the dance floor. Or, at least, I assume it's a dance floor because I can't see an inch of it. The entire space is crammed with men and women dancing in what seems to be one big amorphous mass of humanity.

"Umm, I'm not sure I want to be here," I begin, but Elsa grabs my arm and pulls me along with her. "Elsa, please," I begin to protest, but she turns on me.

"Do you want to stay home moping for your Sovrano?"

I deflate a little. "N-no," I admit.

"This was your idea. Clearly, you want to prove a point to yourself. You've come this far; don't back out now. Let's loosen up a little and have some fun, okay?"

I let her drag me into the sweltering hot cavern.

Seb seems to have disappeared somewhere; thank God. At least, I don't have to deal with him and Elsa getting pissy with each other.

The strobe lights dance over us as she elbows her way through the crowd. She keeps a firm grip on me, until we reach the very center of the dance floor. Bodies push in on us from all sides. Sweat beads my brow and trickles down my temple. My dress clings to my back. Elsa grips my arms and sways in tandem to the music, which is so loud that it pounds through my veins. The beat ricochets about my head. Elsa swings her hips, dirty-dancing with me as she squats, then pushes out her hips and straightens. I notice the men behind her eyeing her up and down as she continues to dance, apparently, unaware of their attention.

"Elsa!" I scream to make myself be heard above the music. "Elsa!"

She glances at me. "Come on, babe, you need to loosen up a little."

She throws her arms around me and grinds her hips into mine.

"What are you doing?" I laugh as she pulls back, then twirls me around and back in. Then she turns her back on me, and once more does a bump and grind.

"Elsa, I need to get off the dance floor." I grip her shoulder.

She turns to me. "Aww, and I was just beginning to have fun."

"Well, I'm not." I scowl.

"Hmm, I know just what you need."

She grabs my hand, and pushes through the crowd, hauling me with her.

We burst out of the throng, and cool air instantly envelops me. I yank my hand from her grasp and push the hair off my neck.

"Phew, it's hot in there."

"I know the best way to cool off." Elsa heads for the bar, and I follow her. She gets the attention of the bartender. "Two tequilas, please." Within minutes, he places two shots in front of us.

She picks up her shot glass, while I eye mine with doubt. "Um, I'm not sure I should—"

"You absolutely should," she insists. "Come on." She picks up my shot glass and thrusts it at me. "Bottoms up!"

She holds up her glass. I take my glass, then clink glasses with her.

"That's the spirit. On the count of one-two-three—"

I throw back the liquor, and the alcohol slides down my throat. It hits my stomach, and tendrils of heat radiate out to my extremities.

"Whoa"—I shake my head—"that was—"

"Good!" she declares. "It was excellent." She gestures to the bartender. "Two more, please."

"Oh, no." I back away. "I'm not drinking more."

"Oh, yes, you are." She picks up a glass and pushes it into my hand. "Come on; you have to keep me company."

I draw in a breath and am about to protest when she whines, "Come on, Theresa, it's our first time out together. We need to celebrate."

"Right." I resist the urge to roll my eyes. "You don't need to get drunk to celebrate."

She stares at me. "Of course, you do." She raises her glass. "Come on!"

I hesitate, and she lifts up my hand, then clinks her glass to mine. "Drink up!"

I blow out a sigh. Damn, I really don't want to get tipsy, but no way is she letting me out of this unless I oblige her. I clink my glass with hers, then throw back the contents of the shot glass. This one goes straight to my head. A delicious warmth infuses my chest. I can't stop my lips from curving up.

"Whoa!" I fan myself. "That's something."

"Right?" She turns to the bartender, but I grasp her shoulder.

"NO more for me. I'm going to the bathroom."

"Hold on, and I'll come with you," she interjects.

I wave her off. "You get another drink. I'll just head to the bathroom and back."

"But—"

I cut her off. "I'll be fine. I just need a minute to cool off." I brush past her and head for the restroom before she can protest. Once there, I join the queue snaking past the restroom doors. It's a full twenty minutes before I return to the bar, only to find Elsa glowering up at Seb.

I walk up to stand between them as Seb reaches down to brush a strand of hair behind her ear. What the—? I stare between them for a full minute, and yet, neither of them notices me. The tension between them is off-the-charts.

"Hello … everything okay?" I finally ask.

Elsa scowls and takes a step back. Seb lowers his hand to his side at the same time.

"Elsa? Seb? What's going on here?"

"What's going on is that your bodyguard seems to think he owns the place, is what."

"I do, actually." Seb looks her up and down. He seems to notice her dress for the first time, and his features harden. "What the fuck are you wearing?" he asks.

"Excuse me?" Elsa opens and shuts her mouth. "What did you just say?"

"You may as well as be parading naked for all that you have on."

"What the hell?" Elsa turns to me as if to say, *is this guy for real?* She rolls her eyes before turning back to him. "Who the hell do you think you are, you asshole?"

"We're leaving," he says through gritted teeth.

"You can take her. I'm not going anywhere." Elsa turns away.

"Don't turn your back on me," Seb growls.

"I'll do what I want, when I want!" Elsa huffs.

Seb's features seem to grow thunderous. He steps forward, but I grip his hand.

"Don't," I say in a soft voice. "Let me handle this."

He glowers at her for a second longer, then nods.

"Elsa," I touch her shoulder, "I think it's time for us to leave."

"I'm just starting to have fun." She scowls at me from the corner of her eyes. "Besides, who does he think he is to order me around?"

"The Sovranos can be a bit overwhelming. Why don't we get out of here, and I'll explain on the way home?"

"Fine." She tosses her hair, most of which has escaped from the messy bun on top of her head. "There's one thing I have to do before we leave." Her eyes gleam.

"Oh?"

She darts toward the bar, grabs a tall glass of beer, then turns and dumps it on Seb.

16

—————

Axel

I sprawl across her bed.

It had been a bitch getting here, but I had been determined to make it here on my own steam. After Theresa left, I pulled away from Sheena. My legs were shaky, but I managed to walk to the bathroom by myself. Sheena asked if I was sure that she couldn't help, and I assured her that I could take it from there and that she could return to whatever it was she'd been doing. She gave me a funny look but did as I asked. I walked slowly into the bathroom, had a shower, then managed to dry myself and pull on a fresh set of clothes—courtesy of the Sovranos, who've ensured that I have a wardrobe full of clothes. Something I'm not particularly happy about, but until I regain my memory completely and am strong enough to get out of here, I have no choice but to be dependent on them. It hurts my pride to do so, but I'm nothing if not practical. It's the only way I've managed to survive this far.

I need to get stronger, which means I need to focus on my recovery—ergo, I need to pretend to be amenable to whatever the Sovranos have in mind, and that means accepting the clothes and the roof over my head. It's only for a few more weeks, assuming I can will my body to cooperate. And the one thing I'm good at is using my determination to shape events to go my way.

Once dressed, tiredness crept over me. So I slid onto the bed and napped for a few hours. I woke up refreshed, energized, and horny. Thoughts of Theresa filled my mind. Her soft skin, her pink lips, the way her hips sway as she walks, that scent of apple blossoms that fills my lungs every time she's near. She is everything soft and curvy and pliable. Someone I can bend to my will and use to keep myself entertained while I recover. It's why I rolled out of bed, then walked up the corridor and toward her room.

I walked in and found it empty. First surprise, then irritation filled me. I checked the bathroom and her closet and concluded she wasn't there. By then, tiredness started setting in. So, I walked over to her bed, sat, and using the internal phone line, called down to the kitchen, the hub of activity. The staff informed me that she was last seen leaving with Seb.

What the fuck? What is she doing with him? Where is he taking her? And, most importantly, how dare she leave the premises of the house without my permission? Of course, I didn't tell her that she had to stay inside. I didn't warn her that she couldn't head out of the house without informing me. I thought it was understood… Clearly, I was wrong. Clearly, I have to make myself clearer to her.

Tiredness overcomes me again and I stretch out on her bed and close my eyes. The next thing I hear is the sound of the door to the suite being pushed open. I have just enough presence of mind to reach over and switch off the bedroom light.

I hear her footsteps approach. She's humming under her breath. Wherever she's been, it's put her in a good mood. Did she fuck him? Did she allow him to have his hands all over her? I ball my fists at my side. I track her progress as she walks inside the room. It's dark outside, and while the light from the living room illuminates her up from behind, I'm in darkness so she doesn't seem to notice me.

She walks toward the bathroom, bumps into a chair, and almost falls.

"Whoops," she hiccups, as she rights herself. "Sorry, sorry," she apologizes. To the chair? I arch an eyebrow as she straightens, then weaves her way in the general direction of the bathroom again. She stops halfway and kicks off her heels. She reaches for the hem of her dress, then yanks it up and over her head. She throws it toward the bed where it lands on my face, covering my mouth and nose. The scent of apple blossom, mingled with her sweat, fills my nostrils. Every pore in my body seems to pop. My groin hardens. She unhooks her bra and lets it fall to the floor. Then she shoves her panties down her shapely legs and kicks them aside, giving me a flash of her curvy behind before she disappears into the bathroom. The sound of the water from the shower reaches me.

Fuck! I adjust myself, then push off the bed. Thankfully, my legs feel strong enough to hold up my weight, at least, for the time being... Barefoot, I pad over to the bathroom and glance within to find her inside the shower. She hums to herself as she raises her arms. The shower water pours down her shoulders, down her back, in the valley between those perfectly-shaped arse cheeks. Fucking fuck. A bead of sweat runs down my spine. I approach her, then pull open the door of the shower stall and lean against it.

She hums under her breath, then turns. Eyes still closed, she soaps her breasts, running her hands along the sides, underneath them, before trailing her fingers down her waist to play with her pussy lips. She slides her finger inside herself, then adds another. She moves the fingers in and out of herself, in and out. Her breasts rise and fall. I raise my gaze to her face to find her eyes still closed. She bites down on her lower lip as she continues to pleasure herself.

I drag my gaze back to her pussy to find her finger fucking herself with three fingers now. Fuck! I slide my palm inside the waistband of my pants and squeeze my cock. As she thrusts her fingers in and out of herself, I drag my hold up my shaft, then again, and again.

My breath comes in pants, the steam from the shower envelops me, and sweat beads my shoulders. I increase the intensity of my actions, keeping pace with her. Her hips twitch; and her torso curves. Fuck, she's close. She leans into the wall at the back of the shower as my dick lengthens further. I stroke myself harder, faster, and that's when her entire body seems to freeze. I jerk my chin up, take in the way her features contort, how her eyes are still closed, her eyelids crinkle as she opens her mouth in a soundless cry.

"Fuck, you're beautiful," I groan as I come.

That's when her eyelids fly open. Her gaze widens. And she opens her mouth again, no doubt, to scream. I pull my hand out of my pants, close the distance between us, and thrust my hips into hers. I push my chest into those gorgeous breasts, then fit my mouth over hers.

All of her muscles seem to lock, her entire body freezing in surprise. I thrust my tongue in between her lips, and that's when she comes alive. She pulls her hand from between us and digs her fingers into my shoulder. I'm sure she's going to push me away, but instead, she locks her leg around my waist and pulls me closer. I slap my palms into the wall on either side of her head. I tilt my head, deepen the kiss, and she moans. I absorb the sound as I push my already erect cock into the softness of her core. I twine my tongue with hers, then bite down on her lower lip. A groan bleeds from her mouth. The sound goes straight to my head and suddenly, I need to have her. I shove my wet sweatpants down my thighs, then notch my cock against her entrance. I slow down to glance into her flushed features.

"Open your eyes," I order.

Her eyelids flutter open, and she stares at me with those green eyes. I search her features. "Do you want me?" I growl. "Do you, Theresa?"

She swallows.

"Say the word, and I'll leave you."

She hesitates.

"If I take you now, there's no going back," I warn her. "I won't stop until I own you, possess you, break you." Then I whisper, "Until I make you mine."

Her pupils dilate until only a circle of green remains at the circumference of the iris.

"Axel…" She licks her lips. "Axel…"

I nudge the crown of my cock against her wet opening. "What's it gonna be, Theresa? Do you want my cock?"

"Yes!" She tips up her chin. "I want y—"

I thrust forward, and she stiffens.

"That hurt." She gasps as she squeezes her eyes shut.

I dig my fingers into the wall, firm my thighs, and hold myself there. The warm, wet flesh of her pussy envelops my dick, and fuck, if I don't come all over again. I stay there until her breathing evens out, and she opens her eyes again.

She cups my cheek, and a wave of tenderness runs through me. I pull out, then slide back in. Her pussy instantly clamps down on my cock, and heat radiates out from the point of contact between us.

"Fuck!" I push my forehead against her. Pain pricks around the wound at my temple, but I ignore it. "You're killing me, Sunshine."

She pushes her breasts into my chest, and the sensation of her hardened nipples digging into my chest sends me over the edge. I pull out, then drill into her, this time thrusting all the way inside. Her entire body jolts.

I begin to fuck her in earnest, watching her features closely. Every time I bury myself in her, the flush on her face seems to deepen. Every time I hit that spot deep inside her, she moans. Her eyelids flutter closed, and I snap, "Eyes on me."

It seems as if she opens her eyelids with great difficulty and peers up at me from under her eyelashes. Her eyes are stormy with lust, with arousal, and fuck, if that doesn't turn me on even more. I grip her thighs just under her butt and haul her up. She wraps her legs around my waist as I impale her again. My biceps twitch, my thigh muscles protest, but I push aside the pain.

"Oh, God," she groans. "Oh my God, Axel."

I grit my teeth as I tilt my hips and slam myself into her. Her body stiffens, her eyes roll back in her head, and that's when I press my entire body into her. "Come," I order, and she opens her mouth in a wordless scream as she detonates. Her pussy squeezes down on my cock, and I groan as I shoot my cum inside her. We stay that way until my thighs tremble. Some of the adrenaline fades away, and my leg muscles quiver.

Fuck. I fucking hate that I'm still so weak. I pull out of her, then squeeze her thighs so she lowers her legs. Then I drop to my knees in between her thighs.

"What are you—" She groans as I lick my tongue up between her pussy lips. I lick away the blood, and the taste of my cum mixed with hers coats my palate. I thrust my tongue inside her wet channel and weave it in and out of her. The sweet scent of her arousal surrounds me. I squeeze the backs of her legs as I swipe my tongue around her clit. She gasps, then digs her fingers into my hair, even as she tries to move away from my questing tongue.

A moan bleeds from her lips, and I increase my pace. I tilt my head and plunge my tongue inside her soaking wet channel. Her knees quake, and her entire body jolts. "Oh my God," she gasps. "Oh God, Axel."

She clings to me as I bury my nose in her pussy, draw my fill of her scent, then drag my tongue up to her clit.

"Who does this pussy belong to?" I growl.

"You," she moans, "you, Axel."

I urge her to throw her leg over my shoulder, opening her even more for me. I curl my tongue around the engorged clit, and she huffs. I squeeze her arse, then drag my finger down the valley between her butt cheeks. I bite down on her pussy as I slide a finger inside her back hole, and her muscles stiffen. I glance up to find she has squeezed her eyelids shut.

"Open your eyes," I growl, and her eyelids flutter open. She holds my gaze from under heavy eyelashes as I thrust my tongue inside her pussy. I curve my finger inside her back channel, and she shudders.

"Who does this arse belong to?" I snap.

"Y… you," she stutters.

"Damn right." I swipe my tongue up between her pussy lips again and again, then plunge my tongue inside her channel.

Her thighs tremble, and she sways. "Axel," she whispers "I'm going to—"

"Come," I command, and her entire body shudders. Her back curves, and she throws her head back as she shatters.

17

———————

Theresa

I float down from the orgasm to find I'm leaning into him. Water beats down on my back. Some of the spray coats his shoulders and trickles down his back. He's massaging my ass cheeks as he stares up at me. His mouth and chin glisten. That's my cum, I realize. My cheeks heat. He rises to his feet, pulls his sweats up around his waist, then stares down at me.

"That's the last time you leave here without my permission," he growls.

"Excuse me?" I blink. Some of the sexual haze retreats. "I'm not your prisoner."

"Is that right?" He laughs. The jerk laughs at me.

"Why are you laughing? I didn't make a joke."

"You might as well have." He smirks. "You don't leave here without my consent, and that's final."

I try to pull away from him, but his grip on my hips tightens. Water from the shower pours over him. His hair sticks to his forehead, and his features stand out in contrast. I glance at the bandage at his temple. "Your dressing is wet," I point out.

"Fuck that." He scowls. "What were you doing with him?"

"With who?"

"Seb," he spits out his brother's name as if it's a bad word.

"So you've been spying on me?"

"Don't answer a question with a question."

"How about I not answer your question at all?" I sniff.

He grabs my hips and fits me to the cradle of his pelvis. The thickness at his crotch stabs into my core. "You will answer the question."

"And if I don't?"

He peers into my face. "Trust me; you don't want to find out what happens if you don't."

I hold his gaze, and those blue eyes of his bore into me. I flinch. "Nothing happened with Seb. You know that, right?"

He doesn't reply.

"Besides, Seb has his own issues. My friend Elsa and he seem to have taken an instant dislike to each other. In fact, she dumped a pint of beer on him earlier. It was quite entertaining." I laugh.

He stares at me with a strange look in his eyes.

"What?" I redden. "What is it? Do I have something on my face or something?"

"You're fucking gorgeous, and I'm not just talking about your looks, Sunshine. There's an innocence to you, and it's not just the fact that you were a virgin. "

"Gee, thanks," I mutter.

"It's something else." He shakes his head. "You have a thirst for life, an optimism, a happiness that radiates from you that is so very infectious. You make me want to have hope."

"Wow…" I swallow. "That feels very much like a compliment."

"You confuse me." His scowl deepens. "I can't figure out what makes you tick."

"And that's bad?"

"That's ... not good for my peace of mind," he growls. "You're not good for my peace of mind. When I found you'd gone out, I lost my mind. I hated that I wasn't strong enough yet to walk out of the house and go after you. I hate being this helpless. I hate that I need to rely on others to protect you. That I have to be in this house that belongs to someone else. That I have to be dependent on others, knowing they're probably plotting against me as we speak."

"They're your family; if they wanted to hurt you, they'd have done it by now."

"Or maybe they're waiting for me to be strong enough so I can put up a fight as they take me down."

"You don't trust anyone, do you?"

"I trust you." His gaze widens. He seems taken aback by his words. To be honest, so am I.

"You don't have to be jealous of anyone else where I'm concerned. You are the first man I've been with, Axel. You've seen the evidence of that with your own eyes." I peer up into his features.

His jaw hardens. His gaze seems to grow even more stormy.

"Why are you so angry?" I cup his cheek. "All this bitterness inside of you, all this pain, where is it coming from?"

His brow furrows. For a second, I'm sure he's going to answer my question, then a mask seems to drop over his face. He releases me and steps back, only to sway. I grip his shoulder to right him, and his features grow even more angry. He spins around and heads out of the shower. He makes it to the door before his knees seem to grow too shaky. He grips the doorframe and draws in a breath.

I reach behind me and turn off the shower before I walk over to him. By the time I reach him, his features are pale.

"You okay?" I reach out to touch him, but he shrugs it off.

"I can walk on my own steam."

"I have no doubt," I murmur.

"Don't humor me." He firms his lips.

"I believe you. I'm only trying to help."

"Well, don't." He takes another step forward, then another. I glance down at myself and realize I'm dripping water all over the carpet. Shit. I turn and hurry back into the bathroom. I dry myself quickly, then shrug into a bathrobe, before I return to him. I catch up with him as he nears the door to the hallway. His clothes are dripping, and his breathing is labored. He grips the frame of the door and draws in a breath.

"Let me help you, please," I plead.

He doesn't answer me. Simply takes another step forward, then another.

His pace is slow, and he seems to be growing more tired with each passing minute. Halfway up the corridor, he sways. I grab his arm, and this time, he doesn't shake it off. I throw his arm across my shoulder, wrap my arm around his waist, and help him back to his room.

"Why don't you sit in that chair, and I'll help you out of your clothes?"

He doesn't protest, and I shoot him a sideways glance. His face is paler, his cheekbones more pronounced. He has his gaze fixed on the chair. He seems to be slowing down with each step, but we finally make it to the chair. He lowers himself into it with a sigh, then leans his head back and closes his eyes. I undo the buttons of his shirt.

"Lean forward," I murmur.

He obliges me without complaint, and once more, I rake my gaze across his face. His eyes are closed, his breathing labored. Clearly, he's in pain. I push his shirt off of his shoulders, then reach for his sweatpants. "Uh, you'll need to lift your hips so I can help you out of these."

I pull his sweatpants down, and his thick cock swings free. He sinks into the chair, and I pull his sweats completely off. He places his head against the back of the chair, and his chest rises and falls. Moisture gleams across his shoulders and slides down the demarcation of his pecs. It slips down his sculpted chest, around his belly button, and catches on the trimmed hair at the base of his cock. My mouth waters, and before I can give myself the chance to change my mind—after all, I'm already down here—I wrap my fingers around his shaft and it jumps in my grasp.

"What are you doing?"

I tip up my chin to find him staring down at me. His blue gaze is direct as he surveys my features. Without breaking the connection, I lick my tongue around the crown of his dick.

He draws in a harsh breath, but otherwise, there's no change of expression on his face. I lick the slit on the head, and his nostrils flare. I close my mouth around his shaft, and his gaze intensifies. I tilt my head and take in as much of the length as I can. He buries his fingers into my hair and tugs. Pinpricks of pain radiate across my scalp. My nipples tighten. My core clenches. He tugs on my hair so I'm forced to pull back until the head of his cock is poised between my lips. Then he pushes forward, and his dick slides down my throat. I gag, and tears squeeze out of the corners of my eyes.

"Why is it that seeing your tears turns me on?" he murmurs, almost to himself. As if to punctuate his words, his shaft thickens, filling my mouth. I force myself to relax my jaw as he begins to fuck my mouth in earnest. Of course, with Axel, even a blowjob is not something he'll allow me to give him. He has to be in control, even here.

I balance myself with one hand on his thigh as he pulls me forward. His dick slides down my throat. I draw in the dark, musky scent of his, and moisture laces my core. My pussy throbs, and my lower belly clenches. I dig my fingernails into his thighs and glance up at him. His gaze is intense as he speeds up. His chest planes flex, his shoulder muscles knot, and the tendons of his throat move as a growl rips from him. His hold in my hair tightens, his cock pulses and he comes, shooting his warmth down my throat. He seems to come until his cum fills my mouth. I try to swallow, but it overflows from the corners of my lips.

He pulls out, then hauls me up and fixes his mouth on mine. His lips clash with mine, and he licks his arousal off of my mouth. He thrusts his tongue in between my lips and sucks from me. He kisses me so deeply, so intensely, my head spins. I plaster myself to his chest and throw my arms around his neck as I push myself into him.

The room seems to tilt, and I open my eyes to find he's on his feet again. I try to protest, but he doesn't release my mouth. He carries me to his bed, places me on the mattress, and follows me down. He pulls me to him as he continues to kiss me. My head spins. Darkness flickers at the edges of my vision. When he finally releases me, I gasp. Oxygen rushes into my lungs, and I sink into the pillow.

We stare at each other, and something seems to shift. He cups my cheek and brings me in for another kiss. His lips touch mine. He shares my breath but doesn't deepen the kiss further. He brushes his mouth against mine as if learning its outline all over again. He leans in closer until his thighs touch mine, his hips cradle mine, and his chest brushes against my breasts. My nipples tighten, and one side of his lips curves. He pushes a strand of hair away from my temple. "I'm not sorry I took your virginity," he whispers.

"I don't want you to be sorry that you took my virginity," I reply.

"I don't want you to leave this house without telling me."

"Okay," I whisper.

"When the household staff told me that you'd left with Seb, I was sure that I was going to kill him."

"And now?"

"I'm sure I'm going to kill him."

I chuckle. "I just needed to get away from here," I explain. "When I saw you with that … that woman—"

"You mean Sheena?" He smirks.

"Whatever." I huff. "When I realized that she was going to help you bathe—"

"She didn't."

"Oh?" I blink.

"I asked her to leave right after you did."

"Oh…" I glance away. "But you meant to convey the impression—"

"That she was going to help me shower and more, yes."

"So did she?" I turn my gaze on him. "Did she help you shower and more."

"Already told you. I asked her to leave right after you. She's only my physiotherapist and nothing more, so you don't need to be jealous of her."

"Who says I'm jealous of her?"

His smirk widens. "It's cute when you deny the emotions that are written all over your face."

"They are not."

"They are." He wraps his fingers around my neck, and a shiver runs down my spine.

"When you get this … assertive, it turns me on," I whisper.

"I know," he replies with such confidence that I resist the urge to roll my eyes.

"Jeez, is there anything that you're not sure about?" I ask.

"Myself. I'm never sure how I'm going to react around you." He increases the pressure around my throat, and a thrill grips me. My breasts seem to swell, and my thighs tremble.

"Axel," I protest, "you need to rest."

"I'll rest when I'm dead."

I frown. "That's not funny. When that bullet hit you and you crumpled to the ground, I thought my heart would stop beating."

"You did?" He presses his thumb into the base of my throat where my pulse beats rapidly. "You didn't even know me then."

"I knew that you had stepped in front of me and taken the bullet meant for me. Nobody has ever done anything like that for me. Speaking of..." I touch the bandage on his temple. "Don't you need to change this bandage?"

"It's waterproof."

"Oh." I lower my hand and place my palm against where his heart beats in his chest. He leans in and presses his lips to my forehead. A warmth squeezes my chest.

"What was that for?" I murmur, then yawn.

"That was to show you"—he kisses the tip of my nose—"I'm not a complete asshole"—he presses a soft kiss to my lips—"and I do have it in me to be tender"—he presses a kiss to my chin—"on occasion."

He leans back and glances at my face.

"I know you're not as much of an alpha-hole as you pretend to be," I murmur.

"Alpha-hole?" He chuckles. "I like it. You may refer to me as alpha-hole from now on."

I yawn again. "I should have known that you would take that as a compliment."

"If the shoe fits." He raises a shoulder as he draws me onto his chest.

"Aren't you supposed to be recuperating? Won't I hurt you if I put my weight on you? Isn't it better if—"

"Hush." He tucks my head under his chin. "Sleep now."

I open my mouth to protest, and instead, end up yawning again. Sleep tugs at the edges of my conscious mind. I close my eyes and am instantly asleep. When I wake up, I'm alone in his bed and naked.

What the—? Did he carry me to bed? Is he strong enough to do that already? Clearly, he's almost fully recovered.

I glance around the room and find it empty. It's only the indentation in the pillow next to me that indicates that someone else occupied the same bed as me.

I swing my legs over the side, grab the bathrobe from where it was thrown down next to the bed, and shrug it on before heading to my room to freshen up. Finally, I discard the bathrobe, step into my jeans, and shrug into a sweater. I pull on thick socks, then my trainers, before I head out of my room. When I peek inside Sheena's room, then Axel's, I find them both empty.

I head down the flight of steps and toward the study, which is the only room I haven't been to before. The sound of voices reaches me as I near the doorway.

"What are your intentions with Theresa?"

18

Axel

"Intentions?" I lean back into the couch.

I woke up at the crack of dawn, knowing I needed to start exercising again. Theresa was curled into my side. I had carried her to bed last night, and she hardly weighed anything. Still, by the time I had reached the bed, I was exhausted.

She slept with her head on my chest and her leg flung over me, her cheeks flushed and her eyelashes a dark fan over her cheeks. Her breathing had been steady and she seemed at peace. I had reached out to touch her face then stopped myself. I do not do tenderness. I do not want to feel this drawn to her. She's simply a woman who happens to be a welcome distraction while I work to get my strength back.

Yeah, sure. That's why I wasn't able to stop myself from taking her virginity. Or from holding her later in bed. That's why I held her all night as she slept. There is something between us, no doubt about that. Already, my feelings toward her are softening. Already, I find myself wanting to kiss her again before I crawl between her thighs and feast on her luscious pussy, right before

I thrust into her sopping wet channel and fuck her so hard, she'll never want to be with any other man again. What the fuck? Since when did I begin to feel this possessive about her?

It's best that I get away from her and try to find perspective. And that's why I managed to withdraw my arm from under her neck, then pulled away from her. She stirred, and I had frozen. She settled down, and I swung my legs over the side of the bed. After pulling on some clothes, I felt steadier and much stronger as I made my way to the door. Guess that's what a night of uninterrupted sleep with no nightmares can do to you. And the sex helped too. My arms and legs felt limber, and my mind was clear as I headed down the corridor. I reached the exercise room and started in on my daily routine.

By the time I finished working out, Massimo made an appearance. He informed me that Michael and the rest of the Sovranos were waiting to meet me in the study. I wanted to tell him to fuck off, but hell, I do need their help. So, I agreed to meet them.

I took my time showering and getting changed, being careful not to disturb her. Just because I was going to be agreeable didn't mean I had to rush to follow their orders. With a last look at the sleeping Theresa, I walked down to meet them, by which time nearly half an hour had passed.

To Michael's credit, when I walked into the room, he didn't seem angry or upset. If anything, he seemed to be in a particularly good mood as I prowled over to the settee. He leaned back in his chair, and as soon as I was seated, he asked me what my intentions were with Theresa.

Now I hold his gaze as I fold one leg over my other knee. "That's why the lot of you have come here? To ask me about my personal life?"

It's Massimo who answers from his perch by the fireplace. "Firstly, you're our brother, so it means, yes, all of us are concerned about your personal life."

"And even more so when it seems to concern a person under our protection," Adrian adds as he leans back against the wall by the window.

The brothers are stationed at various points around the study. It might seem casual to an untrained observer, but there's no doubt in my mind that they have taken up positions such that they cover all of the exit points in the room. Add to that, the meathead standing guard outside the door, and if I were to try to leave now, they'd definitely stop me. Not that I'm going to attempt that particular move. And not only because I'm not yet back to full strength. I'm curious about their interest in Theresa. They seem to treat her like she's their younger sister or their ward.

"Vowed to protect?" I tilt my head. "Is that why Seb, here"—I jerk my chin in his direction—"decided to take her out without informing me?"

"Informing you, huh?" Seb smirks. "Who is she to you that you need to be informed about her every move?"

"I'm her—" I open my mouth, then shut it.

"You're her?" Michael's smile widens. "Go on; I'm listening."

"She is someone I protected once already with my life," I point out.

"An action which you claim you don't even remember taking."

"It's not a claim," I say through gritted teeth. "I still don't remember the events of that day."

"Fine," Michael raises his hands, "I'll grant you that. All the more reason I have to wonder why it is you have taken such an interest in Theresa."

My muscles stiffen. "Question is, why is it that all of you are so interested in Theresa?"

"Xander cared for her," Seb growls, "so she is under our protection."

"And I'd never let anything happen to her," I counter.

"We agreed to have her move in under the same roof as you, only because it's easier to guard both of you this way." Seb walks toward me. "It's why, when she called, I agreed to accompany her to Venom."

"Venom? You took her to a nightclub?"

"Relax, it's owned by us," Seb drawls.

"I don't give a fuck who owns it. Who gave you permission to take her to a nightclub?"

"We definitely don't need your permission for that." Michael smirks. "Unless, of course, you're telling us otherwise?"

"Otherwise?" I scowl. "What do you mean?"

"Oh, I don't know. The way you're going all possessive over her, makes me wonder if you don't have more of a vested interest in her?" Massimo retorts.

I lean back against the couch. "I'm sure I don't know what you mean. I have no interest in her."

"Hmm..." Luca's brows draw down. "The way you were eyeing her up seemed to indicate there was more than just a passing interest on your end."

I tilt my head. "I admit, when I regained consciousness and realized what I had done, it intrigued me. I'm not the kind of man who'd take a bullet for anyone else, let alone a woman I don't know at all. It made me wonder why I had reacted so. It's the only reason I asked for her to be moved here to the same place as me. Also, I hoped that seeing her would help me regain the missing bits of my memory, but other than that?" I glance between the brothers. "Nope, I have no interest in her."

"So, you won't mind if we decide to find a suitable match for her from within the Cosa Nostra?" Seb drawls.

Motherfucker. Every muscle in my body tenses. My shoulders knot. I glare at Seb, and his grin widens.

"Well?" he asks. "Since you're not interested in her, you won't mind if we secure her future, right?"

I glower at him. My stomach knots. My guts feel like they have been put through a wringer. I force my muscles to unwind, one at a time, unclench my fingers, then jerk my chin. "Nope, I don't mind at all."

"But I do," her voice rings out. I turn to the doorway as Theresa walks into the room. Her features are pale, her back erect. "What I very much mind is my future being discussed when I'm not in the room."

She pauses next to Michael.

"Do I not have a say in my own life?" She tips up her chin at him. "As Xander's brother, I expected that you'd, at least, give me the choice in who I want to spend the rest of my life with."

"Of course, it's your choice," Michael rises to his feet, "but you can't blame us for being worried about you. We loved Xander, and we know that he'd want you to be happy."

"And I know what will make me happy."

"You do?" Michael's brow furrows.

She nods. "I know who I want to marry, and it's someone Xander would have approved of."

Michael holds her gaze. The silence stretches. The hair on the nape of my neck rises. It can't be. Surely not. She wouldn't go there, would she?

I glare at her, but she keeps her gaze averted from mine.

"Who is it?" Seb finally inquires. "Who is this person you want to marry?"

My heart begins to race. The pulse pounds at my temples. No fucking way is she going to do this. Oh, no. I rise to my feet just as she turns and points a finger at me.

"Him," she says in a clear voice, "I want to marry him."

. . .

Theresa

"The fuck?" He glares at me. "What did you say?" He clenches and unclenches his fingers in what I realize is a nervous tic. He takes a step toward me, and Luca grabs his shoulder.

"Let me the fuck go." Axel tries to shake him off, but Luca holds onto him.

"What the fuck did you say?" Axel glowers at me.

"Watch it," Luca says in a hard voice.

"No, *you* watch it." Axel seizes Luca's collar.

Luca's features contort, he pulls back his fist, and my heart slams into my chest.

"Wait!" I close the distance to them. "Stop, Luca, please." I twist my fingers together. "Please don't hurt him."

The two glare at each other, then Luca lowers his fist.

The breath rushes out of me. The adrenaline drains out of me somewhat as I turn to Axel. "I … I owe you an explanation."

"You think?" Axel says through gritted teeth. "Tell them you didn't mean what you said."

I hesitate.

Axel's brows draw down.

"Do you know what you're doing?" he says in a low voice.

No, I don't. It's why I'm standing here, trying to break up a fight between two grown men who, individually, are twice my weight, at least. A chuckle bubbles up, and I clamp my lips together. I'm not going to get hysterical. I'm not.

"Theresa," his tone hardens, "you don't want to do this."

"Stop threatening her." Luca scowls at him. "Give her a chance to complete what she's saying."

Axel stares at me a second longer, then he shakes off Luca's hold. "I'm listening," he snaps.

"I…"

Axel holds my gaze, and the courage seems to drain out of me. A trembling grips me. My heart thuds so hard in my chest, I'm sure it's going to break out of my rib cage. "I..." My knees seem to give way from under me. I sway. Both Axel and Luca step forward, but Axel reaches me first.

He grips my forearm. "What the hell?" His scowl deepens. "Have you eaten anything today?"

"I..." I shake my head. "No, I haven't. I woke up and uh, came in search of you."

"And to think, I'm the one who was shot. You need a keeper, you know that?" He guides me to a chair and pushes me onto it.

"I'm fine," I protest. Sweat breaks out on my brow, and I lean back into the chair.

"You're not bloody fine." He lowers himself onto his haunches in front of me. "Deep breaths," he says in a brisk voice. "Are you feeling faint?"

"No," I murmur, "just a little weak."

"Someone, get her a glass of orange juice," he orders as he peers into my face.

I close my eyes because I can't bear to see the concern in his eyes, which is so at odds with the rest of his attitude, and also, because I'm actually feeling a little lightheaded. It's probably from the adrenaline that had rushed through me when I'd made that bold statement—the one I hadn't even been aware I was going to say until I heard the words emerge from my mouth. But once I heard it, it felt right. I'd known from the moment I set my eyes on this guy, I'm not going to let him get away. And while marriage might not mean the same thing to him as it does to me, it's one way of trying to form some kind of connection with him, right?

Footsteps sound, then I sense Axel lean in closer. "Here," he orders, "drink this."

I open my eyes to see him holding out a glass of orange juice in my line of sight.

I glance from the glass to him.

"Go on," he holds it to my lips, "take a sip."

I drink from it. Only when I have drained the glass does he lower it and place it on the table next to me.

"Better?"

I nod.

"Good. Now you can take back what you said earlier."

"Axel," Michael warns, "let her speak."

Axel firms his lips.

"I… I can't speak when you're glaring at me."

"I'm not glaring at you."

"Yes, you are." I squirm around in the seat.

"Why don't you say your piece looking into my eyes, eh?" I scowl.

"Don't intimidate her," Seb admonishes him.

"Yeah, give her some breathing space, will you?" Massimo adds.

Axel rises up to his feet. Jesus, I'd forgotten how tall he is. And despite the weight he's lost over the last few days, his muscles are still defined enough that the T-shirt he's wearing clings to his shoulders.

He folds his arms across his chest and bares his teeth.

I flinch. "Wh … what is that?"

"What?" he says, still with his lips drawn back.

"That ... that look on your face."

"I'm smiling." He pulls his lips wider.

"It's scaring me."

"Don't scare her." Luca takes a step forward.

"Yeah, step back, will ya?" Seb snaps.

"Fine." He takes a step back. Like literally, one step back. "Good?"

"Nope," Luca walks toward him. He reaches for Axel, who blocks his arm.

"Don't fucking touch me, you wanker."

"Why don't you back away then?" Luca bares his teeth.

Axel moves back, putting about five feet of distance between me and him.

"Is that better?" Luca asks me.

"Don't talk to her." Axel scowls at him.

"Are you fucking kidding me?" Luca turns on him. "First, you try to frighten her—"

"Good." Axel's grin turns predatory. "She should be scared of me."

"Hey," Seb prowls over to flank Axel on the other side, "don't threaten her."

"You can't tell me what to do," Axel retorts without taking his gaze off of me.

Seb places his hand on Axel's shoulder, and Axel responds by kicking his legs out from under him. Seb hits the floor on his back with a thud that echoes around the space. The next second, Luca is on Axel, and Massimo has closed the distance to the two. He throws his massive arm around Axel's chest, holding him in place as Luca pulls back his fist, only to stop an inch from Axel's face.

"Go on," Axel growls, "throw the first punch, motherfucker. Give me a reason to smash up your face."

Luca's features darken. He tightens his fist with such intensity that the skin stretches across his knuckles.

"Luca," Michael warns. Luca draws in a breath. He glares at Axel one last time, then lowers his fist and steps back.

Axel's grin widens. He turns to face me. "Well, then," he lowers his voice to a hush, "what was it that you asked earlier?"

I tip up my chin and look into his eyes with a boldness I don't feel. "Will you marry me, Axel?"

Every muscle in his body seems to tense. The skin around his eyes tightens. His nostrils flare, and a pulse, wildly throbbing, appears at his temple.

"And if I say no?"

My heart begins to race. My chest hurts. A bead of sweat slides down the valley between my breasts. What else did I expect? That he'd confess he feels a connection with me and agree to my stupid proposal?

"Are you … saying no?" I whisper.

We stare at each other. He opens his mouth, and this time, it's Michael who raises his hand. "Think carefully, brother," he says in a hard voice. "You may be one of us, but we still haven't forgiven your indiscretions toward us."

"Nor have we forgotten," Massimo rumbles.

If Axel hears them, he doesn't let on. He simply holds my gaze. His blue eyes seem to burn with an inner fire. It's as if he's reached into the depths of my soul and knows what I'm up to. Knows why I suggested this insane idea.

The silence seems to go on and on. My nerve-endings stretch so tightly, I'm sure I'm going to scream any moment. My mouth dries. My throat feels itchy. And still, he doesn't speak. Damn it, why doesn't he say something … anything?

"Axel," I burst out, "forget what I said. It was a moment of madness. It was a stupid suggestion. It was—"

"Yes."

"Eh?" I blink rapidly. "What did you say?"

"I said, I'll marry you."

My pulse rate ratchets up. The blood pounds at my temples. "Wh … what?"

"I'll marry you, Sunshine," his eyes gleam, "on one condition."

I try to speak, but no words emerge. I open and shut my mouth, then settle for staring at him.

"Don't you want to know what the condition is?" he murmurs.

I shake my head. Whatever it is, it can't be good. Of course, a man like Axel wouldn't just agree to something, not unless he gets something out of it. It wouldn't be enough for him to simply marry me. He'd have to milk the situation for his benefit.

"Lost your courage?" His grin widens. "Doesn't matter. I have enough for the both of us. I'll marry you, so long as," he turns to Michael, "I get an equal stake in the *Cosa Nostra* business."

Luca makes a noise at the back of his throat. The rest of the men stare at him like he has lost his mind.

Only Michael doesn't react, then he tilts his head. "Each of the brothers, me included, gets a portion of the profits from the *Cosa Nostra*. You, too, will receive yours."

"You'd share the profits with him?" Luca snaps. "This *stronzo* hasn't done anything to warrant it."

"He's one of us," Michael says calmly, "he's entitled to a share of the proceeds."

"He hasn't taken the risks we have." Luca leans forward on the balls of his feet. "He didn't help build the business. He hasn't earned his share."

"He will." Michael fixes Luca with a hard stare.

"There's one more thing," Axel drawls. "I want a seat on the board of the cryptocurrency venture."

"The board of Trinity only has three representatives, one each from the Cosa Nostra, the Bratva, and the Kane Company," Seb points out.

"Not my problem." Axel raises a shoulder. "That's my price for marrying her."

A hot sensation stabs at my chest. Am I so repugnant that he needs to be paid to marry me? What was I thinking, asking him to be my husband, in the first place? I knew he wasn't like Xander, but maybe somewhere, deep inside, I hoped that he shared, at least, some of the tenderness that had attracted me to Xander. Perhaps my sub-conscience has been clinging to the hope that Axel really is Xander returned to me. Maybe I hoped that he would not only agree to marry me, but that he'd also confess he felt something more than lust for me. Did I mistaken how he'd touched me last night? Did I mistaken our chemistry for something more?

I lock my fingers together. "What makes you think you have the power to negotiate when, really, it doesn't matter to them if you marry me or not?"

"You sure about that?" He shoots a glance at Michael. "The Don wants to see you happy, Theresa. You're under his protection, after all. And he, more than anyone, knows that both partners need to willingly enter matrimony for the other person in the marriage to be happy. So," he raises his shoulder, "you see, I very much hold the power in this negotiation."

"She's not a commodity to be bargained over, you fucktard," Luca growls.

Axel grins. "Developing a conscience, are we?" He moves to stand by me, so he's facing the rest of his brothers. "Let's not forget how Michael kidnapped his bride and forced her to marry him, or how Christian held his bride-to-be captive until she agreed to be his. Seems I'm only following in the footsteps of my older brothers by putting down a price for this transaction."

Michael opens his mouth to speak, but Axel raises his hand. "Before you ask, yes, more events from the past have filtered into my memory, though in this particular case, it was one of the household staff gossiping that cued me in to just how screwed up my blood family really is."

The tension in the room ratchets up.

"You're treading a dangerous line, little brother." Michael widens his stance. "My magnanimity with you will go only so far; don't push it. You won't like the consequences, just like the household staff are about to find out."

Axel and Michael engage in a staring match. I squeeze my eyes shut.

Transaction? He called me a transaction.

I'm not naive. I've grown up in the Cosa Nostra. So I'm aware that marriages are normally used to further business interests. Or personal interests. They are rarely ever built on love or any such human emotions… Still, to be labelled as an asset to be exchanged as part of an arrangement—one that I opened the gates to with genuine intention… It hurts. Hell, it's bullshit, to be honest.

I jump up to my feet. "I will not be used as a pawn," I snarl.

"Is that right?" He stares down the length of his nose at me. "And am I not a pawn for you too? Is that not why you proposed to me?"

"I proposed to you because…"

"Because?"

"Because I couldn't not." I lower my chin to my chest, as if that can smother the words I'm about to utter. "You remind me too much of him."

"So the only reason you want me to marry you is so that you can hold onto the memory of your dead boyfriend?"

"He wasn't my boyfriend," I protest.

"Your dead … love, then," he drawls. "If it looks like a duck, if it talks like a duck, then it's a duck, Sunshine."

"Stop with that nickname already," I hiss.

"Oh, I'm just getting started." He smirks, then glances up toward Michael. "What say you? Do we have a deal, Don?"

19

Axel

What the hell are you doing? Why are you turning this entire exchange into a transaction? You know why she asked you to marry her. Because she felt the same connection you did.

Because when I looked into her eyes, I saw myself reflected in them. Because when I kissed her, it felt like my entire body responded. When I took her into my arms, it was as if I had come home. And when I buried myself in her, it was the single most erotic experience of my life. It was as if something had been missing in me, something I didn't even know about. Something that propelled me to take her virginity—a first for me.

Not lying when I say that I have kept away from inexperienced women. I've preferred those who know the score. Know that all I can give them is a one-night stand. That's all they were looking for from me anyway. A good hard fuck and they'd be on their way.

With her, I knew things were going to get complicated. Not only because I would be her first, but also because one taste of her, one whiff of her scent, one glance at those mesmerizing eyes of hers, and I was a goner. I knew there was no walking away from her. For now, at any rate. How could I, when everything in me wanted to claim her, to make her mine? And she offered me the way to do so. When she said she wanted to marry me, I panicked. Hell, I'm in the prime of my life. No way do I want to be tied down by just one pussy. But the thought of anyone else having her when I haven't yet had my fill of her? That is unacceptable.

All I need to do is to fuck her out of my system, and then I can be on my way. Not that I can allow her or the Sovranos to figure that out. Between them, they must have slept through most of the female population in this city; but for some reason, they felt protective toward Theresa. Which means, I have to play their game so they don't see me as a threat. Which, face it, is going to become more and more difficult the longer I stay on. There's only so long I'll be able to hide my real nature from them. Ergo, the only way to have her is to pretend to marry her. Once I have her in my bed, I can scratch this itch that seems to grip me every time I see her.

And, to be clear, I don't intend to stay married to her. Once I've had enough of her, I'll walk away.

Of course, there's also the fact that I shot at Christian … and missed. How the hell could that have happened? I remember enough about myself to know that I never miss. And yet, I didn't hit him. So, I have to wonder, was my intention only to throw a scare into him? Is that why I blackmailed his wife into spying on the Sovranos?

Clearly, I need information on them. And what better way to get that than by staying close to them and marrying the woman they are sworn to protect? This way, I'll have the advantage. I'll be able to use Theresa to manipulate the Sovranos, and they won't dare hurt me.

Not that I think I'm in any danger from them. They regard me as their brother, so chances are, they won't kill me. Doesn't mean they aren't going to pump me for information. They're just holding on until I'm back to full strength, which will be very soon. Try as I might, I can't hide the fact that I'm recovering quickly. So, I need another way of ensuring my safety, and Theresa is my insurance.

All in all, it is to my advantage to marry her.

"Well?" I narrow my gaze on Michael. "What do you say?"

Michael widens his stance. He surveys my features before he turns to Theresa. "Is this what you want?" he asks in a gentle voice.

"Yes." Theresa nods.

"Are you sure?" His jaw firms. "Axel is not Xander."

"I … I know." She swallows. "I still want to marry him."

He drums his fingers on his chest. "All right, then." He turns his gaze on me. "You'll be invited to the next meeting of the Cosa Nostra."

Seb inhales sharply. "Motherfucker!" He glares at Michael. "Are you really going to do this, *fratellone*?"

Michael ignores him. "I'll also set up a meeting with the leaders of the Bratva and the Kane Company and let them know that you will be the spokesman for the Cosa Nostra."

Seb looks like he is about to protest further, then firms his lips.

"Are you sure about this?" Massimo asks slowly.

"I have my reasons," Michael murmurs.

"Fuck that," Luca snaps. "This asshole flounces in, and after trying to kill Christian, he not only gets a seat at the table with the families, but also a cut in the most lucrative venture we have ever set up?"

"It's what Xander would have wanted." Michael shoots him a sideways glance. "Feel free to leave if you're not on board."

"You know what? I think I will." Luca pivots on his heel and takes a few steps forward, then pauses. "There's something I need to do first."

He careens around and slaps his palms into my chest. Pain ricochets up my neck.

"Fuck me." I stagger back. Why the hell am I still so weak? This fucking gunshot wound. I fucking hate being this defenseless. I straighten as Luca raises his fist. I throw up my arm and manage to block his blow. Luca raises his other fist when Theresa jumps up.

"Stop it," she cries out.

Massimo wraps his arm around Luca's chest and hauls him back. "The fuck you doing, *stronzo*?"

"Teaching this *pezzo di merda* that he doesn't fool me. He may have pulled the wool over all your eyes, but mark my words, this *testa di cazzo* is going to turn on us. And I, for one, am not going to stand by and watch him take a piece of our hard-earned future when he has sacrificed nothing for it." Luca glowers at me.

"He's our brother," Michael says in a hard voice. "He's entitled to his part of our legacy, no matter that he's as much of a fucktard as you."

"Have you forgotten that he almost killed Christian and blackmailed Aurora?" Luca tries to shake off Massimo's hold, but he doesn't let go. "Fuck," Luca growls, "release me, *stronzo*."

"Only when you get your temper in hand," Massimo retorts.

"I can't believe you're siding with this motherfucker," Luca spits out. "Thought you, at least, would see through this *fetente*."

Massimo hesitates and loosens his grip.

"You know I'm right." Luca makes eye contact with every brother. "He's taking us all on a ride, and Michael is not able to see it. But surely, you do, Massimo, don't you? You can see why it's wrong to let him in on our family business. And in such a short period of time."

Massimo scowls. He glances at Michael, then at me. "No, I don't think it's wrong."

"Me neither," Seb says slowly.

"Same here," Adrian adds.

Luca stiffens. "You're going to regret this, all of you." He scans the faces of his brothers again. "He's going to turn on all of you, and when he does, don't say I didn't warn you."

If they only knew how right he is.

Michael blows out a breath. "I know you've always wanted to be Don. And I know it was a disappointment to you when I made Seb the Capo, but this is precisely why I haven't given you more responsibility. You're too hot-headed, Luca. You say what's on your mind without thinking it through."

"Being passionate is the only thing that differentiates us from common criminals. We are the Cosa Nostra. We have a reputation of being the most cut-throat, the most dedicated to our cause."

"And it's precisely that which has stopped us from becoming more powerful," Michael murmurs.

"Thinking with your gut is a strength—"

"If you're able to match it with cold logic, something which you've been unable to master."

"And you have?" Luca shoots back.

Michael tilts his head. "Not yet. But I know when I need to give something up to achieve a higher goal."

"Yet, when it comes to Axel, you're letting your emotions get the better of you? You're going by what you think Xander would have wanted, instead of what makes sense."

"And you're letting your ego get in the way of giving up short-term gain for long-term success."

The two glare at each other, then Michael draws in a breath. "You're simply going to have to trust me in this situation," he says in a hard voice.

"And you're going to regret trusting him." Luca flexes his shoulders, and this time, Massimo releases him. Luca glares at me one more time, then turns on his heels and stalks out the door.

Silence descends on the gathering. Michael rolls his shoulders. "You'd better be who you say you are." He turns on me. "If it turns out that you're lying to me—"

"I'm not." I crack my neck. "Besides, now that I'm marrying Theresa," I allow my lips to twist. "I'm marrying into the family. Surely, that's enough proof that I intend to stay and see things through?"

Michael's gaze intensifies. His forehead furrows.

"You don't seem convinced, brother," I drawl. "Having second thoughts?"

"I never have second thoughts." Michael jerks his chin. "No doubt, you are keen to exercise your authority as part of the Cosa Nostra."

"Indeed." I draw myself up to my full height. A headache begins to thrum at my temple, but I ignore it.

"And I'm sure you'll want to marry Theresa at the earliest opportunity."

"Y-e-s," I say slowly. What the hell is Michael up to now?

"And what about you, Theresa?" He turns to her. "I assume you don't want to wait too long to be married to him either?"

Theresa glances between us, then nods.

"It's settled then." Michael's eyes gleam. "Theresa and Axel will be married in a month's time."

"A month?" I burst out. "Isn't that a bit soon?"

"Why wait, when both the bride and bridegroom are willing?" Michael smirks.

"Now, hold on." I rub at my temple. "Aren't there preparations to be made for the wedding and such?"

"Oh, after two speed weddings in the family, trust me, we have the drill down to a science," Massimo murmurs.

My knees seem to buckle from under me, and I'm not sure if it's because

I've pushed my body to its limit, or because the thought of being tied down to one woman, albeit in a wedding that I don't consider to be real, is catching up with me. I move back until my back hits the wall.

"Let's not be hasty now." I hold up my hands. "Let's think this through, shall we?"

Theresa turns on me. "Apparently, it takes the thought of getting married for you to lose your confidence?"

"Lose my confidence?" I scowl down at her. "What gives you that idea?"

"Oh, I don't know, maybe it's because your face is pale, and there's a sheen of sweat on your forehead."

I touch my forehead, and motherfucker, she's right. I wipe off the moisture, then raise a shoulder, "I haven't lost my confidence."

"Oh, good, so you'll be fine if we get married in a week?"

I stiffen. "I thought Michael said a month." I scowl in his direction. "Didn't you say a month?"

"I said a month."

"And I say we get married before you lose your nerve." She holds my gaze.

"Lose my nerve?" I glower at her. "I never lose my nerve."

"Good!" She flips her hair over her shoulder. "So we'll get married in seven days."

Half an hour later, Theresa has left. My brothers sprawl about the living room. I lean back in the sofa and glance toward the bar where Michael is pouring himself a drink. "Can I get a whiskey before you all start this interrogation?"

"Interrogation?" Seb drums his fingers on his chest. "Whatever gave you the idea that we're going to interrogate you?"

"Considering I revealed to you that I've begun to recall what happened before I was shot, it's not that far-fetched a conclusion," I drawl.

"Has he always spoken like he's reading from a dictionary, or is this the first time I noticed it?" Luca glowers at me.

"First time you noticed it," Adrian retorts.

"Didn't Michael ask you to fuck off?" I ask mildly and am rewarded when Luca's jaw hardens.

"Fuck you too, asshole!" he snaps.

"Beginning to sound like a broken record, *Lucasshole,*" I retort.

Adrian chuckles, then turns it into a snort. Luca glares at him, and Adrian raises his hands. "You have to admit, that was inspired."

"Will the two of you cut it out?" Massimo scowls between us. "You're beginning to give me a headache with your bitching."

"He started it." Luca and I point at each other.

The fuck? Christian may be my surviving triplet, but Luca sounds a lot more like me. Probably why he can see through me. Unfortunately, we both have a lot in common when it comes to losing our cool. Only difference is that I've learned to rein in my anger, while Luca has very little filter. In a way, it means he says what he thinks so he wears his heart on his sleeve. Which makes him less of a threat, as compared to Seb, who watches me with a cool gaze. He's a cool customer, that one. Holds his cards close to his chest. It's clear, now, why Michael chose him to succeed him. He's a man who doesn't let his expression give away much.

"So, what happened on the day you gate-crashed Christian's wedding? Why did you point a gun at Aurora, and why is it that you stepped in front of Theresa when she was shot at?"

I rub my jaw. "Good questions—ones I've been asking myself, to be honest."

"So, you don't remember what happened on that day?" Seb frowns.

"Not yet; the memories filter back when I least expect it."

"What is it that you remember, so far?"

"As I mentioned earlier, I know I was sent on an assignment. I know the man who called me was my partner. Or my boss; I'm not sure. But he and I worked out the details of the assignment. Initially, part of it was using Aurora to get more information on you guys, which is why I approached her in the first place."

"And Christian. Why did you shoot at him during the Christmas getaway?"

"Clearly, I don't see the lot of you as friends." I rub the back of my neck. "The details are fuzzy in my head, but suffice to say, when I think of the Sovranos, I'm not filled with love and sunshine."

"Surely, after that confession, you're going to shove this guy where the sun don't shine?" Luca growls.

Michael, who's been pouring his drink at the bar, turns to face the room. "How do you feel about us now?"

I stiffen. The scars on my forearm itch.

"Still want to take us out? Still want to put a bullet in each of us when you get a chance?" He places his glass on the counter, then prowls toward me. He stops in front of me, then pulls out his gun and holds it out to me with the handle facing me.

The room goes silent. Tension ripples off the other men.

Michael holds my gaze as I stay silent. A beat, then another. Then I reach out and take the gun. There's a slither of movement as every one of my brothers pulls out his gun and aims it at me. Only Michael doesn't move a muscle. I hold his gaze for a second longer, then snap open the cylinder. I pour the bullets into the palm of my hand and hold the gun out to him.

Michael takes the gun and slides it into the back of his waistband. He holds out his palm, and I drop the bullets into it. He pockets the bullets, then holds up his hand. "Down boys," he says mildly.

The men put away their guns. Adrian relaxes against the wall, Massimo sprawls back in the arm chair, and Seb raises his glass and drinks from it. Only Luca stays where he is, every muscle in his body tightly wound.

"I still don't trust him." He rotates his neck, and his joints pop.

"The feeling is mutual," I drawl. A wave of tiredness washes over me. Fuck, guess that adrenaline rush didn't do me any favors. Every time I think I'm almost recovered from being shot, my body signals otherwise. Thank fuck, I'm sitting. If I were standing, I'd have to find the nearest seat and collapse into it. As it is, I lean back in the sofa. I spread my legs and drum my fingers on my chest. "So, did I pass your little test, Don?"

"I'm not sure yet," he replies.

I blink, then chuckle. "At least, you're a straight shooter. I like that."

"And you've bought yourself some time by marrying Theresa." He raises his glass in my direction. "Sorry, *fratello*, I'd offer you a drink, but it's not wise to mix alcohol with whatever you're on."

I raise my gaze toward the ceiling. "Fuck my life."

Seb smirks. "No, that happens when you get married in seven days."

20

Theresa

"Seven days?" I throw up my hands. "What was I thinking? Why did I have to suggest such a short time frame? And why did he agree to it?"

"He wasn't going to say no; not when you challenged him in front of his brothers," Cass says in a soothing voice.

"I only said seven days because I fully intended him to panic and say no."

"But he didn't?" Elsa stares at me with wide eyes.

Yeah, after I pulled that stunt where I suggested that Axel marry me in a week, and he agreed, I walked out of there in a daze. I didn't even wait to see if Axel was okay. I had seen how pale he was, noticed the lines etched around his mouth. I knew he was in pain and wanted to help him, but honestly, after the stunt he pulled, when he basically used me as a bargaining chip with the Sovranos, I figured he deserved it. So, I walked out of there and headed to my room, where I promptly lost my shit. I called Cass and insisted that she come down. Then I dialed Karma's number, but she didn't pick up, so I called Elsa and insisted that she come over to see me after she closed the shop for the day.

Now, I glance at her. "Nope," I shake my head, "he agreed." I raise my shoulders. "Who'd have thought that?"

"So, you thought he'd balk at the fact that it was such a short timeline? That's why you suggested it?" Cass leans back against the settee.

"I was positive that he'd turn me down."

"So, you didn't really think he would agree, huh?"

"I wasn't sure," I confess. "I mean, he decided to use me as a negotiating tool in order to get a piece of the Sovranos' profits, but I thought that if I crunched the timeline, it would scare him off."

"And did it?" Elsa asks.

"Clearly, not." I rake my fingers through my hair, then begin to pace. "But why would he agree? He could have said no."

"Why would he say no, when he clearly wants a part of the power that the Sovranos wield?"

"He didn't have to agree to marry me." I raise a shoulder. "He's one of the Sovrano brothers. Eventually, he'd have gotten what he asked from them."

"Maybe not quickly enough, though," Cass murmurs. "You probably crunched his timeline by half with your proposal."

"Argh!" I squeeze my eyes shut. "What possessed me to come up with that? I mean, I could have simply bedded the guy. Why did I have to propose to him?"

"Because you want to make sure that he never leaves you?"

"Clearly, I'm still suffering from PTSD from Xander leaving me." I lower my chin to my chest. "I think that's why, when I found my control over the situation slipping, I blurted out the one thing I should've never voiced aloud."

"Perhaps it's good that you spoke your mind." Cass rises to her feet. "This way, everyone knows where you stand."

"But I have no idea where he stands."

"He's going to marry you, isn't he?" Cass walks over to me. "He won't go against the Sovranos. He's given them his word on the wedding. And besides, as you said, he wants to have a say in the business. He won't risk pissing them off."

"But he doesn't love me," I slap my hand over my mouth. Did I say that out loud? Why the hell had I said that aloud?

Cass and Elsa stare at me.

"Forget I said that," I squeeze my eyes shut. "Damn it, it's so mortifying."

"Are you in love with him?" Cass finally asks.

"Of course, not," I open one eye, "I barely know him, how can I be in love with him?"

"She's in love with him," Elsa declares.

"You aren't confusing him with Xander, are you?" Cass asks softly.

"No. Yes." I shuffle my feet. "I don't know, okay? I mean, rationally, I know he is not Xander. But then he'll say or do something that'll remind me of Xander. I mean, his accent is different, of course, and so is his build, but there is so much more about him that is familiar. Then I have to remind myself that Xander is dead, and that simply breaks my heart." My features crumple.

"Oh, sweetie." Cass closes the distance between us and hugs me. Footsteps sound, then Elsa hugs me from the other side. I sniffle as the tears run down my cheeks.

"Damn it, I'm tired of being sad. I don't want to spend all of my time mourning Xander. I need to let him go. Besides, he'd hate to see me cry over him. He'd want me to move on with my life. He'd want me to be happy."

"And that's what you're doing." Cass leans back so she can see my face. "You're fighting your way forward. Although, I admit, your methods are unconventional, but at the same time, I don't blame you. If I were in your shoes, I'd probably do the same thing."

"And you, Elsa?" I turn to her, "Now that you know exactly what kind of situation I'm in, what do you think?"

"I…" Elsa shakes her head. "Honestly, I'm still getting my head around it." She walks over and sinks into the seat. "I'm not really surprised that you're a part of the *Cosa Nostra*."

"You're not?"

She shakes her head. "I mean, you managed to buy the space for the flower shop."

"There are others who could have afforded it too."

"Outright," she reminds me. "You wouldn't have been able to do that, unless you had help."

"I'm sorry; I sort of lied to you about that."

"You know how bad of a liar you are; I wasn't fooled for an instant." She tosses her head. "And then, more recently, you had all of those people dropping you off and picking you up, and they had Mafia stamped all over their tailormade suits."

"Who are we talking about?" A new voice says from the doorway.

I turn. "Karma!" I cry out. "You came!"

"Of course, I came."

"But I didn't leave you a message when I called."

"I saw your missed call, then heard what happened from Michael."

"Ah…" I hunch my shoulders. "So you heard about my—"

"Upcoming nuptials, yes." She grins, and as she walks toward me, I can tell that she's mentally taking measurements. "Figured you'd need my help with the dress."

"Oh my God!" I peer into her face. "Can you believe this? I'm going to get married. I am. Going to. Get married." I shake my head. "What the hell was I thinking when I proposed to him?"

"Hold on a second…" Karma stares at me. "You proposed to him? YOU proposed to a Sovrano?"

"Yes?" I say tentatively.

Her gaze widens. "And he agreed?"

"Technically, he didn't have a choice, but... Yes?" I venture.

She bursts into a laugh, "You've achieved the impossible, you know that?"

"No, not exactly." I frown.

"The Sovranos have egos bigger than ... than—"

"Their dicks?" Cass offers.

"Which are sizable." Karma nods. "Also, how do you know about their dicks?" She furrows her forehead.

"Lucky guess?" Cass says in a droll voice. "I haven't worked with them all these years without having some idea of their voracious appetites."

"Hmm…" I scowl at her. "You mean to say, you haven't seen Adrian's—"

"Nope." She makes a popping sound at the end of the word.

"I'm sure that's going to be remedied soon enough." I waggle my eyebrows at her.

"Not happening," she says in a firm tone. "And don't try to change the topic." She turns to Karma. "You were saying?"

"That you've set a record of sorts, by proposing. The Sovrano men are way too dominant to not want to take the lead in their wedding proposals, but you did it. You can be proud of that. Only…" She chews on her lower lip. "You need to be careful."

"Careful?" I tilt my head. "How do you mean?"

"As you said, he didn't have much of a choice but to agree to marry you. I assume the rest of the Sovrano brothers wouldn't have let him walk away if he had said no?"

I shrug my shoulders, then nod. "I still don't understand what you're getting at?"

"You hurt his ego, babe." Karma touches my shoulder. "I one-hundred percent support what you did. Hell, it's about time someone came along and took the brothers down a notch, but it's not without consequences."

"Hold on…" Elsa jumps up to her feet. "Are you saying that he might hurt her?"

Karma turns to her. "You must be Elsa. I've heard so much about you from Theresa."

"Oh, shoot, you guys haven't met before, have you? Elsa, meet Karma, Michael's wife and, Karma, this is Elsa, my life-saver who is also my friend."

"I'm her employee, actually," Elsa laughs, "and it was Theresa who literally *did* save my life when she gave me this job. And hold on … isn't Michael the Don of the *Cosa Nostra*?"

"Oh, so you've been reading up on the Sovranos?" I chuckle.

She shoots me a sideways glance. "I may be new to this city, but you can't go a day without hearing all about the Sovranos and how the Don killed his father to take over his current position... Oops…" She firms her lips. "No offense meant." She turns to Karma.

Karma raises a shoulder. "None taken."

"So it doesn't bother you, uh, being married to a man who has killed?"

"Elsa." I gape at her.

"It's okay." Karma's lips kick up. "I *am* married to the Don of the Cosa Nostra, after all, and it does bother me. Except, I know that Michael is often in situations where if he doesn't make the first move, he won't live to see the next day, and I love my husband too much for that to happen."

"So you turn a blind eye to what he does for a living?" Elsa asks.

"I embrace what he does." Karma holds up her hands. "Being part of the *Cosa Nostra* is a part of Michael, as much as being a designer is in my DNA. I couldn't ask him to leave it any more than I could give up working with fabrics. And it's because I know Michael so well that I'm confident Axel won't hurt you physically." Karma glances at me with a considering look on her face. "If he did, he'd have the rest of the Sovranos to answer to. No, he won't do something that obvious."

Elsa scowls at her. "Then? Do you think he'll hurt her mentally or emotionally?"

"It's possible," Karma says slowly. "I reckon, he'll get back at you in some form, though. How and what? That, I don't know, but you'd best watch out for it."

"But she's going to be marrying him." Elsa folds her arms across her chest. "Doesn't that put her in a vulnerable situation?"

"Possibly." Karma holds my gaze. "Either way, you need to be on alert with him."

"You're beginning to worry me, Karma." I run my fingers through my hair. "I understand what you mean when you say I hurt his ego. It's only after I blurted out the proposal that I realized what I had done, and it was too late by then. But surely, once we're married, he'll come around?" I take in her features —the way her brow is pinched, the worried look on her face.

"You really think he's going to get back at me for this, don't you?"

"Yes"—she lowers her hand to her side—"but if you watch out for it, there's no reason you can't turn the tables on him."

"Okay, stop…" I rub my temple. "You're beginning to give me a headache."

"I know it's a lot to take in, but if you're forewarned, you can use it to your advantage."

"How do I do that?"

"Defeat him at his own game," she replies.

"What game is that?"

"Whatever it is that he initiates with you."

"That's not very helpful." I try to laugh, but the sound comes out strained.

"I don't know him very well," Karma says in a soft voice. "Not as well as you do."

"Which isn't saying much." I twist my fingers. "How do I even begin to figure out what he's up to?"

"Oh, if you pay close attention, I'm sure you will see the signs, and once you know where his mind is at, I'm sure you'll find a way to keep ahead of him."

"You have more confidence in me than I do." I laugh uncertainly.

"You can do this," Elsa says with vehemence. "If anyone can figure out a way to survive, it's you."

I turn to Cass. "What do you think, Cass? You've been silent all along."

"I'm worried." Cass narrows her gaze on me. "I won't bullshit you by saying otherwise, but I also know you're smart enough to beat him at his own game."

I scowl. "So you do think that he's going to try to get back at me, as well?"

"I would be surprised if he didn't," she admits. "But we have your back"—she turns to the other women—"don't we?"

"You bet," Elsa replies.

"We're here in your corner," Karma adds. "If he does anything, and I mean anything, to cause you grief, you pick up the phone and call me, and I'll make sure Michael reins him in, okay?"

"Okay…" I blow out a breath.

"Good." Karma tilts her head. "Now about that dress... What color were you thinking?"

21

Axel

I'm getting married. What the bloody fuck? I'm getting married. How the hell did that happen? Oh, I know, it has something to do with a curvy, green-eyed sprite who dared to ask me to marry her in front of those … those men. Men who are my brothers, but who abandoned me and my mother as surely as their father did. So what, if none of them knew of my existence? It's their father who sent my mother away in exchange for assets that would further his business.

My mother was the only daughter of the head of the *Camorra*, arch rivals to the *Cosa Nostra*. She had fallen in love with my father, despite the fact that he was married. She moved to be with him, despite the fact that her family would never accept her back. By the time she was pregnant with me and my brothers, she realized just how abusive he could get with her.

After my brothers and I were born, she wanted to leave my father. In response, he negotiated with my mother's father for her return. He insisted that she leave the children behind, but she refused. Finally, he agreed to let her take one of the triplets—me—along with her.

She left, and when her family had disowned her, she decided to strike out on her own. No small decision for a Mafia princess who had been brought up in the lap of luxury. She moved to London, and with no skill to support herself, she turned to the world's oldest profession. A cliché maybe, but my mother had been determined to survive without the help of her family. She also insisted that I go to a good school. She worked herself to the bone to ensure that I had the best education available. Pun intended.

She made no secret about how much she despised the *Cosa Nostra* and the *Camorra*, and anything to do with the Mafia, really. It was the one thing she made me promise—never to have anything to do with them. What she neglected to mention was that she was one of them, as am I. She hadn't told me anything about my background, or my father, or about my triplet brothers. Not until she was on her deathbed. Even then, she waited until the very last minute, when she sensed her imminent death, before she finally told me about the circumstances surrounding my birth. Then, she breathed her last.

I knew it was inevitable that she would die early, the way she had been working so hard, and let's face it, women in her profession aren't known for their longevity. She had poured all of her hopes, dreams, and ambitions into me, and a part of me knew that she wouldn't survive for long. Still, no matter how much you try to anticipate it, no one is prepared for death.

My mother had been struck down by a fast-spreading cancer. She refused treatment, something I had found out only later, for she ensured not to tell me about it. Of course, as a teenager I was wrapped up in my own life. Still you'd think I would have spotted that my mother was suffering from cancer. But she managed to hide it well. It wasn't until she was near the end that I realized just how sick she was. At that point, it was hard to ignore how skeletal she'd become, and I hated myself for missing it. I held her hand and looked into her eyes as she passed.

When she was finally still, anger gripped me. I glanced into her lifeless features, and a rage of the kind I'd never experienced before swept through me. She had given me everything materially possible; everything except love. She ensured I had a good education, yet not once had she simply spent time with me, just been with me the way a mother would be with her child. She burdened me with her expectations, her aspirations and wishes.

What about me; what about what I wanted? Yes, it's selfish, I know that. She had sacrificed everything for me, and yet, as I sat there, still holding her hand that was growing increasingly cold, a desolation had swept through me. She had left me without once telling me that she loved me.

I was a reminder of her past, perhaps. I was someone through whom she thought she could vindicate herself, and I hated her for that. And I hated myself for thinking that way. I was so angry with her for screwing me up in the head. I was upset with her for not taking better care of herself. I was frustrated that I wasn't old enough to stop her, that I was unable to keep her from working herself to death, and…

I hated myself for not noticing sooner. She insisted that she was fine, and I believed her. I lived the life of a carefree youth, someone who had everything going for him, who was going to achieve all of his dreams… The kinds of dreams that she had wanted for me.

I swore then I would avenge her. I would track down those who were responsible for destroying her. I would find the man who had lied to her and caused her to get pregnant, which led to the events that had ruined her. I would find my father and ensure that he suffered as much as she had. As much as I had.

It was what led me here. All of the images from my past pour through my mind, and for a second, I have complete clarity.

I remember now, how I tracked down my father. And when he was killed before I had the opportunity to avenge my mother, I was forced to refocus my attention on my brothers.

I had already approached Christian's now-wife Aurora in London and coerced her into helping me. When her father had taken ill and she returned home to become the Sovranos' doctor, that only made it easier.

Then, Christian put himself in my crosshairs when he fixated on Aurora. I could learn more about him than anyone else because he spent the most time with her. When the two of them became separated from the rest of the family, and thus, were unprotected, I had my opportunity to strike.

And I had help. I straighten. On my side, I had an ally who was more powerful, stronger than the Cosa Nostra, and with as fierce a motive as mine to take them down.

It's why I must go through with this sham of a marriage—something I didn't anticipate, but which I can use to my advantage. It's why I will use my soon-to-be wife to get back at the *Cosa Nostra*.

I throw back my head and laugh. It's perfect, actually. I couldn't have planned this set-up better.

I'm going to leverage this marriage to my benefit and take full advantage of the perks that come with it too. I roll off the bed where I flung myself down after returning from the meeting with my brothers. It's only a short flight of steps from the study downstairs to my bedroom, but the catch-up with them and the events of the day took it out of me. I'm healing fast, but I'm nowhere near my former health, and while I'm pushing myself to get in shape, I also know the dangers of overdoing it. So, I forced myself to return to my room and I took a nap. A bloody nap in the middle of the day… Like I'm a helpless infant, but at least, I feel refreshed. And I'm going to need my strength for what I have in mind.

22

Theresa

I stand under the shower and let the hot water flow over my shoulders, my back, and down my legs. I raise my head to the spray and revel in the steam and warmth that envelops me. The talk with the women both reassured and unsettled me.

At least, Karma is taking care of my dress. And Cass has assured me that I need not worry about the wedding arrangements. She said she and Nonna will handle that. Of course, I had a clear vision about the flower arrangements, and Elsa helped to bring that to life. She also promised to make arrangements with a friend of hers who runs a macaroonerie—yes, that's, apparently, a thing, a shop specializing in macaroons. Which means, all I have to do is turn up in a few days.

Cass says the venue will be the family church in Palermo, which I already anticipated. The Sovranos are sticklers for tradition, except apparently, when it comes to planning weddings, when they are happy to get married with extremely short timelines. Where other brides need months, and sometimes years, to plan their weddings, the Sovrano brides have to make do with days to plan everything. I remind myself that this is my fault.

At least, I have a week. And I could have had a month if I hadn't opened my big mouth. Either way, that's generous compared to Karma and Aurora, who were both married within 48 hours. The Sovranos have enough clout that getting a marriage license on such short notice is no big deal. So the marriage preparations are all in hand.

It's really what Karma hinted at later that makes me uncomfortable. Will Axel really be upset that I asked him to marry me in front of his brothers? Is that an affront to his ego, as Karma warned? Will he try to get back at me for it? If so, what will he do? And since I'm living under the same roof as him, is that even advisable?

He won't kill me—nah, as Karma pointed out, bodily harm is not in the mix, but it's the other stuff he can do to me that worries me— how he can make me melt with a glance, how he can touch me and I'll feel it all the way to my toes, how he glares at me and a shiver runs down my spine; how he'll lower his voice to a hush and something inside me insists I obey him. Damn it. Basically, I'm putty in his hands. I don't stand a chance against him. So how the hell am I going to survive being married to him? Again, what the hell was I thinking when I flung the proposal at him, and in front of everyone else?

I groan and lean my forehead against the wall of the shower. Clearly, I have a death wish. It's why I challenged his ego. Of course, he's going to be miffed. But is Karma right? Is he going to take revenge for what I did? I know I left him with little choice but to agree to my proposal. It's why I raised it in front of everyone.

No, I didn't planned it—not consciously—but my subconscious is way ahead of me at the moment. He's recovering so much more quickly than anyone expected. And no way could I let him go after he recovers. I needed to find a way to tie him to me, to buy some time while I figure out how to win him over. No, I did the right thing. Too bad, if his ego is hurt. He'll just have to deal with it. And if he decides to take it out on me… Well, I'll just have to deal with it. I'll need to plow through the next few days, until I get to the wedding. Once we're married, I'll have to find a way to get into his good books, if that's even possible. I straighten, then wash the shampoo from my hair. I switch off the shower and turn, then scream.

"What the h-hell; what are you doing here?"

He simply watches me from under his thick eyelashes. Those blue eyes of his seem to glow with an inner fire. He's wearing a short-sleeved, white T-shirt which clings to his shoulders. I can't help but take in the patchwork of scars and tattoos on his right forearm. I lower my gaze to where the material of the jeans molds to those powerful thighs. Jesus, whatever his profession was, it definitely involved a lot of physical activity. What does he do anyway? Is he a part of some other rival gang? Is he a mercenary? An assassin, maybe? Not sure why, but something in the way he's always on alert, the way he came awake from the coma, only to jump out of bed and take on the man who had attacked me in his room… I'm still not over it. That kind of strength means he's had special training, but where? With whom?

"What's going on in that mind of yours?" he rumbles.

"N-nothing." I straighten my spine. I'm not going to hide. This is my bathroom, damn it. He's the one who's intruding, not me. Besides, I made the first move, surprising him with the proposal, and now I need to face whatever the repercussions from it are.

I step out of the shower stall completely naked. He rakes his gaze down my chest, pausing on my breasts for a few seconds before he continues his visual journey over my stomach and down to my pussy.

My thighs clench, and I resist the urge to cross my legs. Instead, I prop my hand on my waist and tip up my chin. "See something you like?" I attempt for a casual tone, but my voice comes out in the form of a squeak.

He doesn't reply. Rather, he takes his time with a leisurely perusal as he drags his gaze back to my chest. My nipples bead, and my breasts hurt. Damn it, if only he'd close the distance between us and crush me to the hard planes of his chest.

By the time he raises his gaze to my face, I'm flushed.

"Well?" I demand. "I asked you a question."

"You're not my type, but I'll shag you on our wedding night."

My jaw drops. "What the hell?" I snap. "Do you have to be so uncouth?"

"Would you expect anything else from me?"

"I'm not sure what to expect from you, to be honest." I raise a hand, then let it drop.

"I gotta admit, I didn't expect you to propose to me either," he murmurs.

"And yet, you agreed?" I fold my arms around my waist and his gaze, once more, lowers to my chest. I resist the urge to look down, knowing my stance must lift my boobs and make them pop out a bit further.

"You knew I didn't have a choice." He takes a step forward. I flinch. *Don't sidle back; don't allow him to find out how nervous you are around him right now.* I dig my bare feet into the floor and hold my position.

He arches an eyebrow, then closes the distance until he's right in front of me. The heat from his body pours over me; the scent of him surrounds me. His blue eyes bore into me, and my breath catches.

"I'm not scared of you," I declare.

His lips twitch. "You should be." He drags his finger down the curve of my breast, and a moan wells up my throat. I bite down on my lower lip as he draws a circle around my nipple. I feel the touch all the way to my core. My toes curl, and a shiver runs down my spine.

"What are you doing?" I whisper.

"Checking out my merchandise."

Anger suffuses my veins. I lift my hand, but he's too fast. He grabs my wrist; the next second, he's turned me around with my arm behind my back, so I'm facing the mirror. He hauls me to him, throws his other arm around my waist, and holds me immobile.

"Let go of me!" I gasp.

"Why should I?" He slides his palm between my legs and cups my pussy. "After all, you're going to become my wife."

"I'm not yet your wife," I remind him.

"Semantics," he drawls. "You opened the floodgates; now you have to deal with the aftermath."

"You could have refused, you know," I say in a tight voice. "It was a stupid suggestion on my part, said in a moment of craziness. You didn't have to play along."

"Oh, now she admits that it was a mistake."

"I never said that it was a mistake," I retort.

"And I never back down from a challenge." He slides his finger inside my channel, and I draw in a breath.

"You're fucking soaked," he growls. "Does it turn you on when I'm rough with you, Sunshine?"

Yes.

Yes.

"No," I snap, "of course, not."

"Your body says otherwise." He slides another finger inside my pussy. He adds a third, then begins to weave them in and out of my sopping wet channel. The slurping noises that my flesh makes as he thrusts his fingers in and out of me fills the space.

My cheeks heat. "Let go of me." I wriggle my hips, but his hold on my arm tightens. He pulls me even closer, and the ridge of his arousal stabs into the valley between my butt cheeks. I freeze, and a laugh rumbles up his chest.

"A little late to be playing the scared damsel, don't you think?" He grinds the heel of his palm on my clit, and a shudder grips me. He continues to thrust his fingers in and out of me, in and out. He curves his fingers inside me, and a moan bleeds from my lips. "That's it," he murmurs, "let go of all your inhibitions, Sunshine. There won't be any place for being shy in our marriage."

Marriage? Hell. I'm sure I'm going to regret what I said for every moment of my life.

I open my mouth to protest, but that's when he releases my arm. He brings his hand up and around to pinch my nipple. My entire body jolts. "Ohmygod," I moan, as he continues to strum my nipple. He moves his hand to the other breast and tugs on the nipple. My head falls back against his chest. I bring my arm up and around his neck, then thrust out my breasts, as he adds a fourth finger inside me, filling me, stretching me. He continues to weave his fingers in and out of me, as I wrap my other arm around his waist. His muscles undulate under his skin as he lowers his mouth to where my neck meets my shoulder. He sinks his teeth into my skin, and I yell. I rise up to my tiptoes, as he lowers his other hand to my pussy.

"Come for me, Sunshine, come all over my fingers." He pinches my clit, and I explode. The orgasm crashes over me, and I scream. Moisture coats the space between my legs; sweat beads my forehead. He pulls his fingers out of my pussy and thrusts them into my mouth. The taste of my arousal fills my palate, mixed with the salty taste of his skin. I lick my tongue across his fingers, and his chest muscles contract.

I open my eyes to find his features flushed. His nostrils flare. "I don't know whether to fuck you or punish you for what you did," he growls.

"Why not do both?"

He blinks, then a chuckle rumbles up his chest. "You have spirit. That's good; you're going to need it for what's in store for you once we're married."

He releases me so suddenly that I stumble.

Turning, he stalks toward the door of the bathroom.

"Wait, what did you mean by that?" I take a step in his direction when he comes to a stop.

He glances at me over his shoulder. "Why are you so impatient? Why don't you wait until we're married? You're bound to find out."

I scowl back. "I told you—you don't scare me."

"Good, that means I don't intend to hold back on my perversions."

23

Axel

"Fifty-one, fifty-two, fifty-three…" I count as I balance the weight of my body in plank position. "Fifty-four, fifty-five, fifty-six." My biceps tremble, and my thighs scream in protest. Fuck, if I haven't become a complete weakling. I used to be able to hold this position until the count of one-thousand. Now, apparently, I can't even get to one-hundred.

"Fifty-seven, fifty-eight, fifty-nine," I grunt as my core protests. The blood thuds at my temples. Sweat breaks out on my forehead as I try to maintain my balance. "Sixty, sixty-one, sixty-two." My head hurts, my quadriceps groan, and every muscle in my body seems to seize up. Sweat drips down my temples and down my chin to plop onto the floor below me.

"F-u-c-k," I growl as my arms give way from under me. I face-plant on the floor and lay there unmoving. My breath comes in pants; my muscles are on fire. "Fuck, fuck, fuck." It's going to take me time to build up my endurance again. And I'm getting married in a few days.

It's been a full day since I walked out of Theresa's bathroom, after making that statement about my perversions. My intent was to scare her, and I must have succeeded, for I haven't seen her since. To be fair, I've been throwing myself into my rehabilitation. I work with Sheena on the prescribed exercises, then throw myself into working out in my own time. I know I'm pushing it, but I don't care. I need to keep myself occupied, or else, I'm in danger of walking into her room, throwing her down on her bed, and burying myself inside her sweet pussy... Something I want to resist until we're married. Not that it matters. I already took her virginity, after all. I pause. Hold on a second —is that why she wants to marry me? Because I was her first?

Theresa doesn't strike me as a traditional girl. I wanted to find out more about my future wife, so I used the phone loaned to me by the Sovranos to search her online.

I didn't find much of a presence on the social media networks. I did, however, stumble across the Instagram feed for her shop *The Tilting Tulip*. All of the pictures were of flowers. Apparently, the woman doesn't believe in showing her face to the camera. There was one picture which showed her back and that of another girl with #bestsisterever. And another, where her profile was visible on screen. The picture shows her working on an arrangement of tulips, a beam of sunlight accentuating her hair and the flowers. There was something arresting about the image. The photographer captured the serenity on her face as she focused on the flowers. Has she ever looked at me with that much singular attention? A hot sensation stabbed at my chest. I couldn't believe that I was jealous of flowers.

I clicked out of the Instagram feed at once. All I learned was that she loves what she does. Judging by her nearly thirty-thousand followers and the comments on the pictures, her flower shop is also doing really well. She looked gorgeous in the picture. So vital, so full of life... Thank God I had stepped in front of her and took the bullet for her. If it had hurt her in any way, I never would have been able to forgive myself. After all, it was my fault that the shooter had her in his crosshairs.

Now that I'm able to recall the events leading up to my shooting at Christian, I confess, it's only confusing me more. Who is the person who shot at her? Were they aiming at me? Or maybe, Christian? No, it was meant for me. It had to be; so why did they shoot at her instead? Unless they wanted to send a message. To me or to the Sovranos?

My head spins, and it's not entirely due to my overexertion combined with my recent head wound, which is not fully healed. This entire situation is a mess. It reeks of being a trap. But that's not possible. Whoever shot at us wouldn't have expected me to step in front of her. Or did they shoot at her, knowing I'd get in front of her? No, that doesn't make sense. And why would they shoot at her, anyway? Is it because she's under the protection of the Sovranos? Was the intention to show them that their security doesn't hold up to scrutiny? I push myself onto my back and stare up at the ceiling.

And why did the Sovranos accept me without punishing me for what I did? Is the fact that I'm marrying Theresa enough reason to stop them from coming for me in the future? Can I trust Michael to deliver on his promise of giving me a seat at their table?

I push up to my feet, and my legs hold up my weight. Thank fuck. I walk into the bathroom, take a quick shower, then pull on a pair of pants and a shirt. All made of the finest material, perfectly altered to my size and measurements. You have to hand it to the Sovranos—they know how to embrace a lifestyle many desire, yet very few can access.

The kind of life my mother left behind... And one which I'm entering in flagrant contradiction of her wishes. But I have to; it's the only way to get revenge for what these bastards did to her.

They're responsible for her early death, and I'm going to get my revenge for it through marriage. Once Theresa is in my grasp, the Sovranos will experience the kind of emotional torment that my mother went through. *But she is innocent; she isn't responsible for what happened to your mother.* Well, too-fucking-bad. She'll be collateral damage in the plan I'm enacting— a plan for which I'd rather she be compliant than not. Which means, it's best I try to put her at ease. At least, until the wedding.

I pull on my socks and shoes, pocket my phone and wallet—also provided to me by the Sovranos, since I wasn't carrying any forms of ID on me when I was shot. Much as I loathe to use money provided by Michael, I don't have a choice. It's only a matter of time before I'm involved in the day-to-day affairs of the Cosa Nostra. I'll be pulling more than my fair share of weight in their business then. Besides, part of their wealth does belong to me by birthright. After all, I was born into it as much as they were. They owe me for everything that happened to my mother. So no, I have zero guilt in using their resources to get what I want.

I head out of my room, up the corridor, past the door to Sheena's room, which is shut, and into Theresa's suite at the end of the corridor.

I raise my hand to knock on the door, then change my mind. Best to use the element of surprise. I twist the doorknob, walk into the living room of the suite, and find it's empty. I check the bathroom and the bedroom, but she's not there. The scent of her envelops me, and the blood drains to my groin. Fuck. Where the hell is she? I explicitly told her not to leave the house without my permission. Bet that's precisely why she decided to go out. Couldn't stop herself from trying to defy me, eh? I twist my lips. Another challenge she's thrown down at me, and this time, I'm going to show her the consequences of going against me.

I rise to my feet and begin to pace, slowly. Does she think I'm not strong enough to leave the house? Well, she hasn't reckoned with how much I've been pushing myself. I may not have one-hundred percent of my normal strength, but fuck, I'm no longer a weakling either.

I pull up Seb's number on my phone and dial.

"Yes, it's me."

24

Theresa

"Perversions?" Elsa's eyes round. "Did he say … per-ver-sions?"

"Shh…" I glance around the crowded nightclub, but thankfully, nobody's paying any attention to us. Yep, I decided to tempt fate by asking Elsa to accompany me to Venom again.

"Well…" She draws from the straw of her frozen margarita. "Did he elaborate further?"

I shake my head.

"But he did say *perversions*?"

I scowl at her. "If I didn't know you better, I'd think that you were having too much fun with that word."

"I am." She drinks some more of the margarita. "Have you imagined what he meant by that? What all he could do to you? How rough he could get? How he could spank you, or tie you up or—"

"Stop!" My cheeks heat. "And no, I haven't imagined any of that."

"Liar." She laughs, then drains the rest of her margarita, before leaning over the bar counter. "Get me another margarita, please?"

"She's had enough," a voice says from behind us.

Both of us turn at the same time to find Seb glowering at her. Yep, I had wanted to leave the house, knowing fully that it would piss off Axel, but that was the general idea. I was so mad at him for making me come on his fingers, for scaring me with his threats. If he thinks I'm going to back down because of the thought of some rough sex after marriage, he can think again. My thighs clench, my toes curl, and moisture beads the space between my legs. OMG, just the thought of what he could do to my body has my heartbeat ratcheting up. My pulse beats at my temples. I rub my damp palms on the skirt of my dress just as Elsa raises an eyebrow at Seb.

"You can't tell me what to do," she drawls.

"Oh?" He smirks.

"You're not my keeper," she insists.

"But I am the person responsible for the safety of both of you." He folds his arms across his chest.

"You mean you're responsible for Theresa's safety," she corrects him.

"You're here with Theresa; ergo, I'm responsible for your safety too."

The two of them glare at each other for a few seconds. The silence stretches, and neither seems to want to back down.

I slide off the stool. "Thanks for bringing me here, Seb, especially as I know it means going against Axel's orders."

Seb smirks. "It's because it goes against his orders that I couldn't resist. Also, he can't order me around. I don't answer to anyone."

"Not even to the Don?" Elsa asks.

He hesitates. "He's the only exception."

"Wow…" Elsa's gaze widens. "But would you go against the Don on certain occasions?"

"The Don is not unreasonable; there isn't much we disagree on."

"So, you would go against the Don if the situation warranted it?"

"Why are you so curious about it?" Seb scowls.

"It was just a question." She glowers back at him.

"Well, you shouldn't be this curious about things that don't concern you."

"Hey!" She draws herself up to her full height, which still means she comes up to the height of his chest. "You're my friend's designated bodyguard-slash-chauffeur tonight, which means it's totally within my purview to find out everything about you."

"You mean, *you* want to find out more about me?" He smirks.

"It means, I want to make sure that you are, uh ... qualified in your role of chauffeur-slash-security guard. Speaking of, why don't you stand at a distance?"

"Why should I stand at a distance?"

"Because you're frightening the rest of the men away."

"Men?" Seb's face grows thunderous. "What men?"

"My question, exactly," a familiar voice cuts through the noise of the bar.

"Oh, hell." I squeeze my eyes shut and mutter under my breath. "It can't be." *Please, please let it not be him.*

"You thought you could slink away without asking my permission, and I wouldn't follow you?"

I glance over my shoulder at the tall, dark, massive, glowering man whose blue eyes are alight with an emotion I dare not try to name.

"How did you manage to leave the house?" I frown.

"I'm well enough to walk, or didn't you notice?" he retorts.

"I know you're getting better, and believe me, I'm happy about that."

"Are you?" He tilts his head. "Somehow, I can't help but think that you wanted me out of commission long enough to not be able to walk on my own two feet up the aisle for my own wedding."

I gape at him. "I would never —" I take in his angry features, the skin that wrinkles around his mouth, the firm set to his jaw. "Wow!" I throw up my hands. "You really think I planned it so you'd embarrass yourself on your wedding day?"

"Didn't you? Isn't that why you pushed to have the wedding so quickly?"

My cheeks heat. "I only suggested a shorter period of time because we both wanted to get married, and I didn't see any reason to wait."

"Were you afraid that I'd change my mind?"

"Well, you won't, now that you have a chance to get a piece of the *Cosa Nostra* business." Bitterness fills my chest, and I push it aside. "How did you find me here, anyway?"

"Lucky guess?" He raises a shoulder.

"Stop treating me like I'm stupid." I sense Seb shuffle his feet and turn on him. "You told him, didn't you?"

He raises his hands. "He called me, so I didn't have a choice."

"You couldn't have given him the wrong address?"

"I figured, you still had a head start on him, giving you enough time to enjoy yourself before he tracked you down."

I glower at him, but Seb has already turned back to Elsa. "What do you say we head out to the car and wait for these guys to join us?"

Elsa pops her head around him. "I assume this is Axel?"

"Oh, shoot, I forgot you guys haven't yet met." I glance between them. "Axel this is my friend and colleague Elsa. Elsa, this is Axel, the man—"

"Who you're going to marry; I know." She thrusts out her arm. "Pleased to meet you."

Axel reaches out to take her hand, but Seb steps between them. "That's enough."

Her gaze widens. "Whoa, whoa, whoa. Back off, asshole. I was merely being civil."

"You can say hello without touching him," Seb replies in a tight voice.

"I was only going to shake his hand, jerkaloupe."

Seb's forehead creases. "Is that an insult?"

"What do you think, you big oaf?"

"I think it's time to leave and give these two a few minutes alone."

She scowls at him, and he stares back with a placid expression on his face.

Finally, she blows out a breath. "Is that okay with you, Theresa? I can stay if you want."

Axel's muscles bunch. I sense the anger vibrating off of him, and for some reason, I want to calm him down.

"It's fine," I murmur. "I'll be fine."

"You sure?" She peers at me closely. "I can stay; honestly."

"No." I shake my head. "Really, I've got this."

She stares at me a second longer, then nods. "We'll be out in the car."

"We'll just be a few minutes," I reassure her. She brushes past Seb, whose features darken. He stomps off after her.

"What's gotten into him?" Axel stares at Seb's retreating back.

"Who knows?" I turn to face him. "Now, do you want to tell me why you came here?"

"I don't know…" He crowds me so my hip hits the bar. "I think the time for talking is over. In fact, I'm positive I don't want to talk about anything right now."

"You don't?"

"I thought it was time to give you an idea of the kind of man you're marrying."

"Oh, I know the kind of man I'm marrying." I tip up my chin. "A lying, conniving, double-crosser who won't hesitate to betray his own brothers."

His face darkens. "Take that back."

"No."

"I'm warning you, Theresa, if you don't apologize for that, I'm going to have to punish you."

A thrill runs down my back. Shit, why is it that the thought of unleashing the beast inside him turns me on so? Why is it that the thought of him losing control and jumping on me and having his way with me turns my insides to jelly? My toes curl. I raise my hand to push back a strand of hair from my face, and my fingers tremble. "I'm only saying what we both know is true. Besides, you don't scare me."

"So you keep saying." He bares his teeth. "Last chance, Sunshine."

"Ooh, I'm so afraid." I pretend to shiver, then yelp when he grabs my wrist.

He turns around and drags me through the crowd. The people in front seem to step aside as he shoulders his way to the end of the bar, then turns up the corridor, and passes the queue of women waiting to get into the restroom.

"Jesus, what the hell do you think you're doing?" I yell.

He doesn't reply, simply increases his pace as he hauls me past the row of curious faces. He reaches the guys' restroom and barges inside, pulling me in his wake. "Out," he snaps.

The man who's been washing his hands at the basin opens his mouth to protest. Axel growls, and the man pales. He turns around, brushes past us, and scampers out.

"That goes for you too." Axel jerks his chin toward the man who's been pissing in one of the urinals. This guy doesn't even protest. Without bothering to zip himself up, he turns and runs out, followed by the man who is drying his hands under the electric dryer.

Why the hell is it that the men's restrooms are always empty while the women's always has a queue? One of the everlasting mysteries which I know I will not solve today. I try to pull my hand from his grasp, but Axel doesn't let go. Once the last man has left the restroom, he turns and locks the door. The sound of the latch falling into place echoes around the space.

I gulp. "Let go of me!" I gasp.

"Nope." He yanks me toward the sinks, then pushes me against the counter before crowding me from behind.

I stare at my flushed appearance in the mirror. My hair is messed up, and my eyes glitter with fear Excitement? Both.

He pulls up my skirt from behind, and I freeze, "What are you—?"

He grabs my panties and tears them off.

"What the—?" I turn my head to find him stuffing my panties in his pocket.

He slaps my ass.

I gasp, too shocked to say anything.

He spanks my other ass cheek, and I yell, "What do you think you're doing?"

"Teaching you a lesson."

He raises his big palm again and brings it down on my ass cheek, this time with enough force that I rise up to my tiptoes. A line of fire seems to unfold from the point of contact, before zipping straight to my core. My pussy clenches, and my nipples tighten. No way. No fucking way am I turned on by what he just did.

I open my mouth to protest, but before I can make a sound, he spanks my other ass cheek with enough force that my entire body jolts. He raises his hand and holds my gaze in the mirror. "Tell me you're sorry for disobeying me."

"No."

C-r-a-c-k. He spanks me with such force that another line of fire, this one even more intense, zips up my spine.

C-r-a-c-k, c-r-a-c-k, c-r-a-c-k. He spanks both my ass cheeks in quick succession, and I can't stop the groan that spills from my lips.

"Fuck," he growls. I take in his flushed features, the color that burns high on his cheeks. The dark pupils of his eyes seem to have expanded until only a blazing circle of blue can be seen around the circumference.

"You fucking get to me, you know that?" he says in a low voice. "Since the first time I saw you, I've been acting out of character. Since I smelled you, I can't get your scent out of my head. Since I tasted you, I want fucking more."

He massages my throbbing ass cheek, and a moan wells up my throat.

He thrusts his finger between my legs, and I gasp.

"Fucking hell." His gaze intensifies. "You're so damn wet, so hot, so slick."

He shoves two more fingers inside me, then curls them.

"Ohmygod!" I throw my head back against his chest, then push my ass into the swollen length at his crotch. I writhe and grind against the throbbing thickness as he continues to work me. He brings his other hand around to cup my pussy. "Who does this belong to?"

"What?" I blink.

"Who does your cunt belong to, Sunshine?" he says in a hard voice, simultaneously pinching my clit with such force that I see stars.

"Tell me," he demands, "who does your pussy belong to Theresa?"

"You," I moan. "You, Axel, you."

"Damn-fucking-right."

He pulls his fingers out of me, only to turn me around. He kicks my legs apart, drops to his knees, and thrusts his face between my thighs. He eats me out, devours me, slurps on my pussy, circles my clit with his tongue, then shoves four of his thick fingers inside my already squelching channel. Too much. Too full. And he doesn't even have his cock inside me yet.

He squeezes my hip, then slides one leg over his shoulder, before attacking my pussy with renewed vigor. This time, he pumps his fingers in and out of me, as he bites down on my clit. That's when the climax sweeps over me. The orgasm slams into me, and I cry out as I come. I slump over him, and he rises to his feet. He notches his knuckles under my chin. "Open your eyes," he commands.

I flutter my eyelashes open and meet his piercing gaze.

"You're mine, Theresa. Mine to fuck. Mine to possess. Mine to do with as I please. You feel me?"

"Yes," I swallow. "Yes, Axel."

"Good." He circles my wrist with his fingers then unlocks the bathroom door and heads out with me in tow. As we pass the still long line of women, they can't take their eyes off of him—not that he notices. He pulls me along at such speed that I have to half-run to keep up. By the time we reach Seb's car, I'm panting.

The two men exchange glances, then Seb jerks his chin toward the car. "Get in, and I'll drop you back at the house."

Axel opens the back door for me, and I slide in; he follows. He throws his arm around me and pulls me close, and I have to admit, I don't try to move away this time. I bury my nose in his neck and draw in his dark, edgy scent. Somehow, that entire demonstration of possession hasn't put me off. It was quite hot, actually.

I sense Elsa glance at me from her seat in the front of the car, but I don't raise my head. I don't want to explain why I'm clinging to him like I can't get enough of him. Damn it, I'm going to marry him. Surely, it's allowed.

Seb eases the car out onto the road and accelerates.

Then a thought strikes me, and I pull back. "How did you get here?" I ask.

"Adrian dropped me off."

"Ah." I subside. The rest of the trip passes in silence. I shoot glances at Axel's face, but he's staring out the window. His jaw is hard. A nerve throbs at his temple. Clearly, he's still angry at me. Or maybe he's mad at himself. To be fair, though, while he made me orgasm, he hasn't found the same kind of relief. I place my palm over his crotch, and the thickness in his pants makes me gasp. He stiffens, but he doesn't stop me when I begin to knead him through his pants. His shaft lengthens, and the heat sears me through the cloth. He widens his legs, allowing me more access, and I slide my fingers up and down his length. His muscles bunch, and his shoulders flex. I squeeze his cock, and it seems to jump under my ministrations. A plume of heat seems to pour off of him. It slams down on my shoulders and pins me in place. I draw in a breath, and the scent of him—sweat and musk and testosterone—fills my lungs. A trembling grips me. I squeeze my legs together to contain the yawning that claws at my insides. The next moment he grips my pussy. A cry rolls up my throat, but he's already there. He fits his mouth over mine and absorbs the sounds. Heat flushes my skin. Goddammit, I'm in a car with my employee/friend in the front and one of the Sovrano brothers, and I can't keep my hands off this guy. I can't stop him from eating my face or playing with my clit.

Another groan rolls up my throat, and he deepens the kiss. He thrusts his tongue inside my mouth, and my eyes roll back in my head. A shudder ladders up my spine, and the climax sweeps over me. A bead of sweat slides down my back as I give into the pleasure completely. The orgasm seems to go on and on, then just as quickly fades away. I slump in his grasp, completely boneless. He continues to kiss me for a few seconds more, then softens his lips, until he's nibbling on my lower lip, kissing the edges of my mouth, my chin, my nose. When he finally sits back, I gaze at him, unable to compute what just happened.

Did I just come from him just kissing me? Okay, he may have had some help because he was playing with my pussy, but for heaven's sake, I wasn't even undressed. Under my palm he's rock hard and so big. He smirks, an amused look in his eyes.

Jerk! Bet he's gloating that he made me come so quickly. I pull back my hand, scoot over to the door, and for the remainder of the journey, glance out of the window.

Thankfully, he doesn't speak either. Neither do Seb and Elsa from the front of the car.

All too soon, we're parking in front of Axel's temporary home. I'm about to follow him out of the car when Elsa leans over the back of her seat. "You sure you're okay, T?" she murmurs. "If you need any help—"

"She doesn't," Axel snaps.

Elsa frowns. I shoot him a scowl. "Don't answer for me."

"I can if I want to."

I blow out a breath. Elsa's brow wrinkles. "Theresa?" she prompts. "Do you want me to come in with you?"

"No." I shake my head.

"No," Axel and Seb say at the same time.

"What the hell?" Elsa throws up her hands. "I'm asking Theresa, you guys." She side-eyes Seb. "And you, mister, have no right to speak," she snaps.

Seb merely raises an eyebrow. Before he can say something and make things worse, I rush in with, "I'm fine, Elsa; I promise."

She doesn't seem convinced. "You don't have to do this, Theresa. You don't have to marry him."

I do, though. How can I explain it to her? This man is my last chance to feel connected to Xander.

And that is really, really the wrong reason to marry someone. I push the thought away. "I'm good, promise." I lean over and kiss her cheek. "I'll be in touch."

I slide out of the car behind Axel, and he slams the door shut. Seb drives away, leaving me alone with Axel. I follow him to the door, which he unlocks with a set of keys.

I'm inside, and he's locked the door behind him before I finally realize what he just did. "Hey," I call out as he begins to climb the stairs, "where's the rest of the household staff?"

"I gave them a few days off."

"And Sheena?"

"I'm taking a break from the physiotherapy sessions."

A ripple of fear runs up my spine. So, I'm alone with him? I can't be alone with him. Not that it would stop him from doing whatever he wants in the privacy of his or my room. But still, knowing that Sheena was here and that there were other people around had provided me with some modicum of safety, which has just been pulled out from under me.

I burst into a run and take the stairs two at a time. "Is that wise?" I pant as I draw up close with him. "Taking a break, I mean? Surely, you need to keep exercising—"

"Which I'm doing on my own."

"But it's too soon after being shot; you need an expert to monitor your progress and help you and—"

"I'm improving by leaps and bounds, the doctor says." He pauses at the top of the stairs so quickly that I bump into him.

He turns and grips my shoulders, staring down at me from his elevated height. "At this rate, I'll be back to my former strength in a few days."

"That … that's great."

"Not for you."

"Excuse me."

"Not that it matters." He looks me up and down. "I have plans for you, Sunshine."

"Don't call me that." I tug out of his grasp. He releases me, and that increases the churning sensation at the pit of my stomach. A hot sensation coils in my chest. My pulse begins to race. Why do I feel so nervous? I'm going to marry this guy. Most likely, I'm going to spend the rest of my life with him, so why am I so afraid of him?

His gaze intensifies. He stares at my mouth, and my throat goes dry. I step up onto the top of the staircase, forcing him to take a step back.

This also decreases the height difference between us. Not that it helps, because I still have to tilt my head all the way back to meet his eyes.

He smirks, and hell, why do I find that so hot?

"I'm not afraid of you." I toss my hair over my shoulder.

He barks out a laugh. "I'll remind you of this when I finally have my way with you."

My nerve-endings stretch, and something inside of me seems to snap. With a low snarl, I throw myself at him.

25

———————

Axel

She crashes into my chest, and it's a good thing I've moved away from the top of the staircase; chances are good I might have tumbled down.

I grab her around the waist and haul her to me as she raises her hand. Her palm connects with my face, and my neck snaps to the side. Anger courses through my veins, and adrenaline laces my blood.

"What the fuck?" I grate out as I carry her up the corridor. "What's wrong with you?"

"You," she yells, "I'm tired of your stupid threats. If you want to do something that is going to shock me, then I dare you to go through with it."

She raises her hand again, but this time, I grab her wrist. I twist her hand behind her back as she pants.

"Fuck you," she spits out, "I hate you."

"Good."

Color splotches her face. She snaps her head forward, and I manage to evade it, barely. Must be a combination of my still-not-close-to-optimum state and her acting on pure adrenaline.

I lower her to her feet. "Calm down," I grate out as I grab her other hand and pull it behind her back.

I pull her close so her breasts are flattened against my chest. Her chest heaves, her hair flows around her shoulders, and she glares at me, her green eyes spitting sparks.

"You're fucking gorgeous, Sunshine," I murmur.

Her nipples pebble against my chest, and goddammit, if they got any harder, they'd surely poke right through the fabric of her dress.

"I want to fuck you so hard that you'll forget all those insults that you like to spew at me."

"Why don't you then?"

"Oh, I'm not going to let you get away that easily."

"Wh-what do you mean?"

I lean in close enough for our noses to bump, then I lick my tongue up her cheek.

She shivers.

"Why the fuck are you so responsive to my touch?" I stare at her through half-closed eyes.

"This is my response to how repulsive I find you," she says through gritted teeth.

"Is that right?"

She bares her teeth.

I laugh. "Your body says otherwise. If I shove my hand between your legs, will I find you wet, Sunshine?"

"Fuck you."

"Not yet." I smirk.

She struggles in my grasp, every move of hers bringing her core in close contact with the already massive erection that tents my crotch. She must feel it too, for her color heightens further.

"Let go of me, you … you *stronzo*," she hisses.

"Now, now, be nice." I shackle both of her wrists with one hand. With the other, I press down on her shoulder.

She sinks to her knees, then glowers up at me. "What do you think you're doing?"

"Less talking; more sucking," I drawl.

Her mouth opens, and fuck, I don't want to hear one more thing from her. If I do, I'll lose my control and simply throw her down and bury myself inside her, and I don't want to do that. Not yet. If I do, I might never want to leave the hot, squelching, moist place that is her cunt, and I can't have that. Not if I want to ensure that I have her so hungry for me, she'll do anything I ask without question. And I need that level of subservience if I want my plans to fall into place.

I lower my zipper, and my cock springs out. Her gaze widens, but before she can say anything I've thrust my cock into her mouth.

Heat, tightness. A shiver runs up my spine. Fucking hell, she is a siren. Every part of her body stills for a few seconds, her gaze lifted to mine. Her green eyes glow with an inner light that, if I'm not mistaken, is a combination of anger and arousal. Fucking hell, I set out to … frighten her, maybe? To try to harness that spirit of hers, but damn, if she doesn't seem to revel in the level of darkness that stirs inside of me.

I ease my cock further inside, and it hits the back of her throat. Then, before she can gag, I pull out and stay poised again with my cock at the seam of her lips.

Her shoulders rise and fall, and her pupils dilate. Without breaking the connection of her gaze, she closes her mouth around my dick. She hollows out her cheeks and—"F-u-c-k!"—a shudder runs up my spine. I bury my fingers in the back of her head and tug on her hair. She gasps around my cock, and my balls tighten.

Sweat breaks out on my forehead.

"Jesus-fucking-Christ," I growl, "your mouth is going to be the end of me."

I press forward on the back of her head, and my cock slides in. I pull her back, then wrap my fingers around her throat. The next time I push her forward, my cock slips down her throat.

"Fucking hell, I can feel my cock glide down your throat; you know that?"

Saliva drools from the corners of her mouth. Her pupils dilate as she grips my thigh to steady herself. I pull her back, then forward, and again. She moans ,and the vibrations travel up my dick, coil low in my belly. My groin tightens, my balls draw up. "Fuck, I'm going to come," and that is a record. I've never come this fast. Never. But Sunshine has a hold on me that I can't explain. Something about her seems to break through my barriers and causes me to lose control. Something I need to be careful about if I want to get through the rest of my mission.

I tighten my hold on her hair and haul her toward me. I empty myself down her throat, and she swallows it down. When I pull out, I stare at her swollen lips. The evidence of my cum and her saliva streaks her chin. I haul her to her feet, then fit my lips to hers.

26

Theresa

I expect the kiss to be hard, possessive, almost punishing. Instead, he presses his lips to mine and holds them there. Softness. Tenderness. He nibbles on my lower lip, and my entire body shudders. He cups my cheek as he licks my lips.

"The taste of you and me combined drives me mad." His voice rumbles up his chest. Pinpricks of pleasure set off from the point of contact between my nipples and his hard chest planes. A whine bleeds from my lips, and he presses his lips to mine in a hard kiss this time, before he pulls back.

I sway toward him, and he rights me with a grip on my shoulder.

"Okay?" he asks.

I open my mouth, but no sound comes out. Am I okay? No, I'm not. I just let him fuck my mouth, and I didn't try to stop him. Oh, I may have made a few token protests, but let's face it, I wanted him. Wanted his hands on me, his lips on mine, his breath combining with mine, his tongue inside my mouth, his cock stuffed inside my pussy. My core clenches.

A slow smile curves his lips. "If I touch you, will I find you wet?"

"You know you will," I grumble.

"Good." He pushes the hair off of my face, then straightens the collar of my dress. "Good night, Theresa." Turning, he ambles up the corridor and turns into his room.

Huh?

I stand there, blinking rapidly, not quite computing what just happened. My pussy spasms, and that emptiness in my lower belly beckons. Hell, no. He did not just walk away without making me come, did he? He shuts the door behind him. What the hell? I walk toward the door, push it open ,and step inside. He's already thrown off his jacket and is about to yank his Henley over his head. As I watch, he pulls it off and tosses it aside, then turns to me. "Do you want something?"

"Yo-you … left me out there."

He tilts his head.

"I … you … I didn't…"

"I didn't get you off?"

I nod.

"I did so twice earlier." He raises a shoulder.

"Argh!" I throw up my hands. "That doesn't count, and you know it."

"Too bad. It's best we keep our distance until the wedding now."

"Excuse me?" I gape as he reaches for his belt. He unhooks it, then the button on the waistband of his pants, then lowers his zipper. Before I can say anything more, he shoves down his pants and kicks them aside. His dick jumps free. Thick and long, it points upward and lays against his lower belly.

What the hell? He's hard again? And, of course, he doesn't wear boxers. I mean, I've never seen him wear boxers. Maybe he didn't buy any boxers? I mean, maybe whoever bought him the other clothes forgot to buy him boxers? Makes it easy for him to whip out his dick with minimal fuss. A chuckle wells up, and I swallow it down.

He arches an eyebrow. "Something funny, Sunshine?"

I shake my head.

He reaches for his cock and pumps it once. I feel the tug all the way to my core. My toes curl. My mouth waters. Even from this distance, I can see the moisture glisten on the crown of that monster shaft.

He squeezes the base of his shaft and watches me, as if waiting to see what I'll do next. When I don't move, he drags his fingers up the length.

A moan bubbles up my throat. Shit, shit, shit, if I stay here, I'm likely to fling myself at him again, this time, with the hope of riding his cock.

And yet I can't drag my gaze off his crotch. Or how his biceps flex each time he swipes his fingers up his shaft. His balls seem to grow thicker, heavier, larger. His thigh muscles ripple.

"Sunshine," he says in a low voice, "either get in here and get me off, or leave."

"Wait, what?" I tip my chin up. "What do you mean, get you off? Don't you want to—"

"Fuck you?"

I nod.

"Nah…" His lips twist. "Gonna wait until we're married now, remember?"

"B-but … but…" I squeeze my thighs together. "I don't wanna wait," I whine.

"I know." He chuckles. "That's the general idea."

"So, you did all that earlier"—I stab my thumb over my shoulder—"to—"

"To turn you on."

"But you won't let me come."

"Nope." He makes a popping sound with his lips. Of course, my gaze darts to his mouth. His gorgeous mouth. His plush, puffy mouth, which he used to bring me to orgasm earlier.

"You got me off earlier. What's changed now?"

"What's changed is that I realized it's only a few days until we are to get married, and I think it's important we spend that time apart."

"You do?" I pout.

He begins to pump himself harder, and I watch in fascination as his dick gets bigger. I swear, it gets thicker and longer and so hard that the head is almost purple. Moisture pools between my legs, and I reach for the waistband of my skirt. I slide my fingers inside and toward my clit when.

"Stop," he orders. "You will not touch yourself."

"Excuse me?"

"You heard me." His lips turn up in a wide smile. "You will not come until I give you permission!"

"What?" I laugh. "Who are you to command when I come?"

"Your soon-to-be husband," he says in a harsh voice. He pumps himself with such ferocity that his muscles bulge, his chest planes flex, and his entire body is wound so tightly, I'm sure he's going to come any moment. I need to leave; I do. I need to get out of here before I do something I'll regret. I try to move, but my feet seem to be stuck to the floor. His gaze holds mine. The skin around his eyes crinkles, sweat beads his forehead, and his features contort as, with a grunt, he comes. My heart slams into my chest, and my pussy clenches in on itself. Fuck, that was hot, so hot. When my foot hits the ground, I realize I've taken a step forward. That's when one side of his lips kicks up.

Asshole. That entire performance was for my benefit. He wanted me to be turned on. He wanted me to see what I was missing. Jerk. *Stronzo.*

Xander would have never done this. He wouldn't have treated me like I was a piece of merchandise, like his possession to do with whatever he wanted. He never would have been mean to me.

And he didn't care enough about you to even try to kiss you.

It's that thought that finally snaps me out of my sexual haze. I spin around, dart out of the room, and up the corridor to my suite. I don't stop until I'm in the bathroom and have thrown off my clothes and stepped under the shower. Oh hell, what am I going to do now? How am I going to survive until the wedding?

I shove my fingers between my thighs. He told me I couldn't come without his permission, but he's not here, is he? He'll never know if I make myself come. Fuck him. I thrust my fingers—one, two, three—inside my cunt. I thrust them in and out of me, in and out. I curve my fingers inside my channel, but it's not enough. I add a fourth finger, and damn it, it doesn't feel the same. Shit, shit, shit. *Doesn't matter; keep going.* I weave my fingers in and out, but each time it feels like I'm about to climax, I can't relax enough to let go. Damn this, and damn him! Has he conditioned my body so much already that I have to obey him even when he's not here? I turn off the shower, dry myself, then pull on my sleep shorts and camisole and crawl into bed.

Sometime later, my eyes snap open. It's still completely dark outside. I reach for my phone, and the clock on the screen indicates it's four am. I put the phone back, try to go back to sleep, but I hear the sound of something in the distance. I sit up and try to listen. There's silence. Maybe it's my imagination. I lay back in my bed, but now I feel wide awake. Damn it. I swing my legs over the side of the bed, then pull on a pair of thick socks. I grab a hoodie and shrug into it, then make for the door. As I pass Axel's room, I hear the sound of a low scream. I stop at the door, press my ear to it, and that's when I hear him cry out again. I open the door and slip inside.

27

Axel

The line of fire lights up the space in the gap between the door of the wardrobe and the floor. It flickers and dances as the heat in the closet builds up. I'm scared, so scared. I press back into the wall of the closet and close my eyes. I don't want to die. Please, I don't want to die. Smoke creeps in from under the door, and I cough. My eyes water. I need to get out of here, but how do I do that? If I reach for the door, on the other side, there will be fire. I press my sweaty palms into the wall behind me. There's no escape. The only way is to move through the door. Either that, or I'd be roasted alive here. Sweat pops on my forehead and slides down my temple.

I have to try to get out of here. But Mum said that she would come for me. She told me to wait here, while she finishes working. I told her I don't like to hide in the closet, but she said we don't have a choice. She has to work, and all she could afford right now is this room. And she can't have me outside. That would upset her client. I told her I would go outside to play, but she said I'm too small to be out on my own. She doesn't think it would be safe for me to cross the road on my own to go to the playground. So, I had no choice but to hide myself in the closet. She said she won't be long. And I believe her.

My ma has always come through for me. She's always there to pick me up from school and to drop me off. And she makes sure I always have enough to eat, and she buys me toys I love. I didn't want to hide, but she promised that this would be the last time. That after this, we would be moving to a bigger place where I'd have my own room. Just this one last client she had to take care of, and we'd start packing right after and be off. I didn't want to agree, but she finally coaxed me into the closet.

Soon after, I heard the sound of voices and knew her client had arrived. Then the usual grunts and groans started, and I plugged my fingers in my ears just the way that she had taught me. I even saw a mouse in the corner of the closet and laughed at it. I reached for it, but it scampered off.

I guess I fell asleep after that, but now I woke up to the heat, the sweat trickling down my back ... and the fire ... the sparks that dance through the slats on the door. I open my mouth to cry out, but my throat is so dry. I don't want to die; I don't want to die. I draw in a breath and burst out coughing. The smoke is building in here; it's too much. Too hot. Can't breathe. My lungs are burning. My skin feels like it's going to catch fire at any moment. I have to get out of here. Have to. I reach for the door, my fingers brush the hot metal, and I scream.

"Axel," I hear her voice. "Axel, you're safe"

"Mom?" I croak.

"It's me, Axel."

I snap my eyes open and meet her worried gaze.

"Axel?" Her forehead furrows. "Are you okay?"

I try to speak, but my throat is too dry. I draw in a breath, and my lungs burn. My heart is racing so fast, I'm sure it's going to break out of my ribcage. Sweat beads my brow and trickles down my temple.

"Axel?" she asks with hesitation. "I think you had a bad dream."

My entire fucking life, so far, is a bad dream. Until the day I met her. That's when everything changed. That's when I realized what was missing— that I need to own her. And I will. Only, I need to use her to further my end goal. I can't let go of that. Not when I have spent my entire life working toward it.

She reaches for me. I grab her wrist and haul her to me, flip her onto the bed and lean over her, all in one smooth move.

She stares up at me, her breath coming in pants. "A-xel," her chin wobbles, "are you okay?"

No, I'll never be okay. Not when I have to use the one good thing I have found in my life for my own selfish means, even knowing I will lose her because of it.

"A-xel, please," she whispers. "I only came in because I heard a noise and wanted to make sure you were okay. I didn't mean to disturb you, honestly."

I take in her pale features. The moonlight that slants in through the crack in the curtains highlights the red strands in her hair. Her green eyes are dilated. I lower my head and sniff at her neck. Her sweet orange blossom scent fills my senses. My cock instantly lengthens; my groin hardens. Fuck, she is potent.

"Axel, don't—"

She tries to scramble away, and I lower the weight of my body onto her, pinning her in place.

She must feel the thickness of my arousal, for she freezes. Every muscle in her body tenses. Her lips tremble.

"Everywhere I look, you're always there. Every time I try to turn away from you, I'm drawn back. Every time I want to stop thinking of you, you pop up in front of my eyes. Why is that?"

"I ... I don't know." She swallows. "I swear, I didn't mean any harm coming in here."

"So you say, when the fact is, you know exactly how to hurt me."

"I hurt you?" She frowns. "I'm not the one who insisted I should move into this stupid house and away from my family."

"Do you miss your family?"

"And if I do? As if you'll let me return to them."

"Do you want to return to them?"

She hesitates.

"Do you?"

"Yes," she bursts out, "I'm getting married in a few days, and I'd rather spend these last few days with my family in my childhood home, okay?"

A tear drop squeezes out from the corner of her eye, and I bend down and lick it up.

She shudders. "Why did you do that?"

"Fuck if I know." I peer into her features. "Fuck if I know why I do half the things I do around you. Fuck if I know why I'm sporting a constant hard-on when I think of you." I tilt my hips, and my already lengthening cock stabs into the soft flesh between her legs.

Her breath catches in her chest. She stares up at me with those fucking huge eyes of hers. She licks her gorgeous lips, and damn it, I'm lost. I lean in closer, unable to resist the temptation of tasting her just one more time. Just a sip, and I'll let her go. Besides, I'm still not going to let her come. This is simply a way of tasting her one last time. Then, I'll stay away until the wedding.

I lower my lips to hers when she bursts out, "What was your dream about?"

"What?" I blink.

"I heard you cry out. And when I walked in, you were thrashing around in your bedclothes. And you called out for your mom."

I stare at her for another second, then pull away. I sit on the side of the bed and lower my arms between my legs. "Get out," I say tightly.

"What?" She frowns.

"I said, get the fuck out of my suite."

"You don't mean it."

I glare at her, "Do I look like I don't mean it?"

"You … you look shaken."

"Oh?" I arch an eyebrow.

"Was it the shooting? Is that what you were dreaming about?"

I laugh. "If you think taking a bullet would cause me nightmares—" I shake my head. "On the other hand, perhaps it's the fact that I took a bullet for you that's causing me those dreams."

"Don't try to change the topic."

"I'm not," I drawl.

"I know it's difficult to talk about it, whatever it is, but maybe it will help."

"What will help is if you get your arse out of here."

"Thought you liked my ass?"

"Don't push it, Theresa," I say in a tight voice. "If I were you, I'd get the fuck out of here while I still can."

"Why can't you talk about it, Axel? You called for your mom, so you must be remembering things about your childhood."

"The one thing I'll never forget is what happened in my childhood," I snap.

"I'm sorry for whatever happened to you," she murmurs, "but at least, you're remembering everything. So that's a good sign, right?"

"What would be a good sign is if you got the fuck away from me at the moment."

The silence stretches for a second, then another. I shoot her a sideways glance and find her glancing at me with a hurt look on her face. Something hot stabs at my chest.

Goddamn it, this is what I was afraid of. Developing feelings for her. Wanting to take care of her. Needing to own her and keep her. *No, no, no, that's not possible.* There is one thing, and one thing only, that I want from her. And that is her subservience. Her ability to be the key to destroying the Sovranos. It's what I've worked toward, and I will not allow her to upend my plans, not when I have come this far. I rise to my feet. "I'm going to the bathroom, and when I come out, I want you gone."

I walk away from her.

Behind me, I hear her feet hit the floor, then footsteps approaching me.

"Axel, please," she pleads, "can't you, at least, share a little of what happened in your childhood? Does it have to do with the scars on your right forearm. Is that why you keep playing with your lighter when you're stressed, even though you don't smoke?"

What the fuck? How could she have noticed that? People seldom notice these details. They see something, and their minds complete the details. But Theresa—she spotted it right away. Anger lights a fire up my spine. How dare she try to find out everything about me? How dare she pay such close attention to me? How dare she walk into my room when I'm at my most vulnerable and then try to win my trust? I will never let anyone close. Those kinds of relationships are not for me. Not when I have one reason, and one reason only, to be alive. Revenge for what the Sovranos did to me and my mother.

"Axel, please say some—"

I turn around close the distance between us, then grab her by her neck and haul her toward me. I crush my lips to hers with such force that our teeth clash. A shudder grips her, then she's kissing me back with as much intensity. She opens her mouth, and I thrust my tongue inside. I suck on her tongue, drag my tongue over her teeth, and drink of her deeply. Then, I release her and step back so suddenly, she staggers. I grip her shoulder and right her. "You can leave and go home, if you wish, until the wedding." I turn and stalk into the bathroom.

By the time I return to the room, she's gone.

28

Theresa

What was that about? He was dreaming, no doubt about it. And he was crying out for his mother. I heard it. In that brief moment, his voice sounded frightened and childlike. It struck a chord in me, and I wasn't able to stop myself from trying to soothe him. I tried to reassure him and his eyelids flew open, and for a few seconds, he looked at me without comprehension. In those unguarded moments, I saw something in his eyes—helplessness, anger, and fear. So much fear. He was afraid for his life. Something happened to him when he was a child, something that scarred him for life and made him the man he is today. Cynical and unable to trust anyone. Someone who isn't even able to open up to his brothers. Oh, he's ready to do business with them, all right, but anything more than that is off the table.

As soon as he realized I had seen past the usual barriers he puts up against the world, and when I pushed him about the dream, he told me to get out. In all honesty, part of the reason I reminded him about the dream is because I knew that he was going to kiss me, and if he had, I might never have left the room. Which, maybe, wouldn't have been that bad, considering I was so turned on by him that I wasn't able to sleep earlier. But I didn't want him to kiss me just then. Not when I had finally glimpsed the man behind the monster, the human behind the unfeeling brute that he likes to pretend to be.

He lashed out at me then, tried to hurt me, and when I still tried to push it, he shut me up with that kiss. Oh my God, that kiss. He never can lie to me when he kisses me. He meant this kiss to be hard and punishing, but all I felt was his passion, his frustration, his need to connect with me, his need for me…

He yearns for me, that much is clear. He wants to do things to me… He… I squeeze my eyes shut. Oh my God. He wants to possess me, to crawl under my skin, inside my heart, into my head, occupy my every thought, be my breath, my sight, become the one thing I can't do without.

And I'll let him. I won't stop him. This is what he meant by his 'perversions.' I have no doubt now. I'll let him do to me whatever he wants. I want what he can do to me. Question is, will I survive it?

"Theresa?" My sister bursts through the door of my room.

I moved back in with my parents first thing in the morning because he told me to leave, and because I couldn't face another run-in with him so quickly after last night. I packed my bags and called Seb, who drove me home without a comment. He promised to be back within the hour to take me to the shop. Not that I don't want to spend time with my parents, but I can't keep away from the shop either.

The shop is my one accomplishment, and I intend to make sure I take good care of it. I don't intend for anything to sidetrack me from my business, not even once I'm married. So I've decided to show up to help Elsa, given I have the entire day stretching out in front of me without him to distract me.

"Sara," I turn to her, "what are you doing back from university?"

"What am I doing back from university?" She rolls her eyes. "You're getting married, T, and you thought I wouldn't come?"

"I didn't mean that," I murmur as I take in my sister's hair, which is dyed in a shade of—is that delphinium blue? Jesus, did she actually color her hair blue? Her face is wreathed in a big smile as she launches herself into my arms. "Oh my God, T! Oh my God, you're getting married! I can't believe you're getting married."

"Um," I pat her shoulder, "it was, ah, very sudden."

"I'll bet." She pulls back in the circle of my arms, then stares down at me from her much taller five-foot-nine-inch height. "Who is he?" She waggles her eyebrows. "Is it true that he is one of the Sovranos? That's what Mom told me. When are you going to introduce me to him?"

"Um…" I shuffle my feet. "You're going to meet him at the wedding."

"But that's still a few days off."

"It's only three days away." I scowl at her. "Besides, I won't be seeing him until the wedding."

"Really?" She blinks rapidly. "You're not going to see him before that?"

"Nope."

"You won't miss him?"

I hesitate.

"Aww," she pats my cheek, "look at you, so much in love. And all along, I thought after Xander you wouldn't be able to—" She claps a hand over her mouth. "Shit, didn't mean to blurt that out."

"It's okay." I grimace.

"No, it's not." She slaps her forehead with her palm. "You know me. Always saying things without thinking them all the way through. Shit, why can't I learn to be more like you?"

"You don't want to be like me." I wince.

"Why not?" She frowns. "You're petite, gorgeous, curvy, you run your own successful business, and now, you're marrying one of the most powerful men in the city."

"The jury is out on that," I murmur.

"What do you mean?"

"He's not one of the existing Sovrano brothers."

"Eh?" She tilts her head. "You're not making sense."

"He's, ah, Xander's long-lost triplet."

She opens and shuts her mouth. "Are you serious?" she finally chokes out. "Didn't Xander's twin Christian get married very recently?"

"Yep, and I'm going to marry Axel, his triplet. His *long-lost* triplet."

"Oh?"

"Y-e-a-p." I step back from her. "A triplet who, likely, hates all of his brothers and is only marrying me as a way of consolidating his position within the Cosa Nostra."

She blinks rapidly. "So you mean you're marrying him because—?"

"I want to," I murmur. "In fact, I'm the one who proposed to him."

"Get out of here..." She laughs. "You proposed to one of the *made* men of the Cosa Nostra?"

"So?" I scowl at her. "Can't women propose to men?"

"Of course, they can. It's just, you—"

"What about me?" I fold my arms across my chest.

"I mean, it's just you, Theresa. You have always been shy and self-effacing and—"

"Just because I'm the quiet one, doesn't mean I don't know what I want."

"I didn't say that—"

"Then what do you mean?"

Sara blows out a breath. "I'm not trying to fight with you, big sis. I know you and I, in the past, have not always seen eye to eye—"

"That's putting it lightly," I scoff.

She chuckles. "You really have changed since I last saw you."

"Which was, like, almost a year ago."

"Not my fault." Sara tosses her head. "Every time I wanted to come home, you encouraged me to stay on at university, to take on a few more credits, to study as much as possible."

"I know." I shuffle my feet. "I must have come across as so callous to you, right? Pushing you so hard."

"You meant well." Her tone softens. "I understand why you're so keen for me to ace my university results."

"If you do, you'll be able to find a job in a company... Maybe in a city like London. And you could be completely independent, away from the influence of the *Cosa Nostra*."

"You want me away from the *Cosa Nostra*, yet you are marrying into the clan?" she murmurs.

I draw in a breath. How do I explain it? "From the moment I saw Xander, I felt sure I was going to marry him. Then when he died, I ... I thought my world was coming to an end; until Axel stepped in front of me and took a bullet for me—"

"Hold on, someone shot at you?" she exclaims.

I shuffle my feet. "I don't think the bullet was intended for me, anyway." I shake my head. "The point is, as soon as I saw him, I had this inexplicable reaction to him. I felt an immediate connection, as if he were the piece I'd been missing all along."

"But—" she begins to say, and I hold up my hand.

"I know. Axel is not Xander. The more I get to know Axel, the more it's clear how different they are as people. And yet..." I lock my fingers. "Yet, I can't get it out of my head that this is my chance at happiness. I never took the initiative with Xander, and I don't want to make the same mistake with Axel. I feel like I've been given a second chance, and I don't want to waste it."

"Haven't you thought, it's because Axel looks like Xander that you should, maybe, walk away from him? That you may be marrying him for all the wrong reasons?"

I stare at her. "Are you only twenty-one?"

She chuckles. "I sound like an old woman, right?"

"No." I shake my head. "You are right, though. Those are all valid questions I have asked myself, but each time, I arrive at the same answer. That I want to marry Axel. I want to be with him. Maybe it's him I'm attracted to. Maybe it has nothing to do with the fact that he looks like Xander. I saw Axel, and it was like *colpo de fulmine.*" *A bolt of lightning.* I bite the inside of my cheek. "It wasn't like that with Xander. Oh, I thought it was, but what I felt for Xander pales in comparison to what I feel for Axel." I pull my hair up off of my shoulders. "Either way, fact is, I don't have a choice. This, the *Cosa Nostra* and Axel, are my future. You, on the other hand, don't have anything or anyone holding you back."

I take her hand in mine.

"You're starting with a clean slate, and I want you to see the world first. To discover what's out there and decide for yourself what kind of a future you want. If, after that, you decide that you want to return to Palermo and settle down here, that's fine. But I want to make sure that you have the options I never did, know what I mean?"

"Oh, T..." Sara squeeze my hand. "You're incredible. I'm so lucky to have a sister like you."

I blink rapidly. "I can't believe you're all grown up and about to graduate from university."

"Just because I color my hair blue doesn't mean that I'm still a kid."

"I know." I laugh and tug on a strand of her hair. "It suits you. It's quite striking, actually."

"Right?" She shakes the hair back from her face. "I figured I'd throw caution to the wind for once."

"As long as it doesn't interfere with your campus placements," I warn her.

"Oh, please, they look at my grades,my IQ, and acumen, not to mention, the way I get algorithms to bend to my will."

"I know you're a math whiz," I murmur. "Half the time, I don't know what kinds of problems you're solving in your head or how you manage to see those numbers and discern patterns among them."

"It's easy, really. All you have to do is take a step back and absorb the entirety of the problem that they pose to you. Then, you have to listen to what they're trying to tell you and—"

"Stop." I raise my hand. "It's all Greek to me."

"It's algebra, actually," she offers.

"That too." I laugh. "I don't know how the two of us could be so different. Me, the straight-laced one who loves flowers and the way they allow me to express my creativity, and you, the talkative nerd with the old soul who can bounce into a room and own it, not to mention, ride roughshod over numbers."

"Jeez, that was almost erotic."

"Shut up." I slap her shoulder.

"Speaking of, have you slept with Axel yet?"

I bite the inside of my cheek.

She stares.

"Oh my God." She claps her hands. "Theresa and Axel, banging in a tree. F-U-C-K-I-N-G," she sings at the top of her voice.

I scowl. "Shut up! See? This is why I don't like telling you anything. In some ways, you still haven't grown up at all."

"Theresa and Axel banging in a—"

I slap my hand over her mouth, or at least try to, for she ducks, then jumps up and races toward the door. " F-U-C-K-I-N-G."

Heat sears my cheeks. I jump up, lunge forward, and grab at her dress. I manage to grip the back of her shirt and tug. The shirt tears with a ripping sound.

Sara screams. "Mom, look what T did. She tore my shirt."

Footsteps sound, then my mom pops her head through the door. "Hush, your father's trying to take a siesta after lunch. And aren't you girls grownups? Surely, you can sort things out without squabbling like you were ten."

"Mom, Theresa and Axel are—"

I manage to slap my hand over her mouth this time. She tries to speak but the noises are indecipherable.

"What are you doing?" My mom frowns at me. "What is Sara trying to say?"

"Nothing," I say at the same time that Sara nods frantically. She gestures with her hand, says something, but again, the noises that emerge don't make sense.

"What is she trying to tell me?" My mom comes inside the room. "Is this about Axel and the wedding?"

I nod.

"Well?" My mom looks between us. "Are you going to remove your hand, so she can tell me?"

I shake my head.

"Don't be silly." My mom's scowl deepens. "You can't indefinitely gag your sister like this, you know?"

I nod. "She was saying that Axel and I are getting married."

"And?" She eyes me with a funny look.

"And … he's taking me on a honeymoon." I cringe. What the hell? That's a big, fat lie. Okay, maybe not, but I certainly don't know if he has a honeymoon planned. Or if he's even going to be strong enough to travel. Although, seeing how he stormed across town and to the nightclub, his recovery is progressing by leaps and bounds.

"Is he now?" My mother's face breaks into a big smile. "After your father and I married, we honeymooned on the Amalfi Coast. It was so hot, and we had this small beach house by the sea. We swam every day, ate dinner and—"

My sister digs her nails into my forearm. She widens her gaze at me.

"I'll release you, only if you promise to stay quiet," I hiss as my mother continues to relate the same story she has narrated to us over and over again throughout our lives.

She nods vigorously.

"Not a word out of you, you hear?"

She holds up her pinkie in the gesture of making a promise.

I lower my hand, and instantly, she bursts out, "Theresa and Axel banging in a—"

I leap toward her. She screams, dodges my outstretched arm, and runs around my mother, who watches us with a bemused expression. She hides behind my mother, and I try to reach around to grab at her. She screams again and takes off running, and I chase after her. "Wait until I catch you, you stupid girl. I'm going to pull on your hair and make sure you regret this for a very long time."

I chase her all the way to the front door, which she throws open and darts out, only to collide with Cass who was about to knock. Both of them stagger.

"Catch her," I yell.

Sara screams again, darts around Cass and runs off, past Karma, who turns to watch her take off out down the garden path, before she turns up the road.

I make to go after her, but Cass grabs my arm. "Hey," she chuckles, "was that your younger sister?"

"You mean, was that my pain in the ass sibling, then yes, she is." I glower at the now empty garden path.

"You two fight a lot growing up?" Karma asks as she draws abreast with us.

"All the time, and apparently, nothing has changed." I shake my head. "What are you two doing here, anyway?"

"Your wedding dress." Karma beams. "We're here to take you for a fitting."

29

Axel

"Nikolai Solonik." The man holds out his hand.

I ignore him and drop into my seat next to Michael. We're in a dingy space behind an Italian restaurant in Palermo.

Nikolai's jaw tightens, but he doesn't say anything as he takes his seat. He's dressed in a custom-fitted suit, his hair cropped close at his temples. Asshole resembles an investment banker, except for the tattoos which peek out from under his collar. For that matter, so do the two men standing behind him, who he doesn't bother to introduce. He doesn't need to, though. The facial resemblance declares that they are brothers.

"Sorry I'm late." An older man walks into the room. He must be in his mid-forties, with grey threading the wings at his temples. Like the other men in the room he, too, is dressed in a dark suit. Me? I opted to dress in jeans and a hoodie.

"JJ Kane." The man jerks his chin at me as he folds his height into the seat next to Nikolai.

"And here I thought, meeting in the room behind an Italian restaurant was something they did only in the Mafia movies," I drawl.

"It's the best Italian restaurant in Palermo." Michael shrugs. "Makes it convenient for us to adjourn for lunch."

"Food is important for you Italians, eh?" I shoot him a sideways glance.

"Hold on, you don't consider yourself Italian?" Nikolai leans back in his seat.

"I grew up in London; I consider myself English."

"You sound English," JJ offers.

"But you're of Italian origin?" Nikolai pushes.

I glare back at him. "My mother was a Mafia princess, if that's what you're asking," I say in a hard voice, "but I'm not Italian." I hold his gaze, and he nods.

"Yet, here you sit, by the side of the Don of the *Cosa Nostra*?"

A nerve throbs at my temple. "Your point being?"

He raises his hand. "Just making conversation," he says in a mild voice.

"I have a suggestion for you. Don't," I shoot back.

The silence stretches in the room. The men behind us shuffle their feet. Behind Nikolai, his brothers don't move a muscle. I swear, I haven't even seen them blink since I walked in here. Do the Bratva have a special school to which they send their men to be trained?

"Xander's loss has been hard on all of us," Michael finally murmurs, "but we have been fortunate to be reunited with his triplet, Axel." Michael surveys the two men seated opposite us. "I called this meeting, in good faith, to introduce both of you to the newest member of our family. Axel is also going to be a board member in our three-way partnership that encompasses the online businesses that we are running."

"You're going to make him a board member in Trinity Enterprises?" Nikolai straightens.

"You have a problem with that?" I smirk.

He scowls at Michael. "Take a number, triple it, and I guarantee, the three of us will come into enough money to increase our sphere of influence on a global scale," he snaps.

"I believe those were my words, and I stick by them," Michael replies.

JJ strokes his chin. "So you're bringing in your brother, but you continue to split the profits three ways?"

Michael nods.

"Still, your family would effectively double its representation, which doesn't seem fair."

"I'm not part of the family," I say in a hard voice.

Both Nikolai and JJ turn to me.

"Are you not a Sovrano?" Nikolai scowls at me.

I open my mouth to protest, and he raises his hand. "Like it or not, you are Xander's triplet. The Sovrano blood runs in your veins. You may have disputes with the rest of the family, but for the purposes of this discussion, you are one of them."

I squeeze my fingers into fists. He's right. It's something I have known since my mother revealed my background to me, and yet, it's also something I have refused to accept. Not when I have made it my life's ambition to destroy this family.

I glare at Nikolai, who glowers back at me.

Behind me, I sense Luca shift his stance. Seb takes a step forward, when one of Nikolai's brothers jerks his chin in his direction. Seb pauses. The tension in the room ratchets up. One of Nikolai's brothers locks his gaze on me; the other continues to watch my brothers carefully.

JJ stiffens.

Nikolai's jaw tics.

Next to me, Michael stays relaxed. "Down, boys," he says in a casual voice. "We can't afford to fight amongst ourselves."

JJ watches us warily.

Nikolai continues to glare at me.

Then JJ shakes his head. "You're right; we need to find an amenable solution."

"Nikolai?" Michael asks, and there's a tone of warning in his voice.

Nikolai holds my gaze for a few seconds more, then he turns to Michael. "I agree, we need to find a peaceful solution. When you agreed to splitting the profits three ways, the tacit agreement was that all three partners would have equal representation on the board, one from each of us."

Michael stays quiet for a few seconds. "That's true."

"What are you trying to say?" Nikolai asks.

"I'm saying that I'll take a step back from the enterprise."

"What?" Luca exclaims. "You'd give your place on the board over to him?"

Michael blows out a breath. "That's exactly what I'm saying."

Nikolai glances between us before he leans back in his chair.

JJ whistles under his breath. "You are giving up your seat on the board to him, ol' chap?"

Behind me, Seb moves restlessly, but unlike Luca, he doesn't express his opinion. Likely, it will be at a meeting with the brothers only, where he lets rip. If I had a brother, I'd want him to be like Seb. Or perhaps, like Adrian, who seems the calmest of all of them. Michael's the Don, Massimo takes too long to make decisions, Luca is the opposite, being too hot-headed, and Christian… Well, Christian hates me, and rightly so, after what I did to him and his family and…

What the fuck am I doing, thinking about my brothers instead of celebrating my victory? I should feel happy, right? The first step in my plan to destabilize the Sovranos is underway. I should move in quickly, take over the meeting, and set plans in motion to reap the benefits of the work done by the company so far.

Instead, I sit here quietly as Michael turns to me. "Fact is, I only took on a leadership role at Trinity Enterprises, because I'd promised my wife I'd focus more on legitimate businesses and phase out the illegal ones. A goal we all share." He glances about the faces at the table. "Now that this business is up and running, I want to focus on the other parts of the organization and accelerate their transition to being above-board. Taking this on, along with everything else that I have to do to steer the *Cosa Nostra* forward, has been a lot for me."

"It has?" I frown. Why is it that Michael doesn't view declaring this in front of his one-time enemies a show of weakness? Why does it not come across as a sign of vulnerability? If anything, his being honest about his inability to manage it all makes him seem more in control.

"I'd rather spend more time with my wife," he offers.

"What are you saying?" I scowl.

"Yeah, what exactly are you getting at, Michael?" Luca says in a hard voice.

Michael rises to his feet and walks over to the head of the table. He folds his arms across his chest and glances at his brothers—and no, I don't include myself in that category. "I know you guys trust me to make the right decision," he says in a matter-of-fact voice.

None of my brothers say anything to the contrary.

He turns to JJ and Nikolai, glancing at each of them in turn. "And I am a man of my word."

"I have no reason to doubt that," JJ confirms.

Nikolai merely raises an eyebrow.

Michael glances at me. "It's why I'm resigning from Trinity's board, effective immediately—"

"What the—?" JJ looks taken aback.

"*Cazzo*," Luca exclaims, "you're really going to do this, aren't you?"

I sense Seb wanting to say something, but he stays quiet.

"What the hell are you trying to do here?" I force out the words. "If this is some kind of delaying tactic—"

"It's not." Michael's lips kick up. "I'm giving you my position in Trinity."

"Don, what are you—" Luca begins to protest, but Michael holds up his hand.

"Can you give me a few minutes with my brothers?"

He addresses the question to JJ and Nikolai, who glance at each other, then they rise and leave the room, along with Nikolai's brothers.

Michael turns to us. "Axel will represent the Cosa Nostra on the board of Trinity. I will step down. It will remain a three-way partnership, the profits being split among three parties. That should satisfy the Kane Company and the Bratva. As for us"—he glances sideways at Luca—"with Xander gone, the proceeds will continue to be split among the seven of us within the Cosa Nostra, so the status quo is maintained. Does that answer your questions?"

30

Theresa

I come awake with a start. I'm not sure what woke me up, but it's still dark outside. I reach for my phone and check the time: two am.

Earlier, after trying on my wedding dress—which is beautiful; Karma outdid herself—Cass, Karma, and I headed out for drinks. We only had time for one round of drinks, then Cass and Karma had to leave. They mentioned the Sovrano brothers were meeting at Michael and Karma's place, and Karma wanted to get home before Michael returned, and Cass said that she had to get there to help with the food and drinks for the evening.

I'd asked if Axel was going to be there, but neither of them knew. They had invited me to accompany them, but I declined.

Also, I didn't want to return to my parents' place. There are only two nights to go until the wedding. And tomorrow night, I'll definitely have to spend at home, as I won't want Axel to see my dress before the wedding. Which means, I can spend tonight back at Axel's place.

I had left him, wanting to spend time with my family, but I can't stop thinking of him. To be honest, I haven't even slept properly since leaving him behind. I also wanted to check in on him and see how much he's improved since I last saw him. Besides, it's not wrong to want to spend time in your soon-to-be husband's home, right?

Strange, how I already think of the place as Axel's, even though it was Xander's first. Have I really replaced Xander with Axel in my head so quickly? No, don't answer that.

Either way, Karma didn't protest when I asked her to drop me off at Axel's place.

She asked if I was sure about wanting to spend the night there, and I said yes. After making me promise that I'd call Seb first thing in the morning and have him drop me off at home, she left, promising to have the dress with the final alterations delivered to my parents' home by tomorrow afternoon.

The household staff let me into the house before retiring for the night. Axel, himself, wasn't there, and while the staff had left dinner warming for us, I wasn't been hungry enough to eat. I walked over to Sheena's room—yeah, that's how desperate I was for company, that I wouldn't have minded hanging out with Sheena—but she wasn't in her room either. In fact, all of her things had been cleared out from her room. Huh? Had she left? Was her physiotherapy work with Axel already done? Of course, he hadn't mentioned it.

So, I returned to the kitchen, pulled a tub of ice cream from the freezer, popped some microwaveable popcorn, and then carried the whole thing back to what was my room, where I had watched reruns of *Friends* all evening while I finished off the feast.

When I still wasn't able to sleep, I walked over to Axel's room, crawled into his bed, and instantly fell asleep.

Now I swing my legs over the side of the bed and straighten. My stomach grumbles in protest, and I wince. Damn it, why did I have to finish off that tub of ice-cream? Seriously? The entire tub? I press a hand to my stomach, but that doesn't help. Maybe some herbal tea? Yeah, that might do the trick.

I had taken off my jeans before falling asleep, so dressed in my underwear and T-shirt, I walk down the staircase. Reaching the kitchen, I make myself a mug of herbal tea, then walk out and up the stairs. I pass the floor on which our bedrooms are located, then reach the top floor.

I have avoided coming up here so far, but somehow, it feels like it's time. The air here feels slightly musty, the stillness even more resounding. The hair on the back of my neck prickles, and a shiver runs down my spine. I cross the short hallway and push open the double-doors to Xander's studio.

Starlight pours in from the floor-to-ceiling windows and the massive skylight that makes up a big chunk of the ceiling. The silver glow illuminates the paintings that are stacked against one wall. Against the other wall, I can make out the shape of canvasses, and to the side, there is a massive fireplace.

I feel around on the wall and hit a switch. Light pours down from two floodlights, one at either end of the studio, to illuminate a half-finished canvas.

Goose bumps pop on my skin. The hair on the back of my neck rises. That … that must be the painting he was working on before his life was cut short. My hand trembles, and some of the hot tea splashes over the side and singes my skin. I yelp, then raise my hand to suck on my hurt skin. My gaze is, once more, captured by the figures on the canvas.

I walk toward it, trying to make out what I'm seeing.

There are three figures on the canvas. Three men of similar height with wide shoulders. The one on the right is dressed in a suit, the one in the middle is wearing jeans and a button-down shirt, and the one on the left is wearing jeans and a hoodie. All three have dark hair. The one on the right has piercing blue eyes, the one in the middle has blue-grey eyes, and the one on the left has eyes which are almost indigo in color. All three have similar features. All three look like Xander… No, the one on the right looks like Christian, but the other two could be Xander times two. They look so similar, like what Xander and Axel might have looked like if they stood next to each other, except for the slight variation in eye color.

Hang on a second. Xander never knew about Axel's existence. He died before Nonna confessed that entire story about Axel's existence, so how the hell did he come up with the idea of drawing a picture with all three of them? I take a step forward, then another. I reach the canvas, which is massive—at least, six-feet by six-feet in size. I glance between the image of the man in the center, which is Xander—there is no mistaking his blue-grey eyes—and the one of the man I'm sure is Axel. How did Xander know to draw his eyes that color? Did he know of Axel's existence? Had the two of them met? Is that how he knew to paint Axel's eyes that exact shade of indigo? I reach up my free hand to touch the image when, "Hello, Sunshine," his voice reaches me from behind.

I yelp and lose my grip on the mug, which falls on the draping that has slipped off the canvas, and comes to a stop.

I jump back, staring at the tea which has splashed onto the canvas. "No, no, no!" I bend, try to use the drape, which is made of some kind of liquid-resistant polyester, then the hem of my T-shirt to mop up some of the liquid. But the T-shirt is too short. *"Cazzo!"* The canvas is too heavy for me to move out of the way so I yank off my T-shirt, then sink to my knees and try to soak up the liquid.

A shadow falls over me, and I know he's standing behind me. But I don't turn. I continue to try to wipe up the tea from the canvas. Sweat beads my forehead, and it's not only from my ministrations to the painting. When it's clear I'm doing more harm than good, I finally straighten. The heat of his body instantly coils around me, and I shiver. Damn it, why did I think it was a good idea to take off my T-shirt?

There's a click, then the hiss of a lighter. I glance over my shoulder to find Axel standing behind me. The flame from his lighter burns white under the glare of the spotlight. He walks to the doors of the studio and yanks them closed. The thud of the doors closing reverberates through the space. I jump.

Without taking his gaze off of me, he reaches out and hits the light switch. The spotlight shuts off, leaving only starlight and the flame from the lighter glowing in the dark. It throws his face into relief, all hollows and planes and a jaw so hard it could have been hewn from granite.

A shiver runs down my spine.

He takes a step forward, then another. Reaching me, he bends forward, and I push back until my hip bumps against the canvas. He straightens my fallen mug, then draws himself up to his full height.

"Wh-what are you doing here?" My voice trembles. Damn it, why am I so nervous in his presence?

"I might ask you the same thing," he counters.

"When did you get back? I ... I didn't hear you," I reply.

"Answering a question with a question, Sunshine?" He leans toward me and his dark, masculine essence, combined with the scent of alcohol and cigars, envelops me. My belly flip-flops, and my nipples tighten. I only have to smell him for my entire body to turn into a mass of need.

"If you answer my question, I'll answer yours." I tip up my chin. His blue eyes darken until they seem like the sky at night.

"When you get sassy, it's a fucking turn-on. It makes me want to shut you up with my cock down your throat," he growls.

"Gesù Cristo." My thighs clench, my toes curl, and a pulse flares to life between my legs. I shouldn't be aroused by his filthy words, but dammit, I can't get rid of the images his words have painted in my mind.

His nostrils flare. "I returned from my meeting to find my wife-to-be asleep in my bed. So innocent. So pure. Your lips were parted, your cheeks flushed as you slept. You had thrown off your covers, and I couldn't take my gaze off of your creamy thighs, the shadowy region between them, only partially covered by your blanket. I wanted to lean over and run my nose up your inner thigh."

Heat flushes my chest.

"To bury my face in your pussy and draw your scent inside. To push your panties aside as I thrust, first my fingers, then my tongue inside your channel, until you were wet and wriggling under me. Then, I wanted to bite down on your cunt until you came."

The pulse between my legs speeds up until I can feel it in every part of my body.

"And while you were still in the throes of orgasm, I would have thrown your legs over my shoulders and slammed my cock inside you in one smooth move. I would have buried myself up to the hilt. I would have stuffed myself inside you until you had felt me in your throat."

A moan bleeds from my lips.

"But I didn't. I didn't want to disturb your sleep. So instead, I walked out and came up here to my dead triplet's studio. That answer your question?"

My throat hurts. My scalp tingles. A bead of sweat slides down the valley between my breasts.

He straightens, and I draw in a breath. The air rushes into my lungs, and I gasp.

"Your turn…" He tilts his head. "What are you doing here?"

"I…" I swallow. "I wanted to talk to you."

He rolls his shoulders. "No, you didn't."

I frown. "I promise, I came here to talk to you. I had Karma drop me off, and tomorrow morning, Seb is coming to pick me up at eight, so—"

"Don't lie." His voice cuts through the space between us. "Don't fucking lie, Theresa."

I swallow.

"Tell me why you came here today."

I shake my head.

He holds up the lighter so the flame is directly in front of my face.

"Axel," I gulp, "why are you so angry?"

"Angry?" He chuckles. "You think I'm angry because my wife-to-be came to visit me two days before our marriage so I could fuck her silly? Why should I be angry because of that?"

I draw in a sharp breath. "That's not true. I didn't come here to sleep with you."

"Who said anything about sleeping?" He reaches out and tucks a strand of hair behind my ear. His touch is gentle and yet threatening at the same time.

"You … you don't scare me, Axel," I finally say, but my tone is timid, the words hesitant.

Axel's lips twist, and it's not a nice smile. "I think I am going to change your mind tonight, baby."

He steps back, then prowls over to the back of the room. He raises the lighter to what looks like a sconce in the wall. The candle in the nook lights up, and he moves on to the next, and the next, until a row of candles on the back wall have all been lit up. He continues to light more candles in candle-holders which have been placed in a circle around a chair. When he's done, he flicks off the lighter and pockets it. Then he walks across to the chair and drops into it.

"Why did he have so many candles in a paint studio?" I glance around the place and take in the turpentines, canvasses, oil-based paints, not to mention the wooden frames or the drapings that cover the paintings. "There's way too much flammable material here."

"I placed the candles," Axel clarifies.

I whip my head around. "You did?"

He nods.

"Wh-why would you do that? Isn't it dangerous?"

His lips twitch. "We're about to find out."

At some point, he lost his hoodie, for all he has on now is a grey T-shirt that clings to his wide shoulders. His jeans ride low on his waist, and he widens his legs so the bulge at his crotch is clearly visible. My nipples harden. I don't need to look down at myself to know that they'll be standing to attention. And of course, I had taken off my bra earlier, so I'm naked to his perusal. His gaze, though, stays on mine. It holds me, seems to draw me in. I take a step forward, then another. He widens his stance further then slides his hand inside the waistband of his jeans and begins to rub himself. It's dirty, filthy, and so damn hot. The flesh at the apex of my thighs throbs. My fingers tingle. I want to touch myself. I want to mirror him. I want to slip my fingers inside my aching pussy and get myself off. I raise my hand to do just that, but he shakes his head.

"You will not touch yourself, Sunshine, not until I give you permission."

31

Theresa

"Wh-what do you mean?" I stutter

"Exactly what I said." He lowers the zipper of his jeans, pulls his cock out, and begins to stroke himself. *Don't look down, don't!* My gaze lowers to where he grips his dick at the base, then proceeds to swipe his fingers up to the crown, repeatedly. The wet sound of flesh meeting flesh fills the space.

Heat flushes my cheeks, and my shoulders tremble. *What the hell am I doing here? Why did I come to his house in the first place? And damn it, I'm already thinking of this as his house and not Xander's. That's okay, right? Isn't this what Xander would have wanted? For me to marry his brother? Would Xander have been jealous? Why am I thinking of Xander when I'm standing almost naked in front of his brother who is pleasuring himself, for my benefit? Get out of here. Go away, leave … until the wedding. You're going to see him at your wedding. You're going to marry him, and then you're going to watch him get off every day, you're going to allow him to get you off, to fuck you as much as he wants.* My scalp tingles. All of my pores seem to pop.

I turn to leave, and that's when he growls, "On your knees."

I hesitate. He narrows his gaze.

"Now," he snaps. I blink.

I sink down and ignore the pain that shoots up my thighs when my knees connect with the wooden floor boards.

"Good girl; now crawl to me."

It doesn't even occur to me to refuse him. I lower my hands to the floor and begin to crawl to him. My heart begins to race, my pulse pounds at my temples, and my lower belly cramps with heat as I watch his gorgeous cock lengthen and throb, the head almost purple with desire as he continues to massage himself.

I pause in front of him, and his actions speed up. The planes of his chest grow solid, the veins of his forearm stand out in relief, and a groan rips from his throat.

"Rise to your knees," he orders.

As soon as I do, he comes, shooting his cum across my breasts.

"Fuck," he growls, "that's bloody hot." He reaches over and rubs the white, ropy strands into my skin.

I can't move. Can't take my gaze off the contrast between his dark skin and my pale flesh. He drags his fingers up my chest and locks his fingers around the nape of my neck. "Who do you belong to?" He hauls me up and places his forehead against mine. "Tell me, Sunshine—who do you belong to?"

I swallow. I want to say the words, want to tell him what he wants to hear, but I can't.

"Tell me." His voice lowers in frustration. "Tell me, Sunshine."

"Xander," I say in a whisper, "I will always belong to Xander. You're just a substitute, someone to stand in for him. I couldn't have him, so instead, I decided I would marry you and hold onto the man who looks so much like him, I—" I cough, for he's tightened his hold around my throat. I try to draw in a breath, and my lungs burn. *Shit, what the hell am I doing? Why am I provoking him? Why is it that every time I see him I want to do something to aggravate him? What I'm saying isn't even true.* It's as if I become a different person when I'm with him—a more interesting person, someone who finds her backbone, someone who wants to stand up against him, someone who is falling in love with him. *Hell!* I rear back, but he doesn't let me go. His grasp is so tight now that specks of black flicker at the edges of my vision.

"What did you say?" he asks in a soft voice.

I try to speak, but end up coughing.

"Damn you." He stares into my eyes, his own burning with pain and hurt and something else … something that seems like torment?

He releases me so suddenly that I collapse onto the floor. I draw in a breath, and the rush of oxygen to my starved lungs makes me almost black out again.

"Shit…" He shakes his head. "Did I hurt you?"

He reaches for me. I try to skitter away, but this time, he hauls me up and into his lap. He holds me to his chest. "Sorry, Sunshine," he murmurs. "Didn't mean to scare you like that. But the things you say… It's like you know exactly how to get under my skin."

I curl against him, absorbing the comfort that he offers me. We stay like that for a few seconds, then I nod toward the painting. "Did the two of you meet? Is that how he painted you?"

"We never met," his voice rumbles in his chest. "The first I realized that we were triplets was when Michael mentioned him to me."

"But you knew you had brothers, right? Your mother must have told you?"

"My mother didn't tell me anything, except to stay away from the Sovranos. So naturally, the first thing I did when I left home was to find out everything I could about them."

"Then how?" I fix my gaze on the painting, on the images of Xander and the man who has to be Axel next to him on the canvas. "I don't understand."

"Neither do I, to be honest," Axel admits.

"Maybe he intuitively knew about your existence?" I peer through the gloom at the canvas. "Aren't twins and triplets supposed to sense each other and stuff? Maybe he had a feeling about you. After all, he was an artist, and aren't artists supposed to be more in tune with themselves and the world? So maybe, he kind of guessed about your existence?"

"Maybe he was just doodling or something." Axel blows out a breath. "Though that's not exactly what I would call a doodle." He laughs in a self-deprecating tone. "That likeness is scary; it's like looking into a mirror. And the way he's drawn himself and Christian, I can almost see the three of us standing together in real life. He was a talented artist."

"You sound surprised." I try to sit up, but he doesn't release me.

"I am," he admits. "I knew he was an artist, but that he was this good?" He shakes his head.

"He never bragged about his art. It was a way of life for him, and he wasn't temperamental or anything; he was always so happy, so full of life. Sometimes, though, I thought I caught a glimpse of the conflict inside him."

"Conflict?" Axel pauses. "You think he was unhappy deep inside?"

"He was confused about his sexuality. Or, rather, he knew he was bisexual, but it wasn't something he was open about. I mean, it's not easy when you are born into an orthodox Catholic family, and a Mafia one at that, to come out and proclaim what you are without some kind of backlash."

"You think the Sovranos wouldn't have accepted him?"

"The brothers would have supported him, but Nonna? Not likely that she would have encouraged him to explore his sexuality." I laugh humorlessly.

"Not like he needed their permission." He drags his fingers through my hair. "He could have left home. He could have opted to find out more about himself and forged his own path."

"It's not easy when you have the pull of family behind you. And it's not like the brothers would have let him simply disappear. Wherever he went, they would have kept tabs on him."

"Oh?" He stills. "You think they'd have kept eyes on him, regardless of where he was."

"One-hundred percent." I turn to him. "Once you're a part of the Sovranos, they are not going to just let you leave, you know. They'll make sure they know where you are at all times."

"So they can control you?"

"So they can protect you. The *famiglia* has a lot of enemies, and you can't fight them alone."

"I don't need their help." His jaw hardens. "I've been taking care of myself so far, and I plan to do so for the foreseeable future."

"I know, but don't underestimate their enemies. You are now a Sovrano, and that itself will have drawn the attention of those who want to get even with them."

"You're worried about me?"

"I know you can take care of yourself," I murmur, "but after what happened to Xander—"

"Goddammit, I'm not Xander." He pushes me off his lap so suddenly, I hit the ground.

He rises to his feet and walks past me to the painting. He stares at it for a few seconds, then grips his hair and tugs on it. "Fuck," he says in a low voice, "fuck, fuck, fuck, why does this have to be so complicated?"

"What's complicated?" I rise to my feet. "You're not making any sense, Axel. One second, I'm sure you feel something for me. The next second, I'm sure that you hate me."

"I hate myself." He turns on me, "I hate myself for being attracted to you."

He glances about the space, as if searching for something.

"What is it?" I swallow. "What are you looking for?"

"I fucking hate that I've allowed myself to be trapped in this situation."

"Trapped? Situation?" I frown. "What are you talking about?"

He sweeps his eyes across the room again, then his gaze lights up. He stomps over to a corner of the room where there is a pile of easels stored against the wall. Next to it is a bunch of brushes placed in a brush holder. He pushes it aside and the brushes spill onto the floor. He kicks a blank canvas aside, then throws another over his shoulder. It falls to the ground with a thud. I jump. What the hell is he doing? What the hell is he looking for?

He grabs a plastic bottle containing a transparent liquid and rises to his feet. He walks toward the giant fireplace, then pauses in the stone area in front of the fireplace before he turns to face me.

The light from the candles flows over him, highlighting the hollows under his cheekbones, the grooves on either side of his lips, the lines radiating out from his eyes. His tanned skin glows almost golden in this light. He seems like a pagan god, a deity at whose feet I must worship. An outlaw who will never follow the rules of society. A fugitive on the run from himself. A feral creature who cannot be tamed by the laws of the land. A man who'll never bend, who'll never concede defeat to another.

"Axel," I whisper, "who are you really?"

He bares his teeth, then flips the lid of the bottle. He upturns it on himself so the liquid splatters across his T-shirt, over his arms, his neck, his face. Then he throws the empty bottle aside. The smell of alcohol envelops me, and the hair rises on the back of my neck.

"No," I whisper, "don't do this."

I rush toward him, but it's too late. He flicks the lighter, holds the flame to his shirt, and sets himself on fire.

32

Theresa

"Nooo!" I jump forward. "Why would you do that? Axel, what the hell?" I throw myself at him. I beat at the flames, but it seems to make no difference. "No, no, no." I throw my arms around his neck and cling to him. Maybe if I plaster myself to him I can snuff out the flames. Maybe if I cling to him closely enough, so there's no space for air between our skin, I can put out the fire? "Axel, Axel," I bury my nose in his chest, push my breasts into his chest, and that's when I realize that the flames have gone out.

"What the hell?" I release him and stagger back to find him laughing down at me.

"*Cazzo*," I hiccup, "what's wrong with you? What did you do? What happened to the flames?"

"They are gone."

"Why did you set yourself on fire?"

"A party trick." He raises a shoulder. "I poured the rubbing alcohol on myself and the flames caught. But they don't burn."

"What?" I stare at him, "You ... you..."

"Pretended to set myself on fire."

"Why would you do that?"

"To test you, of course." He smirks. "A test which you passed with flying colors, Sunshine, I—"

The next second, my palm connects with his cheek, and his neck snaps back.

"What the hell is wrong with you?" he growls.

"What the hell is wrong with *me*? What the hell is wrong with *you*?" I yell back. "You set yourself on fire, you set yourself on fire ... you ...you..." I throw myself at him, and I must surprise him, for when I connect with his chest, he lurches back. "You ... you ... *stronzo.*" I bury my fist in his side.

He grunts.

"You *facisa di merda.*" I snap my head forward; he manages to step aside. I stumble forward, but that only pisses me off further. I turn, kick out, and catch him in the shin.

"Hey," he winces, then grabs my shoulder, "get a hold of yourself."

"You get ahold of yourself, you ... you *testa di cazza*. I hate you, I hate you. I. Hate. You." I raise my hand again, and this time, he grabs my wrist, then pivots me around and twists my arm behind my back. He hauls me back against his chest and that dark, edgy scent of his, now drenched with the smell of burnt alcohol, laces my nostrils. The heat of him surrounds me, tugs at me, and I shiver. And that only makes me even more mad.

"Let go of me," I snarl.

"Nope."

I try to kick at his legs, but this time, he anticipates my move and evades me. He yanks me back along with him, until we reach the chair where he was seated earlier. He drops into it and pulls me into his lap again.

"Oh, no, no, no!" I wriggle in his grasp "Let go of me."

"Can't."

"I don't want anything to do with an idiot who sets himself on fire just to ... to..." I burst into tears. Holy hell, I don't want to cry, don't want to cry, not over this asshole who pulled a stunt like that for... What? "Why? Why? Why did you do that?" I finally manage to force the words out.

"Just for the effect?" he ventures.

That only makes me cry harder. "You're an asshole."

I manage to turn around and slap his face again.

"Motherfucker," he growls. My fingerprints are clearly visible on his cheek. *Good*.

"You're completely crazy," I spit out. "What the hell were you thinking, doing that?"

"I wasn't thinking."

"Clearly, not," I say through gritted teeth. "When I saw the flames... I... I ...." I shake my head. "I thought you ... you..." I burst into tears again, and this time, he pulls me close.

He drags me against him, wraps his arms around me, and presses me close to him. He tucks my head under his chin and rocks me. "I'm sorry, Sunshine, really I am. I'm not sure what came over me. But I was tired of being in Xander's studio, sitting in his chair, holding his one-time girlfriend, surrounded by his talent, and I wanted to make a point."

"So you set yourself on fire?" I burst out.

He winces. "I... I have a strange relationship with fire," he murmurs. "It started when I was very young. As you know, my mother became a sex-worker to support us. Initially, she rented a room in London's East End, which is all she could afford. Her clients came to visit her, and normally, she saw them when I was at school or outside playing. Once, though, one of her clients came when I was home from school. I was ill that day, so my mother was taking care of me. This client, though, wouldn't take no for an answer. He barged in, insisted on being with her. So she made me as comfortable as possible in the closet, and I must have fallen asleep. When I woke up, the closet was filled with smoke. I saw the flicker of flames through the slats in the door," he swallows, "and I began screaming for my mother, but there was no answer."

"What happened then?"

"I lost my mind, threw myself against the door, which gave away. I stumbled outside to find the client gone, my mother unconscious from the smoke, and the room on fire."

"Oh my God!" I grip his hand. "How did you escape?"

"I threw open the door, tried to drag my mother out, but she was too heavy. I ran outside screaming just as the firemen burst onto the landing. One of them spotted me right away. He came over and rescued me. I was still yelling at them to save my mother. A second fireman ran by us, and he carried my mom out of the room. Only then did I allow myself to lose consciousness.

When I woke up, I was in a hospital and the same fireman who had saved me was sitting next to me. He told me that my mother was okay and that everything was going to be fine."

"And was it?" I whispered. "Did everything turn out fine?"

"I'm here, aren't I?"

"That's not an answer."

"What was the question?" His lips twist.

"Did things improve after that?" I ask.

"Thomas Sutton—that was the name of the fireman who saved me—he married my mother," he replies.

"He did?" I brighten. "So you found a home and a father?"

"Briefly." He draws in a breath. "Their marriage didn't last long. Turns out, my mother was addicted to the sex, so she couldn't stay faithful. She began turning tricks. Thomas tried to put up with it as long as possible. But their marriage broke up, and my mother went back to whoring, only this time, as a higher-end call girl. She began making enough money to put me through private school. She passed away when I was sixteen, and Thomas became my guardian. He adopted me, and I took his surname. I stayed with him until I turned eighteen."

"So, things still turned out okay."

"If it weren't for the fire, Thomas wouldn't have come into my life," he agrees.

I trace the scars that run up his forearms. "These are from that fire."

He nods. "I admit, I still have nightmares about that sometimes."

"That's why I heard you scream in your sleep the other night."

"Not proud of it," he murmurs, "but I survived."

"It's not a sign of weakness to admit that you are still traumatized by something that happened when you were a child." I cup his cheek. "I'm glad you told me. I think, maybe I understand you a little better now."

"Do you?" he asks, a strange look in his eyes. "Do you really get me?"

"Not completely…" I search his features. "But maybe, I'm a step closer to getting to know you better."

He holds my gaze, and the tension between us ratchets up. He wraps his fingers around the nape of my neck, and I shiver. He leans in close enough for our eyelashes to mingle. This close, I can see the specks of silver in his eyes. Then his nose bumps mine, and his mouth is on mine. He kisses me deeply, thrusts his tongue inside my mouth and robs me of my breath completely. He hauls me closer, grips my hip, slides his palm across my butt and squeezes my ass as he continues to ravish my mouth. He glides his fingers in between my legs and pushes my panties aside. I gasp, then huff when he thrusts his fingers inside my slippery channel. He weaves his fingers in and out of me, and I wriggle under his ministrations.

Heat explodes in my lower belly, and I try to pull away, but he doesn't let me. He continues to cram his fingers in and out of me. Each time he hits that spot right in the center of me, goose bumps pop on my skin. I strain toward him, even as I try to get away from him, but he doesn't give up. He speeds up his actions as he continues to kiss me, with his eyes open, holding my gaze, as he grinds the heel of his hand into my clit, and with his other hand, he pinches my nipple.

He adds another finger inside me, stretching me, filling me, then releases my nipple only to pinch down on my clit. A trembling grips me. That's when he tears his mouth from mine and pulls his fingers out of me. He holds my fingers to my mouth as I gasp.

"Lick me clean," he orders. And I can't help it. I have to do as he commands. So, I open my mouth, and when he shoves his fingers inside my mouth, I drag my tongue around his digits. He pulls them out, then wipes them on my naked chest. Then, he pulls me off his lap and places me on my feet. He stands up and guides me over to where I dropped my T-shirt. He tugs it over my head, ensuring I thread my arms through the sleeves before he straightens the hem.

"Why didn't you let me come?" I hiss. "Why the hell didn't you let me climax?"

"Just because I told you my life story, doesn't mean I'm going to go easy on you."

I shake my hair back from my face. "You're a sadist."

He laugh. "You're right. You're beginning to understand me now."

I pull away from him, and he lets me. I march up to my room, pull on my jeans, grab my phone and bag, and march downstairs. By the time I reach the bottom of the steps, I've dialed Seb's number. Except, Axel grabs my phone and switches off the call. "I'll drive you home."

33

____

Axel

I tuck my button-down shirt into the waistband of my dark jeans. Hey, at least they are dark in color—my one concession to getting married in church. Church? I'm getting married in church, in front of a minister and everything. Jesus H. Christ. Nope, the irony is not lost on me. I'm swearing, using the name of the Lord, while I'm bemoaning the fact that I'm going to take my marriage vows in front of Him. What a bloody farce. I reach for my jacket and shrug it on. My fingers itch, and I grab up my lighter and flick the flame on and off. On and off. I stare at the flame, the hottest part of which is right above the tip of the flame. The yellow heart of it is where it's the least hot. Strange, right?

You'd expect the innermost part of the flame to be the most lethal, yet it's the coldest. It's what I have in common with fire. My heart will not burn for her. Whatever happens to me affects me on the surface, but never penetrates the inner core of me. And that's good. It's the only way I can stick to the plan. The only way I can see this through to the end without my emotions messing everything up.

I straighten my cuffs when the door opens. Nonna steps inside the room. She's wearing a blue dress that flows to her ankles. The pearl-accented stilettos she's wearing add height to her already upright posture. I stiffen and watch as she walks over to stand next to me. "Axel," she murmurs, "I hope I'm not interrupting?"

"And if I told you, you were?"

"It wouldn't make a difference." Her lips kick up.

"That's what I thought." I chuckle. "Why don't you have a seat?"

She turns to face me. "This won't take long."

I lower my chin and survey her from my greater height. Her silver hair is coiffed perfectly, her make-up is flawless, and the lines on her face only add gravitas to her presence. She regards me with her faded blue eyes, no doubt taking stock of me as I do the same to her.

"You're so handsome…" She reaches up and pats my cheek. "*Nipotino mio.*"

"Which means—?"

"An affectionate term for grandson."

"Right…" I shuffle my feet.

"I take it terms of endearment make you uncomfortable."

"No…" I shake my shoulder. "It's just not what I'm used to."

"You're part of the *famiglia* now, and we can be quite expressive."

"You don't say." I wince.

"You sound so English." She chuckles. "And yet, when I look at you, all I can see—"

"Don't say Xander," I snap.

"I was going to say, my husband."

"Oh?"

"He was very like you. Not at ease with overt emotions. He also hated formal wear. In fact, for our wedding, he wore a button-down and a pair of jeans like yours. Unlike you, he also refused to wear a jacket. Of course, it was in the summer so he could get away with it."

I stare at her steadily. "Why are you here, Nonna?"

She reaches up and brushes imaginary dust off my shoulder. "I thought I saw a little of him in all my grandsons, but when I saw you, I knew it was you who is closest in nature to him."

"Is that right?" I murmur.

She nods. "Your force of will, your focus, how you recovered from being hit and focused on getting back on your feet; how you never let being hurt get in the way of everything you want to achieve."

"And what is it that I want to achieve?"

"Trust, of course." She straightens the lapel of my jacket. "In only a few weeks, you had Michael give you a seat at the negotiating table, something he hasn't shared with any of his other brothers. And yet, none of the others openly protested against him."

"Luca did."

She smirks. "That doesn't count. It was expected that Luca would; he's the hot-headed one."

"He's also the one person who I haven't been able to get close to," I admit.

"But the others seem to be impressed by what they have seen of you. Enough to rally behind you for this wedding. They loved Xander and regarded Theresa as the sister they never had. They didn't protest when Theresa decided to marry you. It's interesting that the proposal came from her, don't you think?"

"I'm not sure what you're trying to imply?"

"You swept her off her feet with such speed that she didn't have a choice but to find a way to bind you to her."

"Are you saying that I forced her to propose to me?" I laugh.

"I'm saying that she fell head over heels in love with you. You gave her what Xander never could. You were the face of the man she could never have with the heart of a man she shouldn't have."

"I'm not sure what you are saying." I cross my forearms over my chest, letting my biceps bulge.

"What I'm trying to say is that I know you don't love her, and if you hurt her in any way, I will make sure that you regret ever returning to the family. Not that I think you will, of course."

"Of course." I tilt my head. "I appreciate your watching out for Theresa, but I think you underestimate her."

"Eh?"

"She may be tiny, but underneath that fragility is a backbone, a strength that will ensure that she always stands up for herself, that she'll never let anyone walk all over her. Least of all, me. She is a survivor, Theresa is, and I plan to make sure that nothing ever takes that indomitable spirit away from her."

Nonna stares at me as if taken aback by my words, then a wide smile splits her face. I blink because now she looks beautiful, like the picture of what a mother should be. The mother I never had. Oh, don't get me wrong. My own tried her best to protect me, but even as a child, I was aware that she always fell short of making the right decisions. I was too young to ever steer her back on track, so I could only watch as she imploded her own life. If I'd had a Nonna in my life, it might have turned out so very differently.

"Lean down, boy," she commands.

"What?"

"Lean down." She scowls at me. "How else am I supposed to kiss your cheek?"

34

───────

Axel

I stare straight ahead past the priest, at the beautiful stained-glass window that soars above us. The light from the sun pours through the pane, illuminating the yellows and blues and splintering into the colors of the rainbow which fill the space.

"You okay?" Seb's low voice sounds next to me.

I'm not, but I will be. "Yeah." I nod without turning to glance at him.

"It's okay to be nervous," this from Massimo who flanks my other side.

Yep, the Sovranos had turned out in full force to support me on the day of reckoning, aka, my wedding. My bloody wedding, in a bloody church.

My ma had insisted on going to Mass every Sunday. She might have tried to leave her Mafia roots behind, but her faith in the One Above had never been shaken. It's why, after she died, I never went back. What was the use of believing in God when he had basically decided that your life was going to be a shit show, and no matter how much you prayed, it was going to stay a shit show? What explanation could there be for how my mother's life had turned out? When I dared to point that out to her, she cuffed me on the head and told me never to repeat those blasphemous words again. So instead, I have decided to enter this marriage under false pretenses and have the lie blessed by Him. Well, why not? I've committed enough crimes, so what's adding one more to the mix, eh?

"Axel," Massimo's voice prompts me, "you sure you're okay?"

"Why does everyone keep asking me that?" I run a finger around the collar of my button-down shirt. At least I wasn't guilted into wearing a tie. I blow out a breath, then roll my neck, trying to work out some of the tension in my shoulders.

"It will be over all too soon," Seb reassures me.

"Then all you have to do is contend with the ol' ball and chain for the rest of your life," Luca drawls.

"Shut the fuck up, Luca," Seb snaps.

"Not saying anything that the rest of us aren't thinking," Luca chortles.

"The fuck are you doing?" Adrian admonishes him, "Man's already nervous—"

"I am not nervous."

"Okay, man's not nervous, but he can't help sweating, even though it's freezing right now in church and—"

I turn on Adrian, who raises both hands. "Sorry, *fratellino*, just trying to lighten the atmosphere."

"Well, don't," I growl, then turn back to my perusal of the goddamn window. Tell me again, why the hell did I agree to this? Oh, yeah, because it's the only way to put my plan in motion—to get revenge on the Sovranos, once and for all. And if, during that process, she gets hurt… Well, too bad. There's always collateral damage, after all. Wasn't I the collateral damage in the tussle between my mother and the Sovrano family? And if they hadn't let her go, if my father had been a better man, if my nonna had intervened, my mother might still be alive today. But she's gone, and I'm here, and I'm finally going to get my revenge for her death.

"One tip for you." Seb leans close.

"Not interested," I snap.

"Oh, I think you should listen to this one," Massimo cautions.

"It's about the kiss," Seb adds.

"Kiss?" I shoot him a sideways glance. Like the others, he's dressed in a black suit, with a bowtie and hair slicked back. Together, they look like the quintessential Mafia clan, the kind you'd see in movies. Only, this is my life, and I need every bit of focus I can muster. "You were saying?" I murmur as I take in the slight bulge at his hip under his jacket. Yep, they're all packing, except me. Not that I've had access to one. Not that I asked. Michael offered and I turned it down. I wanted nothing to distract from the wedding, and I wanted all of them to be lulled into a state of complacency.

"The priests here don't like more than a chaste peck on the cheek after the wedding."

"Eh?" I scowl.

"But don't let that stop you from kissing the bride."

"Thanks for the fucking tip." I glower at him.

"You're welcome." He smirks.

I roll my shoulders, and this time, Massimo slaps me on the back. "Relax, champ, you've got this."

Right.

On the pews, people shuffle their feet, someone coughs, a baby cries out and is shushed.

"Think Nonna forgot to invite anyone?" I ask.

"Nope." Seb chuckles. "It's tradition. Whenever a Sovrano gets married, everyone turns out. Somehow, Michael managed to get away with a low-key wedding. Since then, she's sworn that each time one of us gets married, she is going to make sure it's a bigger wedding than the last."

No kidding. Once more, I glance around at the huge arrangements of flowers that fill the space. It's quite beautiful, actually, and the entire place smells like a garden. Roses, lilies, hibiscus, apple blossoms. I stiffen. The hair on the back of my neck rises. On cue, the church organ strikes up the wedding march.

"This is it," Seb whispers, "and just so you know, I have the rings."

The rings that Nonna had chosen and which I had gone along with. To be honest, I barely paid any attention to them when Seb showed them to me earlier. It doesn't matter, really—not when this entire wedding is a sham. So why does everything feel so much more real right now?

A ripple runs through the crowd, and I know she's walking down the aisle. Massimo draws in a breath. "Mamma Mia, she's beautiful."

I refuse to turn.

"*Gesù Cristo*, she's a vision." Adrian slaps my shoulder. "You are a lucky son of a bitch."

I wince and stare straight-ahead.

"Whoa," Seb gasps, "what the hell is she wearing?"

What the fuck? If she's wearing something that exposes too much of her, I'll—I turn to watch her approach and promptly forget to breathe.

She walks toward me dressed in a simple white gown that covers her shoulders with a high collar at the back and a simple neckline that hints at her cleavage without exposing anything. The lace and pearl-covered bodice stretches across her gorgeous breasts. The sleeves are a lace lattice that stretch all the way to her wrists. The dress cinches at her waist, then flows down in a simple A-line skirt to her ankles. It's tight enough to show off her curves without being obscene in any way. On her head, she wears a delicate tiara from which her veil floats over her face. In her hands, she holds a burst of pink and white apple blossoms. Her other hand is threaded through Michael's.

She mentioned to me that her father uses a walker, but I didn't realize she'd asked Michael to walk her down the aisle instead. I should have known about this, right? But then, I wasn't interested in finding out any details about the wedding. Not when it didn't mean anything to me. It doesn't. So why can't I take my gaze off of her as she comes to a pause in front of me? Why is my heart beating so fast? Why is my pulse pounding at my temples? Sweat pools under my armpits as Michael smiles down at her, then leans around her in my direction. "Hurt her, and I'll kill you." His smile widens as he grips my shoulder, then steps back.

I take in the paleness of her cheeks, visible through the lace of her veil.

I turn to face the priest, who begins to drone. I draw in a breath, then another, forcing myself to focus. Focus. All of my senses click into place. The voices fade away. My muscles relax. My vision tunnels. At the right time, I turn to face her and say my vows, as does she. Then Seb hands us the rings. I slide the ornate gold band over her finger and accept the simple gold band on mine.

Then, before the priest has completed his sentence, I close the distance to her. Her green gaze clashes with mine. I raise her veil, and my breath catches. A hot sensation stabs in my chest. She's beautiful, innocent, and doesn't deserve what is going to come. But I don't deserve what happened to me either. I gather her in my arms and kiss her.

Her breath hitches, the muscles of her body tense, then she melts into me. I haul her close enough that her breasts flatten against my chest. Her lips cling to mine then part, and I sweep my tongue inside her mouth. I tilt my mouth, deepen the kiss, and a moan trembles up her throat. I swallow it, suck on her tongue, ravish her mouth for a second longer, then I tear my mouth from hers. The clapping and cheers from the assembled crowd wash over me. I stare down at her trembling lips, her wide gaze as my chest rises and falls.

"What's wrong?" she whispers. "Axel, what are you going to do?"

I bare my teeth as I release her. "I'm going to take my revenge."

She shakes her head, opens her mouth, but I'm already moving. I pivot on my heel, grab Seb's gun from his holster, then turn. I spin her around and haul her to me, then point the gun at Michael.

"Down," I snarl, "get the fuck down."

35

Theresa

One moment, he was kissing me like his life depended on it, like he had never kissed me before— like he meant it, like he loved me. He loves me; he does. I knew it because of the way he slanted his mouth over mine and wrapped his arms about me and held me so close that nothing and no-one could come between us—or so I'd thought—and the next he pulled back, a strange look on his face. A mixture of determination and anger ... and a plea for under-standing? For forgiveness. My heart slammed into my ribcage, my stomach bottomed out, and I knew then that he was going to do something bad. Something that would change the course of all of our lives.

Something I'd never be able to forget in the years ahead. I opened my mouth to scream, but he'd already spun around, grabbed Seb's gun, then yanked me to him. My breath caught in my chest, and my fingers trembled, even as I clutched my wedding bouquet. *This can't be happening, this can't be happening.* My knee almost gave way from under me, and his grip around me tightened.

"Get down!" He waves the gun at Michael. "Get the fuck down."

The whisper of guns being unholstered fills the space. The next moment every single Sovrano brother except Seb points their gun at Axel.

"Put your gun down," Axel growls at Michael.

Michael glances from him to me, then back at him. "What are you going to do with her?" he asks in a low voice.

"She's my wife now." He laughs, a harsh, mean sound that sends a shiver of fear down my back. "I'll do what I want with her."

Michael takes a step forward, and Axel clicks his tongue. "I wouldn't do that if I were you."

I must make a noise, for Michael's gaze darts back to me. He draws in a breath.

"Put your gun down, now," Axel snaps.

Michael bends and places his gun on the floor.

"Kick it over to me," Axel orders.

Michael slides it over, and Axel stops it with his foot. "Now ask the others to do the same."

Michael nods at his men. First Massimo, then Adrian, and Michael's body-guard Antonio place their guns down and kick them in Axel's direction. Luca makes a growling noise at the back of his throat.

"Do it," Michael admonishes him.

With a glare in Axel's direction, Luca places his gun on the floor and kicks it toward Axel.

"Get on your knees now, all of you."

Michael hesitates. I'm sure he's going to refuse, then he lowers himself to his knees.

"Hands behind your neck," Axel snaps.

Michael complies, and Axel glances sideways at Seb. "That goes for the rest of you guys too. On your knees, hands behind your neck."

Seb hesitates, and Axel cocks his gun. "Do as I say, and no one gets hurt."

"Get down," Massimo snaps as he drops down to his knees. First Seb, then Adrian complies.

"I told you he was up to no good!" Luca laughs. "I wish I didn't have to say I told you so"—he points a finger at Michael—"but I told you so."

"Shut the fuck up"—Axel glowers at him—"and get the fuck down."

Luca shakes his head, wraps his hands behind his neck, and sinks down to his knees.

Antonio, Michael's bodyguard, takes a step forward and Axel shoots at him.

There's a scream from behind me, then the sound of people scrambling up from their seats and racing for the door fills the space.

"On your knees, or the next time my shot will find it's mark," Axel says in a hard voice.

Antonio glances at Michael, who nods. He sinks to his knees, as well.

The minutes stretch. Axel kicks each of the guns behind him and into the pews where they scatter in different directions. By the time I risk a glance over my shoulder, the space is empty. Except for Karma, Cass, and Nonna, as well as my parents and sister who are rooted to their seats, everyone else has left.

Axel turns to the priest. "Leave," he growls. The man doesn't need a second prompt; he turns and scampers off and out of the rear door.

Axel begins to back up toward the front door of the church, forcing me to walk backward with him. As we pass the pew where Nonna is sitting, she rises to her feet. "Don't do this, Axel," she pleads with him. "Let her go, come back to us, and all will be forgiven."

"What about what you did to my mother? Do you think she ever forgave you for that?"

Nonna pales. "I tried to tell your father to not let her go, to definitely not accept the deal that your mother's family was proposing."

"And yet, you let him exchange me for increased power and assets." Axel chuckles. "Now, let's see how you deal with the aftermath of one of your own double-crossing you, and in front of the entire world."

Nonna presses a hand to her chest. "You don't mean it."

"Oh, but I do." He laughs, and the sound echoes through the space. "This is going to show you lot as weak. It's only a matter of time before your enemies come after you and try to undermine Michael's power. And if they fail, well, I'm always available to finish off what I started."

"Let her go," Seb growls. "Xander loved her. For your triplet's sake, let her be."

"It's for my triplet's sake that I'm taking her with me. My brother would have wanted her to be well looked after, and that's exactly what I intend to do with her." His arm around me tightens. He increases his pace, and I struggle to keep up with him, seeing as we're still walking backward.

"Please, Axel, whatever it is, we can work it out. You're not a bad man; I know that. You have so much hurt, so much anger inside of you—"

"Emotions that I intend to work off with the help of your sweet, willing body, Sunshine."

I shiver. "If you think I'm going to let you fuck me—"

"Who said anything about you letting me do anything?" He chuckles, and the sound is so dark, so filled with menace that my head spins.

"This is not the real you speaking. This is someone who is filled with the need for revenge. When it wears off, you'll see what you're doing today is wrong."

"Maybe…" His footsteps thud as he continues to walk backward toward the door. "But I intend to have a hell of a shagfest meanwhile, with you, my darling wife."

"If you wanted to fuck me, you could have done so without kidnapping me."

"But imagine how filled with anger and remorse the Sovranos are going to be now that I have their precious "Xander's girl" with me… Not that you were ever his girl. We both know he was too confused to ever give you that status, but you know what I mean. They're going to be shitting themselves, knowing that I'm going to be taking full advantage of my marital status, darling. Again, not that they can do much, considering we are man and wife, in the eyes of God, at least."

Anger fills my veins, and heat flushes my skin. Before I can stop myself, I turn around and slap him. The sound reverberates through the space. There's silence, broken only by the sound of a pigeon's wings flapping in a corner of the church.

Then, he throws back his head and laughs. "Damn woman, you always surprise me. All that sass and fire. Just when I think you're meek, you flash your spirit." He clasps his fingers behind my neck, yanks me up to my tiptoes, and leans in close to me before saying in a low, menacing voice, "I can't wait to rip into your pussy and teach you a lesson on how you need to behave with your husband."

"You are not my husband."

"The ring on your finger says otherwise, sweetheart."

I reach for my ring, and he shakes his head. "Even if you take it off, we can't undo the vows we exchanged in front of the Man Above."

I draw in a breath, then curl my fingers into fists. "I hate you," I snarl. "I hate that I fell for you. I hate that I spent all those days praying by your bedside. If I could do it all over again, I'd wish for you to die."

He yawns. "Save your strength; you're going to need it."

I raise my hand, and this time, he bends and throws me over his shoulder. "Let me go," I yell, "you *stronzo*, you *carogna*, you *fetente*." I try to bury my knee in his groin, but he tightens his grip across my thighs. He turns and jogs toward the door. I lock my fingers, bring my fists down onto his back, but he doesn't even wince. My veil flows down, blocking out the sight of the church, then the tiara comes undone and drops to the ground, taking the veil with it. I push the hair out of my eyes, and glance up to find Nonna swaying. Massimo jumps to his feet and goes over to catch her before she hits the ground. Behind him, Luca and Seb scramble under the pews to find their guns while Michael and Antonio are already on their feet and racing toward us. Then the door slams shut, cutting them off from view.

Axel races down the steps as I wriggle in his hold. "Let me go," I cry. "Let me the fuck go."

He reaches the first car, a Ferrari, and opens the door on the driver's side. Still holding me, he grabs the man behind the wheel, hauls him out, and flings him aside. He throws me inside, then turns and kicks out the legs from the man who's jumped up to his feet. He follows me inside, forcing me to move over to the passenger's side, before he slams the door.

My gown is stuck in between my legs as I reach for the door on my side. He reaches over, and gripping my shoulder, hauls me over the partition between the seats and across his lap.

I hear the locks on the door engage and cry out in frustration. I try to pull free, but he places the gun on the dashboard and spanks my ass, a hard, tight slap that sends a line of fire up my spine.

"The hell?" I freeze.

By the time I think of beginning to struggle again, he's already eased the car onto the road and accelerated away.

"What are you doing? Let me go, let me go." I hit my head against the steering wheel and cry out.

"Damn it," he curses from above me. "Stop struggling or you'll hurt yourself further."

"The hell do you care about that? You kidnapped me at gun point."

"I never pointed the gun at you."

"Oh," I blink rapidly, "I still can't understand why you did it? We were going to get married—"

"We are married."

"I thought you loved me."

"I never said that."

"I thought you cared for me."

"No, you assumed that I cared for you."

"Why did you marry me if you had no feelings for me?" I cry.

"Thought that was obvious." He snorts. "Revenge, baby, at the Sovranos, for what they did to my mother."

"But they didn't do anything. It was their father who was responsible for what happened to you."

"Our father used my mother and me as a bargaining chip to grow his power, and they benefited from what he did. Everything they have now is due to what he did, so even if they weren't directly responsible, they don't deserve what they have. "

"How are you different from your father, when you're using me as a bargaining chip now?"

"Oh, there is no bargaining here. You are my wife now, and you'll do as I say."

"I won't!" I wriggle again, and this time, he lets me sit up. I reach for the door, try to open it, but the lock won't budge. "Goddamn it." I bang at the door, then wince when pain shoots up my arm. "Argh!" I shake out my hand.

"Told you not to hurt yourself, didn't I?"

"Like I give a shit what you want?"

"Oh, you will." He accelerates, and the car seems to leap forward. I'm pushed back against the seat as he zips down the road and takes a turn without slowing. The brakes screech, and even through the closed windows I can smell burning rubber. Ahead, a car barrels toward us, and I scream and close my eyes. He swerves, and the car whizzes by us. I open my eyes, only to yell again as I find that we are on a one-way street, heading in the opposite direction of the traffic. A truck blares its horn as it speeds toward us. I yell, but I can't hear myself as the sound of the truck's horn rises to a crescendo. I slap my hands over my face as he swerves. I fall toward him, only to stop when a band of steel seems to stop my movement. I snap open my eyes and peer through the gaps in my fingers as he turns the car to the left and onto another road, this time hurtling forward in the same direction as the traffic.

I glance down to find he's thrown an arm across me to stop me from falling over.

"Wear your fucking seat belt," he growls.

"And if I don't?"

"I'll tan your hide, Sunshine." He turns to me without taking his hands off the wheel. "Wear the belt or I'm going to do it for you."

The car swerves to the right and into the next lane; another driver honks angrily as he steps on the brakes, and we pull ahead. I turn around to find another vehicle crashing into it from behind.

"Oh my God," I gape, "look what you did."

"No, it's what you did," he snaps. "Wear the damn seat belt or there are going to be many more accidents, and you will be to blame."

Hell, hell, hell. I squeeze my eyes shut, then reach for the belt and manage to lock it into place.

"Good girl." He finally concentrates on the road ahead, and the breath I wasn't aware I was holding rushes out of me.

We ride in silence for a few more minutes. He finally turns onto the freeway that leads out of the city. He guns the engine, pressing down on the accelerator, but I notice he keeps it just under the speed limit. "Guess you don't want to be caught by the cops, eh?"

He stays silent.

"You know, the Sovranos own pretty much the entire police force and most of this city."

His lips twist in a smirk. He continues to drive down the freeway, then takes the next exit off. I frown when, a few minutes later, he turns onto a narrow road.

"Where are we going?" I ask, even though I know he's not going to reply. He doesn't disappoint me. He drives for another good ten minutes, then turns into a field with a white building, and beyond it, a runway. He pulls to a halt next to the building, then switches off the engine. He snatches up the gun and slides it into the waistband at the small of his back. Then he gets out of the car and walks around to open my door.

I scowl up at him; and he arches an eyebrow. Goddamn him for looking so gorgeous, in his white button-down and clean-shaven jaw. A lock of hair falls over his forehead, and he brushes it back impatiently.

"Come on." He jerks his head over his shoulder.

"Why should I?"

"Because I say so?" He bends down until his face is almost at eye level with mine. "Because I'm your husband, and where I go, you go."

"And if I say no?"

"I'll simply throw you over my shoulder and carry you there."

"You won't," I say through gritted teeth, even though I, obviously, know he will.

He reaches for me, and I throw up my hands. "Fine! Step back, will you, so I can get out." He moves back just enough for me to swing my legs out. I rise to my feet, straighten my dress, then brush past him. He slams the door of the car and follows me. He draws abreast with me, then proceeds to take my hand in his. I try to resist, but he glares at me.

"Behave," he warns in that hard voice that sends a thrill up my back. *Gesù Cristo*, why am I still so attracted to him, and after that stunt he pulled back there?

He prowls inside the hangar—and it is a hangar, for I see a plane parked in there. It's a gleaming piece of work, and he walks straight over to it and up the steps, pulling me in his wake. Is he flying out of the country? Of course, he's flying out of the country. If we stayed in Italy, we'd be found very quickly. In fact, I was counting on that. But leaving the country? Now, that's a whole new ball game. How did he found someone who would work with him anyway?

A man greets us at the top of the steps. He's wearing a captain's hat and uniform. He hands over a phone to Axel, who pockets it before they shake hands.

"We're ready for take-off," the captain says in a British accent.

"Good," Axel nods, "we're ready to go." He doesn't introduce me; the man doesn't ask. Instead, he hauls up the steps behind us and proceeds to lock the door for take-off. I glance around at the plush carpet, the leather seats. Axel walks past me and takes a seat. He pats the one next to him. "Sit down and belt up; we're about to take off."

Under my feet, the low thrum of the engines vibrates. I walk over and pointedly drop into a seat on the opposite side of the aisle from him.

His lips twist. "Wear your seat belt."

"So you keep saying." I snort as I fasten my seat belt. "You don't fool me, though. I know that my safety is the last thing on your mind."

"If it helps you to keep believing that..." He raises a shoulder.

"It does." I lean back and close my eyes as we taxi down the runway. "They won't leave you alone. It doesn't matter where you go; they're going to hunt you down and—"

"And what? They'll punish me? Shoot me?"

He pulls his phone out of his pocket, and his fingers fly across the keypad. "We'll see."

Despite the fact, or maybe it's because of the tumultuous events of the morning, but as soon as I close my eyes, I fall asleep. When I wake up, we're landing. There is a trickle of water across the windshield. I straighten, and a jacket falls off my shoulder. His jacket.

I glance over to find Axel is still tapping on his phone. We touch down with barely a bump, and I glance out at the grey light. The clouds seem to hang low in the sky. I fold my arms around myself.

"Wear the jacket." He pockets his phone as the plane taxis to a stop. He rises up to his feet and holds out his hand. I ignore it, then shrug into his jacket. Not because I want to obey him, but because it looks cold out there.

"Are we in London?" I rise to my feet.

"How did you know?" he asks, sounding impressed.

"The rain." I shrug. "And the captain's accent. I'm not stupid, you know. Makes sense that you'd come back to your home turf. Of course, it's probably the first place they'll look for you."

He leans over, and I try to move back, but the seat has me blocked. He proceeds to fasten my buttons, stopping only when all of them have been done up. Then he turns and once again threads his fingers through mine as we head to the doorway. The pilot comes over and opens the door. Instantly, the chill air sweeps over me, and I shiver.

"Cold?" He pulls me closer, and we walk down the steps in tandem. He heads for a car and talks to someone who hands the keys over to him then leaves. I'm so tired that I can barely stay on my feet. I slide into the passenger seat, and put on my seat belt without his prompting. Instantly, I fall asleep. The next time I open my eyes it's dark outside, and we're still driving.

"Where are we going?" I yawn as I snuggle down further into the jacket. Hot air blows in from the vent of the car, and I'm grateful for it.

"You'll see." He slants me a sideways glance, and I notice the shadow on his jaw. Good grief, the man is virile, but I knew that already. He switches gears with his left hand, and I notice the band around his finger. My husband —we're married. Hell, we're married and he kidnapped me. The panic wells up, and I swallow it down. I glance away, close my eyes, and allow sleep to pull me under.

The next time I wake up, I'm in a strange bed in a strange room, alone.

36

Axel

I raise the glass to my lips, then toss back the whiskey. Reaching for the bottle, I top myself up.

"You did well," the man standing on the other side of the bar counter murmurs.

Maybe too well. Now, my entire family thinks of me as having betrayed them. She thinks I kidnapped her, which I did. Though considering I married her, perhaps it doesn't count as a kidnapping? But the very fact that I pulled a gun on the Sovranos before I took her and left seems to point to the contrary.

I pull out the gun from the small of my back where it has been tucked into my waistband and place it on the counter, pointed at him.

He doesn't even glance at it. Asshole simply pushes his glass forward, as if he expects me to fill it. When I ignore him, he reaches for the bottle and tops himself up without acknowledging the snub.

He raises his glass. "Cheers"—he clinks his glass with mine—"to the successful completion of phase one." He tosses back his own liquor, then tops up his glass with my whiskey. Forty-year-old Macallan's, which he definitely does not deserve to partake of.

"Fuck you," I say in a low voice.

He laughs. "Now, why would you say that? Considering you were the one who wanted to have your revenge on the Sovranos. Unless," he tilts his head, "unless you developed familial feelings. And if you did, I don't blame you. After all, blood is blood, and you may have spent your life hating them, but having spent time with them, you may be feeling otherwise inclined."

"I'll do anything to destroy them," I say in a hard voice.

"Ah," he scratches his chin, "is it the woman, then? Honest to God, I didn't foresee that, and I do think of everything, you know. But it seems even I cannot predict human nature or the power of love."

"Love," I scowl, "the fuck you talking about, man?"

"Don't be upset now." He clicks his tongue. "It happens to the best of us. No one can avoid the power and the suddenness of love. When it hits, it hits; it has no rhyme or reason."

"Get to the point, motherfucker."

"Marrying her must have seemed like a good move, a way to get closer to the Sovranos without eliciting suspicion... A brilliant move, if I may say."

"You may not," I say through gritted teeth.

"Kidnapping her in front of the entire town was a master-stroke." He nods his fucking head. "One way to make the Sovranos lose face, something to expose their weaknesses and have their enemies circling around them like vultures. Gotta hand it to you, boy, that's something I wouldn't have been able to think of. But bringing her here?" He purses his lips. "You're sending out a beacon that's going to attract every single motherfucking friend of the Mafia to you. You've painted a target on your head, and by association, mine."

"I have this place guarded."

"Which is no guarantee that it will protect you against the Cosa Nostra."

I scowl at him. "You're beginning to piss me off, Freddie."

His lips kick up. "That was not my intention. You are the strongest member of my team; you know I don't want to lose you."

"Well, fuck that." I swig back the rest of the whiskey. "I have kicked off the beginning of the end of the Sovranos. As for phase two, it will have to wait."

"Ah," he strokes his chin, "so definitely love, then."

I glare at him.

"Enjoy the early days of your marriage, but remember, you owe me, and I always collect, Axel."

I rise to my feet and jerk my chin toward the door. "Fuck off."

"Now, now. Hold on; you're not thinking straight." He raises his snifter of whiskey, and anger squeezes my gut. I reach out and knock the glass out of his hand. It crashes to the floor and shatters. He stiffens, then rises to his feet and dusts off the droplets that have fallen on his jacket.

"I understand you're not thinking straight," he says in a soft voice, "but remember that you need me, Axel. You—"

I reach over, grab his collar, and haul him over the counter. "I don't need anyone, you motherfucker."

He chuckles. "Words spoken in the heat of the moment, but you know better."

I tighten my grasp on his collar. He gasps. His face turns red, and the veins on his neck pop as he tries to take in a breath.

"Read my lips, you motherfucker. I don't need you or anyone else, and if you dare to threaten me again, I will kill you." I release him, and he staggers back. He straightens his collar, then draws himself up to his full height. "You're going to regret threatening the Sovranos and kidnapping her, Axe; mark my words." Turning, he walks out.

I glare after him, then snatch up my glass and throw it at the wall. It shatters.

"Fuck!" I dig my fingers into my hair and tug.

Asshole is right, though. I shouldn't have brought her here; it's too dangerous—for both of us.

But fuck, if I didn't want her in my space, in my bed. I wanted her to myself just for a few days before I have to face the world. Is that too much to ask?

With a little luck, the Sovranos will be too busy facing the aftermath of the problems I left them with to come after us right away. As for Freddie—fuck. It was wrong to provoke the man. He's dangerous. I should have known better, but everything he'd said was intended to goad me, and for once, I let him get to me. It wasn't wise to throw him out, but goddamn it, I'm tired of being on the defensive. I want to take my destiny in my own hands. To face it like the man I am.

Enough hiding; enough planning. It's time to put the final part of my plan into action. To bring down the Sovranos, once and for all, and to have my revenge.

I straighten, reach for the bottle, and pour myself a fresh glass, when the scent of apple blossoms wafts over to me.

I raise my gaze to find her standing in the doorway. She takes a step forward, but I hold up a hand. "Stop right there."

"What?"

"Don't come in here."

Her jaw firms. "Why not?"

"Because I said so, woman." I smirk at the flash of anger in her eyes before nodding toward the shards on the floor. "There's glass everywhere."

"Oh." She purses her lips. "I uh, heard the commotion and came to check."

"You should have stayed in the room, away from me, where it's safest for you."

"Isn't it safe for me here?"

"What do you think?" I raise the glass of whiskey to my lips.

"I think you've had enough to drink."

I chuckle. "I'm just getting started." I grab the glass and the bottle, then walk out from behind the counter and toward her. "Go to bed." I brush past her, then head out of the living room and toward the study. I step inside, all too aware of her following me. I walk over to the chair in front of the fire and lower myself into it.

I raise the glass of whiskey to my lips, take a sip. She walks over to stand in front of me.

"What?" I growl, not raising my gaze.

"Who was that man who left? Was he a friend?"

"An associate."

"Why was he threatening you?"

I jerk my chin up, "Nothing you need to worry about."

"You kidnap me—"

"I married you."

"—and bring me here." She scowls.

"To my home, which is now your home," I add.

"Exactly, so if someone threatens you, then it means my life is also in danger."

I set my jaw. "I'll say this only once, Theresa"—I lock my gaze with hers —"you have nothing to fear. I will never let anyone harm you; you understand?"

37

Theresa

I do, and that's the problem. This man has been nothing but rude to me since we met. Oh, he's made me orgasm, but he's never been open with me. Not about his past, not about why he agreed to marry me—I mean, why he really agreed to marry me. And then he kidnaps me and brings me here, all without giving me an explanation as to why. And yet, there's nowhere else I'd rather be. There's no one else I'd trust more to keep me safe. *How fucked up is that?*

I close the distance between us, and he stiffens.

"I understand," I murmur, "I know you'll keep me safe. I trust you, Axel."

His gaze narrows. Some of the tension seems to leave his shoulders. He drags his gaze across my features, and my breath catches. Something in how he's watching me makes me feel like I'm at his mercy. And I am, make no mistake. I'm in his house, without any of my friends or family, without any money or my purse or my phone with me. I run my suddenly damp finger down my wedding dress which I'm still wearing.

The firelight catches on my ring, and I pause. He seems to see it the same time as me for his jaw flexes. "Come here." he holds out his hand.

I hesitate.

"Thought you said you trusted me?" he murmurs. His blue gaze bores into me, and a rush of heat sizzles over my skin. It arrows straight to my core, where a pulse blooms to life.

"Theresa?" He arches an eyebrow.

I swallow, take a step forward, another, then place my hand in his.

He leans forward and presses a kiss to my fingers. Goosebumps pop on my skin. I wasn't expecting that from him. He nips on my fingertip, then closes his mouth around it. My belly clenches. A moan leaks from my lips, and his mouth curls.

"You are in my home, under my protection. I can promise you that I will guard you with my life, Theresa."

Something hot stabs at my chest. "What if I don't want that?" I swallow. "What if I don't want anything to happen to you?"

"I thought you were angry at me for bringing you here?"

"I still am." I try to tug my hand from his, but he doesn't release it. "Doesn't mean I want to see you hurt."

His lips kick up. "Concerned about me, wife?"

That heat in my chest detonates and spreads to other parts of my body. "I don't want to be," I say truthfully, "but I'd never wish harm on anyone else, including you."

"I think you're lying."

Heat flushes my skin. I pull my hand from his, and this time, he releases it.

"I've never lied to you, Axel. Unlike you…"

A pulse flares to life at his temple. The skin around his eyes tightens. Shit, why did I have to go and spoil the moment we were having there? Anger rolls off of him, and my belly flip flops. Damn it, even his annoyance turns me on. The way he pouts, how his gaze intensifies, how his nostrils flare as his fingers tighten around the glass. I squeeze my thighs together, and the alertness in his gaze signals that he's noticed it. Nothing escapes him, does it? I turn away—because if I stand there longer, I'll sink to my knees and reach for his zipper and—*Argh, don't think about it. Don't.* I walk over to the shelves of books that line the wall and run my finger down the spines: *War and Peace, Pinocchio, The Ugly Duckling, Harry Potter, The Prince* by *Niccolò Machiavelli,* a book of poems by *Lord Byron.* My finger touches the book, and the entire panel swings open.

"Oh!" I gasp as a room comes into view. It's lit only by the light that streams in from behind me.

"You've found my secret, I see."

"Eh?" I gasp, then turn around, trip on my own feet, and almost fall, except he grips my shoulder and steadies me. "You scared me," I say with a nervous laugh. Shit, now I sound afraid. And I'm not afraid. Not of him, but about what I'm going to find in the room behind me. Well, the jury's out on that. "What's in there?" I murmur.

"Wouldn't you like to find out?"

"Are you inviting me in?"

He moves forward, and I skitter back and past the doorway.

"Now you're already in." One side of his lips kicks up. My pulse rate ratchets up. Heat from his body pours over me and slams into my chest. I gasp, and the scent of him intensifies. My toes curl, and my scalp tingles. I've always had this unreasonable attraction to him, but in his home, under his roof, surrounded by his things, his magnetism is potent. If I stand here a second longer, I'm going to throw myself at him and ask him to fuck me. Which is fine; he's my husband, right?

But our relationship is far from conventional, and damn, if I'm going to ask him for anything! I spin around and walk inside the room. Behind me, I hear his footsteps, then the clink as he places his glass on a table. The click of his lighter and the flicker of the flame precede the diminishment of the darkness. I turn to find he's lit one of the candles on a stand.

That's when I realize that he has placed candles on stands and in a circle around a flat table in the center of the room. There is enough space between the candles for someone to walk through. He lights another candle, then another. He doesn't stop until all the candles are lit. The light falls over the table which has a padded surface like it's intended for someone to lay down on it. I glance up at the walls, take in the painting on one side—a woman surrounded by flames. There's something haunting about her face. I walk closer to study her features. Her eyes are half closed, her mouth open, her head thrown back in the throes of—

"Ecstasy," he murmurs, his voice right behind me again.

I jump and press my hand to my chest. "You need to stop scaring me like this."

"You need to actually start trusting me like you say you do."

I toss my hair over my shoulder, then turn away to stare at the opposite wall on which hangs a paddle, a rope, a whip, and some other device which looks like a spreader. A spreader? I scowl. It would lock around the ankles and force the person on whom it is being used to spread their legs.

"Oh…" Heat flushes my cheek. "This is your—"

"Now, not-so-secret room."

I turn to face him. "Is this where you bring your women?"

"Yes."

I bite the inside of my cheek. Why did I expect him to say anything else? Of course, he has had lots of women, but to bring them here to his house? Why did I think that I was the first person he'd brought here?

I turn to leave, and he grabs my wrist. "Where are you going?"

"Back to my room."

"Our room."

"I'm going to sleep in one of the guest rooms. Surely, you must have guest rooms in this space."

"You're my wife; you sleep in my bed."

"So you can fuck me?"

"Do you want me to fuck you?"

I hesitate.

"You're a terrible liar, so don't even try," he warns.

I swallow, not sure what to say. I glance down at where his fingers are curled around my wrist, then back at his face.

"I—" I open and shut my mouth. I can't bring myself to say it. "I—" I try again, then shake my head.

He releases my wrist, only to nod toward the padded table. "Get on it."

"Excuse me?"

"You heard me." He folds his arms across his chest. "On the table, Sunshine."

I turn to leave when he snaps, "Now."

I pause. Damn it, I hate it when he uses that tone of voice. When I can't disobey him. When everything in me insists that I do as he says. I do hate that, right?

"Theresa," he warns me.

I blow out a breath, then stomp over to the table and heave myself onto it. I fold my arms across my chest, mirroring his stance. "Happy?" I huff.

"Part your legs," he commands as he walks over to stand in front of me.

"Wh … what?" I blink.

"Do it." He lowers his voice to a hush, "Or you can always leave." He nods toward the door.

I glance at the door, then back at him. Goddamn it. I slide my legs apart, as much as the gown allows, that is. He stares down at the space between my thighs, and my clit begins to throb. I grip the table on either side of my legs.

He reaches out and presses his palm flat against the center of my chest. He applies pressure, and I lean back on my elbows.

I swallow, and he cups my cheek. "Shh, Sunshine," he croons, "I won't hurt you."

Then, he grips the neckline of my dress and tugs. With a ripping sound, the gown tears in half.

"My wedding dress," I cry out. When I try to sit up, he wraps his fingers around the side of my neck and holds me in check.

"I'll buy you another."

"But I like this one."

"I'll buy you an exact replica."

"But it's *my* wedding dress," I protest.

"And I'm your husband." He pulls apart the two sides of the dress, and cool air floats over my skin. My nipples tighten behind the demi bra that I slipped on earlier this morning. God, was it only this morning that I had gotten married? It seems like another time, another world. He pulls down my bra, and my breasts spill out.

"Fuck," he growls, then bends and closes his mouth around one nipple. He bites down, and I cry out. The pain shoots straight to my core. My clit engorges. He massages my breast even as he turns his head to my other breast. He takes the nipple between his lips and tugs on it. My entire body jerks.

"Oh, hell," I groan.

He raises his head and holds my gaze as he slides his hand down my waist. He grabs my panties and tears them off.

The breath squeezes out of me. I can't speak; I'm just so surprised by the suddenness of his action.

He pushes up to stand over me and rakes his gaze down my exposed body. Then he reaches over, and almost experimentally, pinches my clit.

My entire body hitches off of the table. "Oh my God," I gasp. "Oh, God."

"There's no God here, baby," he says in a hard voice. "Only me."

He thrusts his fingers inside my channel, works them in and out of me, then brings his fingers to my mouth. I wrap my lips around his digits and suck on them.

"I want you." His tone lowers to a hush. "I want you in a way I've never wanted anyone else before."

Warmth pools in my lower belly. Heat flushes my chest. His words shouldn't move me, but they do.

"Axel," I whine, and his gaze jerks back to my face.

"I want to take you the way I've never taken anyone else before."

His words penetrate the sexual haze that swirls around me. "Wh ... what do you mean?"

"Do you trust me?"

I draw in a breath.

"Do you?"

I nod.

Something like satisfaction shows on his features. Then he reaches into his pocket and pulls out a blindfold.

38

Theresa

"What … what is that for?" I squeak.

He tilts his head; I swallow. My stomach folds in on itself.

"Are you g-going to use it on me?"

"You did say that you trust me..." he says in that low, husky voice that sends another tremor up my spine.

"I … didn't think that meant that you'd blindfold me."

"It's only to heighten your senses. Of course, if you're too afraid to wear it —" He lets the words hang in the air between us. I know he's testing me. He wants to see how far I'll let him go before I ask him to stop. But I don't want him to stop. A shiver runs down my spine. Why do I find it so damn hot? Is it wrong to want everything that he wants to do to me?

"Well?" he murmurs. "What do you say, Sunshine? Can I blindfold you?"

I bite the inside of my cheek, then nod.

His muscles relax. Whoa, did he think that I was going to refuse him?

Before I can ask the question, he leans over and places the strip of silk over my eyes. He ties it at the back of my head, and just like that, darkness descends. I can sense my breath, the bead of sweat that trickles down between my breasts, the sound of his footsteps on the floor as he moves away.

"Stay right there," he commands as his footsteps fade away.

The minutes stretch, and I sit up. Where the hell did he go? Why did he have to blindfold me before he left? If it was to enhance the anticipation, then it sure as hell is working. I shuffle around on the table to find a more comfortable position. Just as I'm about to slide my legs closed, his footsteps sound. Something clinks, ice? Did he go to get ice? He places something on the padded table, then returns to stand between my legs.

"Ready, Sunshine?" his gravelly voice rumbles across my nerve-endings.

"Wh-what are you going to do?"

The heat of his body intensifies, and I know that he's moved closer. The pungent scent of the candle strengthens. The hair on the back of my neck rises. He's not going to, is he?

A line of fire detonates in the center of my chest.

I scream. He clasps his hand across my mouth. I bite down on the edge of his hand as the heat zings down to my core, then fades away just as quickly.

He removes his hand from over my mouth, and I gasp, "Did you … did you just drip the hot wax on me?"

"It's called heat play," he affirms. The ice clinks, then a trail of cold so chilly that it's almost hot steaks down my chest. It shoots down to my core and seems to circle my clit, which throbs.

"Oh my God!" I gasp. "What was that? Was that the ice, was it—"

Another stream of heat zings down over my belly. My core clenches, my thigh muscles tremble, and moisture coils in my core. I close my fingers into fists as the heat fades away, instantly leaving me throbbing, sweating, wanting… More… Much more.

"Axel," I whine, "what are you doin—" I yelp as a stream of cold follows in the wake of the heat. I can almost hear the moisture sizzle as it touches my overheated skin. That too fades away, and something soft brushes my lips.

He takes my hand and places it over his shoulder. "Hold on."

"What?" My heart rams into my chest, "What are you going to do, what—" I yell as a zing of fire trails down my chest. Did he just strip the wax off of my chest? My nipples tighten, my belly quivers, and all of the pores on my skin seem to pop. I pant and hold on as he licks his way down my skin. Then he rips off the next trail of wax, and I moan. A trembling starts from my toes and rolls up my legs, my thighs. It seems to coalesce in my pussy before radiating up my spine.

A sizzle of cold zings down my lower belly, then I yell, for he's drawing the ice around my swollen clit. He drags the ice down my lower lips, then slides it inside my pussy, and I throw my head back. I dig my fingernails into his shoulder as he works the ice in and out of me. In and out. The climax roars through me, and I cry out.

My eyes may be blindfolded, but my vision turns technicolor as the most intense orgasm of my life grips me. As it fades away, I slump back onto the padded table. I float down from the climax and become aware that he's pulled the ice out of me. He pauses—to place the candle back?—then he drags the ice across my lips. The moisture seeps into my mouth, and I suck on it. The taste of my cum, mixed with the scent of his skin, fills me. It's dirty and erotic, and damn, if I don't want more.

He slides the ice inside my mouth, and I bite down on his fingers. He draws in a sharp breath, and a growl rips up his chest. The next moment, he's replaced his fingers with his mouth. He swipes his tongue across mine as he yanks the blindfold from my eyes. I blink and take in that blue gaze of his that bores into me as he hooks his arm under my knee. He yanks my leg up and to the side, then positions his cock at my entrance.

"I'm going to fuck you now." He bares his teeth.

Before I can reply, he thrusts forward and buried himself to the hilt. Too much. Too full. He stretches me. He's so deep in me that, surely, I can feel him in my stomach. I open my mouth, and he deepens the kiss. He crams his tongue inside my mouth, and at the same time, he begins to fuck me in earnest. He lunges forward with such force that the entire table screeches back. My body jolts, and the slap of flesh meeting flesh fills the room. He doesn't close his eyes. He holds my gaze as he slides his hand between us and pinches my clit. A scream wells up, but he swallows it. Sweat slides down his temple and plops on my cheek as he pulls out, only to lunge forward again. He hits that spot deep inside of me that I didn't even know existed. He plunges into me, again and again. And again. Each time, he hits that spot, and sensations vibrate out from the point of contact. He drags his hand up my body to cup my breast. He squeezes down on my nipple, and a moan spills from my lips. He drags his hand down my arm and twines his fingers with mine, then tears his mouth from mine.

"Come for me, Sunshine, come all over my cock."

39

Axel

Her pupils dilate, and she throws her head back as her entire body shudders. Her pussy clenches around my cock as she comes and comes. Her orgasm seems to go on and on, and I continue to fuck her through it. Color flushes her neck and cheeks, and she holds onto me as her features contort. Her eyelids flutter shut, and she finally slumps back.

"Look at me," I growl. "Look at me, Sunshine."

She raises her heavy eyelids, and I hold her gaze as I thrust myself inside her wet, hot pussy one last time.

"Fuck," I growl as I come inside her. A trembling grips her, and I brush my lips across hers. A teardrop squeezes out from the corner of her eyes, and I lick it up. I raise my head and peer into her features. "Did I hurt you?"

She shakes her head.

"Was it too much for you?"

She hesitates.

"Talk to me," I order. "Tell me how you feel."

"Like I've been well and truly fucked?" she blurts out.

I can't stop the chuckle that rumbles up my throat. "I like the sound of that, baby."

I kiss her hard, then pull out of her.

She hisses as I straighten.

"Are you sore?"

"A little," she admits, "but I don't mind."

"So you liked the heat and cold play?"

"I was surprised"— she bites down on her lower lip—"but once I got over the initial shock, it was the most intense experience I've ever had." She lowers her gaze.

"Hey…" I notch my knuckles under her chin. "You don't have to be ashamed that you like kink."

"Who'd have thought?" She laughs. "But it definitely opened my eyes to just how over-the-top sex can be."

"And I'm only getting started." I smirk.

"Jeez, I really shouldn't have said that. Now, your already inflated ego is going to get even bigger."

"Not the only part." I chuckle.

She rolls her eyes. "Forget I said that." She slaps me on my shoulder, and I grip her wrist and tug her to a sitting position.

She glances down, and I follow her gaze to where my cum slides down her inner thigh.

"Fuck, that's hot," I reach down and push the thick liquid back inside her pussy.

"What the—?" She freezes. "Did you just push your cum back inside me?"

"Seems like it," I drawl.

She raises her chin, and her pupils are blown, her color even higher than earlier; her lower lip trembles.

"Jesus!" I bury my fingers in her hair.

"That turned you on, didn't it?"

"It shouldn't have," she whispers, "but somehow, every filthy thing you do only makes you more attractive, and I have no idea why."

"Don't you?" I wrap her hair around my hand, then tug, so she has to raise her chin. I gaze into her gorgeous green eyes, and the blood rushes to my cock. "You're so beautiful," I murmur, and the pink on her cheek deepens. "I want to fuck you again." I brush my lips across hers because I can't resist her lush mouth. She shivers, her lips cling to mine, and that's the only encourage-ment I need. I release her hair, only to scoop her up in my arms.

Turning, I walk out of the room, past the dying fire in the study, and up the stairs to my bedroom. I lower her onto the bed, then point a finger at her. "Stay there."

I pull my phone from my pocket and open the security app, making sure all doors and windows are armed and locked down for the night. I place my phone on the table. "Now, where were we?"

"I'm naked, and you haven't even removed your clothes." She scowls.

"Are you complaining?" I chuckle.

"I want to see my husband's body. Is that too much to ask?"

A thrill runs down my spine. My wife. She's my woman. All mine.

I slide the gun from my waistband, then place it on the dresser. I spin around, grip the back of my shirt, and pull it off. I toe off my shoes and socks, push down my already unzipped pants, along with my boxers, and kick them off.

When I straighten, she draws a quick breath. She drags her gaze down my chest, my abs, down to where my cock is already thickening.

"We didn't use a condom," she says slowly.

"We never have. Are you only just now realizing that?" I walk over to stand in front of her.

Her cheeks redden. "I... I was otherwise distracted."

I smirk.

She scowls. "I'm not on birth-control," she points out.

"And?"

"Do I have to point out the obvious—that I could get pregnant?"

"Is that a problem?"

"Do you want me to get pregnant?" Her forehead furrows. "Is that how you plan to get the Sovranos to forgive you for what you did?"

I tilt my head.

"Oh my God. That *is* your plan, to get me pregnant. That's your guarantee for the Sovranos never hurting you in the future."

She bites down on her lower lip again, and fuck, if that doesn't turn me on further. I place a knee on the bed, then bend down and tug her lip from between her teeth. "No one is allowed to hurt you, Sunshine, not even yourself."

Her breath hitches.

"No one except me; you feel me?"

She nods.

"As to your question, no, I didn't plan that far. In all honesty, I got carried away, which is why I didn't use a condom." He peers into my eyes. "Do you want me to use protection?"

"No." She shakes her head. "I want a child. I want your child. I've always wanted to have my own family, and I don't want to wait."

The thought of her having my baby, our baby... My head spins. Somehow, the idea of planting a child in her fills me with primal satisfaction.

I position myself between her legs, then slide down so my mouth is poised over her glistening pussy. I blow on the chafed flesh, and a moan bleeds from her lips.

I drag my fingers up the abraded skin of her inner thigh, and she shivers.

I lick her from back hole to clit, and her entire body jolts.

"Oh my God," she moans. "Ah, Axel." She digs her fingers in my hair, and her thighs squeeze about my face. I grip her hips and drag my finger down to play with her back hole.

She freezes. I thrust my tongue inside her channel, and she jerks. I continue to eat her out as I slide a finger inside her back hole. At the same time, I squeeze her gorgeous breast.

She pushes her hips up and into my mouth, even as she tries to pull away the upper part of her body. I laugh against her pussy, and she moans.

The noises she makes. Fuck, they drive me out of my head with desire. I tear my mouth from her core, then crawl up her body. I urge her to wrap her legs around my waist as I position myself against her opening. I bracket her body with my elbows on each side of her, holding up my weight as I stay poised.

"Look at me," I order, and she raises her heavy eyelids. She holds my gaze as I thrust forward and bury myself to the hilt. My pelvis hits the soft flesh of her pussy, and she pants. She digs her heels into my back and winds her arms about my neck. She buries her fingernails into my shoulders as I begin to fuck her. In and out of her, in and out. I tilt my hips, plow deeper inside her, and her breath hitches. I hold her gaze as I try to drill into her, going as deeply as I possibly can. Her pussy clamps down on my cock, and I stay buried in her.

"I want to crawl inside you and never leave," I growl. Jesus! I sound like a man possessed. Like a man obsessed. A husband who'll never get enough of his wife. I pull out of her, then ram into her with such force that she moves up the mattress. The entire bed jolts; something crashes onto the floor behind me as I hold her gaze. "Come with me." I ram into her, and her mouth falls open.

Her spine curves, and she screams as she comes. I cup her cheek and lower my forehead to hers as I empty myself inside her. My breath comes in pants, and my heart thuds in my chest. I stay there for a few seconds before I fall onto my back, taking her with me. I fold my arms around her and hold her close. "Sleep," I murmur, as I close my eyes.

When I wake up, I'm alone. I glance at the bed, the room, then jump to my feet and barge into the bathroom. It's empty.

"Fuck," I swear as I grab a pair of sweats and step into them. I snatch up my gun and slide it into the waistband of my pants.

Then I snatch up my phone and glance at the security app. Everything seems normal. None of the doors or windows have been opened. My steps slow as I walk down the steps. When I hit the ground floor, I hear her singing. Huh?

I walk toward it, and the scent of coffee and bacon reaches me. My stomach rumbles, and I head for the kitchen. I walk inside to find her dressed in my shirt that hits her mid-thigh. She's piled her hair on top of her head in a messy bun with tendrils curling about her shoulders. I lean a hip against the doorway, watching as she bumps and grinds as she sings the words of a song I don't recognize, "F-i-r-e ... oh. F—iii-r-e, oh."

I chuckle under my breath, then walk over to her.

"F-i-rr-e, oh. Fiiii-r-e, oh," she sings again.

I lower my head until my mouth is next to her ear. "Very appropriate." I smirk.

She yells, then drops the spatula she was using to scoop the bacon onto a plate.

40

Theresa

The spatula clatters on the counter, and drops of fat singe my skin. "Ouch." I grimace and bring my hand up to my mouth to suck on it.

He catches my wrist. "Let me." He lowers his mouth to the back of my hand and drags his tongue across the reddened skin.

Goose bumps pop on my skin. My toes curl. He closes his lips around the hurt skin and sucks on it. I feel it all the way to my core. He continues to lave my skin, and my nipples tighten. Hell, I was just in his arms, in his bed, and he was inside me several times last night, but apparently, I haven't had enough of him.

I try to pull away, but he doesn't let me. He lavishes attention on my hurt skin like it's the most important thing in the world. The way he gently holds my wrist with his other palm cradling my elbow—the contrast between the darkness of his skin and my more pale one is almost obscene.

"I'm fine," I insist, but all he does is walk me toward the sink. He turns on the tap and holds my arm under the running water. The pain instantly fades away. A sigh spills from me.

"I'm sorry I surprised you," he murmurs. "I saw you in my shirt and stopped thinking."

My cheeks burn. I shoot him a sideways glance to find him focused on keeping my arm under the running water. A-n-d, he's bare-chested. He's wearing pants that ride low on his hips. His biceps bulge as he keeps my hand trained under the tap. Gosh, he's ripped. I felt those cut planes of his chest last night, but seeing him in the light of day, standing in front of him in all his gorgeous glory, sends vibrations of lust shooting down my spine.

"It's nothing," I insist. "It barely even hurts anymore."

He switches off the tap, then raises my arm to examine it. "It's best to put an anti-burn ointment on it so it doesn't scar."

"It'll be fine." I try to pull away again. Not that he lets me.

He levels that hypnotic blue gaze on me, then guides me to a chair at the kitchen counter. "Sit," he commands, and I sink into the chair.

"I'm really okay," I plead.

"Let me be the judge of that." He points a finger at me. "Don't move." He walks over to one of the shelves at the far end of the kitchen.

I drag my gaze on those powerful thighs of his that are outlined in the pants, and my belly trembles. His butt is compact, his waist trim, and at the small of his back, he wears a gun tucked into the waistband of his pants. I bite the inside of my cheek. "You're never unarmed, are you?"

"It's just a precaution," he says without turning around.

"You must have felt naked without your gun all the time you were a guest of the Sovranos."

"I managed." He opens the door, removes a first aid kit, then walks over to me. Uncapping a tube of salve, he proceeds to spread it over the splotches of red on my skin. Any remaining burning sensation instantly subsides. The tension oozes out of my shoulders.

He blows on the skin, then glances at me from under those thick eyelashes. "Better?" he asks.

I nod, not trusting myself to speak. Somehow, this, being the center of his attention, is both unnerving as well as something I enjoy far too much. I could get used to it.

He places my arm on the table, then reaches over and cups my cheek. "I didn't mean to hurt you."

"You didn't hurt me." I chuckle. "I was just surprised; didn't expect you to creep up on me like that."

"What were you singing?" He jerks his chin. "Earlier, when I came in, you were humming a tune."

"BTS," I clarify.

"BT who?" His eyebrows knit.

"BTS." I stare. "You don't know who they are?"

"Nope." He smirks. "I take it they're popular?"

"They're only the biggest band in the world right now. They've also won almost every music award there is to win."

"Hmm…" he stares at my mouth, and I wriggle around in my seat.

"They are, uh, like, really influential on social media," I murmur.

"Are they now?" He drags his thumb across my lower lip, and I can't stop the moan that spills from my lips.

"Um, I think we should finish breakfast before it gets cold."

He finally raises his gaze to mine. "I think I'd prefer something else for breakfast, actually."

Moisture laces my core. I glance away, then back at him. "But I already started cooking," I point out, "and it's not good to waste food."

"It isn't, hmm?"

I shake my head.

"Okay, then." He leans in and presses a hard kiss to my mouth. By the time he straightens, my head is spinning.

I stare as he caps the ointment and sets it aside. Then he saunters over to the counter, proceeds to plate the bacon, along with the toast that has already popped in the toaster.

"How do you like your eggs?" He turns to me. "Let me guess, scrambled?"

I nod.

He heads to the refrigerator, pulls out eggs, then returns to the gas range. He proceeds to make the eggs, plates them, and returns with two heaped plates, one of which he sets in front of me. He moves back to the drawer near the stove and grabs cutlery that he slides over to me before he takes his own seat.

"Eat." He points at my food.

I dig in, and the creaminess of the eggs combined with the salty flavor of the bacon fills my palate. "Whoa," I glance up at him, "these eggs are good."

"I had to learn to cook when I was very young. Otherwise, I would have starved."

"Oh..." I glance up at him, not sure what to say.

"She was too busy earning a living. After the incident with the fire, we moved out. She made sure she never brought clients home after that. She also began making a lot more money, but it meant she had to be out of the house a lot. And when she was home, she was always too tired to cook. So I took over."

"How old were you?"

"Six," he replies.

"You were so young..." I pause with my fork halfway to my mouth.

"I grew up fast." His lips twist. "Don't get me wrong. It wasn't all bad. I do have happy memories of being with my mother too. She tried to spend as much time with me as she could, when she wasn't exhausted. I was young, but even then, I could tell how bone-weary she was. I tried my best to make life easier for her."

"But you shouldn't have had to. You were just a child. Those were the years when you should have been carefree and naughty and able to do as you wanted."

"We don't always get what we want, do we?"

I bring the fork to my mouth and slide the food into my mouth.

"You have to go after what you want. What else is there in life, if not our dreams?" I finally say.

"*The Tilting Tulip*..." he narrows his gaze on me. "That was your dream?"

I nod. "I love flowers, always have. Until he retired, my father was the gardener for the Sovrano family home, what is now Nonna's house. I used to go over to their house with him when I was young and would try to help my father while he was pruning their bushes and planting flowers. Those were the best times of my life."

"And your sister? Did she come along too?"

I pause. "How did you know—"

"That you have a sister? I saw her at our wedding. Also"—he rubs the back of his neck—"I saw it on your Instagram feed."

"You stalked my social media feeds?" I stare.

"Also, as the memories started filtering back, I remembered having researched you," he admits.

I place my fork in my plate.

"You began recollecting your past much earlier than you let on." I swallow.

"Indeed, within a few days of regaining consciousness, my recollections started trickling in. I remembered that I had turned up at Christian's wedding with the intention of throwing a scare into the Sovranos. It's also why I waited until he and Aurora were separated from the rest of the family during their Christmas getaway. My intention was to make them feel insecure. To make them realize that they were not as invincible as they professed to be."

"Because you wanted revenge on the Sovranos for what they did to your mother?" I ask.

"And because I needed Freddie put his trust in me and confide about his own activities.

"So what are you going to do now?"

"Now, the Sovranos are my family. Like it or not I'm also one of them." He shakes his head as if he doesn't quite believe he just said those words. "I don't think I can work with Freddie anymore."

"What if he comes back for you?"

"The house is secure." He leans back in his chair. "I wouldn't take any chances with your safety, Sunshine."

I glance away. I'm still not used to him calling me that.

"Hey." His fork clatters as he drops it on his plate. Then he leans over and grips my chin. "What's upsetting you?"

"Nothing," I swallow.

"It's something." He rises to his feet, then comes around and squats in front of me.

"Look at me," he murmurs.

I shake my head, and tears prick the backs of my eyes. What the hell? Why am I feeling teary now? I didn't cry when he pulled a gun on the Sovranos, or when he hauled me out of there, or when I realized that we were boarding a plane out of Italy, so why is it that I feel like bawling now?

I sniffle, and he cups my cheek. "Hey," his voice softens, "tell me what's wrong."

"Why does something have to be wrong?"

"Because you're crying?"

"I'm not crying," I insist, even as a teardrop rolls down my cheek. He scoops it up then brings his fingertip to his mouth and sucks on it.

"Why did you do that?" I scowl.

"Because I wanted to know how you taste? I want to know everything about you, Sunshine. Your laughter, your tears, how you look when you sleep, how you moan when I make love to you, how you look first thing in the morning when you wake up in my bed."

"What about my favorite flower?"

"What is it?" He peers at me expectantly.

"It's a tulip—a black tulip," I add.

"I'll fill the entire garden with black tulips, if it makes you smile. In fact, I'll buy you a tulip farm in Amsterdam if that would make you stop crying."

A chuckle spills from my mouth. "What would I do with a tulip farm in Amsterdam?"

"Fine, I'll buy you a tulip farm in the English countryside..." His brow furrows. "Assuming there are tulip farms in the English countryside?"

"There are a few." I narrow my gaze on him. "Not that I want you to do that." I add, "I'd be happy expanding my business and opening a branch of my flower shop in London."

"You can do anything you want, baby."

"I can?"

"I know you're a savvy businesswoman. I bet you'll have it up and running in no time."

My cheeks heat. I'm not used to praise from him, or from anyone else, for that matter. I've always done my thing, but done it quietly, not wanting to draw attention to myself. Partly because Xander had loaned me the money to open my shop in Palermo, I'd preferred to just focus on the business, not wanting to draw anyone's attention to me. Even though I knew the Sovranos well, thanks to my parents, and to Xander. Still, I'd never been completely comfortable with the fact that I indirectly owed my success to the Cosa Nostra.

"I want to do this on my own."

"You *are* going to do this on your own," he murmurs.

"I mean, I don't want a loan from you. I'd prefer to raise the funding for the shop on my own."

"And your shop in Palermo?" He searches my features. "What would you do with that?"

"My friend Elsa could continue to manage the day-to-day operations. I've already made her the general manager. I'd oversee it, but she could run it."

"And you wouldn't miss it?"

"I'd still be involved," I tip up my chin, "but this is a chance to expand my brand in a new country, and this time, I'd own the place completely."

He holds my gaze, then nods. "Good." He straightens, then holds out his hand. When I take it, he draws me up to my feet. He peers into my eyes, his own gleaming with intent.

My belly trembles, and my thighs clench. "Umm, what are you doing?"

His lips kick up. "Raise your arms."

"Wh-why?"

"So I can undress you, of course."

Heat flushes my skin.

He grabs the hem of my … well, his shirt, then pulls it partway up. "Do it, baby," he coaxes, and his term of endearment slides down my chest and settles between my legs. I raise my arms, and he pulls the T-shirt up and off me.

He takes in my naked body, and his nostrils flare. "Jesus, all this time you weren't even wearing panties?"

"As you may recall, someone tore off my panties last night. And I wasn't exactly afforded the opportunity to pack. Besides, I was in a hurry to come down and start breakfast."

He smirks, then turns earnest. "You don't have to cook, you know?"

"I wanted to," I murmur.

"And I do have a housekeeper who comes in daily to make sure the place is clean and stocked up. She also cooks when I ask her to."

"I'd rather cook for you." I bite the inside of my cheek.

"Why do I find that so hot?" He leans in close enough so our breaths mingle. "Why do I find *you* so hot?" He grasps my hips and drags me up to my tiptoes. "Why do I find every part of you so delectable?" He licks my lips, and a moan bleeds from my lips. He hauls me up, and I wrap my legs around his waist. He kisses me deeply, his tongue in between my lips, his big hands squeezing my butt cheeks as he pulls me into him. He turns, places me on the edge of the table, then shoves aside the plates and the cutlery, all of which crash to the floor.

I start, then groan when he flattens his palm onto the center of my chest and urges me to lay back. He drags his gaze down my breasts, my waist, to the flesh between my thighs.

"Fuck," he says in a hoarse voice, "I can't wait to taste you again, but first..." He reaches over and grabs the jar of honey and holds it poised over my chest.

"What are you doin—" I gasp as he drizzles the honey across my breasts, then trails a stream down to my navel and across the soft flesh between my belly and my pussy. OMG, he's going to ... ahh. He places the jar of honey somewhere above my head, then leans over and slurps up the honey around one nipple.

"Oh, God." I slap my palm against the table as he curls his tongue around the nipple, then bites down on it. A groan spills from my lips as he continues his journey to my other breast. He slurps on the nipple, and I feel the tug all the way to my core. He massages my tits while I dig my fingers into his hair.

"Jesus." I huff. "This is insane."

I sense his lips curve before he proceeds to lick his way down the trail of honey to my belly button. When he laps at the indentation, my entire body shudders. I tug on his hair, and a growl rumbles up his chest. He slides down my body, then proceeds to lick up the honey from below my belly. My core clenches, and my pussy quivers. I want him to lick me there, but if he does, I'm going to come apart right here on the kitchen table. He blows on my swollen flesh, and I almost scream in frustration.

He presses tiny kisses on either side of my core. My scalp tingles. He stays poised over the most intimate part of me. His hot breath sears my pussy. Moisture pools in my channel. I yank at his hair, trying to get him to lift his head. At the same time, I can't stop myself from raising my hips, trying to chase that feeling of having his lips on that part of me which is currently crying for attention.

A low chuckle rolls from his lips, and the vibrations shudder over my skin. My nerve endings seem to detonate, my toes curl, and my nipples grow so hard that pain shivers from them.

"Goddamn you," I snarl, "what are you waiting for?"

He glances up at me from between my thighs. "This." He bares his teeth. "Ask for it, Sunshine."

I firm my lips.

"Do it." He lowers his voice to a hush. "Ask for what you want."

No.

No.

I swallow. "Make love to me, husband."

41

Axel

Heat coils low in my belly. All of the blood drains to my groin. *Husband.* This is my wife. In my house. Laid out for my delectation. Something hot stabs at my chest. My vision tunnels. "Say that again," I growl.

She licks her lips. Then, she draws in a breath. "Fuck me, husband."

"Good girl." I twist my lips.

Heat blooms on her cheeks.

Without taking my gaze off of her, I squeeze the backs of her thighs, then throw one leg over my shoulder. I lower my mouth and lick her from back hole to pussy.

A moan spills from her lips.

I lick her again, and her entire body jolts.

"You're so fucking sweet, baby."

I thrust my tongue inside her channel, and she yells. "Axel, oh my God!"

I continue to fuck her with my tongue as her entire body jerks. She squeezes her thighs around my neck, even as she pushes her pelvis up and into my face. I drag my tongue up her pussy lips, then bite down on her swollen clit. That's when she explodes. She arches off the table and grabs hold of my ears as the climax rips through her. She shudders as liquid heat slides down from between her thighs. I lower my head to lap it up, then climb over her body. I press my lips to hers and kiss her, then tear my mouth from hers. I slide the gun out from my waistband, place it to the side, then shove my sweats down my thighs.

"Open your eyes, baby," I order.

She flutters open her eyelids as I notch my cock to her opening.

"I love you." I lunge forward and into her with such force that her entire body moves forward. The table lurches, and I pull out of her, then slam into her again.

She groans, "Axel." She opens her mouth, and I fit my lips to hers again. I kiss her, thrust my tongue inside her mouth, as I begin to fuck her in earnest. In-out-in, I tilt my hips, thrust into her again, and my balls slap against her flesh. Her breasts are squeezed against my chest, her ankles knotted over my back. I stare into her green gaze as I reach down and slide my thumb inside her back hole. I plunge inside her and can feel my cock fill her, stretch her, and I slide inside her, and fuck, if that isn't the hottest thing I've ever felt. My dick lengthens, my balls draw up, and I groan as I come inside of her. I tear my lips from hers and stare into her eyes as I support my weight on my elbows.

"What are you doing to me?" I whisper. "Why do I feel so completely shaken when I'm with you?"

She presses her palm to my cheek. "You're different here ... so much more open, so much more—"

"Myself?" I turn my head into her palm and kiss the soft flesh.

"Did you mean it?" she asks in a soft voice.

"You mean about being completely shaken?" I turn to smirk at her.

She frowns. "No, what you said before that."

"About what you're doing to me?"

She slaps my shoulder. "Before that." Her cheeks grow pink. "You know what I mean."

"No, I don't." I chuckle.

"When you said that—"

"That?"

"That you love me."

I peer into her face. "What do you think?"

"That you do love me."

"I do," I agree, "I've never felt like this before, Sunshine. Never felt as if my insides were being torn out of me, never felt like I was on the edge of a precipice and about to go into free fall. Never felt like my heart didn't belong to me anymore. Never wanted to protect anyone like I want to take care of you."

She swallows, and a tear drop squeezes its way out of the corner of her eye.

"Fuck..." I stare. "Did I make you cry?"

"No, yes." She glances away then back at me. "That has to be the most romantic thing anyone has ever said to me."

"So, you're crying?"

"They're tears of joy," she explains.

I shake my head, then pull out of her.

"Oh!" she gasps.

I glance down to where my cum slides down her inner thigh.

"Fuck, that's hot." I reach down and push the liquid back inside her.

She draws in a sharp breath. I glance up at her. Her pupils dilate as she worries her lower lip.

"Told you, only I'm allowed to hurt you, babe." I reach up and tug her lip out from between her teeth.

"Why do you do that?" she asks in a low voice.

"Push my cum back inside of you?"

She flushes. "When you put it like that..." She squeezes her eyes shut. "It sounds so filthy."

"Good." I straighten, drag my sweats up, then slide the gun into my waistband before I haul her up in my arms. "And to answer your question, it's because I want to get you pregnant."

"What?" She stares up at me. "You did not just say that."

I chuckle as I walk out of the kitchen and up the stairs.

"Do you mean it?"

"I never say anything I don't."

"Jesus..." She shakes her head. "First you say you love me, then you say you want to get me pregnant."

"We're married," I point out.

"You realize, you have more Mafia in you than you care to admit."

"What do you mean?"

"This entire kidnapping me, bringing me to your home, then fucking the living daylights out of me and trying to get me pregnant. It's like, really possessive alpha-holish behavior."

"Alpha-holish?" I frown.

"Yeah, when you go all asshole and you're alpha, ergo—"

"I'll take that as a compliment." I smirk.

"Of course, you would." She snorts. "And if that isn't acting like one of the Sovranos, I don't know what is."

I frown as I walk into my bedroom.

"I didn't mean to upset you by saying that."

"You didn't upset me." I head into the bathroom. "But it's disconcerting to realize that you're right."

I reach the tub and set her down, then turn on the tap. The water flows into the tub and steam rises.

I straighten and glance down to find her staring up at me. "What?"

"Who are you and what have you done to Axel?"

"Not sure I follow," I reply.

"You're just so much more approachable, so real, so human … so much more; the kind of man I'd hoped to fall in love with."

"But?" I scowl.

"I … I don't think I'm in love with you—"

"Yet." I pick her up by her waist and place her in the tub.

She giggles nervously. "I'm still not used to your moving me around with such ease."

"You're a tiny thing," I point out.

"And you"—she reaches over and grips my cock—"are so big."

An hour later, I gaze at her, fast asleep in my bed. After that comment about my being so big, which fuck, if it didn't go straight to my head, not that it should have surprised me because I'm bigger than most men. And no, I didn't have to measure myself. It's something I've been told by other women. I frown. The thought of being with any of them doesn't sit right with me anymore. Guess I'm pussy-whipped by a tiny, curvy spitfire who has me completely under her spell. Sunshine turns over and sighs. Her fingers are wrapped around mine. I glance at my ring on her finger, and something fierce grips me. I bend down, press a kiss to her parted lips, then pull away from her.

The security app on my phone pings. I snatch up the phone and can't stop the smile that curls my lips. About damned time too.

I press a button on the app, then begin to get dressed.

As I pull on my clothes, I can't take my gaze off of her. She's mine to protect. Mine to cherish. And I'm going to make sure no one ever hurts her. Even if it means that I hurt myself in the process. I get dressed, then grab my gun from where I placed it on the bureau. I head down the steps toward the study, step inside, then come to a stop.

"Hello, motherfuckers."

42

Axel

"You don't seem too surprised to see us," Seb comments.

"I didn't make it hard for you to find me. I guess you could say I counted on it," I drawl.

Luca leans back in the chair behind my desk. He places one leg, then the other onto the surface. "Are you implying that you knew we'd come for you?"

"What I don't understand is why you did it in the first place." Massimo slides a book back into its place in the bookshelf, before he turns to face me. "If you wanted our attention, you had it already. And if you wanted to speak, we could have talked in Palermo."

"You knew this was the first place we'd look for you; that's why you're still here," Seb states.

"You're giving this *stronzo* too much credit," Luca protests.

"Your security arrangements are impressive. Your men recognized us, but once we explained to them that we were technically family, they didn't stop us," Massimo murmurs.

I tilt my head.

"You briefed them to let us in?" Massimo rubs his jaw. "Motherfucker, you did, didn't you?"

"I saw you on my security camera and told them to wave you on." I pull up the security app on my phone and show it to them.

"*Stocazzo!*" Luca swears.

"I'll be damned," Seb says slowly.

I glance between them. "Would you like a drink?" I stalk over to the bar at the far side, then grab a bottle of whiskey and proceed to pour the liquid into four glasses.

Massimo walks over to stand next to me. Seb approaches me and flanks me on the other side. They each reach for a glass. I grab mine and the remaining one, then walk over to my desk and place it in front of Luca.

He folds his arms across his chest and ignores it. I turn, raise my glass in Massimo and Seb's directions, before I down the alcohol.

Massimo and Seb follow suit.

"Good liquor." Massimo turns and snatches up the bottle, then whistles. "Macallan's forty-year-old, eh?"

"I like my whiskey." I raise a shoulder.

Massimo pours more of the alcohol into his glass, then tops up Seb's, before walking over to pour more liquor into my glass.

"So," he places the bottle on the desk behind me, "you going to tell us what this is about?"

"Where's Michael?"

"He couldn't come." Seb scowls as he sips from his glass. "Karma wasn't feeling well, so he opted to stay behind."

"Is she okay?"

"Is Theresa okay?" Luca shoots back.

"None of your business," I say without turning around.

"Ah, but it is, *stronzo*." He swings his legs off the desk and rises to his feet. "You made it our business when you pulled a gun on the Don and left with a woman who is under his protection."

"I confess, I don't see the logic in what you did." Massimo scratches his chin. "Hell, you married her. If you had asked Michael, he would have let you both leave with his blessings."

"And this way, I didn't have to ask anyone." I roll my shoulders. "I left with what's mine."

"After you threatened the Don in front of the entire town and in church." Luca clicks his tongue. "Either you're very foolish or—"

"You have a plan," Seb cuts in. "By drawing attention to us and making us seem weak, you ensured that every single rival clan looked at this as the opportunity to go on the offensive against us."

"In fact, you counted on it." Massimo takes a sip from his glass. "You hoped we'd be so preoccupied by attacks it would take us time to regroup."

"I had hoped it would land you in enough heat that it would delay your coming after me, yes."

"Something which, clearly, didn't work. As you can see…" Luca rounds the desk, grabs his glass, and stands next to Massimo. "We're here to take the two of you back to Palermo."

"And if I refuse?"

"This isn't us asking," Seb says in a mild tone. "We have come to accompany you back to the bosom of *la famiglia*, whether it's with your consent or not."

"Oh?" I take a drink of my whiskey. "It really is good, isn't it?" I tilt my head. "Although, it's nothing like the one-hundred-year-old whiskey, which isn't for consumption by the likes of you."

"Likes of us?" Luca's features darken. "What the fuck is that supposed to mean?"

"He's trying to get a rise out of you," Massimo warns.

"Well, he's succeeding," Luca growls.

I turn to him. "You realize you're the vulnerable point in this entire family? The one who talks without thinking. Who shoots before he's ready to face the consequences of his actions."

His features distort. The next second, he moves, but my gun is already in my hand. We aim our guns at each other.

"*Cazzo*," Massimo scowls, "put 'em down, you *stronzos*."

Neither Luca nor I move. We glare at each other. Luca's jaw is hard. The skin around his eyes tightens. A nerve pops at his temple as he holds my gaze.

"Put down your guns," Seb snaps. "Let's talk this through without killing each other, shall we?"

"I don't know, from where I am, a bullet in his thick, fat head seems like a better use of my time than trying to parlay."

"You're pushing your luck, you *testa di cazzo*," Luca growls.

I allow my lips to curl in the semblance of a smile. "Like I said, you're the weak link in this chain. If there's anyone who will bring down the Sovranos, it's you, asshole."

Luca's lips firm; his fingers tighten on his trigger.

I laugh. "You going to shoot me, motherfucker?"

"I'm fucking tempted," Luca says in a hard voice.

Massimo glances between us. "Put down the guns, you *coglioni*."

Luca winces.

"At some point, I'm going to need a translation of the expressions you guys seem to bandy about with such alacrity," I drawl.

"Stand down, both of you." Seb scowls. "This is getting fucking tiring. Let's talk like adults, so I can head back home."

"What's the hurry?" I shoot him a sideways glance. "Have someone waiting for you, eh?"

"None of your business," he replies. "Are you guys going to stop acting like irresponsible *faccia di merda* or what?"

"I know what *merda* means," I mutter.

"Congratulations," Luca snorts, "the only word you understood is the one that translates to *shit*. Figures."

I eye him with scorn. "What are you, seven? If you're trying to insult me, you could, at least, come up with a better one than that."

"How about *fetente*?" Luca scowls at me. "That's an improvement, actually. You're more of a *fetente* than a *pezzo di merda*."

"What the hell does *fetente* mean?"

"At least your accent is good." Massimo nods in my direction.

"Stinking pile of shit," Luca offers helpfully.

"Like I said, your insults are immature." I shake my head.

"Says the man who pulled the most juvenile stunt of the century." Luca chortles.

"Fuck you, man," I growl. I shouldn't let his ribbing get to me, but damn, if I can't feel the skin under my collar grow hot.

"Fuck me?" Luca laughs. "Fuck you, motherfucker."

"So, you do know how to insult in English, eh?"

"Fuck!" Seb scowls between us. "Lower your guns. Both of you. Right now."

"First you," I snap.

"First you," Luca says at the same time.

"*Gesù Cristo*, clearly, Luca is not the only hot-headed one in the family anymore," Seb growls.

Luca and I glare at each other for a few seconds, then both of us lower our guns at the same time.

I slide my gun into my waistband, while Luca places his on the table.

He reaches for his drink, which he managed to place on the table at the same time that he drew his gun, and I didn't even notice. Bastard's fast, I'll give him that.

"Finally, fuck." Seb rubs the back of his neck. "Let's talk like grown-ups, shall we?"

"On the contrary, let's not." A new voice sounds from the direction of the door.

I swing toward the door, then draw in a breath.

"Told you, you'd regret throwing me out of your house." He presses his gun into Theresa's temple.

"Motherfucker!" I reach for my gun, but he shakes his head.

"Touch your gun, and she dies."

My heart rate ratchets up. My pulse pounds at my temple. A bead of sweat trails down my temple as I take in her features. Her color is pale, her hair flowing about her shoulders. She's wearing the same shirt that I pulled off her earlier. Thankfully, she's also wearing my boxer briefs under it. She swallows but gives no other sign of being nervous. I hold her gaze and try to communicate my strength to her. I must succeed, for she jerks her chin in a slight gesture.

Behind me, I sense Luca reach for his gun, but Freddie shoots at the table. Chips of wood fly out, and Luca swears.

"Keep your hands where I can see them." Freddie jerks his chin in Luca's direction. "And that goes for you too." He narrows his gaze on me.

I hesitate, and he must push his gun into Theresa's temple, for she makes a small sound at the back of her throat. My chest tightens. Adrenaline laces my blood. How dare he put his hands on her? How dare he hold a gun to her? How dare he walk into my house and touch my wife? Anger floods my blood.

My vision tunnels. The blood pumps so hard that I can hear each beat of my heart in my ears.

"Axe!" Seb's voice cuts through the noise in my head. "Don't," he growls.

I swallow down the fear that bubbles up my throat, then raise my hands.

"Good." Freddie smiles. "Now we talk."

43

Theresa

I woke up and found myself alone. So, I dressed quickly in his T-shirt and boxers and wandered downstairs, where I heard voices from the library. Hate to say it, but I decided to spy on the Sovranos and my husband. I know, I shouldn't have, but I couldn't help it. I was curious about the dynamics between them. And I wanted to see how Axel would react to them. Would they actually end up fighting it out? Or would they arrive at some kind of agreement? And would Axel actually agree to return to Palermo?

To be honest, I don't want to return, but I wanted to see how things would play out between them. So, I stayed silent and peeked in on the conversation. I was so engrossed in the dynamics between the four of them that by the time I heard the footstep behind me, it was too late. I turned and recognized him as the man I saw leaving after threatening Axel the other day; by which time, he already had a gun pressed to my temple.

I'm so damn angry for allowing myself to fall into this situation. I'm conforming to the stereotype of the helpless woman in distress, something that the Cosa Nostra has always warned us about. It's why they don't want us involved in the business end of things—there's also their belief that their women make them weak—which is why they prefer us to be hidden out of sight of their enemies. All dolled up and waiting for them when they come home. Even when I thought that I'd be married to Xander, I swore that I wouldn't be a typical Mafia wife. Xander was an artist; no way would he have forced me to be so submissive.

When I met Axel, though, everything changed. I was so attracted to him, so under his spell that I could never deny him anything, anyway. Which is all the more reason why I want to find my backbone, some semblance of being my own person. At least, in other parts of my life.

That's why I decided to stay back and not let them know I was there, so I could get more information on the situation, because, hell, everyone in the Cosa Nostra knows that information is power. And while I'd never consciously keep anything from Axel... Hell, I also wasn't going to turn down the opportunity that had presented itself... And now I've landed in exactly the kind of situation that the Mafia has warned us about. *Cazzo!*

I hold Axel's gaze, take in how his jaw is clenched, how his features are pale and his gaze angry as he glances from me to the man who's holding a gun to my head, then back at me. Is he upset with me? I wouldn't blame him if he were. *Maledizioni,* I'm upset with myself for landing in this quandary.

The man urges me forward, and I take a step toward Axel, then another. The whole time, Axel holds my gaze. The anger bleeds out of his features, leaving an expressionless mask. He holds up his arms, palms face up, as he tracks us. I pause, and the man behind me digs his gun into my temple again. My heart slams into my chest, sweat pools in my underarms, and I can't stop the breath that catches in my chest. Axel notices it, and his jaw tics. His blue gaze deepens. For a second, I spot something like fear—for me?—then it's gone, and the inscrutable look is back on his face.

"Keep moving," the man behind me barks. I walk in the direction he urges me. He grips my shoulder, and I almost stumble, but he rights me with an arm around my waist. I flinch and try to pull away, but his grip tightens.

"Let go of her," Axel says in a hard voice.

"I will," the man drawls, "but you understand, the only way to ensure your cooperation is if I keep her hostage?"

"If you dare hurt one hair on her head, I'll kill you," Axel's tone is impassive, like his face.

The man laughs. "Wonderful. All that passion just waiting to be unleashed. It will make for an impressive finale."

"The fuck you talking about?" Axel growls.

"You know what I'm talking about," the man replies. "You owe me, Axel."

"I owe you nothing."

"I gave you a place in my gang, a purpose. I taught you everything I knew. Hell, I treated you like a son."

"Fuck you," Axel replies.

The man chuckles. "You never could get away from your Italian blood, could you? I tried to teach you to be calm and measured in your approach. To think strategically before you made your move. To make a plan and focus on the end goal. And you were nearly there too." He shakes his head. "But I should have known, the apple doesn't fall far from the tree. In the end, you reverted to your true nature. Like your old man, you let your emotions get the better of you, and now look where that's landed you."

"Who the fuck are you?" Seb scowls.

"You mean your brother hasn't told you?" the man asks, his tone gleeful. "Shit, I do love big reveals. And set pieces. You've gotta admit, it doesn't get more impressive than this, with most of the key players all in one place."

"What the fuck are you talking about?" Luca growls.

The man holds up his hand. "Let's not get ahead of ourselves, shall we?" He turns to Axel. "You want to tell them, or should I?"

Axel's jaw tics. His shoulders flex, but he doesn't move. Doesn't say another word.

"Guess I'll have to do the honors, eh?" The man all but cackles. "But first, allow me to introduce myself. Freddie Nielsen, at your service. If the surname is familiar, it's because I'm related to the legendary Nielsen brothers."

"The fuck you talking about?" Massimo lowers his chin to his chest.

"You know Ronnie and Reggie Nielsen? The well-known English mobsters who also happened to be twins? There was a Hollywood film made about them, with a very famous Hollywood actor playing both lead roles. I do fancy I'm more handsome than him, though. They should have given the role to me, don't you think?"

A bead of sweat runs down my temple. Axel doesn't take his gaze off of me. I hold onto his gaze, drawing strength from it. He won't let anything happen to me. He can't let anything happen to me. He'll save me. I know he will.

"And you are the Sovranos, of course. At least, you're better looking than your father."

Seb stiffens. "You knew our father?"

"Did *I* know your father?" Freddie laughs.

I sense the vibrations roll up his chest and try to put distance between us, but he yanks me even closer to him. My skin crawls, and a trickle of revulsion slithers down my spine. Terror grips my chest, and I stare at Axel, willing him to do something, anything, to help me. His jaw flexes, and the nerve grows even more prominent at his temple. The fingers of his right hand curl slightly. My gaze flicks to his hand, then back to his face. He shakes his head, the motion almost imperceptible, except I've been watching him so closely that I spot it.

"We were partners," Freddie clarifies.

"Partners?" Luca frowns. "Dear old dad didn't do partners. He wouldn't even entertain the thought of any of us succeeding him. He had to die for Michael to finally become Don."

"And why do you think that was?" Freddie waves his hand holding the gun.

All of my muscles tense. Axel's chest rises and falls. His gaze tracks the gun as Freddie leans forward and further into me in his excitement. "He already had a partner, so he couldn't entertain the thought of anyone else cutting in on his empire."

Axel's gaze narrows, the skin around his mouth whitens, his shoulders flex, and he seems like he's about to rush forward and drag Freddie off of me. This time, it's me who shakes my head slightly. *Please,* I plead with my gaze, *please, don't do anything foolish.*

He must understand me, for he nods.

"I don't believe you," Seb finally says. "And even if I did, what difference would that make?"

"What do you want from us?" Luca growls.

"Not you, him." Freddie jerks his chin at Axel. "Shoot him."

"What?" Axel scowls.

"Your brother." Freddie nods in Seb's direction. "You can start with him."

"Why would I do that?" Axel growls.

"Shoot him, or I shoot her." He places the barrel of the gun against my temple again, and I can't stop the sound of panic that spills from my lips. My heart slams against my ribcage. Adrenaline laces my blood.

"Do it," Freddie snaps.

Axel's features tighten. He lowers his hand, reaches for the gun at the small of his back, then he draws it and raises it.

"No funny business now, or I'll shoot your wife." Freddie tightens his grip on me, and I groan.

Axel's entire body goes rigid. "Don't hurt her, you motherfucker," he says in a low voice, "I'll do as you say."

He turns slightly and levels his gun at Seb.

"Cazzo," Massimo swears.

"Knew you'd turn on us," Luca glares at him. "Don't fucking shoot him, you *carogna*."

Axel cocks the pistol, and the sound echoes through the space. Goose bumps pop on my skin. The hair on the back of my neck rises.

"Don't," I manage to push out the word through a throat gone dry.

Seb seems to freeze, every muscle in his body wound so tightly that the tension pours off of him. He meets Axel's gaze, and the two seem to engage in a face-off.

The silence stretches a second, then another.

"The fuck you waiting for?" Freddie bursts out. "Shoot him, you basta—"

A shot rings out. I squeeze my eyes shut and cry out. Something clatters to the ground, then his grip on my waist loosens. I turn to find Freddie staggering back. He has his palm pressed to his side. Blood flows down his arm and drips to the floor. I hear someone screaming from a distance. My throat hurts, and that's when I realize it's me.

Axel moves in Freddie's direction, his gun in his outstretched hand. Freddie pushes me forward. My foot hits the gun that Freddie dropped, and it clatters away. I stumble forward, and Axel swerves to the side and catches me. Seb bends to pick up the gun, then charges past us, following Luca and Massimo.

I stare up into Axel's expressionless face. He's glaring down at me, anger in his eyes.

"Axel?" I venture.

"You're okay?" he says in that expressionless tone.

I nod.

"If anything had happened to you, I'd never have been able to forgive myself." He wipes my cheek, and his hand comes away bloodied.

I press my palm to my face and rub at whatever is there.

"Are you hurt?" he asks.

"No." I swallow. My stomach churns. "I … I don't think it's my blood."

He drags the back of his hand across my cheek again and again. "He touched you," he says in a hard voice. "The bastard dared to put his hands on you. He held a gun to you." He lowers his hand. "I'm going to kill him." He tries to brush past me, but I grab his arm.

"Don't go. Please, Axel, don't go." My voice wavers, and damn it, I don't want to appear weak, but the thought of that monster's blood tainting my skin…? Somehow, it feels worse than having him hold a gun to my temple. A trembling grips me.

"Sunshine?" Axel's features seem to fade in and out.

My hands and feet feel so cold. It's the adrenaline draining away, I realize, but I can't stop my body from swaying. Dark specks flicker at the edges of my vision.

"Theresa," he calls as he grips my shoulders. The heat of his body flows over me, and I lean into him.

"Axel," I whisper, "I… I lo—" Darkness overwhelms me.

44

Axel

"Theresa, baby." I catch her as she slumps against me. "Fuck, fuck, fuck." I hold her close and peer into her features. "Open your eyes, Sunshine." My heart is racing so hard, I'm sure it's going to jump out of my ribcage. My stomach ties itself in knots. Why did she collapse? Is she hurt? I rake my gaze across her face but can't find any injury. "Goddammit." I scoop her up in my arms, then walk over to the settee and lower her to it.

Water, I need water. I glance around, spot a bottle of water on the table, and leap toward it. I snatch up the bottle, race back to her, and splash some of the water on her face. She moans, then her eyelids flicker.

"Bloody hell." I haul her to my chest and hold her and rock her. My heart beat refuses to slow down, and my stomach is still tied up in knots. "You scared me, baby, you fucking made me die a thousand deaths in those few minutes."

"S ... sorry." She coughs. "I think everything just finally got to me." She shudders. "Is he gone?"

"I think the others are still in pursuit, but," I squeeze my arms around her. "I need to go after him and—"

"And what, kill him?" She peers up at me. "Is that what you're going to do?"

"You know the kind of life I live, Sunshine. Death and I are not strangers by any stretch of imagination."

"I won't let you go after him." She grips the front of my shirt. "If something were to happen to you, I wouldn't be able to survive it."

I hold her gaze, then bend and brush my lips over hers. "Nothing is going to happen to me. You, on the other hand," I cup her cheek, "you're fragile and so vulnerable. It's because of me that he came after you. I put you in danger."

"No!" She shakes her head. "You know better than that. When you live in the world of the Mafia, you have to be prepared for something like this happening."

"And yet, you were safe until I came along."

"You don't believe that," she argues.

"I do," I nod. The band around my chest is so tight that I can't breathe. "You sure you're okay?" I search her features. "You sure you haven't been hurt?"

"I'm fine," she whispers.

I place my palm over hers, wanting to hold her close. Wanting to reassure her and tell her that I'll never leave her side again. That we'll always be together. That I'll always be there to take care of her.

Lies. All lies. It's because of me that bastard Freddie got to her. It's because I married her, she came to his attention. It's because I brought her here, I put her squarely on the radar of every criminal who holds a grudge against me.

I drop my hand from hers and try to rise, but she doesn't let go of me.

"Don't," she begs, "please, don't leave me."

I glance down at where she clutches the front of my shirt, then back at her face. I gently try to unhook her fingers from my shirt, but she holds on.

"Axel, don't do it." A tear slides down her cheek. "Please, Axel, please don't."

"You don't know what I'm going to do."

"Don't I?" She swallows, "You're blaming yourself right now for what happened. You think I'll be safer if I'm away from you. You think if you're not with me, I'll be safe."

"It's true." I glance away. "I can't protect you, my own wife." I squeeze my eyes shut. "I promised that you were not in any danger, that I'd make sure nothing happened to you. I failed."

"You shot him." She grips my cheek and tries to turn me to face her. "It's because of you that he's gone."

"It's because of me that he decided to use you as a way to get to me."

"But you saved me."

"I almost got you killed."

"I'm here. So are you. We're both fine. That's all that matters."

"Is it, though?" I turn to meet her gaze. "What about the next time it happens? And the time after that? What if I'm not there to save you the next time?"

"You'll always be there for me." She swallows.

"Not anymore." I tug her fingers from the front of my shirt, then hold her palms between my own for just a second. Her soft skin, the scent of apple blossoms, the feel of her curves against mine... I commit it all to memory before I release her fingers and rise to my feet.

"Axel!" She sits up. "Where are you going?"

"Away from you."

"I'm your wife!" She jumps up to her feet. "My place is with you."

"Not if I divorce you."

"What?" Her voice trembles. "What do you mean?"

I glance at her over my shoulder. "I never should have married you in the first place. It was all a sham; you know that, right? A way to get close to the Sovranos."

"You don't mean it," she cries. "I know you love me. You told me so."

"It's amazing how good pussy can make a man lose his head and say things in the heat of the moment. I—"

She raises her hand, and her palm connects with my face. Pain lances across my nerve-endings, but that's nothing compared to the agony that squeezes my chest.

"What's happening here?" Seb's voice sounds from the direction of the doorway. I turn to find him prowling in.

"Are you okay, Theresa?" He scowls.

"I am now," she says in a toneless voice.

"He knocked out the security guards on his way in," Massimo says in a disgusted voice as he reenters the room.

I glance at my phone and notice the notification on my security app. "I missed the warning that he breached my security measures," I growl.

"And he gave us the slip, *cazzo!*" Massimo rakes his fingers through his hair. "Who is he? If he was our father's partner, then why haven't we ever heard about him?"

"Who the fuck knows?" I raise a shoulder. "And are you actually surprised your father kept secrets from you?"

"What's your connection to this Freddie character?" Luca steps inside and shuts the door behind him. "You'd better come clean, *stronzo*. It's time for you to stop with the lies."

I glance from him to Massimo, who stares at me with a quizzical look on his face, to Seb, who surveys me with a shrewd gaze.

"I don't believe I owe you an explanation."

"Oh, you're hardly in a position to refuse." Luca laughs.

"Oh, but I think I am," I drawl.

Luca scowls, and Massimo's gaze narrows.

Behind me, I sense her drawing in a breath, but she doesn't say anything. I dare not glance over my shoulder at her. If I do, I'll weaken, and I can't afford that. All I have to do is make sure that she is safe… Focus, focus on that.

"Is that right?" Seb says in a soft voice.

"Indeed." I step away, creating distance from all of them. "You see, I think I hold all of the cards here." I glance at each of them in turn, then fold my arms over my chest. "I'm a cop."

45

Axel

"What?" Massimo gapes.

"I knew it." Luca laughs. "I knew you would betray us." He turns on Seb. "Told you, didn't I?"

Seb rubs his chin as he watches me with a moody gaze. "Explain," he finally says. "You're a cop, and you were working with him?" He nods toward the doorway through which Freddie had earlier disappeared.

"Undercover." I blow out a breath. "I was working undercover."

"Undercover?" Sunshine exhales. "So all this time ... when you were in a coma, when you asked me to move into the same home as you, when you married me—?"

"I was undercover," I reply. "I have been undercover for the last five years."

"Five years?" Massimo rubs the back of his neck. "What have you been doing during that time?"

"Building my reputation in the underworld, working closely with Freddie and building his trust."

"A trust that you broke today when you fired at him," Seb points out.

"Too bad I missed," I growl.

"So, you were trying to get enough evidence to put him behind bars?" Massimo asks.

"And the lot of you," I admit. "It's why I married Theresa, so I could have an 'in' to your inner circle. It's why—"

"You wanted a seat at the table with Michael." Luca whistles. "The Don is not going to be happy."

"Is that the only reason you decided to take on this assignment?" Seb folds his arms over his chest. "Seems it was much more than professional interest at stake here."

"That's a brilliant deduction." I snort. "Of course, it wasn't only professional. I had a personal stake in bringing you guys down. It was because of my personal connection that I got this case."

"Seems you would have been too close to the targets to be allowed to take on this case."

"It's amazing how persuasion and corruption can go hand-in-hand within the ranks of the police department."

"They are the same as us." Luca tosses his head. "Fucking pigs, with their holier-than-thou attitude. Ultimately, it always comes down to money and power. Throw in a personal stake, and anything can bend your way."

"So, you wanted to take us down." Seb tilts his head. "That's why you took on this case?"

"What other reason could there be?" I widen my stance. "You guys are the Cosa Nostra, the most wanted criminals in Europe, and you've been allowed free reign for too long."

"Maybe you wanted to know more about your birth family? Wanted to find out about your brothers?"

"I told you, my mother never mentioned the fact that I was one among triplets or that I had brothers, for that matter."

"Perhaps you wanted to find out where you came from"—Seb drums his fingers on his chest—"get to know your family better."

"Perhaps," I concede, "but the main reason I took on the assignment was so I could bring you all down, make no mistake about that."

"You'd do that to your own family?" Luca growls.

"You're not my family," I shoot back. "Your father—"

"Our father," Massimo corrects me.

"Your father turned out my mother when she needed help."

"She wanted to leave," Luca points out. "It's why he let her go."

"After ensuring that he had exchanged us for assets. That's all he was concerned about. Power. And your grandmother? She didn't try to stop him."

"So, for what you think were their misdeeds you want to bring down the only blood relations you have?" Massimo drawls.

"Yes," I say without hesitation. "The lot of you belong behind bars."

"And you, where do you belong?" Theresa cuts in.

"Not with you," I say without looking at her, yet I sense her flinch. My stomach knots, and bile sloshes up my throat. Goddamn it. Apparently, even my body knows when I'm lying. As long as I can keep the expression off my face and make sure that she believes me...

"Why are you telling us all of this now?" Seb finally asks.

"I want to cut a deal with you," I respond.

"Of course, you do." Luca raises his gaze skywards. "This keeps getting better and better."

Seb narrows his gaze on me. "What sort of a deal?"

Luca glowers at him.

"What do you want?" Massimo snaps.

"I want you to take her back to Palermo and make sure she is safe."

Theresa stiffens, but she doesn't say anything.

"Done." Seb nods.

"What the fuck?" Luca rounds on him. "You're actually going to agree without asking him what he is going to do for us in return?"

"What do we get in return?" Seb raises his chin.

"I give a version of events to my bosses that will ensure you guys are cleared … largely." I glance between them. "Of course, one of you may have to take the fall for some of the events, and perhaps do a reduced jail time." I glance at Luca, who glowers at me.

"Fuck you," he snaps.

"Indeed." I blow out a breath. "Look, it's the best I can do, and you know it could have been a lot worse than this. I hold the fate of your futures in my hands." I tilt my head in Seb's direction. "Wouldn't you agree?"

"Of course, we could kill you and make it look like it was Freddie. Without backup, you don't hold much leverage," Seb reminds me.

"Then again, I'm your brother, and I'm married to Theresa, who is under your protection, so..." I raise a shoulder.

He holds my gaze for a few seconds, then he nods. "I'll need to discuss this with Michael."

Tension leaches out of my shoulders. "Of course." I jerk my chin. "I'll be waiting outside."

I head toward the door when she calls out, "So this is it? You're going to leave me without even a goodbye."

I pause, then grit my teeth before schooling my features into some semblance of normalcy. I glance at her over my shoulder and choke out the words, "Goodbye, Theresa." Turning, I stalk out.

46

Theresa

"So, he walked out on you?" Elsa glances at me with wide eyes. "He just left?"

"Y-e-a-p!" I nod.

Damn it, I was dreading this conversation, which is why I have stayed away from my shop since arriving home. Hell, I didn't even go home. Instead, I stayed with Michael and Karma for the week since returning from London. They have respected my privacy and let me be. Which means I've done nothing but sleep late most days, and cry myself to sleep most nights. In between, Cass had taken over the job of getting my food to my room.

Initially, I protested, but she brooked no arguments. She told me I should focus on simply getting my strength back. I was too heartbroken to protest, so I took advantage of the generosity of my friends. It took five days for me to venture out of my room, and a week for me to face up to my life and tell them that I was ready to face the world. I asked to move back into Xander's home, and Michael was more than happy for me to do that. So I have taken up residence in the home of the man I once thought I loved, which later became the home of the man I know I still love, and neither of them are here with me.

It was clear that he was… He still is my future. There is no one else for me, except him. If only he would realize that. I finally made it to work today, and as expected, Elsa is full of questions. It doesn't seem half as agonizing as I anticipated to talk to her about what happened. In fact, it's almost a relief to be able to finally share the events with a friend.

"And this was right after he told you all that he was an undercover cop?" Her voice rises in disbelief.

I nod again.

She blinks rapidly. "And they let him leave?"

"Seb called Michael, but I didn't hear what he said." I raise a shoulder.

"Ah!" Elsa's face flushes.

"You okay?" I peer into her features.

"Of course." She glances around the tiny office we share behind the flower shop. "Is it warm in here? Did you turn up the heat again?"

"No, I didn't." I watch as she goes to the window and flings it open, then leans out and takes in a few deep breaths, before she turns to face me again.

"I have to admit, everyone seems to have behaved in a very civilized manner."

"You mean, considering it was more or less a stand-off between the cops and the Mafia?" I ask wryly.

"We live in Mafia land, so I wasn't surprised you were linked to the Sovranos, but…" She shakes her head. "What are the odds that you'd marry a man who was trying to take them down?"

"I know, right?" I shake my head.

"I can't believe he would leave like that," Elsa says in a soft voice.

"Me neither." I shuffle my feet. A tightness grips my chest, and I fold my fingers together in front of me. *I will not cry. I will not cry.* I will not regress to my state of mind during the first few days when we returned from London. I cried bucket loads, trying to make sense of everything that had happened, and I didn't think there was anything left, but it feels like there's still more in there, waiting for an opportunity to reveal my misery. Dammit.

Karma and Cass have rallied around me, even though Karma has been unwell, suffering from morning sickness in the first trimester of her pregnancy. She lost her first child in the same car blast that killed Xander. So she's trying to be extra careful with this one. Not to mention, Michael won't let her out of his sight.

Christian and Aurora returned from their honeymoon, though the two of them still spend a lot of time together. It feels good to see both of these happy couples. It gives me some hope that true love is still alive in the world. That true love will find a way. I know a bit about what happened with both couples, and I find myself fantasizing about Axel coming back to me, but sometimes, I think I must be delusional.

He sent me away, said he didn't love me. And for what? Because he was angry with himself for not having protected me better? Because he was a coward and couldn't stand the fact that he loved me so much that it hurt him? Either way, he simply walked out on me, with no explanation. Goddamn. I rub my forehead.

"Have you heard from him since?" Elsa asks softly.

I shake my head. "He said that he wanted a divorce—"

"No!" Elsa bursts out. "That cad! How could he do this?"

"Yeah.. " I laugh bitterly. "To be honest, I'm still getting my head around everything."

"Maybe you shouldn't have come in. Perhaps, you should have just taken more time off—"

"And do what?" I sniffle. "I don't want to stay at Axel's place, surrounded by memories and thoughts of what-if. And my mother and my sister have been so supportive, you know? They haven't pushed me for any explanations, but I don't want to go there either. Of course, my sister, Sara, thinks I should just forget everything and move on."

"And would you be able to do that? Move on, I mean?" Elsa murmurs.

I stare at the computer screen of which I've been trying to work through some of the accounts. Yeah, I've been so desperate to keep my mind occupied that I actually decided to tackle the annual taxes. Go figure.

The tears I've held back so far trickle down my cheeks. "Oh hell…" I wipe them away, but they continue to fall faster. "Damn it." I reach for a tissue and blow into it. "I don't want to cry. I don't want to cry over that asshole, but damn it, I do miss him. I didn't know him for very long, but every time I close my eyes, my mind takes me right back to the time we spent together. And how I felt when I was with him."

"How did you feel?" she asks softly.

"I felt … complete, you know?" I wipe my cheek on my shoulder. "I felt grounded, like I had found my mooring. Like I had found something I didn't even know I was missing." I turn to stare at her over the table. "Is it possible to feel so much for someone you knew for such a short time?"

My face crumples. "Damn, damn, damn." I bury my face in my hands and bite down on the inside of my cheek. I so don't want to cry. It doesn't make me feel any better. I only end up with a headache and a stuffy nose after each crying jag, and I really don't want that right now.

"Oh, honey." Elsa walks over and bends to hug me. "I'm so sorry, Theresa, I truly am. I wish I could do something to help you."

"You are." I sniffle, then swallow down my tears. She leans back, and I lower my hands. "I'm fine as long as I keep my mind occupied."

She straightens. "Hey, you can tackle the taxes. I'm not complaining."

I laugh.

"But we need to do something else, something to really take your mind off of everything and help you get over that *stronzo*." She taps her cheek.

"What are you thinking of?"

"Something you're going to absolutely love."

"I am?" I ask cautiously.

"Yes!" She snaps her fingers. "I know just the thing."

"You sure? The last time you tried to cheer me up, I had three men in strange purple suits try to serenade me as I walked the street."

"They were a Mariachi band," she protests.

"Who carried loads of flowers on their backs."

"I was trying to combine it with a marketing stunt for the shop," she reminds me.

"I was really embarrassed when they followed me around on the street. Everyone was watching me."

"Everyone was applauding their singing," she points out.

"The most embarrassing moment of my life." I scowl at her.

"Well, they cheered you up and took your mind off of the fact that our business was really slow, didn't they?"

"Temporarily," I admit. "You also spent money we didn't have," I add.

"But thanks to the stunt, people noticed you and our little flower shop, and business picked up shortly afterward.

"It's true, but that was just a coincidence."

"My ideas always pay off." She tosses her hair over her shoulder. "It's just that it might take a little time to see the benefits."

"Hmm..." I rise to my feet. "Just as long as there are no mariachis, or anyone following me around with flowers, trying to serenade me."

47

A week later

Axel

I walk up the path that leads to my new home. After the Sovranos left with Theresa—I didn't see her after that insulting goodbye that she didn't deserve. Call me a coward, but I knew if I saw her face again, I'd haul her to me and ask her to forgive me, and I couldn't let that happen. For her own safety, it's best that I maintain my distance from her. At least, until I untangle this mess that is my life. I marched into the police headquarters the next day and met my boss. I gave him the abbreviated versions of events—it's always best to stick as close to the truth as possible—and shared just enough information on the Sovranos so he wouldn't suspect that I was trying to hide anything from him. It was helpful that I had information about Trinity and their efforts to move everything toward the right side of the law. Everything was going swimmingly. Well, until I told him I wanted to resign. James was suspicious, of course. He's a cop, and his instincts must have prompted him to ask me if I had fallen in love with the woman I married.

I didn't deny it, nor did I answer the question. I slipped my hand into my pocket and toyed with the ring that I had taken off before walking in there. Yeah, I wasn't able to take it off earlier, nor could I bring myself to start divorce proceedings. I mean, it's only been a week, but yes, I still have feelings for her. Turns out, I can't just stop myself from thinking about her, dreaming about her, wanting her, needing her, tasting her essence on my tongue, sensing her curves under my fingertips. Goddamn it, I'm a goner. I know I hurt her with what I did, but damn, if I didn't hurt myself more.

James refused my resignation. He told me I was too important of an asset. He told me to debrief the assignment to the rest of my team, then to make sure I had written up my notes, including any incriminating evidence to help them crack down on those within the organized crime groups with which I had interacted. Then, he ordered me to take some paid time off, as much as I need, until I've cleared my head, and think about whether I want to continue with the assignment or not. I was too exhausted to argue with him, so I complied. At least, I no longer have to keep in touch with my team and send them updates on my assignment. One less lie to live, for which I am grateful.

I decided to move out of the house which I had occupied throughout the time I was undercover. I had gotten used to the place, I admit, but the fact that Freddie was able to get through my guards and my security left a bad taste in my mouth.

I opted to move into an apartment block in an upcoming suburb of London. Now, I push the door open and walk in. The floor-to-ceiling windows at the end of the living room frame the view of an illuminated London Bridge, and beyond that, the lights of the city spread out. Without bothering to turn on the lights, I walk toward the view. My footsteps echo through the empty room.

I moved in, but I haven't had the motivation to furnish it yet. I left everything in the house when I moved out, since it was all a part of the undercover façade and didn't belong to me. The only furniture I have now is the mattress in the bedroom. I mean, I need a place to sleep, right?

I slide my hand in my pocket, and my fingers brush the hair tie that I've never stopped carrying around with me. I pull it out and stare at the sparkly purple color. So like her—vivacious and full of life. And I sent her away. I'm responsible for hurting her again… And after I swore that I'd never do anything to harm her. I did the right thing, so why am I still carrying around her hair-tie like a love-sick fool? *You know why.* I slide the hair band into my pocket.

A slight noise behind me makes me stiffen. The hair on the back of my neck prickles. Every muscle in my body tenses as I force myself to breathe… I raise my gaze and take in the shadow visible in the glass pane in front. He draws closer … closer… When he reaches for me, I swerve, then turn and grab his outstretched arm, flip him around and lock him in a chokehold.

"Fuck," he swears, "let go of me, you *stronzo*."

He's my height, built like me, and wears a tailor-made suit. He also swears in Italian… Fuck. I release him, and he spins around to face me.

"The fuck, you *pezzo di merda*!" Christian scowls at me.

"That's what happens when you sneak up on me, you wanker," I snap.

"I wasn't sneaking up—"

"You broke into my apartment—"

"The door was open," he points out.

"Fuck." I drag my fingers through my hair. Clearly, I was seriously distracted if I forgot to shut and lock the door to my own apartment. "Fucking, fuck." I brush past him and head for the breakfast counter and the bottle of whiskey that I had placed there. I open it, then chug down a mouthful straight from the bottle.

"Classy," Christian murmurs, as I turn to face him.

"The fuck you doing here?" I growl.

"More like, the fuck you doing here?" He slides his hands into his pockets, and goddamn, but his stance is so similar to what mine was just a few seconds ago. A hot sensation stabs at my chest. I raise the bottle to my lips and take another swig of the alcohol.

"You going to share that?" He jerks his chin in my direction.

"No," I say through gritted teeth as the alcohol hits my stomach. Warmth radiates to my extremities; too bad, my heart is still encased in ice.

He laughs. "Goddamn, but you are stubborn."

"Why did you come here?" I wipe the back of my palm over my mouth.

He widens his stance. "I could say that it's a social visit, but both you and I would know that I was lying."

I tilt my head.

He moves forward and pauses on the other side of the counter. "What are you doing, Axel?" His blue eyes, almost the same color as mine, meet my gaze.

"What does it look like?" I crack my neck. "I'm living my life."

"Not much of an existence, is it?" He glances around the space. "Is this how you plan to live the rest of your life, alone?"

"It's how I've lived thus far," I retort.

"Doesn't mean it has to be this way moving forward."

"So, what, you want me to return to the bosom of the family and embrace my Mafioso roots?"

"I never said that."

"You're beginning to bore me." I pretend to yawn. "If you have something to say, say it. Otherwise, get the fuck out." I raise the bottle of whiskey, and he swoops out and grabs it. The whiskey spills over my sweatshirt, and some of it splashes onto the counter. "Fuck," I swear, "that's good whiskey, man."

He yanks at the bottle again. I release it, and it crashes to the counter. Pieces of glass scatter from the point of impact and crash to the floor.

Anger squeezes my gut, and my heart slams into my chest. Adrenaline laces my blood, and with a growl, I throw myself across the counter and at him. He moves aside, and the momentum carries me over the counter and toward the floor. I manage to twist my body and hit the floor on my back. The back of my head crashes against the wooden planks, and bursts of starlight flash behind my eyes. The just-healed wound at my temple protests, and my stomach churns.

"Fuck." I lay there winded as my asshole triplet stands over me.

"Still not recovered fully from being shot, eh?" He holds out his arm. "Come on; let me help you up."

I grab his hand and tug. He loses his balance and falls toward me, but I roll aside. It's his turn to hit the floor, only he falls on his front, managing to turn his body enough at the last minute so that his cheek smashes into the floor.

"*Stocazzo!*" he growls, then jumps back to his feet at the same time that I do. We circle each other, and I notice that he's bleeding from a cut on his temple.

"You're not strong enough to take me on, you *testa di cazzo!*"

"Try me, you piece of shit." I bare my teeth as I rush toward him at the same time that he moves toward me. We crash into each other and end up with our arms around each other as we grapple. I manage to grab the back of his neck and squeeze. He grips my shoulders and applies enough pressure that pain shoots down both of my arms. Chest to chest, we grunt and try to push the other off his feet. Sweat pours down my temple, my T-shirt under my sweatshirt clings to my back. His gaze narrows; his color is high as he bares his teeth.

"You pulled a gun on my wife, you bastard." He snaps his head forward, and his forehead connects with my nose.

"Fuck," I yell as pain slices through my head. Blood spurts from my nose. "Why the hell did you do that!"

"You shot me, motherfucker," he growls.

I hook my leg behind his knee and yank it forward. He loses his balance and falls back. The impetus carries me along, and we both hit the floor and roll over before we come to a stop, both on our backs. My chest heaves as I draw in a breath. Every bone in my body seems to hurt. A headache builds behind my eyes.

"F-u-c-k!" I curl my fingers into fists and slam them into the floor. "Fuck this shit!"

Next to me, he lays on his back, his breath coming in pants. For a few seconds, we stay where we have fallen, our breathing gradually returning to normal. Finally, I force my eyelids open, ignore the pain that thumps at the back of my head, and stagger to my feet. I shake my head to clear it, but that only makes it hurt more. I hold out my arm.

He raises his gaze to my face and must see something of my inner turmoil there, for he nods, then grabs my hand. I heave him to his feet, and for a few seconds, we stare at each other.

"You okay?"

"You okay?" I say at the same time.

We both laugh, then break apart.

"I'm not sorry I punched you." He jerks his chin.

"I'm sorry I had to blackmail Aurora and pull a gun on her," I offer.

"I haven't forgiven you for it; I may never forgive you for it," he warns.

"Understandable." I shuffle my feet. "You have to understand that I was only doing my job."

"So a cop, eh?" He scratches his chin. "Somehow, I'm not surprised."

"No?"

"Nope. I never questioned that it was my duty to follow the path of the Mafia, but Xander was torn about it. It's what happens when you're an artist, you know. He thought too much. Philosophized a bunch of shit in his head. He questioned himself a lot. It stands to reason that you would be the one to go straight."

"I'm not sure I'm going back."

"No?" He scowls. "Why not?"

I turn away, head toward one of the kitchen shelves, and pull down a bottle of ibuprofen. I shake out two and swallow them with some tap water. Then reach for the spare bottle of whiskey—one of the few things I managed to stock up on. It seemed more of a priority than furnishing the place. I grab two glasses, pour out the whiskey, and walk back to offer one to him.

"Not good to mix alcohol with painkillers," he points out.

"Fuck that." I toss back the alcohol, then pour more into my glass.

Christian takes a sip, then nurses his glass. "That's how I used to think, before I got married. It changed everything." He laughs.

"You love her?"

"Love her?" He chuckles. "I can't live without her. Even now, as I'm talking to you, my mind is on her. I can't wait to get back to her."

"I know how you feel." The words are out before I can stop myself. *Fuck.* I raise my glass to my mouth and drain it. The liquor burns its way down, and the harshness of the world seems to recede a little. I sway as I slam my glass onto the counter. "Uh, I think it's time you left," I blurt out.

"Hold on, back up." He shakes his head. "Did you just say what I think you did?"

"Yeah, I told you to fuck off." I reach for the bottle, and this time, he snatches it away before I get to it.

"You want to fight again?" I growl, then reach for the bottle, but he evades me.

"You can't change the topic of conversation, *fratello*," he mutters. "I know you miss her."

"You don't know anything," I growl.

"That may be the case," his lips kick up, "but I do know what it is to stay away from the woman you love because your ego doesn't allow you to return to her."

"I'm doing the right thing." I grip the edges of the counter. "She deserves better than me."

"No argument there from me." He smirks. "But for some inexplicable reason, Theresa is in love with you."

"Not after how I treated her." I rub the back of my head. "I broke her heart and sent her away."

"Nothing that a bout of groveling won't fix."

"You don't understand." I squeeze the bridge of my nose. "She can do better than me. It's best if I start divorce proceedings and set her free to pursue a future different from mine."

"Oh?" He tilts his head. "So you'll be fine if she decides to fuck someone else? If she meets someone else and decides to share her life with him. If she—"

I lurch forward and grab his collar.

He chuckles. "That's what I thought."

I glare at him, and the motherfucker laughs in my face. "You're a goner, man. You're so fucking pussy-whipped that you're standing here in the darkness thinking about her instead of manning up to your mistake and returning to her and asking her to take you back."

"Fuck." I tighten my grip on his collar. "Fucking fuck."

"You know I'm right." He brings his glass up to his mouth and takes a sip.

"Bloody fucking hell." I release him and lower my chin to my chest. "I'm so fucked."

"Welcome to the real world, brother," he agrees.

"What the hell am I going to do?"

"You're going to clean yourself up and put on a fresh set of clothes, then you're going to return with me to Palermo and throw yourself at her mercy."

"I can't do that," I push away from the counter and begin to pace. "I'm a cop. I don't think you realize what that means. I'm a cop, and you guys are—"

"The Mafia? Thanks for pointing that out." He smirks.

"Though, I may not be one a few weeks from now," I raise a shoulder, "maybe that will make things easier."

"What do you mean?"

"I'm going to resign from my job."

"Why would you do that?" He scowls.

"Because we're on the opposite sides of the law?"

"So?"

"So?" I turn on him. "Aren't you listening to me? I can't remain a cop and be part of only the most notorious criminal family in all of Europe?"

"Why not?"

"Jesus, fuck!" I glare at him. "Are you listening to yourself? I'd never be trusted if it came out that my brother was the head of the Cosa Nostra."

"Why not? A lot of the *fagmilia* are in law enforcement, as well as in the judicial and political system."

I stare at him. "So you want me to become a spy for the *Cosa Nostra* and tell on my friends inside the workforce?"

"It's an opportunity, though I'd never force that on you, of course," he says seriously.

"Thanks," I retort.

"Of course, even if you stay on in the workforce, you can't continue to be undercover. There'd be a conflict of interest."

"I won't be able to turn on my colleagues," I snap.

"You were ready to turn on your family," he points out.

"I was undercover then. Also, I was hell-bent on revenge." I rub at my temple.

"And now?"

"Now, I've accepted that my ties to the Sovranos can't be broken that easily. Especially not, since my wife considers you assholes as being like her brothers."

"We're your brothers by blood; nothing changes that," he says in a soft voice.

"Which still doesn't change the fact that I'm going to have to resign." I rock back on the heels of my feet.

"Perhaps this is a chance to do something totally different," he offers.

"You mean, like start my own security company, or maybe go private?" It's something I've been thinking about lately. I drum my fingers on my chest. "That way, there is no conflict of interest or any such bullshit. I could spend time between London and Palermo, spend time with you guys, while also growing my own business."

"It would pay much better, of course. Not to mention the fact that you are one of the Sovranos, which is going to attract clients who know that you mean business," he adds.

I drag my fingers through my hair. "It could work."

"It will work." He slaps his palms on his hips.

"I'll have to give up being a cop," I say, almost to myself. Of course, I'd already considered it when I offered to resign. But talking about it and realizing that it's imminent, that it's the only way out, to give up the way of life that has defined me so far... Well, it's sobering.

"How do you feel about that?"

I crack my neck, grateful that the ibuprofen has kicked in and my headache is almost bearable now.

"Axel," he prompts, "how does the thought of quitting the police force make you feel?"

"Good." I blow out a breath. "It's the right thing to do."

"Fucking finally." He drains his glass, places it on the counter, then jerks his chin toward my bedroom. "Well, what are you waiting for? Go pack; we have a plane to catch."

48

Theresa

The thud-thud-thud of the beat pours over me and sinks into my blood. For someone who rarely went out on weekends, I have certainly become at home in nightclubs. I'd blame it on Elsa, except really, it was my idea to come here again tonight. In fact, if she knew why, she would have argued to go somewhere else. Somehow, being here reminds me of the day Axel barged in and dragged me to the restroom and had his way with me. My cheeks warm. Heat flushes my skin. Will I see him again? Will he return to me?

I close my eyes and let the music of the nightclub wash over me. The noise in my head fades away to be replaced by the voices of BTS—my guilty pleasure. A remixed version of BTS' *Life Goes On* fills the space. It's true what they say. You find BTS when you most need it. I raise my arms above my head and grind my hips in tune with the rhythm. I move sensuously to the music, bump and grind, widen my stance and dirty dance all the way down until I'm squatting with my thighs spread wide, then I straighten my legs, and jut out butt with my torso almost parallel to the floor before I snap myself up.

Someone slides over to stand behind me; he begins moving his body in tandem with mine. I turn and glance over my shoulder at dark brown eyes—not blue, not eyes fringed with eyelashes so dark they make his blue irises pop in comparison, not cheekbones so high that they could cut into my skin, not a hooked nose or a jaw that's normally set in disapproving lines. And he's blond.

Still, he's cute, I suppose, in a boy-next-door kind of way. And he's tall; not as tall as Axel, but tall enough to be attractive. Younger, though, closer to my age. The music ratchets up in tempo, and he begins to shake his body in earnest.

He shoots me a wicked grin, and I can't stop the laugh that spills from my lips. I increase my own tempo, and we move in synchronicity, our actions mirroring each other's steps. When I move left, he slides right and vice-versa. I laugh again as I let the sheer joy of the dancing overwhelm me. He grips my wrist, turns me around, then pushes me back before pulling me to him. A surprised laugh spills from my lips. The man can dance, all right. He twirls me around then draws me to him, close enough for our bodies to touch.

That's when someone steps in behind him. I tilt my head back, and further back, to meet blazing blue eyes. Angry eyes that bore into me. His features wear a grim expression, his lips set in lines of disapproval. Something blooms to life inside me. *Axel.* He's here.

I open my mouth, but before I can say anything, he grabs my partner by his shoulder and yanks him back so he stumbles away from me. Then, Axel turns him around and buries his fist in his face. That's when all hell breaks loose. Blondie falls over and onto another couple, who back away. He turns with his fists raised. Axel lands an uppercut, and the man reels back. He shakes his head, then lunges toward Axel, who steps aside. The man smashes into another couple, who spring apart. Another man throws a punch at Axel, who ducks, kicks the legs out from under him, when the first man throws himself at Axel again. Seemingly out of nowhere, Massimo steps in and knocks the guy out cold. A third and a fourth guy join the fray as Adrian and Seb wade in to help him.

That's when Axel tosses a guy aside and marches over to me.

"What are you—" I gasp as he grabs my hand. The crowd parts before him as he drags me in his wake. When we reach the end of the dance floor, I refuse to move. I slow him down enough that he turns to me.

"What the fuck is wrong with you?" I yell at him.

"What the fuck is wrong with you?" he roars back. "You let that man touch you. You let him put his hands on you. You were grinding your hips while he held your waist."

"It's called dancing," I point out.

His features contort. He drops my hand, then brushes past me and onto the dance floor. I blink, then jump forward to stand in front of him. "Where are you going?" I pant.

"To kill him."

"You can't just go around killing people."

"Is that right?" he growls. "Asshole touched you. I'm going to rip him apart from limb to limb for that."

He begins to plow past me, and I throw myself at him. "Oh, for heaven's sake! Seriously, enough with that caveman approach."

His jaw tics. "I'm going to grind his body into the ground, then throw you down and fuck you in his blood."

"Oh!" I gasp. A ripple of heat runs down my spine. My nipples harden. That was bloodthirsty and disturbing, and hell, if that didn't turn me on even more.

"Let him go!" I clutch at his hand. "He doesn't mean anything; I promise. I was dancing, that's all."

He lowers his head and peers into my face. "From now on, you dance with no one else but me."

He's so close now, I can see the lines that radiate out from the corners of his gorgeous eyes. The heat of his body flows around me and envelops me. That clean-man scent of his, spiked with his edgy essence, teases my nostrils. I swallow. "It's a little difficult to do that when you're not around, you know?" At least, he's standing so close that I don't need to yell to be heard.

"Well, I'm back now." He grips my arm, and this time, I don't protest as he hauls me off the dance floor.

We walk past the bar, and I spot Elsa. "I need to tell Elsa that I'm leaving." I have to yell again to be heard over the music.

"We'll text her from the car," he retorts.

"I need to grab my coat and purse from the cloakroom."

"I'll get it delivered home."

"Home? What do you mean home?"

"I mean"—he yanks me out of the door and looks up and down the road —"our home."

"Isn't your home in London? That's where we were when you told me you wanted a divorce, remember?"

A car drives up and comes to a stop in front of me. Christian gets out of the driver's seat and tosses the keys at Axel.

"Thanks." Axel jerks his chin.

"Remember what I told you?" He glances between us, then narrows his gaze on Axel. "Don't fuck this up."

"Hold on, so now you guys are on speaking terms?"

"A lot has changed." He pulls open the door on the passenger's side.

I hesitate. A wind blows over me, and I shiver.

"Why don't we get back home, and then we can talk?"

I fold my arms around my waist and scowl up at him.

"You're freezing." His tone softens. "Don't be stubborn, baby, just let me get us home and then we'll speak, okay?"

Damn it, why did he have to use that endearment?

I glare up at him, and he blows out a breath. "Please, get in the car, Sunshine?"

Maybe it's the fact that he calls me Sunshine, or the fact that he says please, or that his tone is soft and the look in his eyes sends a frisson of aware-ness over my skin. Whatever the case, I find myself obeying him. I slide inside the car. He shuts the door, walks around to the driver's side, and gets in. He shuts his door, turns on the car, and the warm air from the heater instantly circulates around my ankles. I shiver, this time because my body is warm-ing up.

"Still cold?" He shrugs out of his jacket and hands it over to me.

I slide my arms into the sleeves, and it's like I'm enveloped by him. Goddamn it, I've missed him. And now that I'm seeing him again, I can't stop my body from leaning toward him. I turn away and glance out the window, as he eases the car onto the road.

"Here's my phone."

I turn to find him holding it out to me.

"You wanted to call Elsa?" he reminds me.

"Ah, of course." I snatch up his phone and dial Elsa's number. It rings, then goes to voicemail, of course. "Ah, Elsa, it's me, Theresa. I'm calling you on

Axel's phone because I left my phone back in the cloakroom. Yeah, long story." I turn my face away and place my hand over the mouthpiece. "Yeah, he's back and uh, he's driving me home. I'm fine. don't worry… Uh, we'll talk later."

I hang up, then place the phone in the cupholder.

We drive in silence until we reach Xander's home. He turns into the driveway and comes to a stop. Why am I not surprised that this is what he meant by home? It's the only home I've ever known. More of a home than my parents' place ever was, and that was because he was here with me. Somehow, it seems appropriate that it was Xander's home before ours… Wait, am I already giving in to him? Am I accepting that this is the home I'm going to share with him? Am I already forgiving him for hurting me like that?

I shove the car door open and walk up the steps of the house. He follows me, draws abreast, then pulls a key from his pocket and opens the door. Of course, he'd have the key. Ultimately, he's a Sovrano, and the brothers will always have each other's backs. They took me under their protection, but who's going to protect my heart from being crushed again by him?

I walk ahead of him and head into the living room. I turn to find him heading for the bar and pouring himself a drink. He turns to me, and we gaze at each other across the length of the room.

I kick off my heels, because damn it, my feet ache, then sit on the sofa.

He walks over and sinks into a chair on the other side of the coffee table.

The silence stretches, broken only by the ticking of the clock in the corner of the room. I glance away, then back at him, to find he's still watching me closely. Goose bumps pop on my skin. He brings the glass of whiskey to his mouth and takes a sip. The tendons of his throat move as he swallows. A flutter of heat ignites in my lower belly. Jesus, this man is sex on a stick. I can't look at him without wanting to jump him. I knot my fingers tighter, then fix my gaze on a spot over his shoulder.

"Why are you here, Axel?" I burst out. "Why did you come back?"

He places his drink on the coffee table, then leans forward. "I've missed you," he says in a low voice. "Every single moment that we've been apart has been agonizing. I couldn't stop thinking about you, Sunshine. Couldn't get you out of my mind. You were my last thought at night and the first in the morning. And in between, I dreamt about your mouth, your skin, the scent of your hair, the little noises you make as you come, the texture of your pussy when I fuck you with my tongue, the way your cunt trembles around my dick when I bury myself inside you. The way you feel like home. The way nothing and nobody else will ever measure up to you. The way I fell for you so quickly, so hard, that I lost all perception of myself. The way I cannot live without you, not for a second more."

His words pour over me, sink into my blood, crawl into every nook and crevice of my body, into my heart, entwining with my soul. Tears prick the backs of my eyes, and I squeeze my fingers even more firmly together.

"You hurt me, Axel. You shattered my heart. You left me without looking back once, like I never mattered to you at all."

"Not true." He leans forward, his hands clasped between his thighs. "It ripped my heart out to do that. It fucking killed me to leave you, Sunshine."

"Yet you did. You didn't even give us a chance to work things out. You simply told the Sovranos to bring me back here and walked away from me."

"I'm so sorry. I thought I was doing the right thing by you. I thought it would give you a chance to try to move on and find a life without me."

"You told me you'd divorce me."

"I wanted to," he admits, "but every time I thought of it, I felt sick to my stomach. It was like my body, physically, wouldn't allow me to do it."

"Is that why you're here?" I finally glance up at him. "Because you couldn't bring yourself to take that step?"

"I'm here because I love you."

49

———————

Axel

"I made a mistake, Sunshine." A ball of emotion clogs my throat, and I swallow it down. "I know I shouldn't be asking you to forgive me, but—"

"Then don't!" She puts a hand out in front of herself, like a stop sign. "Don't ask me to do it."

I draw in a breath. "What will it take?" I force out the words through a throat gone dry. "What will it take for you to look past what I did?"

"I … I'm not sure," she says, still without looking at me.

"Please…" I force my tongue to form the words. "Please, Theresa, tell me what I need to do to gain your forgiveness."

She draws in a breath, then another. "I'm not sure if you deserve to be forgiven," she says in a soft voice.

"I don't." I roll my shoulders. "I know I acted like a *stronzo*."

One side of her lips trembles before she purses her lips again.

My heart begins to race. Maybe there is a chance she'll forgive me… Just maybe, we'll find a way to move forward together. I rise to my feet, and she glances at me. I skirt around the coffee table and take a step forward. She skitters to the side of the sofa. I move forward, and she jumps up and edges sideways. I take in the glittery dress that she wears. I was too full of rage to actually register it at the nightclub, but now I notice how it dips at the cleavage and comes to mid-thigh. As she takes another step back, it slides up to expose the pale skin of her upper thigh. Lust squeezes my belly. Anger knots my chest. "What are you wearing?" The words are out before I have a chance to stop myself.

She frowns. "If that was supposed to be an apology—"

"I know..." I raise my hand. "I know I'm supposed to be groveling right now. And damn it, I came with the intention of throwing myself at your mercy. But the thought of anyone else having seen you dressed like this, the thought that all those men in the club would have seen your legs and the gorgeous hint of your cleavage, is driving me crazy." I dig my fingers in my hair and tug. "Fuck, fuck, fuck, I'm really screwing up things, aren't I?"

Her gaze widens. She swallows audibly as she takes in my features.

"When it comes to you, I'm helpless," I murmur. "I look at you and all I can think is that you're mine. My wife. My property. Mine to do with as I want. Mine to protect and mine to fuck. Mine to love."

Her breath hitches, her pupils dilate, and her chest rises and falls as she holds my gaze. She takes a step forward, then another. She reaches me, then lifts her hand and cups my cheek. "It shouldn't appeal to me, you know, your brand of caveman possessiveness. It shouldn't turn me on to get a glimpse of just how much you want to own me. I've grown up with the Mafia, and I've always known that I'd marry into the mob, and yet..." She shakes her head. "Yet, hearing the filthy words that emerge from your mouth appeals to something deep inside me. It's frightening how much I respond to your overprotective nature. How the thought of you dominating me resonates so deeply within me. It's why I've never been able to refuse anything to you."

I peer into her face, take in her parted lips, the heightened color of her cheeks. I slide my hand inside my pocket and pull out her hair tie. I reach for the flowing mass of hair that streams around her shoulders and gather it on top of her head. Then I tie it into a ponytail that flows down to brush the small of her back.

"Is that my hair tie?" she cries.

"I took it from you the very first time we met."

"At the hospital, when that man broke in?"

I nod.

"You've been carrying it around all this time?"

The back of my neck heats.

"You've been carrying it around all this time?" She opens and shuts her mouth. "Wow!" She shakes her head. "I mean, that's—"

"Stupid," I interject.

"Sweet," she says in a soft voice.

"You turned me into a lovestruck fool, Sunshine." I lower myself onto one knee and take her hand in mine. "You're my inspiration. You fill a void in me I didn't even know I had. Since we've been apart, I've felt so hollow, like my life was already over. It's as if when I walked away, I left my heart behind with you. Every time I breathe, it's like razor blades are cutting through me. I can't sleep, can't eat, can barely focus on my job. All I want is to be near you, to spend all of my time with you, loving you, and proving to you how much I love you."

"Wow..." She swallows. "That's … that's poetic."

"I missed you." I peer up into her features, "When I wasn't with you, I went crazy with wanting you. All I wanted to do was reach out to you and hold you and kiss you and feel you, and have you melt into me, and hold you so tightly our skin fused together. I know it won't be easy to be together. I know I'll drive you crazy with my over-the-top possessiveness. I'll want to control you, possess you, and direct every aspect of your life, and when I overstep the line, you have my permission to tell me off."

"I do?"

"You bet. Just tell me to sod off anytime I get too overwhelming for you. In fact, I want you to promise me you'll let me know whenever I overstep."

"O-k-a-y"—she tips her head—"though, I'm still not sure what you're saying."

I slide my hand into my pocket, pull out a ring, and slide it onto her finger.

"Oh…" She opens and shuts her mouth. "Is that—"

"Marry me," I murmur.

She glances down at the platinum band with the single emerald in an antique setting.

"It was my mother's." I lower my head and kiss the ring on her finger. "And now it's yours."

Her chin wobbles, and she stares at the ring for so long that I begin to worry.

"Theresa?" My heart begins to thump in my chest. "Will you be mine?"

A teardrop trails down her cheek, and my stomach ties itself in knots.

"Don't cry, Sunshine, please. You know I can't bear to see you in distress."

"So why did you leave me?" she cries. "Why did you walk away from me?"

"I was foolish. I wasn't thinking straight. All I could think was that he could have shot you. That I was responsible for pulling you into my world and painting a target on you. That if anything were to happen to you, I wouldn't have been able to live with myself. It's the moment I realized just how much I love you, that you're my entire universe. I'm nothing without you. Nothing. You're the reason I want to go on living. You're what makes everything worthwhile. You make me feel, you plug me into this world; you're the reason for my existence, Sunshine."

She swallows, and her chest rises and falls. More tears flow down her face. One of them hits my cheek and trails down. I lick it up.

"There's something else." I catch her eye before I continue. "If I ever try to pull something like this again, deciding you're better off without me and not giving you any say in the matter, I want you to knock some sense into me. Remind me, I'm promising to never do that again."

"I promise, I'll let you know." Then she laughs and shakes her head. "You're crazy, you know."

"Crazy about you." I smile, then grow serious again. "And you're mine."

"I am," she agrees.

"So, you'll marry me?"

"I can't," she replies.

"What do you mean?"

"I was never *not* married to you, Axel. I was yours from the moment we met. I belong to you, only you."

50

Two weeks later

Theresa

I glance at the rings on my left hand—my engagement ring and my wedding ring. One has an emerald in an antique setting; the other is an ornate gold band which compliments the first.

The two go together, despite the fact that they aren't supposed to.

Like Axel and me. He swept into my life with the force of a hurricane and turned my world upside down. And now that I've found myself again, I find that I've changed. He's helped me find a more assertive side of myself—a woman who feels more grounded, more confident. Somehow, meeting him helped me realize that I know what I want out of life.

I want him. I want my business to flourish. I want to grow my brand so it's the best in all of Europe. I want my shop to be the destination for flowers and flower arrangements in my part of the world, if not globally. Big dreams for a girl who grew up in the Mafia and never thought she'd have a chance to spread her wings and explore her talent. But that's how being with Axel makes me feel. Free. Free to explore what I want to do with my life. It's like meeting him gave me a solid base from which to build, a framework to my existence that I was lacking before and not even realized until he'd come into my life.

This past week has been the happiest I've ever been. We've agreed that, for the time being, we'll stay in Palermo, where it's safer, since the team guarding the Sovranos can also protect us. This frees up Axel to make the arrangements necessary to create his own security company. There's also the fact that Freddie is still out there somewhere, and until he is located, it feels prudent to stay close to family. Of course, Axel will travel to London, as needed, to foster the growth of his business, as most of his contacts are in the UK.

I look up and at the painting of the three of them that hangs in the study. The Sovranos agreed that Axel and Christian could decide what would be done with Xander's paintings. They were in agreement that the portrait of the three of them would stay in Xander's home—now our home, and Axel and I wanted it in a place where we could look at it every day.

As for the other paintings, the two of them decided they'll auction them, with the money going to a trust that the Sovranos set up in Xander's name. The interest earned from the proceedings will be used to fund artists around the world who are talented but need the extra help in getting their art out in the world. Axel and Christian will head up the trust themselves.

A shiver runs down my back. Heat envelops me a second before my husband's voice reaches me. "I still don't understand how he could have known that he was one of a triplet." He wraps his arms around my waist and pulls me up and flat against his front. Every ridge, every hard plane of his chest, is imprinted into my back as he tucks my head under his chin. "Do you think he knew?" Axel asks.

"No. I don't know." I wrap my fingers around his forearm. I love the fact that, even though he's a Sovrano, Axel refuses to dress in formal wear. His preferred style of clothing is a pair of jeans and a sweatshirt. I'm especially partial to the grey Henley that he's wearing today. I turn my face and rub my cheek against the soft material that clings to his pecs. I breathe in that dark, edgy scent that is so very Axel. Strange, I never noticed what Xander smelled like. Maybe that relationship wasn't all that I thought it was. Maybe it takes the real thing to let you know how many times you thought something was real but it wasn't.

Axel's grip around me tightens. "Damn, but I can't get enough of you, Mrs. Sutton."

Despite officially becoming part of the Sovranos, Axel chose to keep the surname he'd taken after being adopted, and I took his surname.

I turn in his embrace and wrap my arms around his waist. "And I, you." I tip up my chin. "I can't believe how happy I am. Like my life is only just beginning."

"You are my life"—he lowers his head and brushes his lips against mine —"my heart, and my everything."

"And that is something I'm still getting used to. Who'd have thought that under that mean, alpha-holish exterior lies a heart that is secretly romantic?"

"It's you." He peers into my eyes. "You bring out the best in me, Sunshine."

I lean up on tiptoes and press my lips to his. He tilts his head and deepens the kiss. A moan builds in my throat. My nipples tighten, heat coils low in my belly, and I press up against him, trying to plaster as much of my body to his as I can.

A groan rumbles up his chest. He slides his hands down my back to cup my butt and fit my hips to his. He may talk sweet, but when it comes to the carnal side of our relationship, his dominance seems to have intensified.

He hauls me up against him, and the thick, rigid column of his arousal throbs against my core.

"Axel," I moan, as I wriggle to get even closer.

"How about we ditch going to the dinner and stay here, and I can fuck you in our bed?"

He kisses me again before I can reply, and by the time he's pulled away, my head is spinning.

"I know what you're trying to do," I murmur against his lips. "You're trying to distract me."

"Am I succeeding?"

"Yes… I mean, no. I mean…" I pull back and scowl up at him. "We can't not go. We haven't seen any of the family in nearly five days."

"Not complaining." He lowers his head, and I evade him.

"We have to go. I promised Nonna."

His features harden at that.

"You have to make your peace with her, Axel."

He scowls.

"You know I'm right."

"Doesn't mean I need to do so."

"You know you want to. She's an integral part of your past. By mending your bridges with her, you'll be able to move forward."

He blows out a breath. "You're not selling this to me."

"You love your family, Axel."

"Do I?" He frowns.

"I know you do." I laugh.

"I admit, my brothers are not a bad lot. Hell, I even have more in common with Luca than I realized."

They've discovered a love for the shooting range and have even put their differences aside and trained there together, which is good, because Luca is the most unpredictable of all the Sovrano brothers. Axel and Christian, too, have spent time together, and while Aurora is still not comfortable around Axel, she concedes she understands he was only doing what his undercover assignment required when he threatened her.

"Aurora and I spoke on the phone and she'll be there, as well, today. I want to see her and Karma and Cass," I whine.

He narrows his gaze. "So, guess I'm not getting out of this one then?"

51

Axel

"Will you pour me a drink?" Nonna murmurs.

My fingers tighten around the whiskey bottle, then I pour the liquor into my glass. Theresa and I arrived at Nonna's house for dinner, where she was instantly swept away by Cass and Karma, who wanted to show her the latest designs that Karma was working on.

Nonna's butler/chef/companion Gino informed us that Nonna was getting dressed, and Michael was on the phone in the library, so I wandered over to the bar in the living room to pour myself a drink.

Also, it's a delay tactic to avoid facing the rest of my brothers or my grand-mother right away. Yep, I'm a coward that way.

I know it's important, from the point of view of safety, that we stay here in Palermo so the Sovranos can lend their considerable protective detail to keeping Theresa safe, and I appreciate it, but damn, if I am not going to get my security firm up and running quickly so I can do it myself. I've already reached out to a few friends for help, including Karina Solonik, now Karina Beauchamp, who runs one of the most efficient security agencies that I've worked with in the past. In fact, if things go according to plan, the two of us will be collaborating very soon on the next few assignments. I was mulling over the possibilities when Nonna asked me to pour her a drink.

Now, she walks over to stand next to me. I ignore her, knowing it's rude and probably childish of me to do so, but fuck that. If she wants a drink, she can pour it herself.

"I'm so sorry I hurt you Axel, truly," she says in a low voice. "I'd give anything to go back in time and stop your father from what he did."

"But you can't, and now it's too late." I take a sip of my whiskey, and the liquor trails a stream of fire down my throat.

"Let me make amends," she pleads. "Please, Axel, let me try to do right by you."

"I'm not sure you can do anything to make me forgive you." I firm my lips.

"Haven't you ever made any mistakes? Haven't you done wrong to someone else and had to ask them to forgive you?"

I draw in a breath. I had asked Theresa to forgive me. I begged her to give me a second chance. And while she was initially hesitant, I won her over. If she hadn't forgiven me— I squeeze my fingers around my glass so tightly that the skin stretches across my knuckles. If she hadn't forgiven me, I'm not sure what I would have done. I wouldn't have been able to go on with life. I wasn't joking when I told her that I wouldn't be able to live without her. She found it in herself to forgive me after everything that I had done to her. Can I find it in myself to extend the same courtesy to Nonna? *After all, she is your Nonna. Surely, you can do right by her?*

Some of the tension fades from my shoulders. A weariness grips my chest, and I turn to her.

"Yes." I clear my throat. "I've made a lot of mistakes, not least of all, toward my wife. She was big-hearted enough to forgive me, and now I believe I should do the same for you."

Some of the stress on her features fades, and one side of her lips curves up. She extends her hand and grips my arm. "Thank you, Axel."

"Don't thank me; thank Theresa," I mutter. As if knowing that I need her presence by my side, she appears in the doorway of the study. She glances between me and Nonna, and her features break into a smile. She walks over to stand next to me. I wrap my arm around her and pull her into my side.

Nonna's smile widens. "I'm so happy that the two of you found each other."

"Ah, about that…" Theresa shuffles her feet. "Should we tell her?" She glances up at me from under her eyelashes.

"Tell me what?" Nonna frowns.

"I suppose we may as well get it over with." I blow out a breath.

"What is it?" Nonna's gaze narrows. "Are you going to tell me, or should I guess?"

"Oh, no need to guess." Theresa inches even closer to me. "We're pregnant."

"Pregnant?" Karma squeals from the entrance of the room. She marches in, followed by Michael who is close on her heels. Reaching us, she throws her arms around Theresa. "OMG, OMG, that was quick, you guys, but I'm not complaining. Now I'll have someone else to talk to and share notes with."

She squeezes Theresa's shoulders, then kisses her on both cheeks, before stepping back.

"*Grazie, Maria Santa!*" Nonna raises her gaze skyward, before she, too, steps toward Theresa and kisses her on her forehead. "I'm so happy for you." She turns to me. "For both of you. This is the most wonderful news. Not one, but two of my grandsons are going to have children. It's…" She sniffs. "It's incredible. My heart is bursting with happiness." She moves toward me, "Bend down, will you, boy, so I can kiss your cheek."

An hour and a half later, after we've had dinner, my brothers and I move back to the library. The women, including Theresa, have retreated to Nonna's bedroom, where she invited all of them to look at family photos. She invited us too, but we opted for cigars and whiskey instead. If that seems a little chauvinistic, well, it was unintentional. Except, I'm now part of a Mafia family, so guess it's par for the course. A part of me, though—that part which is Italian and steeped in Mafia tradition—thoroughly approves. Sometimes, it's easier to talk shop without having the women around, and I say that from a place of wanting to protect them, especially my woman, from the dangers that are a part of the world that I belong to.

I pull out my lighter and hold the flame to Michael's cigar, then Seb's, Massimo's, Christian's and Adrian's. By the time I reach Luca, he's already lit his own with a match. I light my cigar, then slide the lighter into my pocket and take a puff.

"So, how does it feel?" Michael asks as he blows out a cloud of smoke.

"The cigar is exceptional," I reply.

"It should bloody be; they're Cubans. Three hundred dollars a pop," Seb chuckles.

"Nothing but the best for the Sovranos," Massimo drawls.

"And you know that's not what I meant," Michael murmurs.

I blow out a cloud, then regard my cigar. "What can I say? I already knew."

"So, you suspected it when you remained in London and sent her home?" Seb asks.

"No." I take another puff. "I wasn't thinking straight then. The thought did cross my mind, but I pushed it aside. On some level, I always knew it was a possibility. Also, I think I knew I was going to return to her; I just needed time to sort my shit." I raise a shoulder. "What can I say? I panicked."

"I'd say it happens to the best of us, except you acted like a *coglione*," Luca growls. "No, strike that—you are a *coglione*, a *faccia di merda*, a *testa di cazzo*."

"I assume all of it means the same thing?"

"Yeah, you're a motherfucker," Massimo translates.

"I'd say fuck off, but I deserve it." I raise a shoulder, then take another puff of my bloody good cigar.

"What the fuck?" Luca stares at me. "Not even a smart-ass comeback in that pompous British accent of yours."

"People love this accent, I'll have you know. It's part of my charm."

"You need that charm with the kind of face you have. Of course, it doesn't matter, now that you're off the market," Luca chortles. "Better you than me, brother." He raises a glass.

"So, you two are getting along, I take it?" Seb eyes us with curiosity.

"A temporary truce." I raise my glass and clink it with Luca's. "We ain't best buddies, but anyone who's such a good mark with a gun can't be all that bad."

"I don't trust you one-hundred percent yet," Luca smirks, "but given you've left the pigs, I admit, your knowledge will more help us than not. So, sure. Why not? I'll table our difference of opinion for the moment."

"Will wonders never cease?" Seb scratches his chin. "Hot-headed Luca, actually agreeing to act in a mature fashion. *Cazzo*, it's fucking scary, man."

"Fuck you too." Luca raises his middle finger at Seb, before taking a sip of his whiskey.

"One thing doesn't compute." I narrow my gaze on Michael. "Somehow, I'd have thought you'd be more upset when you found out that I was working undercover, and that I'd married Theresa to get into your inner circle."

"That's true." Luca turns to Michael. "Why is it, *fratellone*, that you didn't lose it and take a gun to this bastard here? It's not only because he's our brother that you stayed so calm when we told you of his true identity, is it?"

Michael puffs on his cigar and blows out a cloud of smoke. "What do you think?" His lips twitch.

"I think that you already knew that our brother was an undercover cop," Seb offers.

"*Che cazzo!*" Luca glances from Michael to me, then back to Michael. "I'll be damned!" He shakes his head. "6ou knew, *fratellone*?"

"Fuck me," Massimo says softly. "Why am I not surprised?"

Michael glances around the room. "I made enquiries. I had to find out why it was that a brother we never knew we had, had chosen this moment in time to turn up in our lives."

"So, you knew all along?" I move around in my chair, trying to find a more comfortable position.

"I had enough information to deduce that you were undercover. However, you had covered your tracks well enough that I couldn't fit all of the pieces together," Michael retorts.

"I'm guessing, then, that the only reason you offered me your seat on the board of Trinity is because you knew I would eventually turn it down?"

"What?" Luca straightens. "You don't want to be involved with Trinity?"

"I may have left the force, but I'm a cop at heart. I doubt the heads of the Kane Company and Bratva would be comfortable doing business with me. Besides, I'm setting up my own security agency. I won't be able to do justice to Trinity."

Luca gapes at me, then he turns on Michael. "You knew this would happen," he says in an accusing tone. "You knew Axel would choose to distance himself from Trinity. That's why you chose to offer it to him?"

"I had an inkling." Michael leans back in his seat, a pleased look on his face "The profit sharing among us never would have been affected, regardless of who sat on the board, but it was about trust. By giving Axel a seat at the table, I was extending a gesture of trust."

"You knew it would go a long way in binding him to the family?" Seb speculates.

"I had hoped," Michael confesses.

"And here I am." I chuckle.

"*Stacazzo.*" Luca rubs the back of his neck. "So what now? Who's going to take on the stake in Trinity?"

"That's for the five of you to decide," Michael addresses that remark to Luca, Seb, Christian, Massimo and Adrian.

"You're leaving the decision to us?" Luca's gaze widens. "Is this another of your tricks, Don?"

"No tricks." Michael laughs. "I figure it's time to delegate more so I have more time to spend with my wife."

"*Cazzo!*" Luca reaches for his glass of whiskey and drains it. "I'll be damned. Although I suspect this is another of your short-term moves for long-term gains."

"Only time will tell." Michael's grin widens. "One thing I didn't see coming? Freddie." He turns to me. "What's his gig? Why did you go under-cover to work with him?"

"We had information that he partnered with your father and on the crime that defined his career, so to speak. I wanted an in with his gang as a way of getting more information on you guys," I reply.

Michael stills, and his gaze narrows on me. "Are you saying he partnered with our father on the kidnapping of the Seven?"

He's referring to the kidnapping of seven boys in England which made waves many years ago.

Silence fills the space. The men watch me, their cigars forgotten. I puff on mine and wait for the ash to build before I finally tip up my chin. "Freddie Nielsen was the mastermind behind that incident. He approached your father with the idea, as he needed the manpower and the organization to pull it off—"

"All of which, our father had in excess," Michael concedes.

"The two of them were involved in the crime that made headlines around the world," I add.

"A crime which ensured that no one would dare challenge our father for a very long time." Michael's jaw tics.

"Not until you came along, that is." Seb jerks his chin in Michael's direction.

"And thank fuck for that," Luca adds. "Not that I didn't respect our father, but he never would have given up his position. I wager, he'd have killed all of us, if it would have guaranteed he could maintain control."

"What Freddie and our father did changed the lives of those seven boys forever," Adrian cuts in.

"They were rescued, of course," I point out. "Someone from within the organization squealed to the police, and the kids were rescued."

"No telling how the incident could have scarred them for life," Adrian muses.

"It was many years ago. The Seven are all grown up and now head up one of the most influential financial services firms in the UK. Of course, it helps that they came from highly-privileged backgrounds. Well, six of them did. The seventh? Well, he just worked harder and made his first million by the time he was eighteen."

"You know a lot about the Seven?" Michael narrows his gaze on me.

"You could say that. I have worked closely with someone, an associate, who is now married to one of the Seven."

"Interesting." Michael blows out another cloud of smoke.

"Isn't it?" I place my cigar on the ashtray without spilling the pileup of ash at the end. "She also happens to be Nikolai Solonik's sister."

"No fucking way." Massimo sits up straight.

"Niko's sister is married to one of the Seven?" Michael tilts his head. There's no change of expression on his face, but it's clear he finds that information very interesting. No doubt, he will find a way to use it to his advantage. Which is what I intended. Nothing like showing the value you can bring to a relationship, even with your own family, for them to take you more seriously.

Michael raises his glass in my direction. "Good move, *fratellino*." He smirks. "You're smarter than I gave you credit for."

"One thing I wonder about..." I place my fingertips together. "Our father gives up one of his eight sons, only to kidnap seven boys and hold them to ransom. Makes you wonder if it's a coincidence?"

"You mean the fact that we are seven and so are the Seven?" Adrian muses.

Michael crosses his ankle over the knee of his other leg. "Who knows what he was thinking? There is no trying to find logic in the actions of a power-hungry ego-maniac, is there?"

I smirk and am about to speak when he holds up his hand. "I know what you're going to say, and I don't deny that much of my life has been dedicated to growing my own power base. Were it not for meeting Karma and realizing there's more to life, I could have gone the same way."

Just then, the doorbell rings, followed by a hammering on the front door.

"The fuck?" Seb scowls. "Who the hell could that be?" He places his glass on the table, then walks to the doorway. I spring up and follow him, with the rest of my brothers right behind me.

The doorbell peals again, then someone bangs on the door even more urgently. "Help!" A faint voice reaches us. "Help me."

Seb hastens his speed, until he reaches the door and pulls it open.

Elsa stumbles forward and would have fallen, but Seb grips her shoulder and steadies her. The cold rushes in through the open doorway, and she shivers.

"Help me, please," she raises her tear-stained gaze to his. "They're after me."

To find out what happens next read Mafia Vows HERE.

Read an excerpt from Mafia Vows

Elsa

"Open up!" I bang on the door! "Open the hell up."

I hear footsteps approaching, but it's not quickly enough. My heart hammers in my chest, and adrenaline laces my blood.

"Help!" I yell. "Help me, please."

I raise my fist to bang on the door again, when it's flung back. I stumble forward and smash my face into what feels like a brick wall. A wall that emanates heat, which slams into my chest, pours over my shoulders, and pins me in place. My breasts swell, my thighs clench, and all the pores on my skin pop. I know who it is, even before I raise my head and those golden-brown eyes meet mine.

"Help!" I pant. "Help me, Seb."

His hand grips mine, he glances past me, and his gaze widens. "Cazzo," he swears. The next second, he hauls me inside the house, pulls me out of the path of a bullet, then throws me down on the floor. The breath rushes out of me as he covers my body with his.

"What the—" I gasp as shots ring out over me.

"Get down!" he yells into the room, before he lowers his head so his cheek is plastered to mine.

My breath catches in my chest, my pulse rate ratchets up, and a trembling grips me. I lay there as the shots seem to go on and on. When they finally stop, silence descends. Something crashes to the floor inside the house, and I flinch. He wraps his fingers around the nape of my neck and holds me in place. It should feel threatening, but instead, some of the panic abates. The heat from his body pours over me and sinks into my blood. Sweat beads my brow, and it's as if I've stepped into a sauna. His chest rises and falls, and I can feel every ridge and every cut of his sculpted muscle that digs into my back. His big body surrounds me; he's all around me. I should feel claustrophobic, but instead, I feel protected, safe, and secure. Then his weight is gone.

Cool air flows over me. The sound of people moving, of footsteps approaching us, of voices raised in concern, pours over me. I try to move, but my body doesn't obey. Try to open my mouth to speak, but nothing comes out.

"You okay, Frozen?"

Huh? Did he just call me what I think he did? He grips my shoulder, turns me over, and once more, I'm staring up into those golden eyes. It's the first thing I noticed about him, because they're startling. Bottomless orbs of power that can see right through to my insecurities. He's so goddamn gorgeous with those thick eyelashes, sculpted cheekbones, a nose that's hooked enough to lend him an air of arrogance. That pouty lower lip that hints at the sensuality that clothes him, that thin upper lip that warns me that he could be mean. Cruel. He could cut me off at the knees with the charm that radiates from him, and surely, fills any room that he enters. He'd chew me up, spit me out, and damn, if I wouldn't enjoy every bit of sensation that he'd wring from me.

"Frozen," he prompts, "are you hurt?" He runs his hands down my torso, my waist, over my hips and that's when something inside me sparks to life.

"Don't call me that, and stop touching me, you oaf." I slap his hands away. "I'm fine."

"Don't look fine." He scowls. "What the hell were you doing outside the door."

"Getting shot at; what do you think?" I glower back at him.

"You could have been fucking killed," he retorts.

"Not going to happen. I like my life, thank you very much."

I try to sit up, but he flattens his palm on my chest and pushes me back down.

"Hey," I protest, "stop manhandling me."

"Not letting you move until you've been checked out by a medic."

"I'm fine!" I huff.

"I'll believe it when a doctor tells me so."

"Hey, guys." I glance up as my friend Theresa's face comes into view. "Thank God. Please, can you tell this jerk that I'm fine and that he can let me up?"

"Umm…" She takes one look at his features, and her eyebrows shoot up. "I think he's right."

What? I scowl at her, but she's too busy waving at another woman, who walks over to us. She's wearing a simple, dark-colored dress that hugs her curves, before dropping to below her knees. Her eyes are intelligent, and her hair is pulled back from her face.

"I'm Dr. Aurora Sovrano; would it be okay if I check you out?"

I glance from her to Theresa, who nods vigorously. "You're safe with her," she assures me.

I turn back to the doctor and nod at her.

She smiles, then glances over to the man who's behind her. "Can you get my medical bag, baby?"

"Sure, honey," the tall, broad-shouldered man, who looks very similar to Seb, and even more like Axel, spins around and disappears inside the house. I take in Aurora's wedding ring. Guess they're married. Somehow, the very cozy endearments of 'baby' and 'honey' still feel out of place in relation to one of the Sovranos.

Aurora sinks next to me and reaches over to take my pulse. By the time she lowers my arm, her husband has returned and hands over her medical bag, before stepping back. The doctor pulls out a small flashlight and shines it in my eyes.

Then she checks my heartbeat with a stethoscope, performs a few other tests, and pronounces that I'm fine. "You'll need to get that cut dressed, though," she points to my forehead.

For the first time, I become aware of the throbbing hurt above my eyebrow. I touch it and wince. When I glance at my fingers, they are bloodied.

Seb rises to his feet and holds out his hand. "Come on; let's get that cleaned up."

"Umm,"—I fold my arms across my chest—"no, thank you."

He merely stares down at his proffered palm, then back at my face.

"What?" I scowl. "I'm not going anywhere with you."

"You do have to get that cleaned up," Aurora says in a reasonable voice.

"Not going with him." I nod in his direction.

"I'm not letting you go anywhere until I ensure that your wound is bandaged," he retorts.

I glower. He holds my gaze. Those gorgeous golden orbs of his bore into me. Damn it, he's not going to back off, is he? Well, too bad. I'm not going to simply fall in line with whatever he asks me to do.

The next second, I gasp, for he's bent down, wrapped an arm around my back, the other under my knees, and straightened with me in his arms.

"What are you doing?" I hiss.

"You could have done this the easy way, but you left me no choice."

"Let go of me!" I shove at his chest.

"Once I've seen to that cut on your forehead."

I glance up to find Aurora stifling a smile. *Traitor.* I mouth the word at her as he marches toward the inner part of the house and past the rest of his brothers, who are deep in conversation—presumably plotting the end of whoever was crazy enough to shoot at the house of the Nonna of the Don of the Cosa Nostra. OMG, someone was shooting at me. Someone was trying to kill me, and if Seb hadn't pushed me out of the way, they might have succeeded.

A trembling grips me, and my teeth begin to chatter. I try to squeeze my lips together, try to curl into myself, to bury myself in his shirt, but nothing makes it better.

"Shh…" He holds me closer to his chest. "It's okay; you're safe."

For some reason, I believe him. Nothing can hurt me as long as he has his arms around me. I shouldn't feel secure in the embrace of one of the Mafioso who rule this city, but it's precisely because I know what he does for a living that I'm confident he wouldn't hesitate to hurt anyone who'd dare to come after me.

"Wh-who was that; who shot at me?" I ask, mainly because I want to stop the line of thought that's buzzing through my mind.

"Whoever it was, he doesn't have much longer left to live," he answers in a grim voice.

I swallow. A shiver runs down my spine. The menace in his voice is a reminder of how his way of life is so different from mine. The confidence with which he speaks is also a turn-on. I shouldn't find the violence that's inherent in him so appealing, but my elevated breathing, the way my pulse flutters as he tucks my head under his chin, the moisture that laces the flesh between my legs—all of it insists otherwise.

He shoulders his way inside a bathroom and comes to a stop in front of the sink. I try to pull away from him, but he only tightens his grasp around me.

"Hush," he says in a voice that brooks no argument. "Calm down first."

We stay that way for a few seconds, during which time I allow myself to relax in his embrace. Allow myself to rub my cheek against his shirt, to draw his musky, edgy scent into my lungs, and close my eyes and pretend it's okay that a well-known Mafioso is comforting me after someone shot at me. Jesus, someone shot at me.

"Feeling better?" His voice rumbles against my cheek.

I nod, and he lowers me onto the counter.

He peers into my face, then swears. "You're still bleeding."

He grabs a fresh cloth, wets it under the tap, and presses it to my wound.

I wince, and his jaw hardens further. He takes my hand and presses it against the washcloth. "Hold it there," he orders as he moves away. Every time he speaks, authority drips from him. It must be nice to know that whatever he says, us mere mortals will obey.

He reaches up and grabs a first-aid kit from the shelf above the sink. Then he shakes out cotton balls and a bottle of antiseptic. He moves to stand between my legs, and when I lower the washcloth, he presses the antiseptic-soaked cotton ball to the wound.

I hiss out a breath.

A pulse tics to life at his jaw, and his features seem to grow stormier. His actions, however, grow gentler. He dabs at the blood, tosses away the bloodied cotton ball, and repeats his action with the next. When he's finally satisfied, he places butterfly bandages on the cut.

"There." He surveys his handiwork. "Does it hurt?"

"No," I say truthfully. "It's just a surface cut."

"On your face." He scowls. "He hurt your face."

"Technically, I think I hurt it when you pushed me down and threw yourself on top of me and—"

He glares at me, and I forget my train of thought. My stomach twists. My heart begins to race in my chest, and I know then I need to get away from him. Being this close to him is making me forget the reason I knocked on the door to this house in the first place. It's fortunate that he's the one who opened it and I collapsed into his arms. I couldn't have planned it better if I tried.

Wariness trickles down my spine. I lean back from him, trying to put distance between us. To my surprise, he steps back, and I slide down to place my feet on the floor and straighten. Unfortunately, that also means my breasts brush his chest. Heat sluices down my spine, and my breath catches.

Every muscle in his body seems to tense. The tendons of his throat move as he swallows. Is he as affected by my proximity as I am by his?

"How do you feel?" he growls.

"I'm fine, really." I peer into his features. "You, however, seem agitated."

His lips firm, and he wraps his fingers around my wrist. Goose bumps pop on my skin. Little frissons of sensations arrow out from the point of contact. "Wh-what are you doing?" I croak.

"Accompanying you back to the others."

Before I can object, he's turned and pushed open the doorway of the bathroom and walked out. He drags me along, and I could protest, but weariness grips me, and I allow him to tug me along. We reach the living room, where the group of men I saw earlier are talking in low voices.

The doctor sees us and rushes forward. She surveys my forehead and nods. "Good job."

Seb grunts.

"Do you need a painkiller?"

"No," I say at the very same time that Seb snaps, "Yes."

She glances between us, then pulls out a pad from her handbag, writes out a prescription, and hands it over to me. Before I can reach for it, jerk face, here, has snatched it from her and pocketed it.

"Hey!" I scowl. "That's my prescription."

He ignores me and nods in the doctor's direction. "Thanks, I'll take care of it."

"I'm sure you will." The doctor turns to me. "You take care, and if you need anything, make sure you call me. Seb has my number." She smiles again, then pats me on the shoulder. She turns to leave, and Theresa runs over and hugs me.

"Oh my God, you gave me a scare. Are you okay?"

"I am." I squeeze her shoulders. "Sorry I barged in on your dinner like this. I didn't know where else to go when I realized that I was being followed."

"You were followed?" Seb snaps from behind me.

I draw in a breath. I will not lose my temper. I will stay calm.

"What's it to you?" I shoot him a sideways glance. "And in case you haven't noticed, I'm speaking to my friend."

"Axel's calling you." He nods over her shoulder. I follow his gaze to find that, sure enough, her new husband is calling out to her.

"You sure you're okay?" She peers into my face. "If you want me to stay with you—"

I shake my head. "No, go. I don't want to keep you."

"I can stay, really," she insists.

"I'll be fine." I kiss her cheek. "Go, be with your new husband."

"You sure?" she whispers.

"I'm sure." I step back.

Her features break into a smile, and she turns and almost skips across the floor to where Axel waits for her. The two of them lock lips in a kiss that seems to go on and on.

"Pussy-whipped motherfucker," Seb snorts.

"What do you mean?" I turn on him. "They're in love."

"Like I said, pussy-whipped," he says with a smirk.

"Jesus, why do men have to be so macho when it comes to admitting that two people can be in love?"

"Because love is an illusion?" His lips firm. "It's one way that women and men con each other into believing that they have feelings for each other, when really, all they want to do is jump each other."

"You don't believe that, do you? If that were true, how do you explain Theresa and Axel, who are not only in love, but married? And the doctor who is married to Christian, not to mention your oldest brother Michael and his wife?"

"They got lucky, I guess?" He raises a shoulder. "Doesn't mean most people do."

"What do you have against falling in love?"

"It's not for me," he says in a tone that brooks no argument.

"With that grumpy attitude of yours, I'd be surprised if anyone were rushing to fall in love with you," I mutter under my breath.

"I heard you." His grin widens. "You're feisty, aren't you?"

"Hate that word." I toss my hair over my shoulder. "I think I should be getting along."

"I'll drop you at home."

"I can see myself home; thank you very much."

"You're not going anywhere without me." He closes the distance between us.

Just then a scream sounds behind us.

Seb

I glance over her shoulder just in time to see Nonna swaying on her feet. Cassandra, our housekeeper has her arm around Nonna. She staggers under the weight of the other woman. In two quick steps, Adrian reaches her and steadies the both of them. Nonna presses a hand to the side of her chest, and her fingers come away bloody.

"Fuck!" I race toward Nonna, Elsa right behind me.

Adrian and Cass lower her gently to the settee, and she leans her head back against it.

Aurora reaches her at the same time as me. She places her medical bag on the floor and sits next to Nonna. She takes Nonna's pulse, and her features shudder. "Call an ambulance," she tells Christian, who grabs his phone and walks off to the side as he dials.

"Here." Elsa shrugs off the scarf she is wearing and gives it to Aurora, who uses it to staunch the flow of blood.

Nonna's eyelids flutter. She glances over the faces of all those assembled.

"It's good that everyone is here." She coughs.

"Don't try to talk, Nonna." I sink to my knees next to her and take her hand in mine. "Save your strength."

"Don't stop me, Seb." Her lips kick up at the edges. "You've always been the most stubborn of all my boys. Once you get an idea in your head, you won't stop until you've found a way to make it happen. I wish I could have been around long enough to see you get married."

"You will be around long enough to see me get married."

"You promise?" She squeezes my hand. "Promise you will get married. Promise you won't let what happened to you get in the way of finding true happiness."

"Why are you talking like this?" I bring up my other hand and envelop her thinner, more fragile one between both of mine. "You'll be around to see the rest of us boys get married."

She smiles sadly. "I had hoped so, but I don't think I will be alive that long."

"Nonna…" I begin to protest when Christian interrupts.

"The ambulance is on its way; it should be here within four minutes. I'm going to open the door so they can come right in when they arrive." He heads for the doorway.

Nonna tilts up her chin in my direction. "Promise me that you will get married within the next month."

To find out what happens next read Mafia Vows HERE.

Get your exclusive bonus scene from Mafia Crown featuring Axel & the Sovranos HERE

Start the Arranged Marriage Mafia Series with Mafia KING, Michael & Karma's story HERE

Read an excerpt from mafia king

Karma

"Morn came and went—and came, and brought no day…"

Tears prick the backs of my eyes. Goddamn Byron. His words creep up on me when I am at my weakest. Not that I am a poetry addict, by any measure, but words are my jam. The one consolation I have is that, when everything else in the world is wrong, I can turn to them, and they'll be there, friendly, steady, waiting with open arms.

And this particular poem had laced my blood, crawled into my gut when I'd first read it. Darkness had folded within me like an insidious snake, that raises its head when I least expect it. Like now, when I look out on the still sleeping city of London, from the grassy slope of Waterlow Park.

Somewhere out there, the Mafia is hunting me, apparently. It's why my sister Summer and her new husband Sinclair Sterling had insisted that I have my own security detail. I had agreed...only to appease them...then given my bodyguard the slip this morning. I had decided to come running here because it's not a place I'd normally go... Not so early in the morning, anyway. They won't think to look for me here. At least, not for a while longer.

I purse my lips, close my eyes. Silence. The rustle of the wind between the leaves. The faint tinkle of the water from the nearby spring.

I could be the last person on this planet, alone, unsung, bound for the grave.

Ugh! Stop. Right there. I drag the back of my hand across my nose. Try it again, focus, get the words out, one after the other, like the steps of my sorry life.

"Morn came and went—and came, and... and..." My voice breaks. "Bloody asinine hell." I dig my fingers into the grass and grab a handful and fling it out. Again. From the top.

"Morn came and went—and came, and—"

"...brought no day."

A gravelly voice completes my sentence.

I whip my head around. His silhouette fills my line of sight. He's sitting on the same knoll as me, yet I have to crane my neck back to see his profile. The sun is at his back, so I can't make out his features. Can't see his eyes... Can only take in his dark hair, combed back by a ruthless hand that brooked no measure.

My throat dries.

Thick dark hair, shot through with grey at the temples. He wears his age like a badge. I don't know why, but I know his years have not been easy. That he's seen more, indulged in more, reveled in the consequences of his actions, however extreme they might have been. He's not a normal, everyday person, this man. Not a nine-to-fiver, not someone who lives an average life. Definitely not a man who returns home to his wife and home at the end of the day. He is… different, unique, evil… Monstrous. Yes, he is a beast, one who sports the face of a man but who harbors the kind of darkness inside that speaks to me. I gulp.

His face boasts a hooked nose, a thin upper lip, a fleshy lower lip. One that hints at hidden desires, Heat. Lust. The sensuous scrape of that whiskered jaw over my innermost places. Across my inner thigh, reaching toward that core of me that throbs, clenches, melts to feel the stab of his tongue, the thrust of his hardness as he impales me, takes me, makes me his. Goosebumps pop on my skin.

I drag my gaze away from his mouth down to the scar that slashes across his throat. A cold sensation coils in my chest. What or who had hurt him in such a cruel fashion?

"Of this their desolation; and all hearts
Were chill'd into a selfish prayer for light…"

He continues in that rasping guttural tone. Is it the wound that caused that scar that makes his voice so…gravelly… So deep…so…so, hot?

Sweat beads my palms and the hairs on my nape rise. "Who are you?"

He stares ahead as his lips move,

"Forests were set on fire—but hour by hour
They fell and faded—and the crackling trunks
Extinguish'd with a crash—and all was black."

I swallow, moisture gathers in my core. How can I be wet by the mere cadence of this stranger's voice?

I spring up to my feet.

"Sit down," he commands.

His voice is unhurried, lazy even, his spine erect. The cut of his black jacket stretches across the width of his massive shoulders. His hair… I was mistaken—there are threads of dark gold woven between the darkness that pours down to brush the nape of his neck. A strand of hair falls over his brow. As I watch, he raises his hand and brushes it away. Somehow, the gesture lends an air of vulnerability to him. Something so at odds with the rest of his persona that, surely, I am mistaken?

My scalp itches. I take in a breath and my lungs burn. This man... He's sucked up all the oxygen in this open space as if he owns it, the master of all he surveys. The master of me. My death. My life. A shiver ladders along my spine. *Get away, get away now, while you still can.*

I angle my body, ready to spring away from him.

"I won't ask again."

Ask. Command. Force me to do as he wants. He'll have me on my back, bent over, on my side, on my knees, over him, under him. He'll surround me, overwhelm me, pin me down with the force of his personality. His charisma, his larger-than-life essence will crush everything else out of me and I... I'll love it.

"No."

"Yes."

A fact. A statement of intent, spoken aloud. So true. So real. Too real. Too much. Too fast. All of my nightmares...my dreams come to life. Everything I've wanted is here in front of me. I'll die a thousand deaths before he'll be done with me... And then? Will I be reborn? For him. For me. For myself.

I live, first and foremost, to be the woman I was...am meant to be.

"You want to run?"

No.

No.

I nod my head.

He turns his, and all the breath leaves my lungs. Blue eyes—cerulean, dark like the morning skies, deep like the nighttime...hidden corners, secrets that I don't dare uncover. He'll destroy me, have my heart, and break it so casually.

My throat burns and a boiling sensation squeezes my chest.

"Go then, my beauty, fly. You have until I count to five. If I catch you, you are mine."

"If you don't?"

"Then I'll come after you, stalk your every living moment, possess your nightmares, and steal you away in the dead of night, and then..."

I draw in a shuddering breath as liquid heat drips from between my legs. "Then?" I whisper.

"Then, I'll ensure you'll never belong to anyone else, you'll never see the light of day again, for your every breath, your every waking second, your thoughts, your actions...and all your words, every single last one, will belong to me." He peels back his lips, and his teeth glint in the first rays of the morning light. "Only me." He straightens to his feet and rises, and rises.

This man… He is massive. A monster who always gets his way. My guts churn. My toes curl. Something primeval inside of me insists I hold my own. I cannot give in to him. Cannot let him win whatever this is. I need to stake my ground, in some form. *Say something. Anything. Show him you're not afraid of this.*

"Why?" I tilt my head back, all the way back. "Why are you doing this?"

He tilts his head, his ears almost canine in the way they are silhouetted against his profile.

"Is it because you can? Is it a…a," I blink, "a debt of some kind?"

He stills.

"My father, this is about how he betrayed the Mafia, right? You're one of them?"

"Lucky guess." His lips twist, "It is about your father, and how he promised you to me. He reneged on his promise, and now, I am here to collect."

"No." I swallow… *No, no, no.*

"Yes." His jaw hardens.

All expression is wiped clean of his face, and I know then, that he speaks the truth. It's always about the past. My sorry shambles of a past… Why does it always catch up with me? *You can run, but you can never hide.*

"Tick-tock, Beauty." He angles his body and his shoulders shut out the sight of the sun, the dawn skies, the horizon, the city in the distance, the rustle of the grass, the trees, the rustle of the leaves. All of it fades and leaves just me and him. Us. *Run.*

"Five." He jerks his chin, straightens the cuffs of his sleeves.

My knees wobble.

"Four."

My pulse rate spikes. I should go. Leave. But my feet are planted in this earth. This piece of land where we first met. What am I, but a speck in the larger scheme of things? To be hurt. To be forgotten. To be taken without an ounce of retribution. To be punished…by him.

"Three." He thrusts out his chest, widens his stance, every muscle in his body relaxed. "Two."

I swallow. The pulse beats at my temples. My blood thrums.

"One."

To find out what happens next read Mafia King HERE

Read Summer & Sinclair Sterling's story **HERE** in The Billionaire's Fake Wife

Read an excerpt from Summer & Sinclair's story

Summer

"Slap, slap, kiss, kiss."

"Huh?" I stare up at the bartender.

"Aka, there's a thin line between love and hate." He shakes out the crimson liquid into my glass.

"Nah." I snort. "Why would she allow him to control her, and after he insulted her?"

"It's the chemistry between them." He lowers his head, "You have to admit that when the man is arrogant and the woman resists, it's a challenge to both of them, to see who blinks first, huh?"

"Why?" I wave my hand in the air, "Because they hate each other?"

"Because," he chuckles, "the girl in school whose braids I pulled and teased mercilessly, is the one who I—"

"Proposed to?" I huff.

His face lights up. "You get it now?"

Yeah. No. A headache begins to pound at my temples. This crash course in pop psychology is not why I came to my favorite bar in Islington, to meet my best friend, who is—I glance at the face of my phone—thirty minutes late.

I inhale the drink, and his eyebrows rise.

"What?" I glower up at the bartender. "I can barely taste the alcohol. Besides, it's free drinks at happy hour for women, right?"

"Which ends in precisely" he holds up five fingers, "minutes."

"Oh! Yay!" I mock fist pump. "Time enough for one more, at least."

A hiccough swells my throat and I swallow it back, nod.

One has to do what one has to do… when everything else in the world is going to shit.

A hot sensation stabs behind my eyes; my chest tightens. Is this what people call growing up?

The bartender tips his mixing flask, strains out a fresh batch of the ruby red liquid onto the glass in front of me.

"Salut." I nod my thanks, then toss it back. It hits my stomach and tendrils of fire crawl up my spine, I cough.

My head spins. Warmth sears my chest, spreads to my extremities. I can't feel my fingers or toes. Good. Almost there. "Top me up."

"You sure?"

"Yes." I square my shoulders and reach for the drink.

"No. She's had enough."

"What the—?" I pivot on the bar stool.

Indigo eyes bore into me.

Fathomless. Black at the bottom, the intensity in their depths grips me. He swoops out his arm, grabs the glass and holds it up. Thick fingers dwarf the glass. Tapered at the edges. The nails short and buff. *All the better to grab you with.* I gulp.

"Like what you see?"

I flush, peer up into his face.

Hard cheekbones, hollows under them, and a tiny scar that slashes at his left eyebrow. *How did he get that?* Not that I care. My gaze slides to his mouth. Thin upper lip, a lower lip that is full and cushioned. Pouty with a hint of bad boy. *Oh!* My toes curl. My thighs clench.

The corner of his mouth kicks up. *Asshole.*

Bet he thinks life is one big smug-fest. I glower, reach for my glass, and he holds it up and out of my reach.

I scowl, "Gimme that."

He shakes his head.

"That's my drink."

"Not anymore." He shoves my glass at the bartender. "Water for her. Get me a whiskey, neat."

I splutter, then reach for my drink again. The barstool tips, in his direction. This is when I fall against him, and my breasts slam into his hard chest, sculpted planes with layers upon layers of muscle that ripple and writhe as he turns aside, flattens himself against the bar. The floor rises up to meet me.

What the actual hell?

I twist my torso at the last second and my butt connects with the surface. *Ow!*

The breath rushes out of me. My hair swirls around my face. I scrabble for purchase, and my knee connects with his leg.

"Watch it." He steps around, stands in front of me.

"You stepped aside?" I splutter. "You let me fall?"

"Hmph."

I tilt my chin back, all the way back, look up the expanse of muscled thigh that stretches the silken material of his suit. *What is he wearing? Could any suit fit a man with such precision?* Hand crafted on Saville Row, no doubt. I glance at the bulge that tents the fabric between his legs. *Oh!* I blink.

Look away, look away. I hold out my arm. He'll help me up at least, won't he?

He glances at my palm, then turns away. *No, he didn't do that, no way.*

A glass of amber liquid appears in front of him. He lifts the tumbler to his sculpted mouth.

His throat moves, strong tendons flexing. He tilts his head back, and the column of his neck moves as he swallows. Dark hair covers his chin—it's a discordant chord in that clean-cut profile, I shiver. He would scrape that rough skin down my core. He'd mark my inner thigh, lick my core, thrust his tongue inside my melting channel and drink from my pussy. *Oh! God.* Goosebumps rise on my skin.

No one has the right to look this beautiful, this achingly gorgeous. Too magnificent for his own good. Anger coils in my chest.

"Arrogant wanker."

"I'll take that under advisement."

"You're a jerk, you know that?"

He presses his lips together. The grooves on either side of his mouth deepen. Jesus, clearly the man has never laughed a single day in his life. Bet that stick up his arse is uncomfortable. I chuckle.

He runs his gaze down my features, my chest, down to my toes, then yawns.

The hell! I will not let him provoke me. Will not. "Like what you see?" I jut out my chin.

"Sorry, you're not my type." He slides a hand into the pocket of those perfectly cut pants, stretching it across that heavy bulge.

Heat curls low in my belly.

Not fair, that he could afford a wardrobe that clearly shouts his status and what amounts to the economy of a small third-world country. A hot feeling stabs in my chest.

He reeks of privilege, of taking his status in life for granted.

While I've had to fight every inch of the way. Hell, I am still battling to hold onto the last of my equilibrium.

"Last chance—" I wiggle my fingers, from where I am sprawled out on the floor at his feet, "—to redeem yourself..."

"You have me there." He places the glass on the counter, then bends and holds out his hand. The hint of discolored steel at his wrist catches my attention. Huh?

He wears a cheap-ass watch?

That's got to bring down the net worth of his presence by more than 1000% percent. Weird.

I reach up and he straightens.

I lurch back.

"Oops, I changed my mind." His lips curl.

A hot burning sensation claws at my stomach. I am not a violent person, honestly. But Smirky Pants here, he needs to be taught a lesson.

I swipe out my legs, kicking his out from under him.

Sinclair

My knees give way, and I hurtle toward the ground.

What the—? I twist around, thrust out my arms. My palms hit the floor. The impact jostles up my elbows. I firm my biceps and come to a halt planked above her.

A huffing sound fills my ear.

I turn to find my whippet, Max, panting with his mouth open. I scowl and he flattens his ears.

All of my businesses are dog-friendly. Before you draw conclusions about me being the caring sort or some such shit—it attracts footfall.

Max scrutinizes the girl, then glances at me. *Huh?* He hates women, but not her, apparently.

I straighten and my nose grazes hers.

My arms are on either side of her head. Her chest heaves. The fabric of her dress stretches across her gorgeous breasts. My fingers tingle; my palms ache to cup those tits, squeeze those hard nipples outlined against the—hold on, what is she wearing? A tunic shirt in a sparkly pink... and are those shoulder pads she has on?

I glance up, and a squeak escapes her lips.

Pink hair surrounds her face. *Pink? Who dyes their hair that color past the age of eighteen?*

I stare at her face. *How old is she?* Un-furrowed forehead, dark eyelashes that flutter against pale cheeks. Tiny nose, and that mouth—luscious, tempting. A whiff of her scent, cherries and caramel, assails my senses. My mouth waters. *What the hell?*

She opens her eyes and our eyelashes brush. Her gaze widens. Green, like the leaves of the evergreens, flickers of gold sparkling in their depths. "What?" She glowers. "You're demonstrating the plank position?"

"Actually," I lower my weight onto her, the ridge of my hardness thrusting into the softness between her legs, "I was thinking of something else, altogether."

She gulps and her pupils dilate. *Ah, so she feels it, too?*

I drop my head toward her, closer, closer.

Color floods the creamy expanse of her neck. Her eyelids flutter down. She tilts her chin up.

I push up and off of her.

"That... Sweetheart, is an emphatic 'no thank you' to whatever you are offering."

Her eyelids spring open and pink stains her cheeks. Adorable. Such a range of emotions across those gorgeous features in a few seconds? What else is hidden under that exquisite exterior of hers?

She scrambles up, eyes blazing.

Ah! The little bird is trying to spread her wings? My dick twitches. My groin hardens, *Why does her anger turn me on so, huh?*

She steps forward, thrusts a finger in my chest.

My heart begins to thud.

She peers up from under those hooded eyelashes. "Wake up and taste the wasabi, asshole."

"What does that even mean?"

She makes a sound deep in her throat. My dick twitches. My pulse speeds up.

She pivots, grabs a half-full beer mug sitting on the bar counter.

I growl, "Oh, no, you don't."

She turns, swings it at me. The smell of hops envelops the space.

I stare down at the beer-splattered shirt, the lapels of my camel colored jacket deepening to a dull brown. Anger squeezes my guts.

I fist my fingers at my side, broaden my stance.

She snickers.

I tip my chin up. "You're going to regret that."

The smile fades from her face. "Umm." She places the now empty mug on the bar.

I take a step forward and she skitters back. "It's only clothes." She gulps, "They'll wash."

I glare at her and she swallows, wiggles her fingers in the air, "I should have known that you wouldn't have a sense of humor."

I thrust out my jaw, "That's a ten-thousand-pound suit you destroyed."

She blanches, then straightens her shoulders, "Must have been some hot date you were trying to impress, huh?"

"Actually," I flick some of the offending liquid from my lapels, "it's you I was after."

"Me?" She frowns.

"We need to speak."

She glances toward the bartender who's on the other side of the bar. "I don't know you." She chews on her lower lip, biting off some of the hot pink. How would she look, with that pouty mouth fastened on my cock?

The blood rushes to my groin so quickly that my head spins. My pulse rate ratchets up. Focus, focus on the task you came here for.

"This will take only a few seconds." I take a step forward.

She moves aside.

I frown, "You want to hear this, I promise."

"Go to hell." She pivots and darts forward.

I let her go, a step, another, because... I can? Besides it's fun to create the illusion of freedom first; makes the hunt so much more entertaining, huh?

I swoop forward, loop an arm around her waist, and yank her toward me.

She yelps. "Release me."

Good thing the bar is not yet full. It's too early for the usual officegoers to stop by. And the staff...? Well they are well aware of who cuts their paychecks.

I spin her around and against the bar, then release her. "You will listen to me."

She swallows; she glances left to right.

Not letting you go yet, little Bird. I move into her space, crowd her.

She tips her chin up. "Whatever you're selling, I'm not interested."

I allow my lips to curl, "You don't fool me."

A flush steals up her throat, sears her cheeks. So tiny, so innocent. Such a good little liar. I narrow my gaze, "Every action has its consequences."

"Are you daft?" She blinks.

"This pretense of yours?" I thrust my face into hers, "It's not working."

She blinks, then color suffuses her cheeks, "You're certifiably mad—"

"Getting tired of your insults."

"It's true, everything I said." She scrapes back the hair from her face.

Her fingernails are painted... You guessed it, pink.

"And here's something else. You are a selfish, egotistical jackass."

I smirk. "You're beginning to repeat your insults and I haven't even kissed you yet."

"Don't you dare." She gulps.

I tilt my head, "Is that a challenge?"

"It's a..." she scans the crowded space, then turns to me. Her lips firm, "...a warning. You're delusional, you jackass." She inhales a deep breath, "Your ego is bigger than the size of a black hole." She snickers, "Bet it's to compensate for your lack of balls."

A-n-d, that's it. I've had enough of her mouth that threatens to never stop spewing words. How many insults can one tiny woman hurl my way? Answer: too many to count.

"You—"

I lower my chin, touch my lips to hers.

Heat, sweetness, the honey of her essence explodes on my palate. My dick twitches. I tilt my head, deepen the kiss, reaching for that something more... more... of whatever scent she's wearing on her skin, infused with that breath of hers that crowds my senses, rushes down my spine. My groin hardens; my cock lengthens. I thrust my tongue between those infuriating lips.

She makes a sound deep in her throat and my heart begins to pound.

So innocent, yet so crafty. Beautiful and feisty. The kind of complication I don't need in my life.

I prefer the straight and narrow. Gray and black, that's how I choose to define my world. She, with her flashes of color—pink hair and lips that threaten to drive me to the edge of distraction—is exactly what I hate.

Give me a female who has her priorities set in life. To pleasure me, get me off, then walk away before her emotions engage. Yeah. That's what I prefer.

Not this… this bundle of craziness who flings her arms around my shoulders, thrusts her breasts up and into my chest, tips up her chin, opens her mouth, and invites me to take and take.

Does she have no self-preservation? Does she think I am going to fall for her wide-eyed appeal? She has another think coming.

I tear my mouth away and she protests.

She twines her leg with mine, pushes up her hips, so that melting softness between her thighs cradles my aching hardness.

I glare into her face and she holds my gaze.

Trains her green eyes on me. Her cheeks flush a bright red. Her lips fall open and a moan bleeds into the air. The blood rushes to my dick, which instantly thickens. *Fuck.*

Time to put distance between myself and the situation.

It's how I prefer to manage things. Stay in control, always. Cut out anything that threatens to impinge on my equilibrium. Shut it down or buy them off. Reduce it to a transaction. That I understand.

The power of money, to be able to buy and sell—numbers, logic. That's what's worked for me so far.

"How much?"

Her forehead furrows.

"Whatever it is, I can afford it."

Her jaw slackens. "You think… you—"

"A million?"

"What?"

"Pounds, dollars… You name the currency, and it will be in your account."

Her jaw slackens, "You're offering me money?"

"For your time, and for you to fall in line with my plan."

She reddens, "You think I am for sale?"

"Everyone is."

"Not me."

Here we go again. "Is that a challenge?"

Color fades from her face, "Get away from me."

"Are you shy, is that what this is?" I frown. "You can write your price down on a piece of paper if you prefer," I glance up, notice the bartender watching us. I jerk my chin toward the napkins. He grabs one, then offers it to her.

She glowers at him, "Did you buy him too?"

"What do you think?"

She glances around, "I think everyone here is ignoring us."

"It's what I'd expect."

"Why is that?"

I wave the tissue in front of her face, "Why do you think?"

"You own the place?"

"As I am going to own you."

She sets her jaw, "Let me leave and you won't regret this."

A chuckle bubbles up. I swallow it away. This is no laughing matter. I never smile during a transaction. Especially not when I am negotiating a new acquisition. And that's all she is. The final piece in the puzzle I am building.

"No one threatens me."

"You're right."

"Huh?"

"I'd rather act on my instinct."

Her lips twist, her gaze narrows. All of my senses scream a warning.

No, she wouldn't, no way—pain slices through my middle and sparks explode behind my eyes.

To find out what happens next read Summer & Sinclair Sterling's story HERE

Read about the seven in the Big bad Billionaires series

US

UK

Other countries

Claim your FREE contemporary romance boxset HERE

Claim your FREE paranormal romance boxset HERE

Want to be the first to find out about L. Steele's new releases? Join her newsletter HERE

Follow L. Steele on AMAZON

Follow L. Steele on BookBub

Follow L. Steele on Goodreads

Follow L. Steele on Facebook

Follow L. Steele on Instagram

Join L. Steele's secret Facebook Reader Group

For more books by L. Steele click HERE

FREE BOOKS

❀ Created with Vellum